In Situ

a science fiction novel

by David Samuel Frazier

For my wife Jolanta.
I can still hear her words ringing in my ears:
"Baby, did ya finish the book yet?"

Since it formed over 4.5 billion years ago, Earth has been hit many times by asteroids and comets whose orbits bring them into the inner solar system. These objects, collectively known as Near Earth Objects, or NEOs, still pose a danger to Earth today. Depending on the size of the impacting object, such a collision can cause massive damage on local to global scales. There is no doubt that sometime in the future the Earth will suffer another cosmic impact; the only question is when.

Pan-STARRS

Prologue

Pan-STARRS

The incessant beeping of her computer finally woke her. Anyway, it was just a short nap and her eyes had only been closed for a moment.

Jennifer Daniels pushed her chair back from her desk, stretched her arms wide and yawned. Her shift was almost over, and she was looking forward to a hot bath, and afterwards, some good sleep.

She had been working all night, detailing a series of images that had been taken by the Pan-STARRS telescope, a part of the most advanced technology ever devised for tracking asteroids and comets.

The telescope was essentially just a huge digital camera that took hundreds of pictures of the heavens nightly, feeding the image data into a high performance computer for analysis. The beeping was normal, just a program Jen had set to signal her when information from a new analytic run had become available. The process had been going on all night—it could wait.

She stood up, walked over to the door, and stepped outside onto a catwalk that surrounded the observatory to try to wake up. It was like stepping into a freezer, especially at this time of the morning. The temperature was not quite 0 degrees Celsius, with a brisk northwest breeze blowing about 15 knots.

But the cold was misleading. Just down the mountain, a half an hour drive, the breezes were tropical, and the Pacific Ocean was warm to the touch.

Jen pulled her lab coat tighter and glanced at her watch—4:13 a.m.

Well, she thought, looking at the lights in the valley below, I'll be heading that way soon enough.

The starlight was just beginning to fade, and she could see the headlights of a line of cars snaking their way up the winding mountain road; tourists driving up to watch the Haleakala sunrise, which was invariably breathtaking. Jen was on top of one of most magnificent peaks on the planet in one of the most beautiful places in the world, Maui.

She was accustomed to working the graveyard shift, although she had never really adjusted to that schedule. Her natural body clock demanded that she function during normal hours, but as she had told others so often, there was something just not appropriate about an astronomer working during the day. Even so, she occasionally took short naps just to recharge so she could totally focus on her work.

Jen took great pride that she had been selected as the Chief Astronomer for the Pan-STARRS Observatory, and the fact that it was located in Hawaii was just a bonus.

The telescope was designed to discover and catalogue never-before-seen asteroids and comets—Jen's specialty. Some of her peers were into black holes or the births of distant galaxies, but Jen was more than content to count rocks speeding around in the solar system. In fact, she had achieved a certain degree of fame in her own, limited intellectual community, for her expertise in them.

The Pan-STARRS darker—perhaps more primary purpose—was to identify any asteroids or comets that could possibly pose a threat to earth in the near future.

Not that Jen or anyone else was seriously concerned. There had not been a globally significant impact event in over 65 million years, so the likelihood of another any time soon was remote at best. It would be like having the only losing ticket in the great cosmic lottery. Jen knew the odds of identifying a real risk to Earth even in her lifetime were miniscule.

As the eastern horizon began to turn pink, she glimpsed the long trail of a shooting star streaking across the sky. Jen shivered, decided she was more than awake enough, and headed back inside to find a cup of something hot and to begin to evaluate the results of her latest run.

"Bless you Jonathon," she said, smiling at her assistant as she walked back in.

He was standing just inside the door with a fresh cup of black coffee, steam still rising off of it.

"Who needs Starbucks when I have you?" she asked him rhetorically, giving him a friendly wink as she took it from him.

Jonathon was normally a pretty cheery guy, but he was not smiling back. Jen took a small sip, holding the cup with both hands to warm them.

"What's wrong Jonathon?" she finally asked.

There was a look of deep concern on his face.

"I put a few photos on your desk with the most recent data printouts. I'm not exactly sure, Doctor, but I think we might have a problem."

Jen looked back at him. Jonathon was just a graduate student, but he was sharp and knew his stuff. She was suddenly worried. He had dispensed with calling her "Doctor" long ago and he wasn't known for beating around the bush.

"What are you seeing?" she asked as they walked over to her work area.

Jonathon held up a twelve-by-eighteen-inch image of the night sky. It was covered with countless dots of light in a rainbow of colors. He had placed a yellow sticky note near one of the brighter, pure white dots, and had drawn an arrow of red ink on the paper, pinpointing it specifically.

"That little devil right there," he said, drawing an invisible circle around it with the top of his pen. He let the photo slide onto the desktop and handed Jen the corresponding printout.

Still preoccupied with the photo, Jen finally focused her attention on the paper. Her face, which had been rosy from the cold, suddenly went pale. Jen collapsed into her chair, clutching the report.

"29 days?" she said, reading it again. "How many times have you run this Jonathon?"

"After I found it in the general run, I ran it three more times, manually re-entering the data of just that NEO from last night's images. Then one more time, calling up data from tonight's observations—all with the same result," he replied, ominously.

Jen looked back down at the printout.

NEO	A 99962
NAME	NEW
SIZE	2.9 KM
IP	99.99 TSI 10
EID	10.18.11 0733 ZULU

"Impact probability of 99 percent? Torino Scale Integer: 10!" she said, staring at the paper, her hands shaking. "Jesus, sweet Jesus! I've got to call the President."

Jonathon barely whispered, "I was hoping you would have a simple explanation."

CHAPTER 1

64,196,324 BCE

If the world was really coming to an end, then Mot wanted to see the evidence of it with his own eyes.

The Astrologers were warning of a giant rock of fire that was coming, visible only in the night sky. When it finally arrived, they said, it would destroy the world in a cloud of fire and ash. The Great One had sent it, the Priests had said, punishment for their "atrocities."

But Mot had certainly never seen this giant fire rock, nor had he ever experienced the guilt of having committed any such thing as an atrocity. In fact, he was young enough that he hadn't as yet even had his parents confirm the selection of his mate; an event that, prior to the announcement of the coming of the giant rock and the ensuing end of the world, he had very much been looking forward to.

Besides, the Arzat Elders had been foretelling the "end of the world" since the "beginning of the world" as far as Mot could remember. Surely this was just another empty threat to get Mot and his young peers to show more respect and to better comply with their wishes and constant demands. In any case, he was determined to find out the truth of the matter for himself.

Mot quietly moved aside the barricade that guarded the main entrance to the Arzat caves and stepped out into the warm night air, careful to immediately seal the opening behind him. He had assistance from the other side.

His friend El had helped him open it and now helped him to move it carefully back into place.

The barricade was essentially just a very large round stone, specifically cut to roll easily in and out of the entrance—easy, provided you had at least two strong Arzats to move it. Its operation was really quite simple, yet complicated enough to effectively confound the predators. They, so far, had never been able to figure out its workings.

Even so, the clan always posted sentries just inside as a safeguard against any unwanted visitors, and particularly any stray Arzats from any other clans who might be foolish enough, or desperate enough, to be out wandering around looking for trouble.

The caves were the most prized possession of the Zanta Clan and had to be constantly protected, not only from the large number of predators that lived in the Arzat world, but from other tribes of Arzats as well. Raids by other groups were seldom attempted in darkness due to the extreme danger, but every measure of security was taken nonetheless, day or night.

Many of the other clans in the region were aware of the prime living conditions Mot's own clan enjoyed, and would be more than pleased, were they able to accomplish it, to annihilate the current occupants and take the caves for themselves.

There were minor skirmishes here and there among the various tribes, but most of the Arzat energies were expended on survival rather than war. None of the other clans, as yet, had ever mounted a successful attack.

There was a distinct advantage in only having one entrance. It made the entire system of caves much easier to protect. The distinct disadvantage was that, if the entrance were ever to be breached by an enemy, there was no line of retreat.

Tonight, it was Mot and El who had been assigned this very important duty of guarding the cave entrance, and Mot had wasted no time convincing his friend to cover his absence and to wait for his return.

Mot had been waiting for this opportunity to sneak out after dark, his rare rotation to guard duty providing the only chance.

Just a short trip, he had assured El, one torch of time, no more. His friend had reluctantly agreed, aware of the fact that he had put Mot up to the adventure in the first place, but not without reminding Mot that there would be severe repercussions if their plan were discovered.

As he emerged from the cave, Mot's senses immediately sharpened.

Although the sun had only just set, its rays of red twilight were already rapidly fading into stars. A moon, half full, had just risen, and hung over the tops of the distant mountains. The sky was the color of embers dying—the deep blue of night swiftly washing over it.

This was the most dangerous time to be out of the protective confines of the tunnels. The Elders had always forbidden venturing out past sunset for that very reason. Only the Astrologers and Priests were ever allowed out after dark, and never without the protection of a large contingent of capable and well-armed Hunters.

Mot knew he could face severe and harsh punishment for his disobedience, but his curiosity had gotten the better of him, so he would probably have gone even if he hadn't been dared to do so by some of the other adolescent males, his friend El being one of them.

Anyway, he did not plan to get caught.

As he stood with his back to the safe haven of the caves, he began to have second thoughts. Before him, the main path through the dense forest that was so familiar to him during the day had become dark and ominous.

Despite his uncanny ability to see in low light, Mot now found that he could make out objects no more than a few sticks away. A torch would have been a comfort and would have helped him to see, but it would be a dead giveaway to every other creature in the forest of his exact location. Mot had reluctantly ruled out the idea of using one for that very reason.

He thought again about turning and tapping a stone on the door of the great cave and having El let him back in, but what was he? A child? Besides, he would never hear the end of it from El or any of his peers if they caught wind of his early retreat. Worse than that, a certain young female by the name of Ara was sure to hear and think him a coward—and that would be a disaster. The mere thought of her caused his heart to race.

Mot cautiously looked up, but was unable to get a completely clear view of the night sky from the entrance. The opening had been purposely and skillfully camouflaged with plants and trees to disguise it, so it blended perfectly into the thick foliage that surrounded it.

Mot knew he would have to venture out to find a better vantage point in order to get a good look at the heavens, and he knew exactly where he needed to go.

As he took his first steps, Mot concentrated all of his being on the dark world around him, and did his very best to bring all of his survival skills into play. His sight was good, but it was nothing compared to his excellent hearing and his ability to sense the vibrations of any kind of movement on the ground. He might be young and foolish, but even he knew that he was risking death. Most of the meals in Mot's world were eaten at night, under the cover of the very dense forest where he now found himself.

He took a few more strides, then stopped and stood perfectly still. Mot flicked his tongue several times, but there was nothing alarming in the air. It was clean and fresh, heavy with water from the afternoon rain, but nothing more. He listened and felt, but could discern no sounds or vibrations of potential threats or unusual movement in the earth. Somewhere, not far off, a large serpent was slithering around on the forest floor looking for prey, but other than that, he could sense no immediate danger close by.

Mot reached to his side and silently slid his hunting stick from its scabbard. He was very proud of it, for had fashioned the weapon himself under the watchful eye of his father who had taught him all the skills necessary to create it. Mot had chosen the best hardwood in the forest, and had worked for more than half a season, painstakingly freeing the weapon's shape from the tree that had grown it, carefully tempering the tip in the Great Fire of the cave. The hunting stick was long and straight, four digits thick on one end, tapering in slightly at the middle, extremely sharp on the other; and wrapped with animal skin in the center for grip. The stick came just to Mot's shoulder when he stood it on its blunt end.

Its scabbard was made from the hide of Mot's first official kill, and allowed Mot to carry the weapon strapped across his back when not in use. His mother and some of the other females had helped him with the tanning process; but Mot had worked equally as hard on the scabbard as he had the hunting stick itself, sewing the pieces of hide together with his own hands, amazed that the texture of the animal skin was so similar to his own.

Soon, Mot still hoped, the scabbard would be marked with a long line of kills that would stand as testimony to his great abilities as a Hunter.

Only just this season had Mot finally reached an age that allowed him to fully participate in the hunts. His father, Url, one of the best Hunters in the clan, had been very proud when Mot had bravely led the effort to bring down a large four-legged tree eater.

When he had earned it, his father had assured him, the weapon would be taken to the Forgers and properly tipped with the blood red metal that they had so recently perfected. Only then, Mot knew, would he be fully recognized as an adult within the Clan; and perhaps more importantly, as a true Hunter.

While he was perfectly able to gut a smaller animal with a swift kick of his leg if necessary, the hunting stick provided Mot with a very important advantage, the ability to keep some distance between himself and his prey. Often, whatever he was attacking might be just as deadly as he, hunting stick or no, perhaps even more so. Sometimes just a minor injury in a hunting skirmish could spell the eventual end for the wounded despite any efforts from the Medicine Men to repair them. Holding the stick now gave Mot courage, the weight of it a comfort, and the further he ventured the more he needed both on this dark night.

Mot listened again, and then cautiously moved ahead, careful to maintain total silence. Another pause, another check with all of his senses.

There was a small plateau of solid rock one hundred steps from the caves that rose high above the thick forest canopy and had a large flat top. It was sheer on all sides and had been used for eons as the Arzat's primary lookout. At night, it was the very place the Astrologers used to count the stars and forecast the seasons. Mot knew he would be able to get a completely clear view of the sky from there.

With only a few more strides down the dark forest path he reached it and quickly crawled up one of its faces, using the sharp tips of his fingers and the toes of his feet to hold fast to the stone; his hunting stick safely back in its scabbard as he climbed.

Mot remained in a crouched position as he reached the top, stopping again to feel for vibrations in the stone and to taste the air for danger, his sharp eyes scanning the dense forest below. Though the moon was only at half, its light cast a hundred degrees of shadow and color over the land. The scales of Mot's skin became translucent blue and green under the glow. He had rarely seen such a sight, having almost never been out of the caves after dark.

Mot unconsciously stood up, completely in awe, and looked deep into the night. Below, the dark canopy of the forest surrounded him, as if he were the only creature on earth.

Despite the partial moon, the stars shone brightly, but one in particular lit the sky. It was not nearly as big as the moon, nor as friendly in color, for it glowed white-hot and angry like a coal from the Great Fire, and trailed white dust.

Mot studied the fire rock for some time, completely mesmerized by the circle of flame that seemed to grow larger under his gaze. He held one hand over one eye and then switched, attempting to focus on the object. He watched for some time, trying to discern any movement across the sky, but could detect none. Still, while he had no way of knowing for sure, it did seem as if the rock was bearing down, heading directly toward him.

Perhaps the Elders are right this time, he thought to himself uncomfortably.

Mot sensed the truth of it to his bones, and it caused him to shiver despite the warm night. He needed to get back. He had promised El that he would only be gone one torch, and he realized that he had probably been out for two or three.

As he turned and prepared to head back to the caves, Mot sensed movement in the forest below. He immediately froze, darted his tongue, tasted the air, and listened.

For a moment, he could hear or feel nothing but own his heart beating, and he could detect no unusual scent, but he continued to hold himself as motionless as the rock he stood on. Nothing.

Then two, maybe three… yes, three animals, hunting as a group. He could feel the scales on the back of his neck rising. Three animals, but Mot could discern only six feet among them as they tromped through the forest, and they were definitely not Arzats.

There was only one other kind of animal that Mot knew of that stood on two legs and hunted in a pack; distant relatives perhaps, but he wanted no part of them. They were nasty and they were deadly and they were relatively intelligent which made them superb predators. Even the bravest of the Hunters feared them. The Arzats referred to the beasts as the Evil Ones.

No one, as far as Mot knew, had ever even killed one. If they got wind of him he would be their dinner. Of that he had no doubt.

Mot again tested the air, but could still not detect their scent. He considered that if he could not smell them, perhaps the creatures had missed *his* scent and would pass by.

He could hear them clearly now, snarling and gnashing their teeth, engaging in their incomprehensible and high-pitched chatter as they tore through the forest floor. Their obvious lack of concern for stealth was testimony to their confidence as predators.

Soon, the beasts were directly below Mot, two of them passing on one side of the rock, the third passing on the other.

He held his breath and remained perfectly still, his heart beating so hard that he felt it was about to explode. Mot struggled to remember all the lessons his father had taught him. He could only hope that he would not be discovered until the three of them had moved on far enough for him to beat them back to the cave. But the trio below him was a group of highly successful hunters. Mot did not try to fool himself that they were anything less. He *would* be detected. It was simply a matter of when. It was safer to assume that, anyway.

Although the sky was clear and the breeze calm, Mot considered that he must have initially been downwind of them, a situation that he sensed was about to change in the predator's favor.

The creatures' footfalls, however, soon passed the rock and were becoming more distant and, fortunately for Mot, were not moving toward the Arzat entrance.

He closed his eyes and focused on the slight breeze trying to detect its exact direction. No question, the beasts had moved down wind of him. A few more paces and Mot knew he would have to risk a run for it.

Mot quietly slipped down the rock and dropped silently back to the forest floor, stopping and listening intently several times along the way. He could still hear them, breaking tree limbs and snapping their jaws, but the beasts had continued moving deeper into the forest, away from his location. The moment Mot judged that he could get to the cave before they could get to him, he would make his move. Maybe he would be lucky.

No sooner had that thought crossed his mind than the threesome stopped suddenly. Mot imagined them sniffing the air, aware that the beasts had probably caught his scent. He immediately began to run, literally for his life.

The long nails on his toes bit into the soft ground of the forest floor and propelled him forward like lightning. Mot was a fast runner, one of the fastest in his clan, but the darkness made it difficult for him. He did his best to move quickly yet quietly the way he had been taught by his father—a necessary skill for an Arzat Hunter—and drew his weapon from its scabbard without breaking pace. But the beasts were on to him, they had sniffed him out, and Mot could hear their angry cries carry through the night as they trampled through the forest and scrambled to intercept him.

As Mot ran the last stretch of path to the cave, he was surprised to see that the entrance appeared to be open; the dull orange glow from the torches that burned further inside dimly lighting his way.

Something was wrong; the barrier was never down, night or day. Mot found himself momentarily annoyed at El, but he didn't have time to question. He could feel the threesome almost at his back, howling with rage, as if Mot had unfairly deceived them.

Then, just a stride or two from the entrance, one of beasts leapt out of the darkness, snarling and roaring. Mot was forced to turn and confront the animal or die. He spun around, baring his own sharp teeth, mustering the best battle cry he could produce, and raised his hunting stick to protect himself. As he did so, the attacker stopped, suddenly suspicious. It craned its head to the side, studying Mot, looking him directly in the eyes as if he were taking Mot's measure. The beast hissed and growled, saliva dripping from its enormous jaws, its breath reeking of spoiled meat, but did not attack.

The creature was waiting for something, and when its partners finally emerged from the forest, Mot recognized the reason. The animal instantly lunged at him now, confident that it had the support of its mates.

Mot knew he was dead, but he was going to make his attackers work for their dinner. He drew back his hunting stick and stepped forward. As the first attacker dove at him, Mot swiftly shoved his hunting stick deep into one of the creature's eyes, so forcefully that the tip emerged from the back of its head. The animal reeled back, tearing the weapon from Mot's grip in the process, its deafening roar filling the night air as it began almost immediately to die. The creature staggered, mortally wounded, and disappeared screaming into the forest.

The other two beasts, momentarily confused, quickly recovered and charged, anxious to disembowel Mot with their razor sharp claws. His hunting stick gone, Mot's only option was to retreat.

He turned and sprang for the cave, but as he did so, he tripped and fell headlong through the entrance, almost impaling himself on one of the eight or nine hunting sticks that were poised and waiting just inside. His remaining attackers, now in a rage and having lost all sense of caution, plunged through after him.

* * *

Mot, dazed and exhausted, rolled to the side and watched with a sense of awe as a group of Arzat Hunters who had positioned themselves just inside the entrance skillfully dispatched his pursuers—each of them very quickly and methodically receiving three or four vicious stabs to the chest and one through the head.

Even so, the creatures did not die right away, and the floor of the cave became treacherous and slippery with their bowels and blood, as the Hunters held them down and watched the beasts scream and squirm until there was no longer any sign of life in them.

When it was over, the Hunters gathered their weapons, stood over their kills, and gave a collective howl of victory that resonated through the cave and shook the walls. The barricade was carefully rolled back into place, two new sentries were assigned, and the Hunters began to disperse to the Main Chamber of the cave.

Mot eventually got to his feet and silently watched as each of the Hunters passed him, their bodies covered in the blood of their victims. In their eyes, a mixture of anger and pride. Anger at Mot for having risked the lives of the entire clan; pride in themselves for having successfully settled the problem that Mot had created.

The Arzat Hunters knew they were extremely fortunate that no one had been injured or killed due to Mot's indiscretion. Mot's own father had been the last to walk past, but he had done so without looking at his son.

It was then that Mot had a revelation. He suddenly and clearly understood what was meant by "atrocity," and that he had just committed one.

CHAPTER 2

In Situ

"Yeeeeessssss!"

Alex screamed at the top of her lungs as she stretched her arms into the sky in triumph.

The sound of her voice reverberated around the high desert canyon and eventually came back as a mere whisper, gently reminding her that there was no one around for miles to hear. The thought made her smile. She liked being alone.

"Yes, yes, yes," she repeated to herself in a lower tone as she looked eagerly back down at the rocky swatch of earth she had been bent over for most of the last two days.

To the layman, the obscure lines on the ground might not have meant much, but to Dr. Alexandria S. Moss, they were a revelation.

Finally, after days of searching, a dinosaur, a real honest-to-god *dinosaur*. Not just any dinosaur either. Finding one out here was easy. They are all over the place. Jurassic, no problem. Stegosaur, Allosaur, Brachiosaur? What do you want? This whole area was a veritable dinosaur hunter's heaven for Jurassic era fossils, and Alex had found more than her fair share over the years. Even a Cretaceous specimen wasn't all that tough. They were all over the place if your eyes were open.

Mostly though, the discoveries came in bits and pieces: a bone-fragment here, a tooth there. But finding a near perfect and totally complete skeleton from the late Cretaceous was like hitting the jackpot, the mother lode of paleontology.

The animal's bones appeared to be perfectly *in situ*, exactly as they had since it had died so many millennia ago.

Far better than that, as near as she could tell, Alex had just discovered an entirely new species. If that were true, she would ultimately have the pleasure of naming her new find, a goal she had been dreaming of her entire career.

Alex and her father had spent many years in these hills looking for this particular type of animal, and now there it was, right in front of her. She had finally unearthed enough of it to determine that it was almost surely complete.

"Needle in a haystack, Alex, needle in a haystack." She could hear her father in her head as clearly as if he were standing next to her. "Patience, Alex, patience!" She had heard him saying it over and over as she had carefully exhumed the first parts of the skeleton.

She wished old Simon could have lived to see this moment.

* * *

Alex had spent the entire fall semester, on sabbatical from the University of Utah at Salt Lake, scouring the remote deserts of northeastern Utah, looking for specimens from the Cretaceous.

Not that this was necessarily a big enough deal to win her "paleontologist of the year" or anything, she thought, but this one was going to be *her* dinosaur. No, *our* dinosaur, she corrected herself. Dad would have been proud.

As she worked, she busied herself concocting potential scientific names for the find. Whatever it would be, it would most certainly include some reference to her father.

The specimen she had discovered was right on the K-T boundary of the Cretaceous-to-Tertiary period change, a geological marker separating the time of the dinosaurs from the present.

It was largely becoming accepted in the scientific community that a massive asteroid had impacted the earth around 65 million years ago, which had led to the extinction of most dinosaurs shortly thereafter.

There was speculation that the K-T asteroid's impact theoretically would have been the equivalent of a billion atom bombs simultaneously detonating, which was almost impossible to imagine.

Alex's father had been obsessed with the idea that there must have been intelligent life before the event. If the 65 million years since was just a drop of time in earth's history; the time of the development of significant mammals, and finally man, was just a molecule. It had never made sense to old Simon that intelligent life would not have developed in the millions and millions of years of evolution during the long reign of the dinosaurs. In fact, if Darwinian Theory was taken into account at all, it made no sense whatsoever.

* * *

The specimen that Alex had found might just prove him right.

Look at the prefrontal lobes on that guy, she thought to herself. She decided that, for the time being, until she came up with a scientific name, she would simply refer to the new discovery as her Einstein-osaur. She laughed at the thought.

Despite her excitement, Alex had to stand for a minute and see if she could shrug off the pain in her back. She had been bent over most of the day, digging in the rocky soil with not much more than the equivalent of a tooth-brush and a chisel.

As she straightened up, she grabbed a bottle of water from her knapsack, threw off her wide brimmed Tilley hat, tipped her head back, and took a huge drink. Water never tasted so good. Alex kept the bottle pressed against her lips until it was almost empty then lifted it away and let the last of the liquid run over her forehead and down her face.

"Hydrate, Alex, hydrate." It was the ghost of her father again. She smiled and shook her head.

Everything Alex knew about this desert she had learned from him. A brilliant paleontologist in his own right, her fondest memories of Dr. Simon D. Moss had been born out here in the high deserts. They had spent countless summers and school breaks all over the west, camping and digging, always on the hunt for that elusive discovery. It got into your blood, and Alex had definitely inherited the paleontologist's blood of her father.

She earned her PhD from Cal Berkley, but had fought for and finally won a teaching job at the university in Salt Lake, near the deserts she had always really called home.

These were some of the best dinosaur-hunting grounds in the world, the high, barren expanses of central and northeast Utah.

As she looked around, Alex felt a cool afternoon breeze cross over her. The rocks were starting to grow long shadows. Her camp was in a canyon just below the dig site at the base of an ancient rock formation. The cliffs overhead topped off around 100 feet above her.

It was only late September, but Alex could already sense the desert beginning to shift toward winter. It was something felt rather than seen. The day had been sunny and warm. Now, as the sun started to sink lower in the sky, the hills and canyons began to cool and color, a million variations of the light spectrum; greens and blues, reds and orange—a gigantic rainbow draped like a blanket over the dull grey rocks.

"There is no possible way I could ever describe this to anyone," Alex quietly said to herself as she stood watching the change. She took a long, deep breath then exhaled in what was almost a sigh.

Alex considered it to be quite normal to talk to herself and others, both living and dead, when she was out on one of her "dig binges," as she liked to refer to them. It was a necessary by-product of self-induced solitude. Sometimes she had arguments with rocks and other inanimate things that were blocking her way. She usually won. Out here, there was no one to ask permission of, no one to seek approval from—total freedom. For her, the desert was a place to gain perspective. When she felt too full of herself or dulled by life with her own species, Alex liked to retreat to the vastness of the high Utah desert and hang out with her dinosaurs.

Only when she wiped her cheek with the back of her hand did she suddenly realize how dirty she was, covered in dust that was millions of years old. The almost white powder became suddenly dark and muddy when wet.

She laughed when she thought about how her face must look—filthy. But she was far away from a mirror at the moment, and since she preferred to work alone, there was no one around that might have any comment about the dark lines of grime she had created with the splash of water. In fact, there was no one around to say anything, which was exactly the way she liked it.

"It's going to take me a week to get this stuff off," she said quietly to herself as she examined the backs of her hands. The grit was already becoming lighter as the dry desert air quickly wicked the moisture away.

She looked at her hands critically, flipping them over as she would if she were preparing for a manicure.

"Man, oh, man," Alex shook her head as she fully realized just how far she had strayed from civilization. She wondered absently, for just a moment, whether or not somewhere, under all of that muck and abrasion, the rather beautiful hands that she had brought with her could be found again.

"What do you think there, Albert?" she said to her newfound fossil. "Think there might still be a woman hiding out under here or have you ruined me forever?"

In fact, the rather sodden female that now stood in the middle of nowhere was quite a beauty. Not that she thought of it much any more, but it had been an issue both in school and early in her career. Doors had been opened and opportunities presented that Alex had often wondered about. Were they more linked to her looks or to her academic efforts? Men were everywhere and interested, some obnoxiously so.

For a short time, she had even become somewhat resentful and suspicious. It had taken her father, as usual, to straighten her out when she had one day protested.

"Alex," he had said in his usual authoritative way, "I'm going to try to tell you this as a man, and not your father. You have a gift of beauty—clearly inherited from your mother, not me—that most young women your age would die for, and most, shall we say 'senior' women, probably envy to no end. The fact that men are paying attention to you is not a problem. When they stop, that will be a problem, because you'll be old and gray like me and wish—oh how you will wish—that you were young again. As far as your performance on professional or academic fronts, just as is true for most anyone who has ever accomplished anything, you will have to learn to become your own best judge and jury. In the meantime, buck up kid, and enjoy the fast and fleeting ride of youth. Besides, being as beautiful as you are can't really be all that bad, can it Alex? You're a very lucky girl."

She still remembered how he had smiled at her with the famously disarming "trademark" Dr. Simon Moss wink.

Alex had never complained again.

Her father had only been gone for two years, and the pain of his mysterious death still lingered. It made her feel older somehow. But at 29, youth was very much with Alex, and she figured that she could still pass for a college freshman in the right clothes and make up. It was almost a certainty if she were to make the rare move of letting her long amber hair fall from the normally "clipped-up for convenience" style that she wore 90 percent of the time. The fact that she was occasionally carded at restaurants and bars around campus she now took as a compliment.

She'd left her hair long, not just because she liked it. Alex could still remember her mother, an actual beauty queen herself when she was in her youth, cutting her own long black hair into what she had told Alex at the time was a "mommy cut."

Her mother had still remained attractive despite the scissors, but even at her own young age at the time, Alex had sensed finality in the move. Her mother had passed from one era to another, from youth to middle age.

Not long after, she had died in a tragic automobile accident, leaving Alex and her father to fend for themselves. Alex had a vague notion that when she finally cut her own hair, she would be passing through her own era. For the moment, she figured that since she pretty much liked the current one, there was no hurry.

The thing about time was that "there's never any going back." Her father, as usual, had been so very right.

But there was one way you could sort of go back, she thought, as she cast her eyes back down at the ground in front of her.

* * *

She had found a unique dinosaur, something that had probably lived somewhere in the vicinity of 65 million years ago. This was a bipedal carnivore of some sort—a theropod that walked upright on two feet—of that she was certain. The elongated head and the heavy jawbone that was lined with what would have been razor sharp teeth were all dead give-aways as to its diet.

Those facts in themselves were not significant. There were plenty of well-known theropods that fit the description: Tyrannosaurs, Velociraptors, Chindesaurs. The list was long. But most were from the Jurassic, or even the Triassic.

This big boy... might be a female, Alex, might be a female... she corrected herself, was something that existed at the edge of the Cretaceous extinction.

Hell, Alex thought, he or she might have even been a witness.

Of course, she would have to carbon date to be sure, but the creature's proximity to the long line of dark iridium-laden sediment around him suggested that he was "right there" when the world had exploded so many millennia ago.

Alex guessed, based on its size and what she could see of its skeletal struc-ture, that it had died as a young adult. He would have stood over eight feet and weighed over seven hundred pounds. But what she found particularly interesting about this creature was the size of its skull, especially in the area of the prefrontal lobes, the thinking part of the brain. It was enormous even compared to Velociraptors—known theropods from the Jurassic thought to have been extremely intelligent.

As Alex bent to get a closer look at the skull, she discovered something else. There appeared to be some sort of damage, a round jagged hole in the back right quadrant. Alex couldn't see any other obvious signs of trauma, but she had only just barely exposed the side of the animal. She shrugged. Ultimately, she knew she would have to get the creature back to the university labs to determine how it had actually died, and with any luck, when it had died.

A part of her wanted to keep working, but it was getting late and she had been at it since dawn. She looked at the sky one more time, then decided to make some notes and further document the find before it got dark.

Despite the fact that she had already been camped for almost a week, Alex had taken her time and had followed good practices not to ruin the specimen. Every move she made during the day was painstakingly logged over the evening campfire; the creature's location and body position diagramed and drawn in exact scale.

Tomorrow, she would call the university and try to extend her sabbatical and enlist the help of some trustworthy colleagues and students to completely excavate the site. Unfortunately, there was no way she could do it all herself, much as she would have liked to. A find of this caliber required a team.

As Alex walked down the slight grade to her campsite to gather her computer and camera she heard the familiar buzzing of a rattler so close that it sounded at first as if she might have stepped on it. She looked around her feet and found the snake directly in front of her, barely three feet away, coiled and ready to strike.

Alex fortunately had frozen in her tracks immediately, or the rattler would have already bitten her. She recognized it as a genus that was particularly venomous, staring at her with its dark reptilian eyes, its tongue darting in and out of its mouth, daring her to move.

"Let the snake decide, Alex, always let the snake decide," her father said to her quietly in his steady calm voice.

The rattler remained curled and ready, its black eyes boring into Alex, its tongue occasionally flicking, testing the air.

Finally, after a minute or two that seemed to Alex like an hour or two, the snake lowered its head, turned and moved off, cutting a fresh track through the loose sand.

Alex felt her breath returning and her heart slowing. She watched the snake until it had completely disappeared into the rocks.

There goes another one of your lives Alex, she thought to herself. Paleontology could be dangerous work. Her father's death was proof of that.

Alex shook the encounter off the best she could and continued down toward her campsite, this time more slowly and more carefully. She grabbed her camera and computer and a thick notebook.

Then, just as she turned to start back up the hill, Alex felt the ground move. At first she thought the shaking might be a small earthquake, but almost immediately after, she heard the muffled sound of an explosion.

Alex paused, listening intently for almost a minute. Nothing.

She shrugged her shoulders. Must be miners working in the area, she thought. She continued back up the path to her dig, keeping an eye out for the rattlesnake, and silently scolded herself for letting the day get by without so much as a note or a picture.

Alex was far fonder of digging than documenting during the day. Her uncanny ability to recall detail was almost photographic, which allowed her to do most of her record-keeping at night around a campfire with a fully charged laptop. Anything she might have missed, she simply made a note of for verification the following morning. Nonetheless, it was a bad habit she knew her father would have frowned upon.

As Alex approached the site, another series of explosions shook the canyon floor. These were much more severe than the first had been, and almost knocked her off balance.

She paused again, listening. There was another muffled explosion.

"This is bullshit," she finally said, exasperated.

Then she heard it, a few small rocks falling down the cliff face directly over her dinosaur. Alex looked up at the canyon wall just in time to see a wide portion of it begin to collapse in a slide. Smaller rocks, then bigger ones, began to roll.

She instinctively sprinted for cover, dropping her camera, computer and notebook in the process. The mountain seemed to fall from every direction, and it was gaining on her. Finally, Alex dove between two of the largest solid rocks she could find and covered her head.

The slide was over in seconds, but the dust persisted and hung in the evening air like dense fog. Alex remained where she was for quite some time with her face buried in her arms. She could not believe she was still alive. Her knees felt like they were bleeding, but otherwise Alex was unscathed.

When she finally emerged from the boulders, she could barely see up the hill. It was a white out. Alex was in shock. She didn't know whether to scream or cry, but she knew that her dinosaur was gone, she just knew it.

CHAPTER 3

Atrocity

"I tell you, he must be banished from the Clan immediately!"

It was Xan, one of the Elders, his body glowing in the light of the Great Fire, his eyes lit with rage.

Mot kept his eyes directed at the floor. He knew that if he even glanced at Xan it might be construed as a death challenge, which Xan would have been all too happy to remedy with a swift thrust of his own lavishly decorated hunting stick.

They were gathered in the Great Chamber. Almost the entire male population of the Zanta clan was present. All of the females, with the exception of Fet the Wise Mother, were purposely excluded, along with the very youngest of males.

The Chamber was circular and had been created during the time of the burning rocks, when the massive lava tubes had formed all of the caves the Arzats now inhabited. For countless eons the caves had served as their home, since the first Great Hunter Orn had been sent by the Creator of All Things to begin the Zanta Clan many thousands of seasons before.

The room was at least fifty sticks across and twenty high, with a hard earthen floor and smooth stone walls that curved upwards forming the large space. In the ceiling, a natural opening of approximately two sticks served as a vent for the sacred Fire that was the centerpiece of the Chamber and was never allowed to go out. The opening was so high that any animal bold enough to risk entry would surely fall to its death in the effort, but the vent had been crisscrossed with long poles, nonetheless, as an additional safeguard. The Fire itself had been purposely set just to the side, so that the event of rain, which was frequent, would not extinguish it.

The Fire, like the cave entrance, was never, almost never, left unsupervised.

On the walls, the words and art of the ancients had been carved into the stone that told the long story of the Zantas and proclaimed them as the greatest of the Arzat tribes. At strategic locations, torches burned and flickered, giving the words and symbols a life of their own.

While both the Chamber and the Fire were most often attended to and used by the females for the preparation of meals, the room also served as the main socializing and meeting place of the clan. The ritual assigning of mates, the telling of the great history of the clan by the Elders, readings from the walls, the Priests' pleas for protection and plenty from the Creator, the forecasts of the Astronomers, the celebration of a successful hunt, formal cremations and funerals all occurred within the confines of the Great Chamber.

The floor was now packed with males of the Zanta clan, some having to stand for lack of room to sit, all awaiting the fate of the young Hunter Mot, their shadows dancing on the walls in the fire light. There were perhaps eight by eight by four of them, all anxious to see what was going to happen.

* * *

The story had rapidly traveled through the caves, evolving from fact to myth in short order.

Mot the "great lizard slayer."

Mot the "great law breaker."

Mot the "brave."

Mot the "coward."

And while there was no one in the room who was not interested in the fate of Mot, son of the great Hunter Url, they were quite content in the meantime to chew on the large pieces of freshly charred meat that had just been passed to them—the result of the unexpected and fortuitous kills that had just occurred this very night.

The hunting, as of late, had not been as productive as usual. Animals had become scarce and their movements more and more unpredictable.

The Astronomers had blamed this change on the fire in the sky. The Priests had blamed the Arzats and their irreverent behavior. The Hunters had quietly blamed themselves.

Regardless of the reason, until this evening, the stores of meat and other foods had been rationed for some time by order of the Council of Elders. The reserve food supply that was kept deep down in the lowest and coldest part of the caves was being depleted at an alarming rate. No Arzat was starving, but all were hungry.

So the unusual circumstances of tonight's kill, and the dire predictions of the Astronomers, had prompted the Elders to order the two animals to be immediately butchered, cooked and distributed. Aside from satisfying their stomachs, the Elders had correctly guessed that feeding the clan might also serve to calm them so that order could be maintained as they debated Mot's fate.

Arzats, particularly in a group, could be emotional and very unpredictable. What the Elders had not foreseen, was that the events of the evening, and particularly the delicious meal Mot had inadvertently provided, had made some of them much more sympathetic to his predicament.

Mot had committed the ultimate of atrocities. He had jeopardized the lives of everyone by breaking curfew and deserting his post. At least, those were the charges. The penalty could be instant death or banishment, the first being far more preferable, for there could be no harsher punishment imaginable than being sent out alone from the caves with orders never to return.

But most of the Arzats that now sat in the Great Chamber were Hunters, after all, and when the story was fully related about Mot's single handed slaying of one of the most fearsome beasts in the forest, it was impossible that there would not be a certain amount of envy and admiration.

Yes, he had broken the law, but hadn't the entire clan just eaten a lavish meal because of it?

Further, many of the Arzats had secretly contemplated a look at the death star for themselves, but none of them had mustered the courage to actually venture out as Mot had.

If nothing else, there was no doubt that Mot carried the blood of Url, famous himself as one of the most courageous and productive Hunters in the clan.

Url squatted on the far side of the room, staring into the Fire, beside himself with grief. Mot was his fifth and only remaining son. Three sons had been lost in hunting mishaps, one in sickness. There were two daughters as well, but daughters were daughters, and they were raised under the complete purview of the Arzat females until they were of age. On occasion, he found himself struggling just to remember their names, which had never been the case for Mot or the four sons who had died. But Url had always felt in his chest that of all his offspring, Mot was the exception. That Za'a, Url's mate, had become pregnant and produced Mot at the end of her reproductive cycle had come as a pleasant surprise to both of them—an unexpected gift from the Creator.

No, Mot would not die like the rest of his sons, Url had assured himself often. He would survive and become one of the greatest Arzats in the history of the clan. Url's certainty had been confirmed by the Astrologers and the Priests, at his request, on several occasions.

Now that dream was dead, for there was one thing neither Url nor any of the clan ever ultimately doubted: the firm, swift and invariably fatal punishment that would be imposed by the Elders for breaking clan law.

None of the Arzats would argue such a verdict, because deep down, they all believed, since they had been taught from youth, that for the great Zanta family to survive and flourish, the words of the Elders—passed from ancestor to ancestor from the days of Orn, whispered to him by the Creator himself, and carved in stone—must be strictly followed. Why laws if they were not to be enforced? There was little room for exception. Exception led to anarchy, and anarchy would lead to the end of the clan.

"Perhaps banishment." Another of the Arzat great Elders, Ag stood to speak, Xan automatically yielding the floor to him due to Ag's seniority. "Mot is young. I agree that what he did was a major transgression, but who among us was not equally curious at his age?"

Ag, one of the oldest of the Elders, was considered most wise, and therefore had the greatest sway with the Council. He was not particularly fond of Mot, but was not past admiring the courage it must have taken him to venture out on his own.

His eyes were the color of blood, ringed with orange and yellow. His skin glistened green and blue in the light, but his scales showed the dry cracks of age. It was rumored that Ag had already seen more than seven by eight seasons. His mid-section was wrapped in the finest of animal skins, a mixture of green and silver textures that were not so different from his own. Despite his age and a pronounced bulge in his stomach, his body still displayed the fine musculature of a Great Hunter—though he had long ago risen high enough in the clan hierarchy that hunting was no longer required of him, and would probably have been unwise. A part of him occasionally missed the excitement of a good hunt, but the ache in his joints as he stood before the group painfully reminded him of his age.

"Perhaps death is enough," he went on, trying to bring swift closure to the matter, his eyes directed at Mot. "Would the Council think that sufficient?"

Death was always so much more final. With banishment, the clan was likely to wonder for weeks about Mot's fate. By suggesting death, Ag felt he was doing the young Arzat and the clan a favor. Besides, he wanted to be done with this issue, as he had more pressing matters to attend to back in his quarters, which had been inconveniently interrupted by the news of Mot's transgression.

A gasp went through the room.

None of the clan would dare to speak out without permission, but that did not stop some low-voice conversations from taking place.

Most of them were silently praying for the death order on Mot's behalf, although not for the same pragmatic reasons as Ag. There was not an Arzat among them that was not terrified of banishment. In the Arzat culture, it was paramount that the bodies of the dead be ritually burned if the individual was ever to have a chance to reach the afterlife. Those who faced banishment were not only condemned to what would likely be a gruesome death, but they would have no hope of ever reaching the next world. It was the ultimate disgrace.

Fet the Wise Mother, who had been seated far to the side, suddenly stood before the group, and another collective gasp rose up in the Chamber. Ag, with his last question, had effectively asked for a vote from the other male Elders, which meant that Fet was not to be consulted on the matter of Mot.

She was clothed in skins even finer than Ag's, and more fully wrapped. Her eyes were golden and piercing with skin that matched, and it was clear even to the younger males that she had probably once been a very desirable mate.

Fet was the only female allowed at the Council as the laws of Orn demanded, for it was natural that the opinion of a female must sometimes, though rarely, be sought. Since Fet was the most senior of the females of the clan, she was also the most highly revered, and therefore allowed to be present.

The fact that more than a few of the males in the room were directly related to her only increased her stature. However, since she had not been summoned to speak, Fet knew she was taking a big chance.

Xan and the other Elders were momentarily taken aback. Even Ag was confused by Fet's sudden audacity. As far as Ag was concerned, this was a very clear-cut matter, except for the question of whether Mot would be banished or killed—and *he* had decided. What more could there possibly be to talk about?

The Chamber went completely still as the entire clan held its breath, waiting for the reaction of the Elders. The crackling of the Fire was the only thing that could be heard for what seemed an eternity.

Finally, it was Ag who broke the silence so that everyone, including himself, could breathe. It had taken him that long to control his anger enough to speak. He looked directly into Fet's golden and unblinking eyes and sent her an unspoken warning.

"It appears that Fet the Wise Mother has an opinion on this issue," was Ag's best effort of saying that Fet now had permission to speak without the immediate threat of him killing her.

“Thank you Ag son of Ta. It is an honor to be present, and an honor to have permission to speak,” her voice was melodic and soothing and her words served as an indirect apology to Ag and the Council for her effrontery.

Fet knew she was taking a chance, but she had seen something in Mot that she liked long ago, and she now had an ulterior motive. When the word of his adventure had been relayed to her it had only confirmed her suspicions that he might be an Arzat worth saving.

Well, perhaps saving, she reminded herself.

When Za’a, Mot’s mother, had asked her for the favor of trying, she had decided to take the risk.

“I will not argue that Mot’s actions did not violate clan law,” Fet continued. “But what real crime did he commit? Who among us would have had the courage to venture into the night alone? Who of us would have had the cunning to beat the great lizards back to the caves? Who of us would have had the fortitude to singlehandedly turn and fight? I know of no one of us!”

Fet paused to let the point sink in. She had just indirectly insulted every Hunter in the Chamber, but she felt she needed to do so in order to ultimately win the argument.

“As far as I have heard, Mot replaced the barrier when he left the caves, and his absence was only discovered by a betrayal.”

Her golden eyes panned the room and eventually fell on young El, who squirmed uncomfortably under her direct gaze.

While upholding the laws of the Elders was always paramount to the clan, logic and emotion ran the other way when it came to loyalty and informants.

Most everyone now knew that it was El who had folded under the scrutiny of one of the more senior Hunters who had passed near the barrier as El stood by waiting for Mot's return. Fet hoped that by mentioning this fact she might take some heat off of Mot.

El, it seemed, was to be given a complete pass on the incident due to the fact that he was directly related to Ag, and only indirectly involved in the actual incident itself. Many in the Chamber turned toward him, staring with intense disapproval. El flinched and cast his eyes to the floor.

"Of all the great and courageous Hunters," Fet continued, "who grace our presence this night and all that have passed into the void, I know of not one who has done battle singly with the great two legged Evil Ones and triumphed!"

There was another huge gasp from the floor. Fet knew she was on shaky ground. Mot had technically broken clan law simply by venturing out, but she could see many heads shake from side to side, and she knew her words were reaching them.

Fet also knew she was risking her own demise, but she was old and tired and had seen the fire in the sky herself. The world was ending so that a new one could be born. If the Zanta Clan was to survive to become a part of the new, then Fet and the other females of the clan had devised the only way she thought it could be done. She was determined now that she wanted Mot to be a part of it.

"I say neither banishment, nor death tonight for Mot. I say let Mot take a place among the others we have chosen for the great sleep. I say let the Creator ultimately decide if he is a worthy Arzat."

Fet was done. They will or they won't, she thought to herself, and then sat down. At least I can look Za'a directly in the eye and say that I tried.

For a moment, the Great Chamber was silent, and then it erupted.

The Arzats had heard the premonitions of the Astronomers and the Priests, and largely believed what they had been told. Still, most of them had tried to ignore the predictions of doomsday and simply carry on with their lives, which had been lived in the same way under the same rules for countless seasons. What was there to do about it anyway? Fet had suddenly reminded them of the coming end of the world in a way that sent panic through the ranks.

"Silence!" Ag said loudly in an immediate attempt to regain control, banging his hunting stick on the floor. "Silence!"

The Chamber gradually quieted, much to Ag's relief. If it hadn't, he was prepared to kill Fet and as many Arzats as it took to restore order—not a pleasant prospect. He was furious at Fet. She had cornered both Ag and Xan, and had effectively rendered their opinions moot, an unheard of usurping of Council authority. If the Council now ordered Mot's death or banishment, given Fet's unforeseen alternative, it might incite a riot. Ag was trapped.

Then, in the midst of all of the chaos, he suddenly had the solution. He would let Url decide. Ag knew Url well and was confident that the great Hunter would side with him. Surely Url would not want his son mixed up with any of this nonsense the females had cooked up regarding some "great sleep."

"Url," Ag called out, "great Hunter and father of Mot, son of Ra, what do you say?"

Url had worked himself practically into a trance during the proceedings. He was almost certain that Mot would be condemned to death and executed this very evening despite Fet's rant. In fact, when Ag had called for Mot's death rather than banishment, Url breathed a sigh of relief.

Since then, he had been gazing blankly at the Fire, which had burned to embers and was in need of fuel. He had hardly been listening, so it took some effort for him to bring his focus back to the present. When he finally looked up, all of the eyes in the Chamber were on him.

"Url," Ag repeated, impatient, trying not to hiss. "Do you have an opinion on this matter?"

Ag longed to be done with this meeting. His legs and back ached from standing, and he needed to relieve himself. If Fet had just kept her mouth shut this issue would have been resolved, and he could be enjoying a good crap and, perhaps later, the attention of the same young Arzat female with whom his evening had originally begun. Instead, he had suddenly been pressed into trying to avoid a clan revolution.

Ag shifted his weight and tightly gripped his hunting stick until he felt the wood choking, imagining it to be Fet's neck. Females! He looked at Fet, and forced his most patient and understanding smile as he waited for Url's response, careful to avoid allowing her to detect the extreme rage inside his head.

Url, who was one of the most successful Hunters in the clan, enjoyed a tremendous level of respect. Without great Hunters, the Arzats would not eat. Many of the stories that were recounted around the Great Fire and carved into stone involved Url and some act of bravery or cunning that had resulted in dinner for the clan.

Tonight, he had been one of the eight who had waited at the entrance and slain the dreaded two-legged lizards. No one in the Chamber doubted that they would someday face Url as an Elder, which gave further weight to his opinion.

Url tried to clear his head. Only once or twice in all his seasons had he been directly called upon by the Council. Any response demanded the proper protocol, and he found himself fighting for the right words. Killing the giant lizards had been much easier. All of the Arzat eyes in the room were on him. Now, suddenly, it looked as if he was to be given a choice regarding the fate of his only remaining son.

He looked over at Mot, carefully weighing the options, and then finally rose to speak.

"Thank you, Elder Ag. Thank you, Council," Url said, slightly bowing his head, "for allowing my opinion, but I do not see how I can be fair in this matter. Mot is my only living son, so my instinct to preserve his life overrules any reasonable judgment I might otherwise have regarding his behavior. And, while I cannot condone his actions, I think I understand them, for I was once young and curious as well. It is said in the stories of the ancients, that our inquisitive nature as a race was the characteristic that led us out of the dark and into the light of intelligence. But the law is the law, and if the Council decides that Mot has broken it, and that *death* is the punishment, I will abide by the decision. With respect, however, if you ask me to vote for my son's life or death, I will vote life—at least for the chance of it."

                                    * * *

Cheers erupted in the Chamber. Fet and Url had won the argument. Ag was forced to quickly lead the Council to vote in favor of allowing Mot to participate in whatever Fet had cooked up as a way of saving the Arzat race and the Zanta Clan.

Personally, Ag highly doubted the process Fet had outlined to the Council regarding long-term hibernation, but, so be it. This allowed him to dispose of Mot without killing him or banishing him, and seemed to satisfy everyone concerned. Url had been the one to finally decide, based on a direct request from the Council, so the appearance of the Elder's ultimate authority had been preserved.

Done with the matter, Ag was the first to depart the Great Chamber, relieved that the Arzats had not rioted and that order had been maintained.

I must retire from this nonsense, he vaguely thought to himself as he headed down the long tunnel toward the communal lavatory. In the meantime, he thought, perhaps a bath in the warm springs with that attractive young female might ease the stress of his important position.

CHAPTER 4

Batter

It had taken about twenty minutes for the air to settle enough to allow Alex to approach the dig site.

She carefully stepped over the loose rocks that covered the area she had been excavating. Several tons of fresh earth was now layered between her and her discovery.

The Einstein-osaur belonged to the mountain again. Her wonderful specimen, even if she could ever find it, would probably have been ground to dust from the force of the falling rocks, along with her computer, her camera, her notes, and all evidence of her discovery.

Alex sat on a large boulder and tried to calm down. She could feel her heart racing, and her head was hot with rage. She listened for the wise words of her father, but there was nothing in the desert air except dust and silence.

After a while, when she thought she could stand it, she looked back over at the debris that now covered her dinosaur and her anger returned.

"Those assholes," she said as she got up and headed back down the hill, walking briskly, the snake now completely forgotten, "those friggin' assholes!"

* * *

Apart from her computer, camera, note book, her precious tools, and her basic supplies, there were three other pieces of equipment Alex always brought to her digs: her pickup truck, her motorcycle, and her gun. The pickup truck was to get her there. The dirt bike was for short errands and scouting. The gun, well, the desert was no place to be without one, especially if you were a solo female.

Her proficiency in the use of all three could be attributed directly to her father and to the fact that she had grown up in the country. Simon had put her on her first motorcycle at five, taught her to drive the ranch truck by age twelve, and helped her learn to properly handle a firearm by fifteen. She was now as good as or better than any man she knew with all of them.

Alex pulled out a ramp from the back of the truck and set it in place, then carefully backed her motorcycle down it. It was essentially a dirt bike, but it had lights and blinkers so she could run it on the street when necessary.

She rummaged around in the cab for a spare backpack and shoved in a bottle of water from her ice chest, her ID, and her Ruger semi-automatic from the glove compartment—checking it to make sure it was loaded.

Alex strapped on her helmet, threw her backpack over her shoulders, fired up her motorcycle, and fishtailed up the road.

Her father had always used motorcycles to hunt for dig sites, and Alex had ridden with him until she had finally demanded a bike of her own. They were much more versatile than four wheelers and could get into and out of places that would leave most ATVs stuck. Alex was an expert with a motorcycle on the dirt and not bad with one on the street. Even so, she was normally a fairly careful rider.

Now she was anything but.

* * *

The afternoon sun was just about to set as Alex swiftly rode toward what she thought was the direction of the explosions. She wanted to find the guys who had ruined her dinosaur before they left for the day.

She gassed the throttle and sped down the gravel road looking for an access in the direction of the blasts. Alex was certain the miners who had set off the charges must be close by.

As she approached the highway, she spotted another dirt road that she had not seen before and took it. It looped through a shallow canyon and rose up onto a plateau, in essence, to the top of the cliff over her camp.

When she reached the summit she stopped the bike, nothing could have prepared her for what she now saw. Below her, in a huge section of flat desert that looked like an ancient lakebed, not more than a half-mile from her campsite, was a vast compound of modular buildings and a lot of heavy equipment.

The complex was situated in a large natural bowl about a mile across in all directions that looked to be entirely surrounded by a high chain-link fence topped with coils of barbed wire.

The sun had just disappeared over the horizon, and lights were beginning to come on around the buildings. A few gigantic dump trucks were appearing like magic from the desert floor, fully loaded and heading for what appeared to be a huge manmade mountain of debris.

Miners, she thought again, confirming her earlier suspicions.

Just as the thought crossed her mind, another series of explosions shook the air.

Alex was amazed that she hadn't been aware of their activity in all of the time she had been working so close by. She tried to remember hearing noises before. It was impossible that there wouldn't have been a lot of it with all of the commotion she could now see going on below her.

Off in the distance, on the far side of the complex, there appeared to be a main entrance with a guardhouse and gate. As she watched, she noticed a large tractor-trailer rig flanked by two black SUVs leaving the facility.

That's where I need to go, she thought.

Alex examined the hill from the top, and found a passage she thought she could rock-hop over on the dirt bike. If she could just get down to it, there was a perimeter road that followed the outside of the fence line. Otherwise, she would have to backtrack out to her camp and take the dirt road to the highway and then try to find the paved access, or she could walk from where she was.

Alex was too pissed for either of the slower options, and it was getting dark fast.

She fired up her bike, took a deep breath, and plunged over the side of the embankment, nursing the motorcycle over several large boulders. Alex had lots of experience traversing rocky terrain, so she was able to successfully maneuver down the hillside and get to the fence line.

Alex realized when she finally reached the bottom that the fence was much higher than she had initially thought. It was at least 12 feet of cyclone topped with another three feet of barbed-wire coil. Every 100 feet or so, signs attached to it warned would-be intruders: BY ORDER OF THE U.S. GOV'T / NO HUNTING OR TRESPASSING / $100,000 FINE OR IMPRISONMENT

The fence held other signs that advised that it was also electrically charged. Uninvited guests were obviously not welcome.

Screw that, she thought. What the hell were they mining anyway?

Alex cranked the throttle and spun her rear tire as she headed toward the main gate, blasting through the gears.

Even in twilight, she realized the dust from her motorcycle could have been seen for miles. This would be no surprise entrance.

As she neared the gate, Alex was shocked to see an armored military vehicle rapidly approaching from inside the complex. Her anger cooled for a moment. These guys looked serious.

She slowed her motorcycle and coasted around the corner of the guard shack and almost ran into two young military men, helmets on and weapons drawn, looking very edgy and nervous.

"Stop the vehicle," one of them commanded with a hand held out, his rifle cradled against his shoulder and pointed directly at Alex.

Alex had already stopped, so she took the hint and killed the motor, very careful to keep her hands in sight. The last thing she needed on this already shitty day was to get shot, and these young men looked quite capable of making a mistake.

"Step away from the vehicle," the same young man ordered her. "Keep your arms raised from your sides and your hands in sight!"

Alex was getting pissed again. What the hell was going on here? This was United States soil she was standing on. She raised her arms nonetheless and got off her motorcycle, slowly stepping to the side.

As she did so, the armored vehicle that she had spotted earlier slid to a stop just behind the two officers and another contingent of eight military personnel exited, all drawing their weapons as they stepped down. A spotlight was suddenly switched on that practically blinded her. It was already getting very dark. When Alex instinctively moved her hand to cover her eyes, she heard chambers loading all around her.

"Can I at least remove my helmet?" she spoke loudly and clearly to the young officer.

He nodded, but continued to hold his weapon high.

Alex carefully unstrapped her helmet and slowly worked it off her head, her long hair falling to her back in the process. She could feel the tension break as she gently set her helmet on the handlebars of the bike and looked the young man directly in the eye.

The officer finally lowered his rifle, glancing at his partner in the process.

"Miss, I need to see some ID, please."

Alex remembered the pistol she had in her pack, right next to her ID. Oh boy, trouble, she thought.

"I am happy to do that officer, but I also wish to inform you that my identification is in my backpack along with a firearm that I am licensed to carry," she said.

Tension again.

Then, out of the corner of her eye, she could see someone running toward the gate from one of the modular trailers.

"Hold on, Sergeant," she could hear him yelling as he approached. It was a voice she knew. "You can stand down, Sergeant. You can all stand down!"

Out of the shadows emerged the face she knew would go with the voice, but it was also a face she certainly didn't expect to see. It was her ex-husband, Tom.

* * *

It had taken several minutes for Tom to sort things out with the guards. Even with him vouching for her, Alex still had to produce her ID and, under much protest on her part, to surrender her prized Ruger to the Sergeant.

After several phone calls from the guard shack, Tom was finally able to clear Alex for entry into the complex.

He had eventually ushered her across the grounds to what Alex assumed was his office.

It was larger than she would have imagined, a full double wide modular. A desk sat in one corner, with a conference table that was more or less centered in the room and surrounded with folding chairs.

The room was quite dark, with the only light coming from a lamp on Tom's desk, as if he had forgotten about the onset of night. Even in the gloom, she could see diagrams and blueprints that were littered all over; blue-taped to walls and draped over the large table.

Along one wall was a series of monitors, which were all conspicuously switched off, with the exception of the one that apparently carried the main gate surveillance.

Alex noticed a coffee maker and a five-gallon water dispenser in another corner and… were her eyes playing tricks on her, or was that someone sitting in the back of the room?

"What are you doing here Alex?"

"No, Tom, I think the far more pertinent question is what the hell are *you* doing here? I've spent a good part of my life here," Alex replied, looking around the room. "What is this place anyway? I thought it was a mining operation when I first spotted it, but clearly it's something more than that."

"This is a classified location, Al. I cannot tell you." Tom slowly replied, spreading his hands, knowing that his answer was not going to fly with Alex. He glanced nervously at the back of the room.

"Can't tell me, huh?"

Calling her Al might have been okay when they were married, but now it made her bristle.

"Classified? What kind of bullshit is this, Tom? Military guards about to shoot *me*—and you can't tell me what is going on?"

She paused, trying to compose herself, now fully aware of the strange presence behind her. To hell with him, she thought. If he wants to be all cloak-and-dagger, so be it.

Alex leaned forward towards Tom.

"Well, this is what I can tell you then: about an hour ago one of your blasts launched a sizable landslide that happened to cover up one of the most magnificent finds of my career, and almost killed me. So I am not so sure, *Tom*, that I am the one who should be doing the explaining about why I am here. And by the way, who the hell is that?" She nodded towards the stranger. "And don't you have any lights in this place?" she continued, totally annoyed.

Alex heard a switch and florescent tubes began to flicker as they came to full power. The stranger in the back had his hands pressed together to his mouth, as if deep in thought or prayer.

Alex glanced at him as she waited for some response. The man was staring at her, studying her. His look gave Alex the creeps.

He was fifty or so, balding, and looked like he had just stepped off a golf course. His face was red from too much sun like one of those poor guys who could never achieve a healthy tan, but continually tried anyway. She imagined that he probably had those goofy sock lines on his legs that ended abruptly at white ankles.

Alex hadn't seen him do it, but it was obvious that he had turned on the lights since the controls were right behind him.

Okay, Tom, not going to introduce me? Fine, she thought, growing more and more perturbed. She turned back towards her former husband and continued her rant, ignoring the stranger.

"I don't really care if you tell me or not, Tom, because you can just bet that I won't rest until I find out. Not only did your guys kill my dinosaur for a second time in 60 million years, but my computer, all of my photos, and the rest of my notes went with it. Suffice it to say that I am more than a little pissed."

Alex let her last statement hang in the air.

She looked at Tom, then the stranger. The room stayed silent for some time.

"Not to mention the fact that then you tried to *shoot me*," she added as an afterthought.

"Alex," Tom pleaded, "no one had any intention of shooting you."

"Oh yeah, let's ask that kid out front."

The mystery man finally adjusted himself in his seat as if he had just finished a great thought.

"Go ahead, Tom, you can tell Ms. Moss."

"That's *Dr. Moss*," Alex said over her shoulder, now even more annoyed. "I'm sorry," she continued sarcastically, "my ex-husband seems to have forgotten to introduce you."

"Ex-husband, hum, very interesting," the man said quietly. "That's very interesting, Tom." He gave Tom a look that Alex couldn't read.

"So, Dr. Moss, am I to assume from your story that you are not a medical doctor but rather a scientist of some sort?" the man continued, obviously playing with her.

Alex didn't reply, she just looked at the mysterious figure as if he were an alien.

"Alex is a paleontologist. One of the best," Tom offered helpfully, trying to break the silence.

"I see. Well, Miss, I mean, err, Dr. Moss, I would certainly like to apologize for any inconvenience we may have caused you," the stranger said.

Alex could feel her face flush red, now she wanted to kill this guy. Okay, smartass, two can play this game. "Wait, I still don't know your name, who the hell are you?"

"Oh yes, so sorry. My name is Batter."

"Batter. Just Batter huh?"

"Think of pancakes, Doctor." He smiled at his own joke, which seemed to allow him to avoid the question of whether there was any more to his name or not.

It was clear to Alex that if Batter had used that line once, he'd used it a thousand times, and he still thought it was funny. He slowly rose from his chair and walked across the room, as if it were a great inconvenience, and held out his hand.

Alex reluctantly took it as if someone were handing her a dead fish. There was something not right about this guy. He smelled like stale bread and Old Spice. Someone had clearly given him too much power for his ego to deal with. His eyes were pale grey, and he looked like a man that lied for a living. But it was his absolute and total confidence that was most disturbing.

"Now, you were saying, Doctor?" Batter said, seating himself uncomfortably close to her at the table.

Alex just stared at him—dead silence again which Tom soon felt the need to fill.

"Alex is one of the finest paleontologists in the country, Mr. Batter. She specializes in the Cretaceous period and teaches… err, I should say she is a professor at the University in Salt Lake. At least, that is, as of the last time we spoke." He looked to Alex for confirmation.

"Tom, the last time we spoke it was not about my career. In fact, I think it had to do with someone you had been cheating with if my memory serves," Alex said, still looking intently at Batter.

"Alex!" Tom pleaded, his face reddening.

Batter was clearly amused.

"Well, Dr. Moss, I'm sorry and quite surprised to say that Tom hasn't spoken a word about you before. Now, as I was saying," he continued, obviously enjoying the domestic dispute.

"No, Mr. Pancake Batter," Alex interrupted, fire in her eyes, "as I was saying, your little operation here just nearly killed me, and it destroyed a one of a kind specimen. That's more than a 'little inconvenience' if you get my drift."

There was a loud knock at the door. Some kind of aide in uniform entered.

"Here is the file you requested, Sir." The aide stole a glance at Alex as he handed the file to Batter. He looked back at Batter, and waited patiently as the older man thumbed the pages.

"Hum… interesting. All right, Corporal, very good," Batter said as he continued reading. "You will return the side arm to the young lady, as well, please," he added without looking up, still combing through the file.

The Corporal reluctantly produced Alex's Ruger and set it carefully on the table, placing the loaded clip beside it. He looked back at Batter as if he were about to salute, then thought better of it.

"Will there anything else, Sir?"

Batter looked up from the file and smiled at Alex. The return of her weapon was obviously some attempt at a peace offering.

"Why yes, Corporal, now that you've asked. Dr. Moss, you must be thirsty. How rude of us not to have offered sooner. Can we get you an iced tea, soda?" He paused. "Perhaps something stronger," he added mischievously.

Alex just looked at him. Who *is* this guy?

"Tom?" Batter asked.

"No, ah, I'm good." Tom twisted uncomfortably in his chair.

"Corporal, two iced teas please for Dr. Moss and… well isn't that interesting… and for Mr. Hancock here, and if you could scare up some bourbon and dump it over some ice for me that would be wonderful." Batter checked his watch. "I think it is way past time for a cocktail."

"Scratch one of those teas and make mine bourbon as well, please, Corporal, straight up." Alex's gaze did not waiver from Batter.

The Corporal remained silent and looked at Batter as if awaiting approval.

Batter was amused.

Intelligent, beautiful, and she has balls. Here is living proof that Tom is the incompetent fool I have always suspected him of being. He laughed.

"Absolutely. Yes, please, Corporal. You heard the lady. And, make mine the same. Tom? Last chance," he added, looking across the table.

Tom shook his head, looking dazed.

"Now, where were we? You were saying, Dr. Moss…," Batter said, turning his attention back to Alex.

Alex watched as the Corporal quietly left the room.

"I was saying that your mining activity has just cost me the most significant paleontological find of my career, and almost killed me in the process. What is going on here? I have been just over the hill for almost a week, and I haven't heard a thing until today. And, what is with all the military? What exactly are you mining?"

"Well, that is a long story, Doctor, but, in short, due to a small problem this operation was virtually shut down for a short period and has only recently resumed."

"No one completely shuts down a mining operation this big without a *big* problem," Alex argued, sensing that Batter was lying.

"Did I say anything about mining, Doctor?" Batter looked at Tom. "Anyway, your unexpected visit may end up being quite fortuitous for you."

"Honestly, Mr. Batter," Alex said, finally exhausted with the game play, "can you get to the point? It's been a long day."

"Ah yes, my apologies, Doctor." Batter paused, and then leaned forward. "What if I were to tell you that we could show you something so incredible that you would forget all about your little dinosaur fossil?"

Alex looked at Tom, confused, then back at Batter. "What do you mean?"

"I mean, Doctor, that the reason we ceased operations was due to a cavern we accidentally opened up during excavation. Well, there was that and some bureaucrats who...." Batter stopped. "Anyhow, the cave contains some things that a paleontologist such as yourself might find very interesting, far more than interesting, actually. In fact, I don't think I would be going way out on a limb to say 'astonishing.' Wouldn't you agree, Tom?"

Tom remained silent, completely surprised by Batter's behavior. Alex had always had a pretty impressive impact on men, but this was... well...

There was another knock at the door, and the Corporal returned, placed the drinks and left.

"Why are there so many military personnel here?" Alex asked again, nodding toward the Corporal as he exited.

"All in good time, Doctor Moss, all in good time. Salute," Batter said, lifting his glass. "I do love a stiff one in the late afternoon, don't you, Doctor?" he said, eyeballing her suggestively. He leaned back in his chair and took a long drink. "Tom, why don't you explain what I am referring to?"

Tom looked dumbfounded. He had never known Batter to be so out of character.

"Well, Tom, I am assuming you can vouch for Dr. Moss and our ability to get *full* security clearance for her?" Batter asked, as if Tom were now the mystery.

"Yes, of course, but...."

"Go ahead Tom." Batter said, waving his hand impatiently. "You can probably tell the story much better than I."

Batter already knew that Alex would clear security. First, her file would have been completely reviewed by the agency years ago before Tom was ever hired and second, because he himself had just checked it again, noting the latest intelligence on her. He was nothing if not thorough. "Don't expect what you don't inspect," had always been his credo, along with, of course, "trust no one."

Tom was just about to speak when Batter's cell phone began to ring.

 Batter looked at it and frowned, recognizing the number.

"On second thought, Tom, I have to take this call. Why don't you just *show* the good Doctor here?" Batter turned back to Alex and offered his hand. "I am sure I will see you later," he said, smiling, hoping he would have the opportunity to personally debrief her.

Batter began to take his call then covered the mouthpiece, "By the way, Doctor, what you are about to hear and see is highly classified by order of the United States government, so unfortunately, you will never be able to discuss anything about it outside of this complex. It would, as they say, be considered an act of treason. Tom will fill you in." He got up and walked towards the door, now totally preoccupied with the call.

As Batter walked out, Alex thought she heard him say, "Yes, Mr. President."

CHAPTER 5

The Big Sleep

After the verdict of the Arzat Council had been passed Fet wasted no time.

She was well aware that she had infuriated Ag to the point that he wanted to personally disembowel her. It was never good to cross an Arzat, especially one as old and ill-tempered as Ag. Fet imagined that given time, he might at the very least try to interfere with her grand plan just for revenge. Because of that, and because Fet honestly believed she had very little time left, she instructed the appropriate females to quickly assemble everyone and to immediately head for the lower caves.

There were about five by eight Arzats in Mot's entourage, including a few torchbearers, a stone carver, some Medicine Men, several of the older females, plus the eight and four adolescents that Fet had originally selected.

Mot was very surprised when he realized that Ara was among them, and might have been pleased were he not so concerned about their fate.

The group slowly worked their way down a long and seemingly endless series of switchbacks. Parts of it were so steep that stairs had been carved into the stone floors.

Even Mot was amazed that the caves could possibly be as long and deep as he was now discovering. Although he had lived in the upper parts of them

51

all of his life, he could not have imagined before this moment their enormous complexity or the vastness of their spaces.

Normally, there would have been a lot of chatter in a group of Arzats this size, but no one spoke, and the procession proceeded in the fog of an eerie quiet.

The group was heading for the sections of cave where the clan's food stores were kept. A very limited number of Arzats were ever allowed there. The entrance was always closely guarded and the area was strictly off limits to the general population.

The penalty for trespassing, like so many other things, was death or banishment. The reserve food stores often meant life or death to the clan, so their storage spaces were treated accordingly, and guarded like treasure. To Mot's knowledge, not even the most mischievous or daring of youths had ever tried to breach the security.

No wonder, it was chilly and very unpleasant. Mot felt the entire world was on top of him, and he began to feel the uncomfortable experience of cold for the first time. Under the dim light of the torches, he imagined that he could actually see his own breath.

The Arzats eventually stopped in a chamber, much smaller than the Great Chamber above, half its size, Mot judged—and cold, very cold. Mot had never felt anything like it. He was no coward, but the prospects of sleeping in such a place were frightening, just based on the temperature alone.

I wonder how long we will have to stay down here, he thought to himself.

* * *

Mot had been elated earlier when the Council had granted him the reprieve, but the details of Fet's alternative had been vague. Anything was better than death or banishment, at least so he had thought at the time. Now, he was beginning to think that this situation might be worse.

But Mot was determined not to show fear and disgrace himself in front of the others, and certainly not in front of his mother or Ara. He felt his body beginning to shake ever so slightly despite his resolve, not realizing that this new sensation of cold was causing him to actually shiver. Mot found himself standing on one foot, then the other, wrapping his arms around his body trying to stay warm.

He glanced over at Ara and the rest of the adolescents, and found them doing much the same, their eyes wide with fear.

In its bowels, the climate of the caves changed, from the relative warmth of the upper chambers, to extreme cold in the lower sections. This condition was a mystery, a phenomenon that worked very much in the Arzat's favor, but had never been explained. Nor had anyone ever felt the need for an explanation. The work of the Creator—the natural chill allowed the Arzats to store food and survive in hard times—was all anyone cared to know.

It was in these chilly lower sections that Fet and the others would execute their plan. They were going to do the same thing with the young Arzats that they had been doing for eons with the clan's food reserves—they were going to "preserve" them.

The females had been working on the details of the plan almost all season, ever since the news had reached them about the death star.

Each time the Hunters had returned with a kill, they had carefully rendered the fat of the animals and stored it. They were going to pack the young Arzats in the fat along with one more very special preservative derived from the roots of one of the ground plants and let the natural cooling of the lower caves take over.

At the same time, Za'a had worked with the Medicine Men to come up with the proper herbs to sedate the youngsters into a deep sleep. The process would slow down their hearts and their breathing to near death, finally stopping bodily functions altogether, and allow the youngsters to silently weather whatever storm ensued in the world above. The animal fat, coupled with the preservative, would protect them and nourish their bodies until the disaster was over, as if they were incubating in an egg.

The Medicine Men had assured Fet and the Arzat mothers that their offspring would be fine for many seasons provided all of the proper measures were taken to perfectly seal them—the seal being absolutely critical to the process.

Large vats of resin from the Ne'e trees had been painstakingly collected and stored for this purpose. The golden resin had been used as a sealant since time began. Properly applied, it produced an airtight cover that was so strong it had to be hammered away later. Meat stored for several seasons could be recovered and eaten, as fresh as the day it had been originally stashed.

The cave did not freeze, which would probably kill the youngsters, but the ambient temperature was very near freezing and very constant, perfect conditions to preserve them in a long state of sleep. The Ne'e resin would be the insurance.

In the floor along one of the walls, eight and four large indentations had been cleared of food stores. The openings were half a stick wide, about a stick long, and half a stick deep—just about the right size if the young Arzats curled up. They reminded Mot of some of the holes in the hot-spring baths. How he wished he were soaking in one of them now.

*　*　*

As Mot stood in the cold, he saw the older females looking at the openings and having a discussion. He began to pray to the Creator that whatever the wise old mothers had planned, they would get on with it so he could get some sleep. The cold was making him drowsy.

Fet put two of the guards to work clearing an additional storage space that had been carved into a wall just above the open spots on the floor.

As Mot watched, he assumed that this would be his bed, though he would have much preferred to be closer to Ara.

The females, after what seemed to be an overly lengthy discussion, finally finished and approached the group. Fet spoke.

"Young Arzats, you have been chosen among the many to survive the great fire rock that is soon to wreck the world. If the Astrologers are correct in their predictions, a great storm will ensue when the rock hits, and much of our world will die, if not immediately, then in the aftermath. I have seen the rock with my own eyes. The Elders have seen it. Mot has seen it. It may be several seasons before the world is ready to sustain our lives once again. We have selected you, the strongest and most able in the Zanta Clan, in the hope that you can live through the disaster that is upon us—by literally sleeping through it—and carry our species and our clan into the next world when the danger has passed."

Everyone looked at Mot, the only one among the young Arzats who had actually seen the coming danger, but he was too cold and frightened to get any satisfaction from Fet's comments or their attention.

Mot was sorry now that he had ever seen the rock, and sorry that he had put himself in this position. He was very tired and just wanted to go to bed. But another thought suddenly occurred to him that caused him to panic as Fet spoke.

"We have prepared a drink that will help you sleep, take it now." Fet said.

A large bowl was produced, and the older females began to distribute a dark liquid into smaller wooden bowls, which were passed to Mot and each of the adolescents. To Mot's nose, the smell was terrible, but when he made the mistake of darting his tongue, his senses got the full force of the brew and he coughed and almost dropped his portion. But he felt the gaze of Za'a upon him, and dutifully sipped the concoction until he had choked down all of it.

* * *

Mot had barely spoken to his mother since his encounter with the Evil Ones; there simply had been no time.

First he had been called before the Council, and not long after he had been led down to into the bowels of the caves. But he knew he had disappointed her and disgraced her in front of the entire clan.

In the Arzat culture, the children were the legacy of their mothers and fathers. The behavior of any offspring directly reflected on the parents and their standing. In this, Mot knew he had failed Za'a entirely.

Nonetheless, he had wanted to ask her, when Fet had finally finished her long speech, one simple question: "How do we get out?" If all of the clan is gone, who will release us? Who will resurrect us?

Of course, the females must have a plan, he thought, trying to reassure himself. If so, he would surely like to know what that plan was. But Mot had looked at his mother and softly probed her mind and knew he must remain silent.

Za'a watched her son from the side of the cave. So handsome, so brave, she thought to herself. What a tragic ending for him. But tragedy was something she was not new to. It was the way of this world, she thought. Za'a was not the only female who had lost children, but most had not lost all of their sons. She would owe Fet a lifetime of favors for tonight. Za'a had asked Fet to save Mot, and Fet had done it on her behalf.

Fet knew that Za'a was past the ability to generate eggs, well past the ability to produce new offspring. There would be no more sons for her.

Fet could fully recall when she herself had experienced the loss of her own womb, so she had great empathy for Za'a regarding her predicament, for what good were females who could not bear sons?

This, at least, would give Za'a some hope that her one remaining son might live.

Like Mot, however, Za'a had stumbled upon the problem of the youngster's eventual release. This had initially caused her great consternation, but she was at heart an Arzat of great faith. The matter would soon be out of her hands and thrust into those of the Creator of all things. Now, it was her job simply to lay the foundation for a chance of her son's survival.

She approached Mot and slowly reached up and gently placed her hand to the side of his head. Za'a could easily have communicated with him without such a gesture, but she was painfully aware of the fact that this was to be the last time she would ever see him, and she wanted the physical connection.

"I feel fear in you my son," she told Mot without uttering a word, "but have none, for I have conferred with the Astrologers and have myself conferred with the Great Creator. You will live again—and thrive."

Mot's head was already beginning to spin from the drugged potion, but he was able to feel the sincerity of his mother's words as they flowed from the tips of her fingers and they helped to calm him. For his part, there was so much he suddenly wished to say, to apologize for and to acknowledge, but he found himself simply replying, "Thank you, Mother. Thank you."

Za'a removed her hand from his temple and moved it into one of Mot's hands. "Here, let me help you, my son."

"Yes, thank you, Mother, thank you," Mot said silently.

Mot suddenly felt like he weighed one hundred stones and fought to keep his footing as Za'a led him to the space that had been cleared and prepared on the wall.

As she helped Mot step up into the opening, he could feel the layers of resin and animal fat around his feet and then around his torso as he settled down inside the sarcophagus. Had he not been so drugged, Mot probably would have jumped out of the hole screaming, begging the council to kill him. It was like stepping into death.

The other adolescents had been similarly assisted and, although he could no longer see them, Mot could hear their frightened pleas, though none of them had uttered an audible word.

Suddenly Mot realized that he had not even had a chance to say goodbye to Ara. This disturbed him to the point that he momentarily overcame his shyness and he let his mind reach out to her.

A few seconds passed, but finally he heard her response, "Sleep well, Mot. I hope to see you soon."

Mot's heart sang. He couldn't believe it. Had Ara actually said those words? He could feel his chest tighten as his hopes soared. He had never had the courage to directly speak to Ara before. And there was promise in her response—not just in her thoughts—but in the way she had delivered them.

"Mot! Mot!" The desperate words of his mother brought him back to the present. "Mot, you must listen to me! Take three slow and deep breaths, and on the third, blow until you have completely emptied your lungs."

How was that possible? He could hold his breath for a very long time, but... Mot wanted to protest, but he was too tired to argue, he just wanted desperately to sleep.

He drew in one huge breath, then blew, another, then blew again.

The last breath, he took in slowly and more purposefully. Even in his highly drugged state, Mot suddenly realized, despite his mother's assurances, that it was probably his last. There was the sweet smell of the cave air, the distinct scent of his mother, the water, the rocks, even the unpleasant scent of animal fat he was lying in, but the one scent he wished to smell most eluded him: the scent of Ara.

He vaguely thought about trying again, but according to his mother's instructions, he blew out purposefully and fully on the third breath, and dropped into a complete and total sleep.

* * *

Za'a stayed with Mot for some time, as did the rest of the Arzat mothers and assistants, watching the young Arzats closely in their drugged state. The Medicine Men moved between them, checking for pulse and breathing. It was critical to get the timing perfect.

As their bodies cooled, and at the moment the youngsters completely ceased any discernible life function, the Medicine Men would order them covered with the animal fat and sealed with the resin of Ne'e.

Mot was the last, his heart was strong.

When they finally came to cover him, Za'a looked at Mot one last time and tried to send him a final message of affection, but there was no response—he was "gone." She looked to the top of the Chamber and made one final plea to the Great Creator to preserve and protect her son, then watched as the animal fat was poured over him and his crypt was carefully covered with a thick seal of resin.

As a final act, the Stone Carver went to each of the holes and chiseled the name of the appropriate individual on the floor next to it.

Za'a watched as he carefully cut the words into the wall below her son, making sure that the carver did it correctly: Mot son of the great Hunter Url.

* * *

When it was finally over, Za'a looked at Fet. "Have we killed them?" she asked without speaking.

Fet felt her gaze and looked back. Her eyes, usually golden, had gone crimson. Her message to Za'a was clear and concise, and yet it avoided directly answering Za'a's question.

"Now we have done all we can do," she replied. "Their fate is in the hands of the Great Creator and destiny."

The two females made the long climb back up through the caves together, the rest of their group following or just ahead.

As they neared the main Chamber, they felt the earth shake, and both of them instinctively knew that they had been right, and had acted just in time.

Fet paused for a moment, slightly unbalanced, but Za'a was there to steady her.

She took Fet's arm and led her back toward the Great Fire.

CHAPTER 6

The ARC

T om walked Alex over to a small ATV vehicle, the kind typically used for hunting or farm work. They were just outside the rectangle of trailers near his office. There was only a vague hint of twilight left in one corner of the sky.

Batter had completely disappeared.

"Tom, what the hell was that all about? Who *is* that guy? And what is all the military doing here?" Alex asked as Tom jumped in the driver's seat of the ATV.

Tom gave Alex a reluctant smile. "Hop in, I'll tell you about it on the way."

"On the way? On the way where?"

"Just get in Alex, would ya?"

He gently tossed her a hardhat with a miner's lantern attached to the front of it and put another on himself.

Lights on, Tom fired up the mini four-wheeler and drove around the trailers and headed directly for a large opening in the desert floor. As they approached it, a huge dump truck with wheels the size of a small house rumbled up the ramp seemingly out of nowhere.

Alex thought for a moment that the giant truck might run them over, but the driver flashed his lights from two stories up in the cab and steered a wide path around them.

"That means there is another right behind." Tom noticed that Alex had an uncharacteristic death grip on the grab bar in front of her, mistaking her excitement for fear. "It's okay, Alex, the drivers know we are on our way down."

"Down? Down *where*?" she asked, her eyes focused on the next truck that had just reached the surface.

Tom looked over at Alex and flashed the very familiar smile that had completely enchanted Alex the first time she had ever seen him.

"I am going to show you something absolutely amazing, and then I am going to show you something I'm sure *you* will find even *more* amazing," he said, speaking loudly over the sound of truck passing them.

They came up over a slight rise and then were suddenly headed down through a massive opening at least four cars wide in the desert floor. It was like entering a steep freeway tunnel, complete with lights and bright yellow directional lines painted on a concrete roadway.

Alex squinted to try to see where the road went, but the tunnel bent back upward after a half mile or so, appearing to level out at what would be several hundred feet below the desert floor, so she could not determine what might be at the end of it.

"I think I am already amazed Tom," she shouted back.

"Just wait, you ain't seen nothin' yet." Tom smiled and winked as he drove down the ramp.

Yes, still "Mr. Charming," Alex thought as she glanced at him.

They hadn't spoken in months, and Alex flashed to their last conversation. Tom had mentioned something about a special assignment he had been working on, but it had gone past her at the time. She had been more concerned about wrapping up a couple of loose ends in their divorce.

During their short marriage of only two years, Tom was always working on some "special assignment" somewhere far away that—as Alex later found out—apparently involved another woman. She had eventually forgiven him since she herself had more or less "stolen" Tom from some other woman he had been seeing at the time they first met. Tom was just that kind of man; the kind women want and are bold in pursuing. Unfortunately, he was also the kind of guy that probably needed to remain a bachelor.

Divorcing Tom had been painful for her but she was a realist. They were both very independent. They would both survive. But she still loved him, and while there was no way in hell she would contemplate ever becoming involved with him again, she counted him on her very short list of best friends. He was a good man, and totally reliable with the apparent exception of his behavior with other females.

One thing was for sure, he was a hell of a geological engineer—one of the best in the world.

"I can't believe Batter is letting me show you this," he said, shaking his head.

They passed another of the giant dump trucks grunting along in low gear as it made its way past them toward the top of the tunnel.

"Why's that?"

"Alex, this project is top secret, and I mean *top* secret. The guys working on this practically have to sign their lives away to be here, and all of them have to pass a super-high level of security. They can't even tell their families what they are doing, or even where they are," Tom said, glancing over at her, as if he were expecting some response.

They passed a rough handmade sign that read "Welcome To Underworld, Population: Not Yet, Elevation Minus 915 Feet."

The tunnel flattened out and they entered an area the size of two or three football fields. It reminded Alex of a super-sized astrodome, complete with very bright lights beaming down in rectangular patterns from overhead. She tried to keep her jaw from dropping.

"Pretty impressive huh," Tom said, noting her reaction. He wheeled the ATV off of the main road and stopped. He just kept quiet and let Alex look.

The place was massive. Alex got out of the cart and let her eyes wander.

What the hell was supporting this, she asked herself as she surveyed the ceiling, which looked to be more than two hundred feet over their heads. They were almost a quarter of a mile below the surface. How had they managed to create such a large space with no visible supports?

"I know what you're thinking. Impossible, huh?" Tom was looking at the scene like a proud father.

"Yes, Tom, this is friggin' impossible," Alex said, her head back, looking up.

There was no doubt in her mind now why Tom had been selected to build it. He was probably one of the few people she knew of in the world that had both the engineering skills and geological background necessary to construct such a project.

"Was, Alex, *was* impossible." He smiled again. "Two words, carbon fiber. Look closely at the rafters. We're building it like a giant egg using carbon fiber beams." Tom raised his head and proudly looked to the ceiling him-self. "Makes the pyramids look easy, doesn't it? It's going to be rated for a 9.0 quake when we get it done."

"But Tom, the expense…," she said as her eyes scanned the structure.

"Nothing is too good for the ole United States government, Alex. They are basically letting me build this thing with no budget constraints. All of those lights, LED," he said pointing toward the high ceiling. "More of your tax dollars at work in places you never imagined possible, right?"

Once Alex had gotten over the shock of the rafters, she let her eyes wander over the facility itself. There were several buildings, some of them eight or ten stories high, set on the floor of the structure. It looked like a small town complete with storefronts and small streets, with the exception that every-thing was painted pure white and it appeared to be deserted. The project looked virtually finished, but for a large gash in one wall where a crew with heavy equipment was working removing debris. Alex could feel the hair on the back of her neck rising.

"So, Tom, here is the obvious question, what the hell is it for?"

The smile disappeared from Tom's face. "It's a doomsday shelter Alex, a doomsday shelter."

Alex just looked back at the place in silence.

"Actually they are calling it an 'ARC'—short for Auxiliary Repopulation Center. This is going to be like a small city when we get it done." Tom kicked a lose piece of rubble away with his foot.

"But why? What specifically is it for?"

"Who knows?" he shrugged. "But no one needs to tell you about extinction events, or nuclear bombs, or world pandemic. Maybe one of those new telescopes spotted something. Maybe some politicians just got freaked out. I don't really know, Alex. All I do know is that I was given an unlimited budget and a very short window of time to get my part of this thing done, with a rather large incentive bonus if I'm on time. Which brings me to our next topic. See that area down near the bottom of the ramp? We were doing some controlled blasting there, trying to get ready to install one of the last reactors…"

"Wait, reactor?"

"Yes, Alex, this place is all going to be powered by a series of small self-contained nuclear reactors."

He pointed to an area where six large cylinders several stories tall were lined up near the gash.

Alex shot him a look of complete disbelief.

"I'm not kidding. They are all chained together. When one wears out it automatically shuts itself down and another fires up. The scientists say that they could theoretically power the entire complex for several hundred years. Just one of them will produce a hundred thousand kilowatt hours a day for fifty years at full power. They're like giant batteries. The boys are working on placing the last one of them now."

"Amazing. I'd heard of them but…"

"Anyhow," Tom continued, "we hit an old lava tube, Alex, and I mean old, millions of years old. Somehow we completely missed it before in the surveys. But what is really interesting about it is what they found *in* it."

Alex felt the hair on the back of her neck rising again, her paleontologist radar was pinging. What *who* found, she thought.

"Anyway, we just had an entire team down here for the last few days clearing it out so that we can get going again and...," Tom paused.

"Clearing it out, *clearing it out*, what did they find Tom—tell me?" she asked, grasping his arm.

Tom looked suddenly uncomfortable. "Well, I spoke to one of the paleontologists...."

"Paleontologists!" she squeezed him harder.

"Come on Alex," he looked at her sheepishly, "there was nothing I could do. I couldn't tell you. I would have been fired immediately. Hell, I might have been shot. He brought in his own people."

"He? He who? Batter?"

"Yes, Batter. He has total authority here, if you couldn't tell. I think he answers directly to the President."

"The President," she said, remembering Batter's phone call. "Okay, okay, you were saying..."

"They found some stuff Alex. One of the scientists told me it might be pre K-T."

"Pre-K-T! *Pre-K-T!*" she was beside herself. "Take me down there, Tom."

"I knew you were gonna be pissed at me."

"No, Tom, I'm *not*," Alex gulped, pissed off at him, but trying to control her excitement. "Please, just take me down there."

Tom was not about to argue. Winning an argument with Alex was next to impossible.

He checked his watch and noted that it was getting late, and he would have loved to propose getting some dinner instead, but he knew better than to try to talk Alex out of going down to the caves now that he had opened his big mouth. Besides, he was still confused by Batter allowing Alex down in the first place. No telling if he would change his mind, if he did, Tom knew Alex would go nuts.

* * *

Tom had been totally astonished by her appearance this afternoon. He had no idea that she had been working so close by, not that it should have really surprised him. Alex was always poking around someplace in that damn desert.

He had been trying to work out a problem with a reactor location with one of his engineers in his office when they heard all of the commotion at the gate, but at first he hadn't really paid attention. There was always some group of curious hunters or hikers that the security guys were chasing off.

When the commotion had continued, Tom had finally glanced up at the security monitor and seen Alex, instantly recognizing her signature stance and her unbelievable body even on the lousy screen. She was crazy, that is what he loved about her, and she was beautiful. The fact that she had no idea just *how* beautiful made her even more attractive. Why, he wondered, had he ever allowed himself to screw up their relationship?

She was perfect, he thought now, looking at her.

* * *

They got back in the ATV and he wheeled them down to an area just a few hundred feet past the main entry ramp and parked. A dozen or so workers were focused on positioning the last nuclear cylinder in place on a cement foundation next to five others that had already been installed.

Tom noticed that their attention was totally diverted to Alex when she got out of the cart. He signaled to one of the foreman who immediately dropped what he was doing and walked their way.

Alex, on the other hand, was staring at a large gash in the side of the wall, where another crew of equipment operators were at work removing what appeared to be the last of some rubble, loading it into one of the massive dump trucks with an equally massive skip loader. In the center of the gash, a rough opening ten or twelve feet wide and equally as tall, dropped into total darkness.

"What can I do for you, Tom?" the foreman offered helpfully, trying not to stare at Alex and failing.

"Andy, meet Alex Moss. We are going to take a short trip down into the cave. Do you guys still have some gear around?"

"Sure Tom, but…," Andy hesitated, "isn't it a little late to be spelunking?" Andy gave Tom a sly grin.

"Never mind Andy," Tom said. "Just help us get the gear, and remind your guys that they are installing a nuclear reactor, not a ping pong table."

"Yes, Boss," Andy said, suddenly embarrassed. "I have a bunch of stuff in my truck. Come on, I'll get you set up."

Andy led them over to a pickup truck and pulled down the tail gate. It was heaped with all kinds of brand new gear; heavy jackets, helmets, ropes, flashlights, and tools of all kinds.

"They were in such a hurry to get out of here they just left all of this," Andy said, waving his hand over the equipment.

Tom fitted Alex and himself with thick coats and grabbed two flashlights.

"Okay, Andy, we aren't going to be long. Alex, you can leave your back pack here if you want."

Alex gulped. There was no way was she going to leave it, especially now that she had her father's favorite gun back.

"Sorry, Tom, what little is left of me after today is in this damn bag, so I think I will just take it along if you don't mind."

"That's fine, Alex. Here, let me help you."

Tom helped Alex zip up her jacket and to strap on her backpack. He handed her a flashlight and smiled.

"Ready?"

Alex nodded. "Why the heavy jackets Tom?" she asked, giving hers a final adjustment.

Tom began to head toward the opening.

"It is very cold in the cave, Alex, in fact, so cold that geologically it doesn't really make sense. The tunnels somehow have acted like their own refrigeration system. The temperature is very constant at around zero-to-one degree Celsius. It's as if they are connected to a bed of ice. Really, I haven't had time to try to totally figure it out."

"How did you find it?"

Tom shrugged. "More like it found us. We were blasting the very last part of the south wall, and when the dust cleared, there it was. Somehow we missed it on all of the surveys. Until that happened, we were right on schedule. We had to shut down for almost a week just to decide what to do about it. The entire facility is almost done, apart from that little delay."

He motioned toward the hole they were approaching.

"But I have to tell you Alex, no one was more astonished than I was at what they found down there. I mean, I am no paleontologist, but even I got excited when I heard about it."

CHAPTER 7

Buck It

They were finally heading home.

Pete Wilson rubbed his eyes to clear the glare from the lights of some oncoming traffic and fought to stay awake. He was seated high up in the cab of a Peterbilt semi with possibly the most important scientific discovery in all of human history trailing along behind in a refrigerated container.

He could only remember a few other times in his life when he had been as excited and dead tired at the same time: his wedding day, the individual births of his three children, surviving boot camp, and finishing his doctorate in physics at UCLA.

Oh, and of course, the day he had been appointed Chief Scientist for all of Area 51.

He glanced over at the driver, a man who went by the moniker of 'Buck,' but whose real name was Don Mills, a fact Pete had uncovered when carefully reviewing the man's file prior to departure from the Utah site.

Buck was not on Pete's official team. He had been forced to use Buck at the last minute, when they had discovered the full extent of the unexpected find in the caves and realized that a refrigerated tractor-trailer would be necessary to transport the specimen they had unearthed.

But Pete had found nothing in Buck's file that would preclude a Class A security clearance—nor had Batter. So here he was, somewhere off Highway 191, heading for one of the most top secret locations on the planet carrying one of the most important finds in history, with some relatively unknown cowboy at the wheel.

"How ya doin', Buck?" Pete asked in his best attempt at a western drawl, as much to be friendly as a test to see how awake his unknown driver was. These were the first real words Pete could remember speaking to the man since they'd left the site.

Buck calmly spit out a pistachio shell he'd been chewing on and flicked it to the floorboards. He reached into a bag he had by his side and placed another large load of nuts in his mouth.

"Doin' fine, Doc," he replied, spitting. "Be doin' better if your boys up front would speed up a bit." Buck punched the clutch, grabbed the gear shift and down-shifted. "How'd ya sleep?"

Pete glanced at Bucks' speedometer then looked out and spotted one of their escort vehicles a few hundred feet ahead of them. He had given the lead driver specific instructions that they were not to exceed fifty miles an hour, and he was happy to see that the driver was following his orders.

Pete had to admit, from his vantage point in the cab of the semi, it did seem like they were only going twenty. He leaned forward so he could get a look out of Buck's side view mirror to make sure the second vehicle was still following.

"Sleep? What do you mean sleep?" he asked, preoccupied with his effort to see what was going on behind them.

Buck smiled and spit another pistachio shell. "Hell, Doc, you been snorin' like a steam engine since we pulled out of Vernal."

"Really?" Pete had no recollection of dozing. He checked his watch and yawned. "Where are we?"

"Just a few miles out of Green River. Another twenty minutes or so and we'll be on the 70. Then we can start making some real time."

Buck was about to be very disappointed, thought Pete, looking out at the stars through the passenger window. There were some low mountains off to the right, but the rest of the land was flat, barren desert. Over towards the east, a quarter moon was rising. He looked back at the road, a long straight-away of two lane highway that looked like it went on forever.

"Don't worry about it Doc," Buck laughed. "That's why I'm drivin' and you're the Doc."

Buck could see the black Suburban suddenly slowing in front of him. He downshifted and hit the brakes. The SUV's red lights flashed off, and the vehicle appeared to pick up speed again. Buck banged the semi back into a higher gear and hit the throttle.

"Probably just seen a rabbit," he said, a little exasperated. "Really, Doc, these guys are driving slow as molasses. Can't you call 'em an' tell 'em to pick up the pace just a notch?" he pleaded.

Pete looked out at the long dark highway ahead of them and weighed Buck's request.

He was just as anxious to get this trip over with as Buck so he could get back to the labs and begin work on the twelve blocks of ice that they had recovered from the site. Each one of them, he already knew from radiological testing, contained the nearly complete remains of a never before discovered species of dinosaur that had lived sometime just before the great extinction. Twelve of them!

On top of that, it was pretty clear from the way the specimens had been mummified and buried that they were sentient, with a level of intelligence that had never before been imagined. He couldn't wait to get started.

It was a miracle that they had even been given time to exhume them. Batter had been insistent from the start that Pete's scientific team would have only seventy-two hours to complete their examination of the site and get out. Despite Pete's plea for an extra day, Batter had stuck to the timeline. At one point, Pete had been so frustrated that he had actually considered trying to go over Batter's head until he realized he couldn't imagine who that would be other than the President himself. Besides, Pete was a military man at heart, and Batter had issued an order not a request, and Batter, as far as Pete knew, was one of the highest ranking "unofficial" officers in the United States government, not to mention the fact that he was completely in charge of Area 51 and, therefore, Pete's boss.

So Pete had immediately pulled in his best people, and they had begun to carefully remove all twelve specimens as quickly as possible. But the working conditions in the caves had been difficult, complicated by the extreme cold. Pete had been forced to bend almost every rule he had ever been taught for the proper collection of scientific evidence in order to get the job done in the short time he had been given, much to the chagrin of his staff of paleontologists.

It had taken all seventy-two hours to cut the stone around the specimens with diamond blade saws so they could take each sarcophagus out more-or-less intact. The resultant cubes were approximately four-by-four-by-eight feet, and each weighed over a ton.

One of the ARC foremen had loaned them a skip loader and an operator to pull each piece out and had helped them to devise a winch and a make-shift skid pad to get the blocks up the long cave corridor and loaded onto the refrigerated truck.

Pete had been offered a C-130 from the military to transport them, but the thought of any kind of aviation disaster with such a precious cargo was too much for him to bear, and personally, he was not fond of flying, so he had turned the offer down.

Now, as he looked over at Buck, loudly snacking on his beloved pistachios and spitting them on the floorboards, Pete began to have second thoughts about that decision.

He picked up his phone and dialed the lead SUV.

"How's everyone doing up there?" Pete asked when one of his team picked up.

"We're fine, Doc. Our driver says we are just about at the junction. Everyone else is passed out."

"Well, I have a request back here that we pick up the pace, and I am inclined to agree with my driver. Can you tell your man up there the new limit is…," Pete hesitated, looking over at Buck and then at the straight highway in front of them, "…sixty? Let's get home."

"You got it Boss, six-zero it is," Pete heard the happy reply from the other end. "See you in a few." The phone went dead and the SUV accelerated.

Buck threw down the clutch and changed gears.

"Thanks, Doc. Maybe we'll even get there now," he said, obviously much happier about the new pace. "Ya know, Doc, you got real lucky snagging me for this run."

"Oh yeah, how's that?" Pete asked, not all that interested.

"I was just fixin' to load up with about five thousand pounds of fresh bison for a run up to Salt Lake when I got the call. You know they actually farm those things now? Anyhow, there is a huge ranch up near Vernal where they grow 'em, slaughter 'em, butcher 'em, and package them all in one fell swoop. Quite an operation. Big money in it too. Did you know that shit is three times as expensive as beef? Can't really tell the difference myself. Leave it to the heath nuts," Buck said, fishing in his bag for more pistachios. "Buffalo," he said disdainfully, shaking his head.

"Well, I guess we just got lucky," Pete said absently, already creating a mental list of things to do the minute they arrived.

"Yep, you sure did. Did you know I'm ex-military, as well?"

"Is that so?" Of course, Pete knew everything about Buck's service record from his file.

"Yep. Drove convoy in the first Gulf War, you know, the war we actually won. Dangerous stuff though. Got blown up a time or two, but here I am." Buck was frowning into his rear view mirror. "Now what the hell...."

"What's going on Buck?" Pete leaned forward to try to get a glimpse into his mirror, but could see nothing but the glare of headlights.

"That knuckle head, he's not... Yep, here he goes..."

"Buck, what's happening?"

"This asshole behind us is trying to pass," Buck said, one eye on the road and one in the mirror. "And here he comes."

Buck watched as a semi behind them passed the rear SUV escort and was moving up beside them. In the distance, he could see the oncoming headlights of another tractor-trailer, plenty of room if the guy didn't hesitate.

"Do it if you going to do it boy!" Buck pulled his foot off the gas, willing the other driver to hurry.

As the semi pulled by, all Pete could see was a series of running lights and the huge fuel tank they were attached to. When he looked forward again he knew they were in trouble.

"Ah shit," Buck said, as he watched the fuel truck try to cut back in early.

Buck downshifted and hit the brakes hard, swerving off to the right of the road, but he was too late. The nose of the Peterbilt dove under the rear of the passing truck, and all Buck could see was an enormous mass of stainless steel heading for the cab.

Pete watched as the fuel truck lifted and came right toward the windshield, smashing the glass as both trucks ran off the road and plowed into the soft embankment.

When they finally stopped moving, Pete looked over to find Buck, but there was nothing but fuel tank occupying the driver's side of the rig where he had been sitting. Buck was gone.

Pete reached up and touched his forehead, and his hand came back red with blood. Apart from that, he found it to be a miracle that he was still alive and the truck still upright. He unbuckled his seat belt, pushed the door open, and slid down to the ground, the smell of fuel almost overwhelming him.

* * *

"Doc. Doc, are you all right?" he could hear Paula, one of his team yelling as she ran to assist him from the SUV that had been following.

"Yeah, I think so," Pete replied, still in a daze.

"Let me see that," Paula said, gently removing Pete's hand from his head.

She scrutinized the wound, and then miraculously produced a Kleenex from her pocket to try to staunch the flow of blood.

"Doesn't look *too* bad, right in the eyebrow. Nothing five or six stitches won't fix. Where's your driver?"

"Well…," Pete started to reply.

"Hey, you guys gotta get outta here," an unfamiliar voice said coming around the truck.

Pete assumed that it had to be the fuel truck driver who had apparently escaped the accident unharmed.

"This thing might blow any second," the man was shouting as he emerged around the side of the wreck carrying a large chrome fire extinguisher.

Pete looked down at his feet and noticed that the ground around them was already becoming saturated with fuel. He ran for the rear of the truck, pulling Paula along with him.

As Pete reached the back of the tractor-trailer, he realized the rest of his team had already converged there with the same thought: the specimens!

The driver of the fuel truck had followed.

"Look Mister, I am very sorry but you've got to get these people out of here. When this thing goes it is going to be big. That fuel up there is pouring all over that hot engine. It could go at any second."

Pete was already pulling the huge doors open on the trailer, ignoring the warning.

"Doc, he's right. We've got to get out here," Pete heard another of his team members say.

"Two of you go stop traffic in both directions," Pete commanded over his shoulder. "We've got to get at least one of these off of this truck."

He turned and looked at his team, and could feel the blood beginning to flow again from his head. Two of the security detail immediately headed off in separate directions. There were nine of them left.

"Let's do it," said a team member named Rich as he jumped up on the trailer. "Which one Doc?" he asked Pete as they stood over the two specimens closest to the back.

It was a helluva question. Yes, indeed, which one?

Pete looked for a moment at both of the blocks, one of them clearly larger than the other, and then decided.

"Let's see if we can at least push the smaller one out."

His entire team fought to slide the icy block, all ten of them, pushing and pulling on the large stone and the straps around it until it was on the lift.

When they got it to the ground, one of the drivers used the winch on his SUV to drag the sarcophagus down the highway out of range of the impending inferno.

Just as they turned to go back for another, the trucks burst into flames. In seconds, the fire had engulfed both vehicles.

They watched from a distance as the flames rose from the two trucks. There were several explosions and the flames leapt higher into the sky with each one. It was all-consuming. No one had any doubt that when it was over there would be nothing left of the other eleven dinosaurs. Even several hundred feet away, they could feel the intense heat converging with the cool night air of the desert, the smell of fuel and burning rubber heavy in the air.

The group was silent. Even the fuel truck driver who had caused the disaster had run out of apologies. He was fully experiencing the shock of having just killed someone.

He sat on the side of the road, perched on his fire extinguisher, smoking a cigarette, his hands shaking.

* * *

Pete and his team sat for over an hour quietly observing the inferno.

He finally looked up when he heard the sound of the immense rotors of a Chinook helicopter overhead, and watched silently as the landing lights came on and it touched down on the highway near the position his team had taken with the only thing they had left: one specimen.

CHAPTER 8

The Doomsday Scenario

The clock on the desk in the Oval Office said 4:21 p.m.

President Arthur H. Long leaned nonchalantly over the couch where he had been seated since lunch with a contingent of Chinese delegates, some of his staff, and a handful of interpreters.

He snuck a look at the time, trying not to be obvious about it.

They had been meeting all day to see if they could reach some agreement on currency, and to wrap up a few details of an extended trade deal.

It was tough work and required his total concentration to keep up with the translations and make sure that no measure of etiquette was breached along the way. So far, they were making good progress.

The President knew it was absolutely critical that the day end well, and he couldn't wait for that moment. He imagined that if he sat much longer his ass was going to stick to his seat.

Another hour or so, he thought, and maybe we can wrap this up.

The Ambassador was rambling on about something in Chinese when the President saw his most trusted aide quietly enter the room.

Now what, Long thought, squirming.

He had given orders that they were not to be disturbed except in the case of a dire emergency. Any interruption could be construed as bad manners, and could easily be taken as an insult that might jeopardize the entire meeting.

The aide stood stoically by the door looking directly at the President, his hands at his sides, with only his index finger pointed to the floor. This was a pre-arranged signal indicating a Level One emergency.

Reluctantly, the President asked one of the interpreters to apologize and say that he needed to be excused for just a moment. He waited until the words had been translated, smiled apologetically, and rose from his seat, the delegation members watching him disapprovingly as he made his way across the room.

"This better be good, Anders," President Long said quietly, trying to stay out of earshot of the rest of the delegates, aware that most of them actually spoke and understood English better than he.

But Long had no doubt that the message would be important. Anders had been working for him since his days as a Senator, and they could practically read each other's minds. Still, he couldn't imagine a scenario bad enough to warrant the interruption, save a sudden all out nuclear war, and the only people he could think of that would really ever have the balls to try something like that were seated right behind him.

"Sir, I think we need to take this outside," Anders said, looking at him seriously, opening the door in the process so the two of them could exit the room.

Long turned to the delegation, bowed and smiled awkwardly, then followed Anders into the corridor. Anders had already set off down the hallway.

"What's this all about?" the President asked, matching his aide's brisk pace.

"It's a woman from Pan-STARRS, Sir. She's the Chief Astronomer, and she has been holding for the last hour. She says she has important news and that *her* 'protocol' requires that she communicate with you directly," Anders replied as they reached another office and a secure line. There was a light blinking on the phone in front of them.

"What the hell is Pan-STARRS, Anders?" the President asked as he began to reach for the phone.

"It's the observatory on Maui, the one that tracks asteroids and comets. I checked before I came to get you, and she's right about the protocol, if...," Anders let the comment hang in the air.

"If what?"

"If there is a high chance of a significant impact within a ninety day window."

"Impact? Impact of *what*?"

"I think maybe you should just speak to her directly, Sir."

The President looked at Anders skeptically, punched the blinking button and picked up the receiver.

"This is President Long."

"Err... Sir..., this is Dr. Jennifer Daniels. I am Chief Astronomer at the Haleakala Pan-STARRS Observatory. I am sorry to interrupt you, Sir, but I have important information regarding the recent discovery of a NEO."

"A what?"

"Sorry, Sir. A 'near earth object,' an asteroid, Sir."

"Go on," replied Long, while he racked his brain trying to remember his briefing on the Pan-STARRS project. He could vaguely recall a lot of scientific jargon about 'near earth objects' and 'impact probabilities,' pretty boring stuff considering what he had on his plate. The briefing had been some time ago.

"Sir, we have strong reason to believe that an asteroid approximately 2.9 kilometers in diameter will strike the earth in less than twenty-nine days somewhere near Mexico in the western Pacific Ocean."

The President sat down, holding the receiver to his ear, searching for something to say, the details of that long ago meeting snapping back into his head in living color.

"Sir?"

"Have you been able to come up with any calculations regarding potential damage?" the President finally managed to say.

"Sorry, Sir, but I have spent the last five or six hours just trying to pinpoint the exact trajectory of the object and to confirm the impact probability before I called."

"And?"

"Well Sir, as I said, as near as we can tell, somewhere around 25 degrees North and 118 degrees West. The impact probability is essentially one hundred percent. We are still working on a precise Torino number."

"I'm sorry, Doctor, I meant, can you say anything about damage."

"Not yet, Sir, as I mentioned…"

"Doctor," the President interrupted as calmly as he could, "can you give me a ballpark idea?"

"Well, roughly, something on the order of several million nuclear devices exploding simultaneously, Sir."

The President looked over to Anders and covered his mouthpiece.

"We need to find Batter."

CHAPTER 9

The Caves

Tom and Alex climbed over some rubble and entered the rough opening, switching on their flashlights almost simultaneously. It was pitch black inside.

Alex stepped carefully, sweeping her light high across the cave's rafters, trying to get a sense of its size. The area they were in was large, with twenty to thirty foot ceilings and almost as wide.

Aside from the hole Tom and his men had inadvertently knocked open in the ARC, it looked as if there were two other natural entrances; one which seemed to lead upward, and one down, all part of some sort of vast natural tunnel system.

"Which way, Tom?"

"That way," he said, pointing his light at the entrance that looked like it went up, "only goes for about two hundred feet and then it's totally blocked by a slide, but this way," he said turning the other direction, "well, you'll see."

Alex followed Tom toward the second entrance.

The cave narrowed considerably and then began to descend more rapidly. As they stepped off into the dark she stumbled into him.

"Watch it Alex," he said, concerned for her safety, "shine your light down so you can see where you are going."

Alex turned her flashlight to the floor of the cave and was astonished at what she saw.

This cannot be, she thought to herself.

She knelt down and looked at the area ahead of her, moving the light from side to side, touching the floor with her hands. Impossible.

"What would have? What could have? No, there must be some mistake," she said to herself. "This has to be a natural phenomenon."

She realized she had tripped on a *step*!

"Amazing huh? Just like I promised," Tom offered smugly.

"This must be some kind of natural rock formation, right?"

Alex was looking at a series of steps that continued into the dark below. They were cut directly into the stone, approximately six feet wide from side to side, a foot and a half deep, and had a drop of about eight inches. Each one seemed perfectly proportioned to the next.

"You tell me, Doctor," Tom replied. "All I know is that one of the guys from the team that was down here earlier today said that they had found pre-K-T specimens and no other evidence of any other occupancy since, suggesting that these were cut, what, over sixty million years ago?"

"That's impossible. What specimens, Tom?"

Alex continued to pan her light over the obviously man-made staircase, which defied logic if the cave dating was accurate at pre-K-T.

"Oh my god! They must have made a mistake," she said. She felt as if her head was going to explode. "Who was this guy you spoke to?"

"I don't remember Alex," he thought for a moment. "Wilson, yes, I think it was a guy by the name of Pete Wilson. Anyway, they didn't exactly invite me along. All I know is that they commandeered a refrigeration truck from town and spent a good part of yesterday and almost all of today loading it up. Heck, they just left a few minutes before you got here. Batter was involved, so he probably knows the whole story. I had other issues so I didn't get down here until this afternoon with my…" Tom hesitated.

"With your *what*, Tom?" Alex asked suspiciously.

Tom's face reddened, "Come on Alex, I am under orders to finish this project a.s.a.p."

"With your *what*?"

"With my demo guys Alex. We're going to blast this area in the morning and seal it. Those explosions this afternoon, that was my crew preparing the fill material up top."

"Jesus, Tom, what's the hurry?" she demanded.

"I don't really know, but there is definitely a *big* hurry. Batter was emphatic that in no way were we to fall any further behind schedule. We've already been delayed almost a week because of this find. He's given me only twenty days to finish."

Alex was shaking.

"You mean to tell me that you guys are going to purposely ruin what is possibly the most important discovery in the history of modern man over a friggin' schedule?"

She tripped again and Tom reached out to catch her.

"Alex," Tom continued calmly, "Batter assured me that the scientists have already recovered or documented anything of importance down here, and that I need to get the project completed. As he said, 'because *that*, Tom, is exactly what we are paying you to do.'"

"Well, Tom, aren't you just a little bit curious about what the rush is? I mean, didn't you tell me that what you are building is some sort of dooms-day shelter?" Alex asked him as if he were some kind of idiot.

"Yes, of course I am, but I haven't been able to discover anything yet that will tell me the real purpose behind it. And I ain't asking. You know how the government is, Alex, cloaked in secrecy. All I know is that they are pay-ing me big money to finish. Maybe the funds appropriated expire if certain deadlines aren't met. I don't know. But, Alex, think about it, hasn't the world always been 'coming to an end' ever since we were kids? Someone in Washington has probably just taken that notion far too seriously."

Alex had to admit that Tom was making some sense. That did not, however, justify the fact that his team was just about to destroy what might be the most significant archaeological-paleontological find in history.

"I haven't even shown you the good stuff yet Alex. You want to see it or stand here and argue all night?"

"Let's go," she replied.

They continued down the stone staircase. Alex noticed that the steps them-selves had the usual slight indentations from years and years of foot traffic on them, but they were cut wider and deeper than modern stairs, which made them somewhat awkward to traverse.

The cave leveled out in places, and the stairs disappeared, then reappeared when the descent got steep again. Where level, the walls were cut near the bottom at ninety degree angles so the path could be kept perfectly flat. No question that they had been intelligently engineered.

Alex also noticed that the temperature was dropping dramatically as they went down. She was glad that Tom had insisted on the heavy gear.

"Here it is," he said. "There is this one last long stairway, and then we'll be there."

Another fifty or so steps down and they emerged into another large chamber. They were now about three or four hundred feet from where they had entered, but Alex wasn't sure how much deeper they were.

It was cold though, very cold, freezing in fact. Alex could see her breath in the beam of her flashlight. She swept it around and spotted several indentations in the floor and several more in the walls.

In some spots, rectangular stones had been cut and put in place like tables or benches. She immediately thought that the room must have been some sort of burial chamber. Several caves seemed to branch off from this main room, but she could only see their black entrances.

"Amazing isn't it?" remarked Tom. "Take a look at the inscriptions in front of the holes in the floor Alex."

She approached the indentations which looked like rows of giant stone bathtubs cut directly into the floor, her heart in her throat. Inscriptions?

She shot her light down at the edge of one of them. Sure enough, I did look as if something had been chiseled into the stone. She crouched down to get a better look. The marks were hard to make out, but they were definitely there. Her mind tried to rebel at the very idea, but the evidence was unmistakable. Whatever beings had occupied these caves not only knew how to carve stairs, but they knew how to write! This had to be manmade, or made by some far more recent ancestor. No way this was pre-K-T.

Alex panned her flashlight around the chamber, but it was hard to see anything clearly.

"Tom, I have to have some better light. I noticed some portable floods in the back of that pickup. We need to get them."

"Oh, Alex, come on," he groaned, "we have to get out of here soon anyway. Here, let me help you." Tom moved toward Alex with his light.

"Tom," Alex said with an edge in her voice, "first of all, you know I am not leaving here until you assholes blow the place up, and second of all, I need some light. Now, are you going to help me or not?"

Tom knew better than to cross Alex. Even he somewhat understood the importance of this discovery, and he had known all along that, once he brought Alex down, he would have a hell of a time getting her out. They were going to be here all night. At least if they went back for the lights, he might be able to get some dinner sent down. His stomach rumbled.

"Okay, let's go get them," he surrendered.

"We don't both need to go. Please, Tom! I am just going to stay down here and have a look around."

"I am not feeling real good about that Alex."

"Oh come on. It'll just take you a few minutes, and it will give me some more time. You said it yourself, I don't have much," Alex countered, pleading.

"Alright Alex," he said, doubtfully. "But you have to promise me that when

I say time is up, it's up. My guys are going to begin closing this up around 5 a.m., so we have until then, but that is it. Agreed?" Tom knew he would probably have to carry her out over his shoulder regardless of her answer.

Alex checked her watch. It was already 8:15 p.m. That would give her eight or nine hours to look around. Not much time, but better than nothing.

"Agreed."

"I am going to see what I can scare up for dinner while I'm up there. Anything else?"

"No," Alex said, suddenly distracted by something she could see on one of the walls. "Go ahead, Tom, I'll be fine. Good luck on dinner, I am starving. Maybe some hot coffee?"

"I'll do my best. Be careful Alex," he pleaded.

"You, too. See you in a minute."

Alex looked toward Tom and shot him a reassuring smile, then watched for a moment as he turned and began to ascend the stairs that led back to the entrance.

"Tom, are you sure that guy said he'd dated this place to pre-K-T?" she called out.

Tom turned back. "That's what he said Alex. I know, it seems incredible to me too. But I have no reason to think he was lying. He was probably just wrong. I'll be right back."

It wasn't long until the light from Tom's flashlight vanished and Alex could no longer hear his footfalls. An eerie quiet fell over the cave, which was quite unnerving in its stillness. Alex shook it off.

He'll be back in a minute, she reassured herself.

"Okay, Alex, game on. What do we know?" She could hear her father's voice speaking to her again. We have stairs and we have some sort of storage or burial chamber with some sort of inscriptions. If it were truly pre-K-T it would pre-date the most ancient writings ever discovered by, oh, only by about 65 million years! By default, mankind would not be the only intelligent beings to ever have lived on earth. In fact, they would be far from the first. If all of that were proved to be true, then even Darwin himself would probably roll in his grave. Such a discovery would pose a monumental philosophical problem for the Christians, the Jews, the Muslims... Intelligent life other than man? *Before* the first human? No way! Most all of the world's religions would have a collective heart attack. This would have to be kept secret or half of the world's culture, more than half, would have to be essentially shit-canned!

Those bastards, that's why they came in here and cleared everything out, and that's why they are going to seal the cave! That's why Batter had no worry letting Tom show me the place, because no one would believe me even if I had some physical proof. They would figure out a way to discredit anything I produced. It would be easy. Why? Because the whole notion is totally impossible, and tomorrow any hard evidence of it will be gone!

Alex suddenly recalled the tractor trailer and the government vehicles she had seen leaving earlier, and felt her stomach turn to knots. She realized that Batter's guys had probably cleaned the place out and loaded the most important specimens on the truck.

I have got to find something I can take out of here, she thought, preferably before Tom gets back.

Now she was glad she brought her pack. There was no way that he would knowingly let her remove any artifacts.

She panned her light into the holes in the floor looking for something, anything, she could take with her.

One thing was for sure, whoever Pete Wilson was, he and his team had done a thorough job. It was clear to her that someone had literally cut any specimen right out of the stone floor, which was very unusual.

Must have taken them hours, she thought.

Most of the spots were completely barren, but in one of them she noticed a splinter of some kind of resin. She reached over and picked it up. It looked like amber, or something very similar.

Alex examined the piece for a moment then shoved it in her bag and trolled around the cave with her flashlight. Obviously, the team had completely stripped it. Nothing else looked unusual, just...

Wait. What is that weird spot on the wall?

The place Alex was interested in was about six feet over the level of the floor, a rectangular indentation that otherwise blended almost perfectly with the wall's stone surface.

She moved towards it, carefully avoiding the large holes in the floor.

"What the hell?"

As she ran her light over it, Alex could see that whatever was covering the hole was translucent. It looked almost like the amber material she had just found.

Then, she could feel her pulse rise. Below the amber material, almost at eye level, she could see the same type of hash stroke writing that was by each hole in the cave floor—a series of symbols scratched into the stone.

God, I wish I had my camera, she thought.

She stood on her toes and ran her hands over the opening. It was smooth and the material looked like it had been purposefully placed there.

How in the hell had they missed this? Maybe I can get some of this material off, she thought.

Alex tried with her hands, but the amber-like coating was as impervious as stone. She needed something like a hammer, but there were no tools that she could see in the cave.

Damn it! I should have told Tom to bring some tools down here. Then she remembered. The gun!

She quickly threw off her backpack and pulled out the Ruger. Perfect, she thought, examining it.

"If you're going to use my favorite pistol as a hammer Alex, at least make sure it isn't loaded," Simon advised her.

She took out the clip and tossed it back into the pack. You're right, Simon, no sense in shooting myself, she thought.

Alex took a soft whack at the material by holding the barrel and striking with the butt of the gun, but it didn't budge. She stepped up on a small out-cropping, a precarious foothold at best, but it gave her a much better angle.

As her light pierced the amber, she noticed something darker in the center of the hole.

Alex pressed her face closer but her hard hat got in the way. She tossed the hat to the floor, and it clattered and rolled into one of the holes.

What the heck *is* that?

She held the light at various angles but still could not see what might be behind the amber façade. It was difficult to hold the pistol and the light and balance on the wall, but she needed to do all three to get the job done.

Alex began to gently tap again with the butt of the gun, and then more forcefully. She realized she was probably going to ruin the weapon but it might be worth it, and that her father would agree.

Finally, after several strikes in the same area she began to see progress. Some of the material was flaking loose, and a long crack was developing.

She gave it some more whacks, and felt as if she were almost through it, before she lost her grip and fell.

Alex tried to react, but she could see nothing behind her. She tumbled backwards into the dark and struck her head on the stone floor.

Alex had only had a millisecond to think about what a stupid move she had made before she blacked out completely.

* * *

It hadn't taken Tom long to make the ascent back to the main construction area, but he immediately sensed trouble when he got there. His crew was circled around an area near the wall where they had been installing the reactor.

Andy looked up when he saw Tom approaching and waved him over.

"What's up, Andy?" The pale look on his foreman's face was not a good sign.

"Look, Tom, over here." Andy pointed at a section of floor. It was wet.

"I don't get it, Andy, did someone spill something?"

"No, we've been working here all day, and this is the first I've seen of it.

The place was as dry as a bone until just a few minutes ago, as far as I can tell. But what's even weirder is that, not only is it getting wetter, but the water is warm to the touch. You don't know of anything that says there is supposed to be a hot spring or anything down here do ya Tom?"

Tom was concerned, "No, there was nothing in any reports that said anything about geothermal springs. There are some in the area, but we haven't run into any natural water during this whole project so far. Of course," he said, gesturing over his shoulder, "those caves weren't supposed to be there either."

Tom moved closer to get a better look. There was no question about it, water was seeping through, a bad sign. Just what he needed, another delay.

"Andy, hand me that hammer, would you?" Tom took the claw end of the hammer and gently tapped on a section of the wet surface. He turned back to Andy. "I have no…"

An explosion of rock threw him to the ground.

A fissure had opened, about a foot in diameter and it was suddenly gushing hundreds of gallons of hot sulfuric water that was headed directly toward the opening of the lower cave.

As Andy helped to pull Tom back to his feet, the fissure expanded and thousands of gallons began pouring out. The water was suddenly a river, moving straight toward Alex.

"We've gotta block that entrance Andy," he screamed above the roar of the water, "Alex is still down there!"

Tom immediately scrambled his crew to try to stop the torrent already beginning to cascade into the cave opening. He fought to stay calm as he issued orders, but his mind kept screaming, I've killed Alex.

CHAPTER 10

Meet Mot

When Alex finally did regain consciousness and managed to open her eyes they were met by another pair across the room not ten paces away.

She immediately wanted to move, run, scream, anything but lie there and wait to die, but she could not. For the first time in her life, she was paralyzed with fear. Her heart felt like it was going to explode and her head was throbbing with pain. She hoped that she was dreaming, but she knew that she was not.

The creature sat there, its eyes boring into her, studying her, circles of amazing red and yellow color around large black pupils that were clearly reptilian. They looked simultaneously intelligent and deadly.

The beast attached to them was enormous, and Alex imagined that it would top seven feet when and if it decided to stand. Its facial skin was translucent and grey—like a giant lizard. The creature sat on the stone floor, legs crossed Indian style, with its hands—if you could call them hands—resting on its knees. Its eyes were somewhat shaded by a large brow which converged at the center and dropped to form a small nose that disappeared into a pronounced upper lip and large lower jaw that was sure to house a number of very sharp teeth.

This was impossible. Such a thing did not exist!

Alex knew she must be dreaming, but she felt quite awake. She tried not to look away, afraid that the minute she did she would be torn limb from limb.

For a while, she just lay there motionless, trying not to blink.

Then the thought occurred to her: if she were going to be the beast's dinner, she probably already would be. If it was a killer or even a scavenger, she would be watching it eat her small intestines right now. In a stare down, however, there was simply no contest, this thing had her beat.

She finally surrendered and looked away and was relieved when the animal seemed to take no action.

Alex noticed her flashlight lying on the stone floor of the cave next to the beast, its lens showing the clear signs of a fading battery. The beam cut weakly through a fine mist that seemed to be growing thicker by the minute, and threw just enough light to allow her to clearly see the creature and little else in the cave.

Alex gulped. This is not going to be fun when that battery dies, she thought. And was it her imagination, or was it getting warmer?

She was still wearing the heavy coat that she had borrowed from Tom's foreman, but now she was extremely hot and noticed that it was downright balmy in the cave. She wondered what had happened to Tom and where all the sudden heat was coming from. She wanted to take off the jacket, but she was afraid to move.

"Ugg," the creature grunted deeply, as if suddenly bored.

* * *

Mot was equally frightened. He had just awakened from what he thought was a very brief sleep, only to find himself trapped in a room with this smooth skinned creature that reeked of some sort of sweet fruit-like smell. He had never seen anything like her or smelled anything like her. Worse than that, he had found himself, aside from this strange female, quite alone.

Where was his mother? Where were the Elders? Where was Ara? Where were all of the others?

When he had first opened his eyes, he had expected to see them, but his vision had been completely blurred from the animal fat he had been packed in. He tried to breathe but realized he could not until he escaped the confines of his resting place.

Mot had fought his way toward the dim light he could see through the amber window and kicked his way out, the animal fat that had held him captive having grown warm and soupy. When the amber finally fell away he had been able to slide from the hole like a greasy piece of meat and almost landed on the creature that now faced him. It took him several minutes to cough enough to get a proper breath.

It seemed to him as if it had only been moments ago that he had felt his mother's hand on his face, only moments since he had been drugged and sealed into that disgusting hole. He resolved that, if the Elders were to give him a second chance, he would never again break any rule.

Now, he was stiff and sore and starving. The only thing that had kept him from pouncing on the female and having her for dinner was her strong unnatural odor and the fact that she was unconscious. His stomach had said eat, but his nose and his instincts had told him to be wary.

So he had taken up a position across the cave as the creature slept and studied her from a distance, considering at the same time a possible way out.

"Perhaps this is a test," he thought. "Perhaps the Elders have placed me in this room with this creature as some sort of test."

While he had pondered the sleeping female and the fact that he had obviously been left trapped in the cave alone with her, Mot had also realized that he was insatiably thirsty.

Once he was able to rise and get his body working, he located a cistern. He buried his head in it and sucked in water until he could take no more. At the same time, he fully washed out his eyes. The water was warm and slightly sulfurous, but it quenched his immediate thirst and helped to temporarily stave off his ravenous hunger.

Then, even in the low light, he was able to locate a pool of deeper water further back in the cave. He waded in and carefully washed himself of the rest of the animal fat, glad to be rid of the obnoxious odor. It felt good to be clean again, and as he moved around, he could feel the strength returning to his muscles as his body warmed. He checked on the female again. When he determined that she still appeared to be unconscious, he quietly found a place in the back of the cave to relieve himself—an act that was, at that point, one of the highlights of his young life.

When he returned, Mot noticed that the empty spots in the floor were filling with water and the level was slowly rising. The water was just about to engulf the female.

At first, he was reluctant to do anything, but he eventually picked her up, sniffing her unusual scent, and carried her to one of the stone tables that had been carved into the cave wall.

She was wearing thick clothing made from hides he had never seen before and had something strange and soft growing from her head. Mot set her down gently and then sat down across from her and tried to think, nervously tapping his foot on the floor of the cave. He was very confused.

Why was it so hot when it had been so cold before?

He looked around and suddenly realized that the cave was indeed filling with water and the flow was becoming more rapid.

Mot was no stranger to hot springs. There had been a whole series of them in the upper caves that the Arzats enjoyed as baths.

It occurred to him that this was what was now filling the cave and heating it. Perhaps it was the heat that had allowed him to escape from the confines of his miserable bed, he thought.

Mot was not overly concerned about the rising water. He would simply go up the way he had so recently come down.

He sat for a while longer and considered leaving the strange creature, and making his way to the Great Chamber on his own.

As he sat, he finally noticed the only form of light in the cave and got up to inspect it. He picked up the object, expecting it to be hot to the touch, running his hands over it, turning it over and over. It was like magic.

How does such a thing exist? Light with no heat? He accidentally pointed it directly into his eyes and saw spots afterward. Mot sat back down with the strange light in his hands and shot it around the room.

Whatever it was, it was way better than a torch, he thought.

Mot eventually set it by his side and considered the female.

Her skin was white and soft and so thin it appeared to be almost nonexistent. She was the size of a very young Arzat. Her clothes were very strange. He had never known any other animals that wore them as the Arzats did. Was she intelligent?

He watched her for a long time, trying to imagine where she had come from. Had the world really ended? Perhaps she had come with the death star. She appeared to be so fragile that Mot could not imagine her living in the world he knew for more than the blink of an eye.

Perhaps she is a god, he thought, watching her more closely.

"Ugg," he had muttered, trying to wake her from where he sat.

Mot was sore and tired from waiting, and oh Great Creator, was he hungry, and the water was rising. Something had to be done.

"Ugg," he said again, fidgeting and making noises. Finally, the creature's eyes had fluttered open.

* * *

Alex looked back, not staring this time but trying to understand what the creature was up to. She felt as if her heart was about to explode with adrenaline.

The beast, its eyes never wavering, suddenly raised its right claw to its mouth, yawned widely and belched. It shifted position, as if it were trying to get more comfortable, then looked down and picked up her flashlight and shined it in her direction.

Okay, Alex, you can relax now, she tried to comfort herself. You are either dreaming or dead because this is impossible. There is absolutely no way this can be happening. And that is no claw, my friend—Mister Opposed Digit.

Even in the dim light, Alex could see that the creature had three long fingers and a 'thumb,' which he was now using to hold her light. Its arms bulged with muscles and were much longer than she would have expected; proportioned to its body much like a human's. Her mind raced to come up with some sort of explanation.

She was lying on her left side on a flat stone bench, perhaps three feet from the floor, her head resting on her arm. The creature across from her might as well have been an alligator or a Komodo dragon, with that one major difference—it had a thumb!

Were the light any better, she might have confirmed her suspicion of the second major difference, that the creature had no tail!

And was it actually possible that it was tapping its foot on the floor? Was it intelligent? Again, she looked into its eyes.

The beast tilted its head, studying her, and then suddenly its tongue darted unexpectedly from its mouth. Alex flinched and the creature flinched in response.

"Arrrrrrrrr," its eyes narrowed suspiciously, then became neutral again. It sat back, still looking directly at her, and began tapping its foot again. Alex did not dare move.

They stayed that way for some time. Alex wasn't sure, perhaps ten minutes, perhaps an hour. Her head was throbbing, she was frightened and she had to pee.

Uh oh, now what am I going to do?

The more she thought about it, the more she had to go.

Minutes passed, the creature sat, quietly tapping. Alex finally could stand it no longer. She either had to urinate right where she was or she had to make a move.

Make a move, she decided.

Carefully, slowly, she raised her head and the pain in it intensified. The creature twitched. She immediately stopped.

"Ew, ew, Zatan. Zatan." The creature said, lifting its arms.

The hair raised on the back of Alex's neck. This thing, whatever it was, had language! Amazing. It seemed to be telling her it was okay to get up, in fact, encouraging her to do so.

"Zatan, zatan." The tone was light, not menacing. It waved its arms, but stayed seated.

Alex carefully pushed herself up, her head on the verge of exploding. She raised her hand and felt for a wound but was relieved to find that there was only a large knot where she had hit the stone. She was extremely hot and the heavy jacket made her feel as if she were in a sauna.

"En tew abba?" the creature asked.

Suddenly she realized that the lizard was actually asking her if she was alright.

Alex shook her head and pointed at her groin.

"Ew, zatan." The creature rose and started towards her.

He was seven feet tall and several hundred pounds of scary reptile. Might as well have been a raptor. Alex's bladder let go.

Mot hesitated. It was clear to him now that he had frightened the Smooth Skin.

In Mot's world, the side-to-side movement of Alex's head was a positive. It meant 'yes' to him, so he hadn't meant to scare her, he was just trying to get her to move. They needed to go.

Suddenly, the most intoxicating smell Mot had ever experienced filled his nostrils and caused him to involuntarily flick his tongue. He stood there, mid-way across the floor, in absolute shock, trying desperately to suppress his almost overwhelming desire to flick again.

Mot stayed motionless, embarrassed about his wayward tongue, bad manners for an Arzat.

Alex could do nothing but look at the beast and continue to pee. It was a mixed blessing. She was so scared on the one hand that she was about to be eaten, and on the other, so glad to finally relieve herself, that she no longer cared that she had done it in her pants.

Then, there was a loud crack somewhere in the distant rock above them, and the warm water that had been slowly creeping into the cave began to rush in.

Mot turned just in time to snatch the flashlight from the floor before it was washed away.

He rushed up towards the stairs. Water was flooding down them and came to Mot's knees, almost sweeping him away. There was no way to get out that direction.

He ran to the back areas of the chamber and looked upward, searching for another exit.

He was not panicked yet. While he had only been in this part of the cave once, his overall experience having lived and played in the caves since his childhood told him that there were usually always several ways out of any large chamber.

Mot quickly reached out and pulled himself up the wall and found an opening. It was about three sticks above the ledge the female was on, and he felt like he could easily carry the creature up to it if he had to.

There was only one problem. The passage was too small for either of them to squeeze through.

Have to try something else, he thought.

He looked down at Smooth Skin and thought that he saw her shiver even though the cave was now warm from the vapors of the rising hot water.

Mot crawled back down the wall and stood directly in front of the female.

"I have to find a way out," he said, trying to send the message directly to the Smooth Skin's mind.

He listened for an answer and looked for some comprehension, but he neither heard nor saw any.

"En ma obba," he told her, pointing to the vent. "Ez emu soo abu." There is no exit. I must find another way.

Alex tried desperately to understand, any fear of the creature now replaced by her fear of the rapidly rising water as it began to swirl up to the ledge.

Then, just as soon as she heard him speak in his incomprehensible language, the creature dove into the water and disappeared.

Alex sat, suddenly alone, looking into the dark, and watched as the beam of her flashlight went completely out of view. She was left in pitch black.

I am going to die here, she resolved.

Mot swam.

He knew he would have only one chance to save the female. He wasn't worried about himself as much. Mot was an excellent swimmer and could hold his breath for almost a torch of time if necessary. So, despite the dire circumstances, he was still confident he would find a way out for himself.

His eyes had a second lid that allowed him to see just as clearly under water as he could on land, and with the magic light he had no problem swimming along looking for an exit.

Mot, he told himself, you must find a way out.

He swam with the ease of a fish, looking and probing. There must be another exit, he kept telling himself.

Finally, he spotted flat water above. When he broke through, he saw it immediately—a stone staircase.

Mot had found the second exit, or perhaps the very same path he had taken with his mother and the others.

Where were the others?

Mot thought for a minute about simply leaving and searching for the clan, but something drew him back to the female.

Yes, he thought, I will try to save her. What if she is all there is?

Mot drew in a large breath and plunged back into the water.

Alex was shaking despite her heavy coat and the warm water that was now up to her waist.

It was pitch black, so even though she knew there were ledges higher up, she could not see well enough to try to reach them.

"There is a tremendous difference between fear and panic Alex," she could hear her father saying. "Fear will keep you alive. Panic will kill you."

Alex ran her fingers over the rock wall, looking for a handhold but felt nothing but greasy stone.

"Easy for you to say, Simon!" she called out into the black.

Alex tried one side and then moved to another, slipping off the ledge in the process. She went under, then came back into the dark, her feet managing to find part of the ledge. She stood back up and stripped off the soaking jacket. The water was almost to her neck, and she felt herself starting to cry.

Oh yeah, and quitting Alex, that will also kill you.

But she still felt herself about to give up. Then below her, through the dark water, she spotted the beam of her flashlight.

The reptile emerged, holding the light to her face.

"You must come with me now," Mot once again tried to communicate directly. "you must come with me now! I have found a way out!"

He looked into the female's eyes. She was calm, but in a vacant sort of way. Mot had seen this many times before. It was the look of someone who had resigned themselves to death.

"Tew toa tato eva!" he told her forcefully.

Mot had no idea if the creature could swim or even hold her breath, but there was no option. He pushed the light into the female's hands and pointed the beam at his face. Mot held his nose with one hand and gestured down towards the water with the other.

"You must come with me now," he thought as strongly as he knew how.

"Tew toa tato eva!" he repeated aloud, and slapped the female as gently as he could, afraid of breaking her.

The water was at Alex's chin, and she had been so close to surrender that she had a hard time snapping out of it, even with the sudden jolt.

Did you just slap me? What the…? Suddenly, Alex totally understood. She looked at the reptile and tried to tell him with her eyes.

"Okay. Okay! I got it!"

Mot took the cue. "Uda?"

"Uda," Alex felt herself answer, intuitively knowing what the creature had said.

Mot drew in a deep breath and observed Smooth Skin doing the same. There wasn't a moment to lose. He snatched the light back from her, grabbed her hand, plunged into the water, and began to swim for both of their lives. He felt her try to kick, as if she were trying to help.

"No," he told her with his mind, "just hold on."

With one arm in front of him holding the light, and one arm trailing, holding onto the female, Mot began to kick rhythmically with both of his feet together, using them like the tail of a large fish.

He did his best to remain focused on retracing his way to the exit, making his way as quickly as he could through a lava tube, but he felt the female growing more and more desperate for air.

"We are almost there," he tried to pass to her, not sure she was receiving his message.

For the second time in just a few minutes, Alex felt she was about to give up. She was terrified and totally at the end of her breath.

The fact that she hadn't had to swim had helped, but she had no idea where they were going or how long it was going to take. Her lungs were trying to defy her mind and draw a breath. She made a vague attempt to rally and shake it off, but it was no use.

Mot knew he was almost to the top. He had been surprised that the female was so short of air. Any Arzat he knew could easily have held their breath many times longer than this trip was going to require. He could sense that Smooth Skin was about give in.

When he was close, he sent another message. "Blow. Blow slowly."

Alex blew, she had no idea why, but she began to exhale, and did her best to do it slowly. She knew at the end of it, her body would overcome her and inhale on its own, water or air, it didn't matter.

She blew and blew, but near the end, she still found herself submerged.

Mot rounded a corner, knowing the flat water was above them. He lunged for the surface and did his best to pull the female up and in front so she would be the first to the top. He pushed up so quickly that he almost launched her out of the water.

She was choking when she emerged, having just begun to fully experience drowning, but there was air and Alex knew she had made it, if she could just get her lungs clear.

Mot rolled her on her side and, as forcefully as he dared, he began slapping the creature on her back. The female coughed and spit water, then finally seemed to get a breath.

He kept slapping her until he was sure she was breathing, then took the flashlight and gently set it on a one of the stone steps so he could see her. Mot lowered himself, crouching, and watched.

Alex continued to cough. When she was finally breathing normally, she rolled over only to find the reptile once again staring at her.

"En tew abba?" he asked, his eyes glowing red and pupils wide.

Alex hesitated a moment, and then began to laugh.

CHAPTER 11

It Speaks

A lex laughed, and then laughed some more.

Perhaps it was the totally impossible nature of her situation. Perhaps it was because she knew she had just narrowly escaped death for the millionth time in her life. Perhaps she was really going nuts, because as she laughed, she thought she could distinctly hear the—whatever-in-the-hell-it-was-creature beside her, laughing as well. It was a deep otherworldly sound that defied description.

She was lying on the remnants of an ancient stone staircase. The opening around her was at least ten feet in diameter, part of some other long lava tube that rose up into the dark until she could no longer see the end of it.

Alex reasoned that there must have been at least two entrances to the chamber, and that her scaly companion had found this second one.

She looked at the water level on the steps below her and could not detect it rising. Even so, she knew it would be prudent to get to an area higher in the cave.

Maybe there is even a way out of this hellhole, she thought.

Alex looked back at the creature.

His eyes were glowing just from the dim beam that was still emanating from the flashlight. She couldn't imagine how they might react to the full light of day, but they were no longer so intimidating.

The reptile was crouching, patiently watching her.

He's every bit of seven feet tall, Alex thought, some weird evolutionary variation of a Theropod, a distant descendant of some line of two-legged dinosaur to be sure, but proportioned very much like a human.

She guessed his weight at three hundred—maybe even four hundred pounds—without an inch of fat on him.

His arms were massive exhibits of muscle, but nothing compared to the musculature in his legs. Alex imagined she could fit her entire body into just one of them if it were hollow.

His feet were large, but in balance and proportion to the size of his legs. He had three toes with long curving nails and one shorter opposed toe trailing behind like a bird's.

Alex thought that if she were to look closely, she would also find that the creature's feet were at least partially webbed, which would explain how he could swim so well.

His hands—yes *hands*—she again pondered, consisted of four fingers each, one of which was definitely opposed to the other three.

But the most extraordinary feature of this beast was his head. It exhibited the largest prefrontal cortex bulge she had ever seen in a dinosaur. If "dinosaur" were even the right classification, she pondered.

Hell, I keep thinking this thing is a "he," but I don't really know if it is male or female.

She then noticed something she hadn't seen before, perhaps because it was hard to see, perhaps because she hadn't looked. The creature was wearing some sort of loincloth made of material that totally blended in with his own skin.

He, oh yes. *That* is definitely a 'he,' she thought as she looked directly in the area of his genitalia and blushed. *He* is wearing clothes! Not much, just a loincloth made of some kind of skin, but clothes nonetheless.

Impossible, she thought to herself once again, vaguely wondering how any kind of material like that could have survived.

Mot grunted, suddenly uncomfortable and even embarrassed by the female's obvious interest in him, although he had been sizing the female up, as well.

In all his short life, he had never seen such a creature. She had skin smoother than the finest animal pelts and she was tiny, as small as a three- or four-seasoned Arzat, yet she seemed more mature. She definitely smelled more mature, no question about that.

From the moment he had first approached her, Mot had never wondered about her sex. But it was her obvious intelligence that confounded him. Other than Arzats, he had never known or heard of any creature that had any real ability to communicate much beyond their own species, and certainly none of them had actual language.

"Uu ta nedo," he said quietly, we need to go. Mot grabbed the flashlight and stood.

Alex heard him, but there was something else she finally and suddenly realized about the creature. She understood him as well. It was not just interpretation from the context of the moment—she had totally *understood* what he had just said!

No Alex, only vampires and certain other weird fictional characters telepath, she admonished herself. She thought that she must be dreaming again, and if she was, she was ready for it to be over.

Mot looked at her one last time, turned, and started up the tunnel.

"Wait!" Alex was suddenly worried that the creature would desert her, leaving her alone in the dark. She fought to get to her feet, her head still throbbing.

Mot paused.

He hadn't exactly understood the word, but he had understood the meaning. This female could apparently communicate like any Arzat; sometimes with words only, sometimes with words and mind, and sometimes with the mind only. This was all very interesting but what he now needed was something to eat and to find his family and the others of his clan.

Ez ta maga, he thought. I need to eat.

"Ez ta maga," he said aloud, glancing back at Alex, but he thought to himself, and if you do not hurry up little one, I am going to eat you!

Mot was tense and irritable and, despite what even he now understood must have been a rather long sleep, he was tired.

Something was not right. He was in a hurry to get to the Great Chamber and find out exactly what had happened, but in his heart he doubted if anything of his past would be there. Mot could sense that something had dramatically changed, and he could feel no presence of the other Arzats.

He especially searched for the presence of Ara, but did not find it. It saddened him. The female creature and the magic light he held were clues that were hard to ignore. Still…

"Teo," he said to Alex. Hurry.

She got the "I am hungry" part and "hurry" but also something about the creature having her for a meal.

Careful, Alex, she thought as she got up to follow, this thing could still rip you from limb from limb.

The two of them climbed up a series of long paths combined with intermittent flights of stairs, Mot leading the way.

He stopped several times, still trying to discern any evidence of Arzats. There was a low rumble he detected, far away under the ground, but nothing of his people. He flicked his tongue. They were definitely getting closer to the surface—he could sense a slight freshness in the air.

The going from here would be simple. These parts of the caves felt very familiar to Mot, and he quickened his pace, despite the fact that the female was struggling to keep up, her breathing stressed from the climb.

Mot glanced back at her as the cave took a sharp turn to the left. As he stepped around the corner he barely caught himself before falling into a deep crevasse. In the process, he lost his grip on the magic light. He watched helplessly as it fell, bouncing from one sidewall to another, finally reaching the bottom.

Mot looked over the edge watched as the light flickered and went out. Now the two of them were in total darkness.

Alex had been doing her best to keep up, mindful that the only real chance she had to escape the caves was her unlikely guide with the reptilian skin.

When the light disappeared, she first thought that the creature had moved too far up the cave for her to see him, so she sped up, suddenly panicked that she would lose all sight of him. She found herself practically running in pitch black, her mind trying to remember the dimly lit path she had just seen disappear.

"Ne!" she heard the creature say in the dark. He was so close that her heart crept into her throat.

This is where I get it, she thought. He is going to eat me.

She tried to move away and immediately felt his hand on her holding her back. She almost pissed her pants again from surprise.

"Ne." Stop, he said again more quietly. His voice was otherworldly, guttural, commanding.

Alex was panicked.

I am not going to just stand here and let this thing eat me. She moved again but the creature grabbed her with both of its arms. The power behind them was overwhelming.

Mot was confused. Why was this small creature struggling with him? Did it want to die? He used his mind to reach into hers further than would be polite, and then understood.

"Ah, I am not trying to eat you little female. There is a huge hole in the floor, which will kill you if you fall into it. Do you understand me?"

Alex stopped fighting. She felt light headed, it was the same sensation she had felt earlier. Her mind, and suddenly, his, had become completely intertwined.

"There is a big hole," the creature said again.

"Where is the light?"

"I'm sorry, but it fell from my hands. It was not done purposely. There is a deep hole blocking the way. The magic light fell in. Do you understand?"

"Yes," she could feel herself answer.

A picture had entered her mind. She could see the crevasse clearly and even the tumbling flashlight as it had disappeared. It was exactly as if she had seen the event herself.

"You can let go of me now. I understand," she said.

Instantly, she felt the creature release her.

There was nothing for a few minutes, besides the sound of both of their breaths and the pitch black.

"What do we do now?" Alex was finally the one to break the silence, although she had asked the question only with her mind.

Mot, in the meantime, had been trying to figure another way out. They hadn't passed any other tunnels since they had left the water, so backtracking was not going to work. The only solution was simple, but dangerous for the female. He would have to carry her down the crevasse, and back up out of it.

Mot was certain that they were on the right track. He could smell it in the air, and the darkness wasn't new to him. Arzats practically grew up in the dark. Torches and small flames were used only when necessary, and much of his upbringing had been carried out in the absolute darkness of the caves.

But this crevasse had surprised him. He had previously been comfortable without light, but that was on very familiar ground. Things had obviously changed in the caves. He would have to be exceedingly careful the rest of the way.

Mot knew he would be much better off if he simply left the female.

Alex could sense that the creature was debating. He was thinking of leaving her, and she would be trapped in the pitch black!

"What is your name?" she asked out loud and in her mind.

The sounds of her words echoed down the crevasse, swallowed in the darkness. She could hear the creature's regular breaths across from her, very close. It was thinking.

"I am Mot son of Url" he finally replied.

It was that same guttural unworldly sound. The creature had spoken to her before, but this was the first time Alex had really heard him, the first time she had really and clearly appreciated the fact that this thing, this whatever it was, as amazing as it was, could actually speak.

But his spoken words had nothing to do with what she was hearing in her head.

"Mot," she repeated aloud. "Well, Mot, my name is Alex, and since I am not interested in having you leave me here, I thought maybe I should formally introduce myself. I would shake your hand but I cannot see shit. Anyhow, we are in this together as far as I can tell, and believe me, you are going to need a friend if and when we ever get out of this cave. Things aren't quite the same in the world as when you went down for your little 65-million-year nap."

Oh great Creator, Mot thought, now completely confused, hearing the chatter, but understanding it only in his head. Definitely a female.

"What is 'shit'?" he asked aloud in his own language, but Alex had understood him in her mind.

"Sorry, that was impolite," she replied.

"We have such impolite words as well, many of them," the creature said. "What is 'shake hand'?"

"It is a way of formal greeting my species uses the first time two individuals meet. There are others, but that is one of the most common ones."

"Are there many in your clan, Alex?"

Alex thought for a moment about how to answer that. Seven billion and counting might overwhelm him, so she just said, "Yes, many."

Mot was taken by surprise by the little creature's response. He sensed that there was more to her answer than she had given, but he could not be sure exactly what she had meant.

Perhaps she has learned to block, he thought.

Blocking thoughts was common with the Arzats—one only revealed what one wanted revealed. Of course, the clan would break down into total anarchy immediately if one could not block his own thoughts. There would be no privacy whatsoever.

In general, a conscious effort was needed for a thought to pass.

"I have never been able to directly speak with another species before. You are very unusual. Where do you come from? Are you from another world? Did you come with the great rock? Have you seen any of the rest of my clan?" He asked her, only with his mind.

Alex was just as perplexed as Mot regarding their apparent ability to communicate non-verbally.

For god's sake, we don't even speak the same language, she thought.

Alex knew she needed to be careful. This creature obviously had no idea about the world it had awakened into. The shock he was about to fully experience might be too much for him.

"No, Mot, I am not from another world, and no, I have not seen anyone from your 'clan.' Have you any idea how long you might have been in your hibernation—your long sleep?"

Mot thought carefully about the question. His mother had cautioned him that things might be very different when he awoke. He now fully sensed that none of his clan had survived, and it saddened him. What would he do?

"No, can you tell me?" was all he could think to answer.

Jesus, Alex, she thought, how was she going to explain what a year is, let alone 65 million of them? You are going to shock this guy to death.

"Many years," was all she finally said.

"I do not understand 'year'? What is a 'year'?" Mot was confused.

Now you've done it Professor Moss. She was furious at herself.

"Calm, Alex, stay calm," she heard her father say.

"It is a way we mark time. It is the time it takes the earth to orbit the sun."

"I do not understand 'orbit.' The Astrologers say when Qa'aa aligns in the same spot a season has passed, is that the same?"

Oh my god! Compose yourself Alex.

"Yes, Mot, that is essentially the same. How many seasons have you lived?"

"I just turned two by eight, and you?"

Alex could actually sense pride in the answer. He's just a kid she thought, a teenager! Okay, he did not count in tens. Come on Alex, remember your math. He is using base eight.

"I am three eights and five."

"You are old!" Mot exclaimed.

That hurts.

"Maybe in your world, not so much in mine. Humans often live—how do I say this?—eight eights, and more." Alex said. She could not think of how to go higher.

"Arzats can live that long as well, but it is rare, and usually just the females."

"Arzat? Was that the name of your people?"

Oops, *damn it*, Alex thought, should have used 'is' not 'was.'

"That is the name of my race. Our clan is the Zanta. I must find the others." Mot's stomach growled. He was so hungry it was causing him physical pain.

"I must get out of the cave. I need to find food."

"Will you help me get out as well?" she asked.

The scent of the female so close to him was almost overwhelming.

I bet she would be delicious thought Mot, then once again put the thought out of his mind.

"It is too difficult. I must go and find my people and food. Then, perhaps, I can come back and get you."

Alex suddenly realized she hadn't eaten since lunch the previous day and she herself was ravenous, so she could certainly understand what was going on with her dinosaur friend's stomach.

She sensed Mot was going to leave her, and believed that, if he did, she would die.

Alex was also strangely aware that her presence was not doing anything to ease Mot's hunger. Dangerous to be around him in that state, but suicide if she didn't convince him to lead her out of here, she thought. She might die with him, but Alex knew she would die for sure without him.

She could tell the creature was determined to see if the world was the same as he had left it and was anxious to see for himself as soon as possible. Alex decided that now was as good a time as any to break the news.

"You are going to need my help, Mot. You have been asleep for a very long time. The world you left has changed. I am sorry to say, Mot, that there are none of your 'people' left."

Mot could feel his temper rising.

What did this creature know about anything? There were many, many Arzat clans—surely some were still around.

Yet, in his heart, he could tell that the smooth skin creature was speaking the truth, at least as far as she knew it. Perhaps he *would* need her assistance. But, they needed to cross the crevasse. How could they? Mot was confident in his ability to climb down and back up, but the female? In the dark of the cave?

"I am sorry I destroyed your magic light, Alex," was all he could think to say.

The sincerity of the statement took Alex by surprise. Little did he know how many more of those magic lights there were in the world he was about to enter. He would be as helpless as a baby out there, and probably be killed almost immediately by the first human with a gun that encountered him.

"Listen, Mot, I know how to find all the food you can eat if you can just get us out of here. As I said, there are many of my kind on the surface, and some of them are very dangerous. But I can help you."

Mot thought about the night he had killed the two footed beast. A creature like Alex wouldn't survive a moment in his world. She would be torn apart, if not by the many nasty animals of the forest, then surely by the Arzats themselves. How could the world she was from be any more dangerous than his?

Mot was totally confused, and this was no time for confusion. He would keep this creature close to him until he found out exactly what was going on above.

"I will have to carry you."

CHAPTER 12

The Way Out

"Alex, you will have to hold to my back. I will climb down the rock then up the other side. Since I will require all of my limbs in order to do this, you will have to hold on to me all on your own. Once we begin, if you let go, I will not be able to save you. Also, while I normally have good vision in the dark, my eyes do need some light to be able to see. Since I have killed your magic light, I have made things more difficult."

Alex realized that both she and Mot had given up speaking aloud. It was much easier to simply exchange thoughts.

"I understand," she silently replied.

Her immense relief that Mot was not going to desert her was short-lived.

How in the hell am I going to hang on to this guy? It'll be like trying to bareback a Volkswagen up a steep hill!

"You have to do it, Alex, so just do it," Simon said to her.

"I am a very good climber, Alex."

There was silence in the cave.

"Alex?"

"Where are you?" she asked.

"Here." Mot reached out and took Alex gently by the arm to guide her. "Just place your arms around my neck and hold on to my back with your legs," he instructed.

I am glad I can't see, Alex thought. This would probably scare the shit out of me.

She reached up and tried to grasp Mot around the neck, but she was too short to even have a chance.

"I will bend down," Mot said.

Alex realized that her previous analogy to riding bareback on a car was right on the money. The creature's neck was so enormous that her arms barely met in the front. She did her best to lock her hands and hold on with her legs. The skin on his back was very course and reminded her of alligator, which helped her to hold on, but on the sides of his body his skin was smooth, and as slippery as a snake's.

She squeezed her legs around him as tightly as she could.

"Are you secure?" asked Mot.

"Yes, I think so," Alex answered, with some doubt.

"You will need to squeeze your legs together, Alex, when we start down, or I am worried that you will fall."

"I am! This is as good as it gets!" Alex exclaimed in her head, suddenly aware of how close some of her extremities were to the dinosaur's very sharp teeth. She could feel the creature's warm breath on her hands.

"You needn't worry, Alex, I have been climbing like this since I was a child," Mot said calmly.

"Even in the dark?"

"Often in the dark. As I said, light would be better, but we have none."

This creature is never going to make it, thought Mot, blocking, so Alex could not hear his complete response.

He turned, carefully feeling his way, moving his body so as not to throw the smooth creature into the black below. His toes caught nicely into the rock, which seemed to be rough, not nearly as smooth as the sides of the cave, and would have made climbing next to impossible with the creature on his back.

One leg, then two, and then he began to descend. Mot could feel the female already struggling to hold on, so he knew he would have to be swift and without mistake.

When the magic light had fallen, he had judged the hole to be eight sticks of eight deep—a relatively easy climb by himself, somewhat harder with the weight of the female pulling him from the wall. He could feel her breath on his back becoming more labored.

Because they were in pitch black, Mot could only guess at their progress.

He moved carefully, testing each foot and handhold as he went. When he thought they were about half the distance to the bottom he paused. The creature was slipping, he could feel it. Some correction had to be made or she would fall.

"Alex, you must take a tighter hold," he told her, his hands and his feet bound to the wall.

Alex was painfully aware of the fact that she was about to fall, but she was at a loss as to what to do about it. She started to slip, then it was over, and she totally lost her grip.

"Kak," Mot said aloud.

He felt Alex slip and immediately swung his right arm around to catch her while he struggled to hold the wall with his left, barely reaching her before he lost her into the crevasse. Mot pulled her up to his side, and then shoved her all the way above his shoulders with his one free hand.

"Swing your legs around my head Alex."

Alex suddenly found herself on Mot's shoulders, his head directly beneath her. She thought she had just heard the creature say "shit" when she had slipped.

"This will make climbing more difficult for me, but should save you from falling Alex. You will have to balance the upper part of your body carefully as I cannot hold on to you."

"I understand," she said. Alex could see nothing.

"Hold on to my head if you need to."

Alex did so, placing her hands on each side of it, amazed at the enormity of his skull. It was like grasping a large pumpkin—with teeth!

Mot continued down, his hands and feet perfectly interpreting the stone wall as he went. Finally, his senses told him the opposing wall must be close behind them.

"Alex, carefully reach behind you with one arm and feel for the other wall. I will hold you."

Mot used one free hand to pinch Alex's legs securely around his neck and took a strong grip on the wall with his other.

Alex forced herself around and pushed her right arm out into the dark. Nothing.

Mot stretched out as far as he could.

"Further, Alex."

Alex could feel one of Mot's hands holding her legs like a vise, so she leaned as far as she could into the black void and was surprised when she actually touched stone.

"Got it! The other wall is only about three or four feet behind us."

"I do not know this 'feet' measurement, Alex, but if you touched the wall it is enough. Hold tightly."

Mot spun and blindly went for the other side, depending completely on Alex's information. He felt himself starting to fall into the black, then both his hands struck the wall and he was able to grip it. He brought one foot forward, then another, and managed two solid footholds. They were across.

This was fortunate, he thought.

While he couldn't be exactly sure, he felt the move had saved them several sticks of descent and as many for the ascent.

"Now we will go up, Alex."

Mot pulled and tugged his way up, slowly, deliberately. With Alex riding on his neck, the climb was difficult, but he had less worry that she would fall. If something had gone wrong now, it would have been his mistake that made it so.

Alex said nothing. She remained fully focused during the entire ascent making sure she didn't slip and go 'ass over tea kettle' back to the bottom of the ravine.

When over a full torch of time had passed, one of Mot's hands finally felt the top. He pulled up, and flicked his tongue to be sure. Yes.

"We have reached the other side, Alex. You may climb off of me. Be very careful and go forward."

Alex reached out and felt for solid ground. When her hands touched the flat part of the cave, she gently tumbled off of Mot's shoulders and crawled along the floor. She could still see nothing in the pitch black.

Mot crawled over onto the floor of the cave as well. He took a good sniff of the air and got mostly the scent of Alex, but there was no mistaking it, somewhere down the tunnel the air was fresh.

"I think we are very close now, Alex."

Thank god. Alex moved to stand up and immediately hit her head on something.

"God damn it!" she said aloud.

Mot, still crouching due to the short ceiling, could only imagine what Alex had done. He had not understood her expletive, but he could sense her pain.

"Careful, Alex, this part of the cave is low. Always test with your hands."

"Now you tell me."

"Follow closely, Alex," Mot said, ignoring her remark. "You may keep your hand on my back if you wish."

Mot led Alex slowly, testing the floor of the cave as he went. If he came upon another fissure, this time he would not see it, he would have to feel for it as he went.

They inched along for what seemed like another hour to Alex, moving mostly upward, sometimes even encountering the same type of stairs she had seen in the first part of the caves.

"I thought we were close," she finally said, exasperated, breathing heavily.

"We are here, Alex," Mot said, stunned by what he had found.

They had just entered the Great Chamber, and although it was still very dark, Mot was starting to be able to see. It now looked to him like the little female had been right. Mot took a deep breath and flicked his tongue. Sadly, he discovered, there was no sign or scent of his clan anywhere.

He trained his eyes upward, and through a very narrow opening, high above his head, he could just make out the night sky.

"This is the main gathering place of my clan, Alex. I know this place well. Can you see the starlight?"

Alex was still in a world of total darkness, but she instinctively looked up, and sure enough, high above her head, she could barely distinguish the fine white points of a few stars. She was exhausted, but the sight filled her with hope. Maybe she was going to make it out of here after all.

"How do we get there?" she asked, worried they would have to climb again.

"Perhaps we will not have to. The main entrance to the caves is nearby," Mot replied.

She followed Mot closely, still completely unable to see. The Arzat, on the other hand, could now see quite well, the small amount of light from the stars was more than enough.

He was happy to discover that the large round stone that marked the main entrance was still in place just as he and his friend El had left it what seemed just hours ago. The rocks appeared to have grown around it, but it was still there.

He placed his body against the barrier and pushed with all his strength, but it would not move. Mot tried again, but without success.

"You may have to help me, Alex."

"Mot, I can't see anything. What are you trying to do?"

"We must roll the rock."

Mot led Alex to stand next to him. She could feel the cold stone, and ran her hands along the surface, surprised and amazed at its size.

"We must push it back Alex. Ready?"

On Mot's command, Alex gave the stone everything she had. Mot strained with her.

At first, nothing happened, then the stone actually moved an inch and stopped. They tried a few more times, but no amount of effort was working.

Finally, Alex slid to the floor, out of breath, and Mot did the same.

"We should be able to move it Alex. I do not understand."

Alex was confused as well. If they hadn't been able to move the rock at all, she would have assumed that it had simply bonded to the wall.

Then, out of nowhere, she recalled once trying to move a horse trailer before they had removed the chocks that blocked the wheels from rolling.

Alex crawled to the other side of the stone and probed. Sure enough, there was a rock the size of a baseball wedged between the floor and the rounded edge of the giant barrier. Alex gave the rock a good tug and it broke free. The stone door, of its own accord, began to slowly roll and almost crushed her hand in the process.

By the time Alex and Mot jumped up, the two of them were facing out onto the entire Utah desert. It was still dark, but the horizon was just beginning to show signs of sunrise. A cool breeze blew into Alex's face and she took a deep breath. They had made it.

She looked out onto the desert floor and began to laugh again. Somehow, she and Mot had ended up directly above the slide that had destroyed her dinosaur specimen. She could see the dark outline of her pickup and her camp just beyond.

Nothing is going to surprise me after this, Alex thought to herself. She looked over at Mot, who was staring blankly into the desert.

Mot continued to gaze outward for some time. He noticed Qa'aa was about to rise. Then he turned to Alex, completely stunned.

"This is not the world I know."

Alex continued to look out at the horizon. The sun was just beginning to peek over the mountains, a slight morning breeze in the air. To Alex, there had never been a more beautiful sight.

"Well, you may be in luck my friend. This *is* the world I know."

"I must eat Alex." Mot was ravenous.

The wind had blown her strong scent directly into his nostrils with almost overpowering effect.

I hope there is something to eat in this world besides this young female named Alex, he thought to himself again, eyeing her.

"Come on," she said, starting down the hill. "I have food in my truck."

"What is a 'truck,' Alex?"

"Follow me. I'll show you."

CHAPTER 13

The Show Must Go On

Tom and Andy stood and surveyed the cave entrance from the project side—their eyes bloodshot, their faces covered in dirt. They were both exhausted and Andy wondered how long either one of them could keep standing before falling over from fatigue.

"I'm sorry, Tom," Andy said without taking his eyes from the cave opening that was now partially blocked with several hundred tons of rock and debris.

A handful of the other crewmembers were gathered not far away, standing or sitting quietly, waiting for more instructions.

Tom's men had done everything they could, but the fissure that had so suddenly opened had continued to pour a deluge of hot spring water—countless thousands of gallons of it—into the cave entrance for several hours.

Tom knew in the seconds after the spring had burst that Alex's only chance of survival would hinge on his ability to stop the flow before too much of the torrent had reached her, but the volume of water had gotten progressively worse rather than better.

His men had dumped truckload after truckload of rock to try to temporarily block the water from running down into the caves, while others had worked on the source, but the ancient spring was stubborn. It had taken several small shots of explosives to dislodge enough material to stanch it.

In the meantime, despite all their efforts, the water had continued to force its way into the cave and down toward Alex.

Tom had considered a direct blast at the entrance, but the percussion would have been just as likely to kill Alex as the water, and who knew if they would ever be able to open it again.

Was she was able to get to higher ground, he wondered. But he knew the likelihood was one in a million. Tom was familiar enough with the caves that he could not imagine where any higher ground might have been.

"I should never have left her down there," he said, almost to himself.

"You couldn't have known, Tom. It was a fluke. I've built three of these damn things now and we have never run into a situation like this. Never!" Andy said, shaking his head.

Tom turned to Andy. "Your guys did a hell of a job."

He glanced at his wristwatch for the first time in over ten hours—6:31 a.m.

"I think maybe we should shut down for today, take 24 hours, and then see where we stand first thing tomorrow. Do you think you could help me get the word out to everyone?"

"I'll do better than that. I will totally take care of it. Go get some rest, Tom," Andy said, truly sorry and still in shock himself.

Just as Andy spoke, a small four-wheeler rolled down the ramp and headed their way. It pulled up beside them, and Batter stepped out.

"Jesus, Tom, what happened?" said Batter as he looked around the project.

"That's my cue to go get started," Andy said to Tom and began walking toward his men.

"I just got word that you guys had a flood," Batter continued as he approached. He looked perturbed and like he had just awakened. "Why wasn't I notified sooner?"

"We had a breach in a completely uncharted hot spring. It happened about eight o'clock last night. Sorry, but we have been working to stop it ever since."

"Interesting," Batter said, then paused, looking around at the carnage from the attempt to kill the water flow. "Well, this whole area has been a total surprise," he continued, clearly annoyed. "Where is the Doctor?"

Tom didn't answer, he just looked in the direction of what had been the cave entrance.

"Oh no, Tom. What happened?"

"I took Alex down for a look at the burial site and she wanted some more light. When I came back up, the spring blew."

"So, she's still down there?"

"Yes."

"Dead?" It was a stupid question, and Batter knew it the moment he asked.

"Judging by the amount of water, I would say there is no way she could have survived. I'm going to clear it and go back in to see if I can recover her body."

"I am very sorry to hear that Tom, particularly since it was sort of my idea for you to show it to her." Batter looked at Tom, then around at the project. "Where is everybody?"

Sort of your idea, Tom thought, irritated. It *was* your damned idea!

"I asked Andy to shut down for 24 hours until we can regroup."

Batter was quiet for a moment.

"We can't do that, Tom."

Tom felt the blood pound in his temples and he turned to Batter. "Why not?"

"Look it, Tom, this is not my decision. It is a matter of national security. We simply cannot afford to stop. In fact, I am in the process of obtaining security clearances for more workers so we can speed this thing along. The ARC absolutely has to be done according to our new schedule. Now, I am very sorry about Alex, but we must keep going."

Should I tell him the real reason, Batter debated, then decided against it. Regardless of the terrible situation, it was not proper protocol. Tom did not "need" to know.

"Batter," said Tom, turning toward him, "I think my wife has just died."

"I thought she was your ex?"

Tom could not stop himself. His fist struck Batter squarely in the jaw and Batter tumbled to the ground from the force of it.

"I probably deserved that," Batter said, holding his chin. He wiped the side of his mouth with his sleeve and was relieved to find that his teeth still seemed to be in place. It occurred to him now that he should probably have been more careful. He was very familiar with Tom's credentials, which not only included the fact that he was one of the best geologists in the U.S., but also that he was a former Ranger.

I am such an inexcusable smartass, he thought, genuinely sorry about the comment.

Pity about Alex, I fully intended to recruit her for one of the ARCs.

Tom stood over Batter, shocked at himself. He looked down at Batter's bleeding mouth and was instantly sorry that he had hit him—but he also suddenly realized he was done—done with *everything*.

"I'd like to see if I can recover Alex," he said, "then I'll just go clear my office."

Batter knew he had to save Tom to save the project. There was no time left to find a replacement.

"Tom," Batter began, still on the ground, "I definitely deserved that. Some people, not the least of which would be all of my ex-wives, have accused me of being a cold-hearted son-of-a-bitch, and they are probably right. But I still need to have you here. We absolutely have to get this thing built and built on time." Batter extended his hand to Tom. "Now, help me up would you?"

Tom was completely taken by surprise. He had seen Batter in too many other types of altercations with contractors and others to imagine him capitulating in any way, despite the mishap with Alex. But Batter was right. Without him, the project would suffer even more delays. Tom knew that Batter was under some sort of gun from his own superiors to finish the complex, but exactly why was a mystery.

He finally reached out and pulled Batter from the dirt.

"I imagine you will want to organize a search team once the water recedes," Batter said to Tom as he looked in the direction of the damaged entrance, still rubbing his jaw. "Go ahead and take the 24 hours Tom, but do me a favor and work out a new time line with as many men as you need to get back on schedule. We absolutely have to get this thing done. Once again, I am very sorry about Alex."

Batter brushed himself off and held out his hand, which Tom shook reluctantly. "I know this is going to be a tough time for you. I wish I had
clearance to tell you what the hell the rush is all about, Tom, but I am sure
you can imagine a reason if you just think about it long enough. Lives may
depend on it. That is all I can say."

Moments ago, Tom had been ready to walk away. Alex was dead. It was
his fault. The rest of this whole undertaking was shrouded in secrecy from
the start. Nothing about it had felt good from the beginning. But Tom saw
a look in Batter's eyes that he had never seen, an earnestness that was absolutely uncharacteristic. Something bad was about to happen to the world,
and Batter, unlike him, knew exactly what it was.

"I have to leave for Nevada today, Tom, but I will be working on those additional contractors while I am in transit. Let me know of any other issues
and I will do my best to help."

Tom could not recall ever hearing such sincerity in Batter's voice.

"I'll send you an email when I work out exactly what we need," he responded. "In the meantime, I need to address this hot spring. I have to see
if I can figure out where the source is, and if it is going to cause any more
problems."

"I'll stay in touch," said Batter as he headed for his ATV.

Tom watched as Batter drove off. He was thinking about all of the things he
needed to do and reached for his radio to call Andy.

First and foremost, he thought, I need to find Alex.

CHAPTER 14

Eat This

I t was Alex's turn to lead. They were in her world now.

She carefully made her way down the broken cliff face and over the loose rocks that covered what she had just yesterday considered the most remarkable find of her life.

How quickly things could change, she thought.

Alex shook her head and glanced back at Mot, who followed her closely, apparently having no problem negotiating the rough terrain. His skin was shining in the morning sunlight, a hundred different shades of greens, blues and grey.

Alex noticed out of the corner of her eye that Mot would pause periodically to scan the area and dart his tongue. She couldn't decide if he was the most frightening creature she had ever seen or the most beautiful.

He's one big-ass son of a bitch that's for sure, she thought to herself.

Alex was eventually able pick her way over the rocks and to locate the very same path where she had so recently encountered the rattler. That event now seemed to her to have taken place eons ago. A part of her secretly wished the snake might appear again just to test Mot's reaction, but she knew he would have more than enough to react to momentarily.

As they rounded a stone outcropping, Alex's truck and campsite came back into full view. She paused, checking to make sure there was no one in the area.

Alex had already determined that Mot's life would depend on her ability to keep him a secret until she could figure out how to *very* carefully and appropriately introduce him to the world.

Mot also surveyed the area. He had stopped and was listening intently, trying to sniff out any possible danger.

Alex could see nothing of concern, but almost instinctively turned to Mot for confirmation.

"Mot, it is very important that no other humans see you. Do you understand?"

"Yes, Alex. I do not sense the presence of any of your species close by."

Mot had already come to the same conclusion himself. Although he recognized nothing of the world in which he now stood, he did sense danger in a way that was equal to or even greater than the one he was used to. While he could detect no immediate direct threats, he still felt oddly as if he were about to be attacked by something he could neither smell nor see. This was definitely not his home.

Where were all of the trees, he kept wondering as he looked around.

The Astrologers and Priests had been right: the world had burned. There was nothing left but dirt and rock. The air tasted thin and dry to him and he noticed that it was slightly more difficult to breathe.

Mot began to wonder how he could ever survive in Alex's world.

"That's my truck right there," Alex said pointing to her pickup.

When they reached it, Alex pulled down the tailgate and slid out a large white cooler. She opened it, and Mot could immediately smell the strong aroma of the food it held inside. Were it not for the extreme discipline he had learned as a child, he might have simply grabbed the entire cooler away from her, the odor of meat tripling his hunger.

Alex was famished as well and dug through the case. She knew she had to feed Mot at once, and felt fortunate that she probably liked meat as much as he obviously did.

She remembered that she had a package of steaks at the bottom and rummaged around until she found them. She quickly un-wrapped the cuts of beef from the white butcher paper they were packed in and held them out to Mot. There were two beautiful 16-ounce cuts of New York steak. By the look on Mot's face, she was certain that he could easily down a dozen of them.

Mot looked at the meat and inhaled deeply. It did not have the strong smell that he was used to, but it was the most delicious odor he had encountered in this new world, with the possible exception of the creature in front of him. He stared at the steaks for some time and then looked up at Alex.

"What do you think Mot?" Alex asked, suddenly worried about his reaction.

"Do you have fire?"

I'll be damned, Alex thought, this guy likes his meat cooked!

She immediately put the steaks down on the tailgate and pulled out her camp stove and set it on the ground. The stove was powered by a small propane tank that was attached to it. She turned on the stove to test for gas.

Thank God, she said to herself as the familiar odor of propane filled the air.

Need a lighter, she thought.

Alex remembered that she had a spare in the glove box along with a pack of cigarettes. She had basically stopped smoking years ago, but old habits die hard, and there seemed to be those moments when there was nothing better than a good smoke; nearly escaping death always being one of them.

"Give me just a second Mot," she said.

Alex went to the passenger side of the truck, opened the door and grabbed the lighter. She flipped open her stash of Marlboros, relieved to find that there were still a few in the pack. As she walked back, she deftly tossed one in her mouth, cupped her hand over the lighter and fired it up. Alex stopped for a moment, inhaling deeply, then blew out the smoke into the desert air. Heaven!

Mot stared at her amazed. He couldn't help but flick his tongue as the odor of the smoke and the steaks and the strange smell from the metal contraption Alex had placed on the ground swirled around him.

"What is that?" he asked.

"Believe me, my friend you *do not* want to know. It's one of the nastiest things ever invented by humans."

Alex shoved the cigarette back in her mouth and bent down, squinting from the smoke. It suddenly occurred to her that Mot might have been asking about the stove, but she was too exhausted at the moment to try to explain how it worked.

Mot watched again as fire appeared from the end of the shiny object Alex was holding, and then the metal box she had placed on the ground jumped to life with flames. Mot flinched.

He was used to a world where fire was created by the heavens and carefully guarded and maintained. The Arzats used fire for many things, but had never mastered making it for themselves. Even in times of extreme heat, the communal Fire was never allowed to go out. Someone was always was assigned to tend it.

The fire Alex created had appeared like magic.

She adjusted the flame on the stove and stood up.

"There," she said, "we'll just give that a minute and then we can throw the steaks on."

She went back to the cooler, suddenly very thirsty, and pulled out a couple of bottled waters. She twisted the cap off of one and offered it to Mot.

He was almost as thirsty as hungry, but had no idea what to do with the object.

Alex noticed that his hand was so large the bottle nearly disappeared in it. He looked confused.

"Like this," said Alex. She tipped the bottle to her lips and took a long swig, nearly emptying it.

Mot watched then tried to copy her, but the result left him choking.

"I am *so* sorry, Mot," she said as she rummaged for a bowl.

"Here, try this."

Alex poured the rest of the contents of the bottle into a plastic bowl and handed it to Mot. He held the bowl with both hands and tipped his head over it, sipping eagerly. It reminded Alex of a horse drinking. Successful, she turned and put the steaks on the camp stove grill. They almost immediately started to hiss and pop.

"How do you like them?"

"I enjoy all meat Alex," Mot said, mesmerized the fire.

"I mean red in the middle or cooked through?"

"No red."

"Well done it will be then my friend. Near as I can tell, you haven't had a meal in a very long time, so I guess a few more minutes won't kill you. I just appreciate the fact that you didn't eat me," she said, only sort of kidding.

"You would taste much better cooked, Alex."

Alex looked at Mot and noticed that his reptilian pupils narrowed slightly.

"And you have a sense of humor," she replied, laughing. She pushed the cooler out of the way and sat down on the tailgate of the truck.

Mot watched as she put the fire stick back to her mouth, the hot end glowing. She took another long drag and blew more smoke into the morning air.

"Oh my god, this is friggin' heaven," she said out loud, her feet swinging.

Alex glanced back down at the cook stove, then back to Mot.

"Here, have a seat Mot," she said, patting the place beside her.

Mot sat, trying to emulate Alex, the truck bed sinking under his weight.

Alex judged again that he must be somewhere around three hundred and fifty to four hundred pounds. She spun halfway around and dug back into the cooler, suddenly remembering that there might be some fruit in the bottom. She removed a plastic bag that contained several apples.

"What else do you eat besides meat?" she asked as she pulled one from the bag and held it up suggestively.

"Oh, many kinds of plants. I have never seen such a thing as this before," Mot said, studying the round object with great interest.

"Try it. It is called an apple," she said, passing one to him.

Mot took the fruit, smelling it before taking a small bite. He was amazed by its sweet flavor.

Alex flicked her cigarette aside and took a bite of her apple as well.

"Pretty good, huh?" she asked, the symbolism not lost to her.

Now I am Eve, she thought. Alex shook her head, still convinced that she might wake up at any moment.

Mot was overwhelmed. Between the instant fire, the meat now charring on the magic stove, the strange metallic object he was now sitting on, and especially the smooth skinned creature that was sitting beside him, he did not know what to think.

"Yes, very good," he said, as if he were lost in his own thoughts. "Are you a god Alex?" he asked suddenly.

Alex almost choked on her apple, then laughed. She looked at Mot and realized that he was totally serious.

"No Mot," she said emphatically, "I am definitely *not* a god. I am flesh and blood just like you. You have been asleep for many years—seasons, I guess you would call them—and much has changed, but we are both of the same world."

She jumped down from the truck and gingerly flipped the steaks with her fingers.

"How many seasons, Alex?"

"Many, many," she said.

She bent down, cupped both hands and scooped as much sand as she could from the desert floor, then let it run slowly back out between her fingers.

"Many, many seasons," Alex said, looking back up at him. He was staring off into the desert.

"I think the meat should just about be done, now let me just find a knife," she said.

She brushed her hands off, once again digging through a box in the truck, and produced a plate and a long sharp knife. Alex pulled the steaks off the fire with the blade, put them on the plate and sliced them into smaller pieces.

"Here you go Mot, be careful, they are very hot."

Mot picked up a piece, carefully smelling it first, and then placed it in his mouth and chewed. Second most delicious thing he had ever tasted, he decided. He was glad he had waited.

It took only moments for Alex and Mot to polish off the entire plate, with Alex being careful to make sure that Mot got the bulk of it.

As she watched him finish the meat—this amazing being with his skin glowing in the sun—she marveled at the creature she had inadvertently discovered. Before her, eating with her, and somehow communicating with her via some sort of weird telepathy was obviously the singular most important discovery in history.

How am I going to protect you, she thought to herself. How long will it take for some wild-eyed cowboy like Batter to screw things up?

Alex hadn't figured out yet how she would introduce Mot to the world of humans but she knew that for the moment, she needed to hide him.

She nervously looked back around the canyon.

Alex thought she could hear the sound of helicopter in the distance and glanced up at the sky. Far off on the horizon, in the vicinity of the project, she could see a massive double bladed transport gaining altitude. Her heart skipped a beat. If the chopper decided to turn their way, anyone aboard it would easily be able to spot them.

She tossed the cook stove into the back of the truck, keeping a wary eye on the helicopter. It was still gaining altitude but did not appear to be turning in their direction. Alex pushed back the cooler and slammed the tailgate shut.

"Mot, we need to get out of here," she said to him as he stood and watched her every move with great curiosity. "There may be humans around, and I am not sure what their initial reaction will be to seeing you, but it might not be good. My father's ranch is not far from here and I think that would be a safe place to go for the time being. Okay?"

Mot looked into Alex's eyes and could see the fear in them.

It was a silly question, given all she had just said. If what she had told him was true, he was somewhere in a far and distant future he knew nothing about. There was certainly no sign of his clan anywhere and he was beginning to believe that none of them had survived. The thick forest he had grown up in and hunted in was gone. What else was he to do?

"Yes Alex," was all he could say. He looked out at the desert, wondering which direction they would be walking.

"Just give me a minute. I've got to see if I can find the spare keys to this truck."

Alex went around to the driver side and opened the door. She fumbled around on the floorboard trying to remember where she had stashed the keys, her originals lost somewhere in the caves. It has to be right here, she thought to herself as she looked under the seat for the spare.

Her father had taught her to always have a spare. Not just of keys, but of almost everything it might be practical to have a spare of. There had to be one somewhere.

She walked to the front of the pickup and lifted the hood. To her relief, she spotted a magnetic key box far down in the left side of the motor. Alex had to reach to get it.

"Howdy there."

Alex froze, her head buried in the engine compartment. The sound of the voice was not more than fifty feet away.

"Howdy there," the male voice repeated, slightly closer.

Alex backed slowly out from under the hood and turned. There were two men in front of her, both dressed almost identically in jeans and camouflaged hunting jackets.

One appeared to be in his late fifties. The other, probably mid-thirties, looked as if he could be the older man's son. They carried shotguns loosely slung over their shoulders. Alex prayed that Mot was not in their line of sight.

"Do you need a hand?" the older man asked. There was something disturbing in his tone.

Alex looked at both of them, still concerned about Mot. She was accustomed to running into people when she was out, even in the remotest areas. Most that she ran into were fine folks, but there was something dangerous about these two that she could instantly feel.

This is why I always carry a gun, she thought to herself as she sized them up.

Unfortunately, her handgun was underwater back in the cave and her shotgun was out of reach in the cab of the pickup.

No matter, she reminded herself, the only time a gun is any good against another gun is when it is loaded, first out and first pointed with the safety off. These men had theirs in their hands.

"No, I'm okay. I was just looking for my spare key," Alex said sheepishly, "seems like I've lost my other one."

Obviously, thought Alex, they have not seen Mot yet or they would be shitting their pants and shooting.

"We saw the hood up," the older man said as he eyeballed Alex up and down in the same obvious way the younger man was doing.

Alex noticed that the older man's hands were filthy, with black lines around his yellowed fingernails. The younger man had tattoos across his knuckles and she could see the tops of other tattoos around his neckline. There was also something odd about their clothes, she noticed, they just did not seem to fit right.

"What are you fellas doing out here?" Alex asked as nonchalantly as she could, her heart pounding.

Both men continued to look at her like ravenous dogs, not seeming to hear the question.

"Huntin' for birds," the younger man finally offered, still looking at Alex as if she were a hotdog and he hadn't eaten for days.

"Having any luck?" Alex was worried. She had to try to appease these guys so she could send them on their way and work on getting Mot out of there. She was still amazed the men hadn't spotted him, but she did not dare look to see where he was.

"Not 'til now," the older man snickered, shooting a glance to the younger one. "Not real smart for a pretty lady like yourself to be out here all alone. You *are* all alone, aren't ya?"

The man craned his head around, looking past the truck.

Alex felt the hair stand up on the back of her neck. Okay, this was real trouble. She prepared to fight.

"My husband is just over the rise that way," Alex indicated over her shoulder, sure that it was obvious that she was lying. "We're paleontologists," she added, trying to bring a note of truth back into her tone.

"Bone hunters, huh?" the older man said. "We get plenty of those around here, that's for sure. Don't see a lot of women doin' it though. Junior, jump over the hill there, and see if this young lady's husband needs a hand." He looked back at Alex and grinned, flashing his yellow teeth.

"Okay, Pop."

Junior gave Alex a good long stare and started up the narrow canyon that she and Mot had come down earlier.

Alex took a deep breath, sure that Junior would spot Mot the minute he passed the truck, but nothing happened as he moved around vehicle and up the hill.

"What's your name?" Alex asked desperate to buy some time. She watched the man carefully, trying to judge if she could get close enough to disarm him before he killed her. If she were going to make a move, she knew she needed to do it before the other man returned.

"I go by Senior," he chuckled, "and that there," he said, indicating the younger man already over the rise, "is my boy Junior. Been so long since we used our real names I practically forgot what they are," he continued, winking at Alex. "Ya know, we been a long time without any female companionship...," he interrupted himself. "Junior, see anything?" he shouted.

"No, Pop," came the answer from a distance.

"Well then, get your ass back down here!" Senior yelled back. "Ya see, as I was saying lady..."

"Alex. It's Alex," she said. Decide, Alex, decide.

"Well, *Alex*, as I was saying. Been a long time since Junior and me had the pleasure of any female companionship. I was just wonderin' if, well, seein' as how it's pretty obvious you're lying about the husband and all...," Senior's eyes narrowed.

"What are you talking about?" Alex asked, but she knew. She felt as if she would vomit.

Junior strolled back. "I didn't see no one, Pop."

He stood by the old man and gave Alex an accusatory look.

"Anyhow, I was just telling the lady here, that if maybe she were a little bit cooperative, that maybe we would be a little gentle, and maybe, we'd even leave her alive."

Senior pulled his gun off his shoulder and pointed it directly at Alex.

"Whaddaya think, Junior?"

Junior's eyes narrowed and he smirked as he also pointed his gun at Alex.

"Sounds good to me, Pop."

Alex was pinched between the two men and the front of the truck. She considered trying to run through them but they were too close for that and just far enough away to blow her face off with their guns. She admonished herself for not trying to take out Senior when she had the chance.

All she could think of saying was, "No!"

"Guess we gotta do this the hard way, Junior," Senior said, moving the barrel of his gun right up to Alex's face.

In what seemed to be less than a split second, a shadow crossed behind the men, then Mot was between Alex and her two attackers, hissing and snarling, holding the long knife Alex had used for the steaks earlier.

A look of surprise, confusion, astonishment, then fear, and finally pain washed over both men's faces. Junior dropped his gun in the dirt and fell to his knees. Senior waved his gun in the air, trying to say something, but words seemed impossible. Blood gushed from his mouth as he tried to speak, then he too fell to the ground, his shotgun firing harmlessly into the desert sky in the process.

Both men ended up face down in the dirt, blood flowing from nearly identical wounds in each of their backs. They convulsed for a moment then stopped moving.

Alex looked at the men, then at Mot, his back to her, still protecting her, the bloody knife clenched in his fist.

Somehow, he had gotten behind the men, knifed them and then moved in front of Alex so swiftly she hadn't seen him do any of it.

Mot glanced back at Alex, then hunched down carefully over the men. He sniffed Senior first, then turned to Junior and did the same. Satisfied, he grunted, stood back up and turned to Alex.

"They are dead, Alex. They cannot hurt you now."

He looked back at the men, then focused on the shotgun Senior had fired.

The males' sudden appearance had surprised Mot. He had first sensed their footsteps, and then smelled them coming down the canyon only moments before they came into view. Mot could tell from their scent that they were human, but apart from that they smelled nothing like Alex.

Then, there had been no time to warn Alex before they had appeared. Mot had immediately found cover under the large metal box Alex called her "truck," and had waited to see what would happen.

Mot looked again at the dead humans, berating himself for not having detected them sooner. Fortunately Alex had told him her species could be dangerous, so he was ready for anything, but as Alex had spoken to the two males it had been hard for him to probe their minds and find out exactly what they were up to.

When Alex had finally said "No," a clear picture had formed in his mind of what they were planning, and he had taken action.

Mot thought at first about trying to fight them, which would have been easy, but he had no idea what the males held in their hands; some kind of hunting sticks he had never seen, some kind of weapons.

Whatever the objects were, it was clear that Alex was as fearful of them as she was of the humans, and Mot had been in too many scrapes before to resort to half measures. Usually, even among Arzats, the conflicts he was used to amounted to kill or be killed. No, he could not afford any mistake. He had silently taken the long knife from the back of the truck, then, as quickly as he could, he had attacked, aiming for what he thought must be the area of the creature's hearts.

Alex continued to stand by the front of the truck, staring at the two dead men.

Senior, in a fit of post mortem nerves, twitched briefly and blood ran from his mouth and nostrils again.

"This is not good, this is not good," she kept saying.

Mot stood over Senior's shotgun studying it with great interest.

CHAPTER 15

Depraedor

I f Batter had cared to, he might have looked down from the Chinook he had commandeered and spotted Alex's white pickup and the four figures around it, but the helicopter was already too high for him to have made out any detail, and he was too engrossed in a phone conversation with the President to have noticed anything anyway.

* * *

Just before he had gone to see Tom he had been summoned on an urgent mission. He was to assess the preparedness of another ARC project that he had been working on for some time in Area 51, a military base in southern Nevada that had become infamous during the fifties and sixties as a highly top secret government facility.

Over the years, many rumors had circulated about the goings on there from government testing on extraterrestrials to the development of flying saucers and various other top secret weapons. But, despite decades of research by curious journalists and the enthusiastic speculation of Area 51 hobbyists, nothing of note regarding its operations or actual purpose had ever come to light.

This level of secrecy was no doubt helped by the fact that there was a standing order to 'shoot to kill' any intruder attempting to breach the complex's twenty-three by twenty-five mile perimeter.

The secrecy was further ensured by the fact that all of the personnel working there had to have a Level One security clearance to do so, with a potential charge of treason hanging over the head of anyone who might dare to violate the government's trust.

Aside from the Area 51 staff, Batter was probably one of the few other men on the planet that was completely familiar with the base's main purpose. During the Cold War, a vast underground complex had been constructed including a secret subterranean railway that ran all the way from Washington D.C. to the heart of the underground facility.

The whole thing was a monumental project that was originally designed to serve as an alternate center of government for the United States in the event—god forbid—that D.C. should ever be attacked by nuclear means.

Over the years, the entire facility had been continually upgraded as new technology came on line and new threats emerged. A huge component had morphed into a major research and development center. The rail, once a high speed diesel system, was now all-electric. The power for the entire operation, once a very complicated system of underground hydro, was now all provided by self-contained nuclear pods. Ventilation systems had been reworked to protect the occupants, not only from radioactive fallout, but from pandemic diseases and biological weapons as well.

The facility was massive and had even amazed Batter when he had first seen it in the '80s. The ARC component had been redesigned to house all of the U.S. Congress, the Supreme Court, the Presidential Administration, and various support staff. All in all, room for over a thousand souls should they be lucky enough to make it there in the event of a disaster. It was like a giant, one level convention hotel without windows.

Families unfortunately, as well as most of the normal support staff that worked outside of the specific parameters of the ARC, were not to be provided for in the event of an actual catastrophe.

* * *

"Yes, Mr. President," Batter had answered once a secure line had been established, and the young lieutenant sitting next to him had given him the thumbs up that the line was safe and open.

"Batter, how well can you hear me?" the President asked, aware that Batter was in the air.

"You are coming through five-by-five Sir."

"Listen, I have two new situations I need for you to assess for me."

"Yes sir."

"The first is this: we may not have as much time to prepare the ARC units as we previously discussed this morning. It appears that there is another smaller asteroid actually in front of the one we first spotted. According to Pan-STARRS, there is 'a shadow' asteroid in front of the Diabolus, and the computers just picked up on it. Apparently, the trajectory is almost exactly the same as Diabolus, but this one is way out in front of it. It's not as big, but big enough. The astronomers are still trying to work out the exact time line and potential impact damage, but suffice it to say that this new asteroid is going to get here much sooner. They are calling this one Depraedor."

Batter's mind was going.

"Batter, are you still with me?"

"Oh, ah, yes, Sir. I got it."

"Obviously, I need to know exactly what you can get ready and what the time line is for all of the ARC units."

"How much time, Sir?" Batter asked, wondering what could be worse than a twenty-eight day notice.

The President paused. "72 hours."

Batter looked at the airman who was assisting him with the call. The young officer had turned away from him and seemed busy with other tasks associated with the operation of the helicopter. There were two pilots up front, but all Batter could see was the back of their helmets. For some reason, he vaguely wondered about their families and how many children they might have.

"Batter, are you there?"

"Yes, Sir. I will get on it, and I'll have a report for you right after I touch down. We had a little snag with Utah yesterday that I am trying to address. Nevada, of course, is always ready, but I will reconfirm that when I get there. I'll check on the status of Colorado and Kansas as well."

There were a total of four ARC units that had been developed. Of them, Utah was the least complete. The original criteria for the three additional units had been that they all needed to have proximity to the Area 51 rail line, away from any major historical seismic activity, and spread out enough to give each of them a chance of survivability should one or more others suffer a close or direct hit from a nuclear attack or—now it seemed—*from a massive asteroid impact event.*

"I'm counting on you, Batter. We are preparing to move personnel soon. I need to know how many, and where."

"Yes, Sir."

"Now," the President continued, "I have one other thing. You know about the K-T samples that were taken from the Utah site last week?"

"Yes, sir."

"Well, apparently the find was astonishing in many respects. In short, the scientists believe they may have finally identified the missing link in their cryogen research. As you know, this had been an integral component of the entire ARC project even before we were faced with this shortened timeline. In any case, if true, they are telling me it might now be possible to complete a cryogenic unit that could actually work long range. I need you to meet with the researchers when you arrive and let me know what you think."

For years, there had been wild speculation about how long it might be necessary to remain underground after an asteroid hit, particularly if it happened to have the magnitude of something like the K-T.

The scientists had speculated that it might be as much as a few centuries before it was safe to venture out on to the surface, far beyond the time that food and supplies would reasonably last in the ARC units.

Were cryogenics actually possible, there might be a way to preserve at least some semblance of the human race into a time when it once again became possible to inhabit the planet.

Batter was only somewhat familiar with cryogenics. He knew of several private companies that claimed they had perfected it, but they were really just a bunch of cowboys milking the Indians as far as he was concerned, and they certainly seemed to be a whole lot better at freezing things than they were at thawing them out.

The government research in cryo, on the other hand, which had initially been pursued for use with astronauts in space travel, was much further along in development. In fact, the scientists at 51 had recently revived a primate that had been frozen for just over a year with minimal cell damage. According to Pete Wilson, everything they needed to produce viable cryo units had been completely vetted with the exception of a fully tested cryo-protectant.

With some misgivings, Batter had approved the construction and installation of several cryo-beds at each of the ARCs, on Pete's assurance that they were "just one molecule away" from perfection.

"May I ask, Sir, what leads them to believe this?" Batter asked.

"Well, apparently when they thawed out that one dinosaur specimen they managed to save—are you ready for this, Batter—its heart started beating!"

CHAPTER 16

Arzat Awake

"Shit! She's gaining consciousness! Let's have everyone out of the room except the anesthesiologists please," Pete Wilson said as calmly as he could, his heart racing.

Pete had been lucky. Despite the terrible and unfortunate accident in the desert, he had not been killed and his team had been miraculously able to save one of the twelve specimen they had originally taken out of the Utah site.

The prize they had been left with was the only remaining evidence of what everyone had thought at the time to be a perfectly preserved, never seen before, specimen of a sentient pre-K-T dinosaur. But "perfectly preserved" were hardly the words to describe what was now happening in the lab.

* * *

Pete had finally been able to breathe a sigh of relief when the helicopter they had called for after the accident had safely reached the base and the sarcophagus had been transferred into secure cold storage. He had given everyone on his team only eight hours to rest before they would begin to examine the specimen in detail.

After he had seen the medics, Pete took a hot shower in his quarters and fell instantly asleep. Then, what seemed to be only a second later, he awoke to his alarm blaring and his head throbbing from the ten sutures it had taken to close the wound he had suffered in the wreck.

An hour later, he and his team started the slow process of thawing and exhuming the specimen. The top layer of the sarcophagus had been like cutting the stone that encased it—some kind of ambergris or near relative that was two to three inches thick.

The second layer had been the big surprise. They had expected the entire block to be frozen solid, but the minute they had broken away a large enough section of the amber, they discovered some sort of goo about the consistency of jello. It was as if the creature had been purposefully packed in it the minute after death.

Whatever the material was, its freezing point was well below 0 Celsius. Someone had thoughtfully called for a shop vacuum. Then, five hours and three fifty-gallon trash bins later, they were looking at a complete dinosaur from the late Cretaceous. Everyone's heart rate had increased. Bones, skin, perhaps even internal organs.

As Pete suspected, this was going to go down as one of the most significant finds ever in the world of paleontology. Scratch that. It was one of the most significant finds in all of human history, period!

Pete was confident that he and his associates would be writing enough material over the next few years to fill a library. The fact that the information would probably all be classified was only mildly disturbing. Those were the rules of the game when you worked for a top-secret organization and he had long ago surrendered to the idea.

Pete was also enough of a realist to know that, had it not been for the governmental construction of the Utah ARC, it was very unlikely that anyone would have ever made such a discovery. After all, they had been working at minus 1,000 feet or so from the surface for god's sake. Then, of course, there had been the accident.

Now, none of that seemed to matter.

The specimen was removed from its ancient stone capsule and placed on a rolling table then transferred to a large and very well equipped autopsy room. Pictures were taken, and various measurements.

The creature would have stood about 6 feet 8 inches and weighed 311 pounds. Some distant relative of the theropods was the immediate theory. It definitely had walked upright. They determined that it was probably an adolescent female. The creature had no apparent tail of any kind—another first—but the greatest mystery was that it appeared to be partially clad in some sort of reptile skin!

One of the younger doctors, a clown by the name of Phillips, had posed for a shot with a stethoscope. When he placed it on the chest of the creature, his face had immediately gone from jovial to serious. He had paused long enough to cause the team member who was taking the photographs to admonish him.

"Come on Phillips, very funny, quit messing around and let me get some more shots without you in the damn picture!"

Phillips had ignored the remark. "Ah, Dr. Wilson, I think you better…" he said as he carefully but quickly moved away from the dinosaur and thrust his scope out to Pete. "I know it's impossible, and you must think I am kidding, but…"

Pete looked Phillips in the eye. There was something unnerving about the way he had looked back.

"Okay, Phillips," Pete finally said, "I'll bite just so you can have a good laugh. You probably all deserve it."

Pete took the scope over to the specimen, placed the instrument in his ears and then, as nonchalantly as he could, he placed the flat part on the dinosaur's chest and listened.

Nothing.

Phillips gave an expectant look his way as if to encourage him, but Pete
was just about to give up when he heard it—a heartbeat deep and distant—
at nine-second intervals. He caught five or six of them before his hands
shook and he dropped the stethoscope from his ears.

"That is impossible," was all he could say.

The next minutes were a blur of activity.

They rushed the dinosaur from the autopsy room to the largest operating
room in the building and placed her on a table that was equipped with thick
leather restraints.

Pete immediately called in every doctor, veterinarian, and animal expert
on base and basically ordered every test it was possible to do without cutting the creature open. They cinched the dinosaur down and started a heart
monitor along with an EEG to report brain activity, and watched in awe as
the brain functions increased steadily along with the heart rate.

Pete was concerned about the consequences of the creature regaining consciousness and the shock it might send her into when she suddenly realized
her new circumstances. He had seen animals often go into shock when they
had recovered from anesthesia in different surroundings.

Reluctantly, he had ordered an IV and prepared to have anesthesiologists
ready to sedate if necessary.

Pete was just as worried that any kind of drug might kill his specimen, especially any kind of anesthesia.

How were they to know what kind of dosage or even if it would work?

One of the other doctors had a lot of experience with gators, and another with primates, but his was only mildly comforting to Pete.

Talk about famous, he had thought. How about being responsible for *killing* the one and only specimen of a living dinosaur ever known by overdosing it with tranquilizers?

He instructed everyone to leave the room except his two anesthesiologists and ordered the doors secured. No telling what might happen. There was a glass gallery just above them, so the rest of the team could still see what was going on.

* * *

Now the beast was actually regaining consciousness, 65 million years after it should have died! It was utterly and completely impossible.

"This is impossible, right?" Pete kept asking to no one in particular as he closely watched the monitors.

No one bothered to answer until the beast began to move.

"Be careful Doc," one of the anesthesiologists cautioned, obviously scared to death.

One of the creature's fingers twitched and Pete was standing very close to the table.

* * *

The Arzat was almost certain she must be in another world. There were strange sounds all around her and a multitude of very unfamiliar and un-pleasant smells that she had never experienced before. And never in her life had she been surrounded with so much pure light. Before she even opened her eyes she could sense that it would be blinding to do so. She instinctively attempted to pull her hand up to cover her face, but her arm would not move.

Perhaps she was still dreaming, she thought. She had certainly felt like she had been dreaming for a very long time. Nothing had happened in the dreams that she could specifically recall—movement, travel, alien voices, and the ever-present cold—but all of the images were vague.

The only thing she could remember clearly was one of the female Arzats handing her something foul to drink.

She felt as if she were stuck in a white cloud, the kind that emerged in the bright sunlight just before a storm.

She tried to move again, but her left arm, both her feet, and her legs were mysteriously pinned down. She started to panic.

Gradually, she opened her eyes. At first she could see nothing, the brightness of her surroundings blurred everything.

She blinked a few times and, as her pupils naturally dialed down to impossibly narrow slits, she was surprised to see a weird creature staring at her, so close to her face that she could have reached out and grabbed it were she not constrained.

She hissed and snarled instinctively.

The creature, whatever it was, seemed equally surprised and immediately took a couple of steps back.

There were other similar creatures in the room as well, but she was not sure of their numbers. She could not really see them, but she could sense them. She was surrounded.

Where were her parents? Where was she?

The Arzat tried desperately to move again. As her eyes became better focused, she attempted to see what was holding her, but she had difficulty lifting her head. It too was strapped down somehow.

She strained to look down her body, and was further upset to see that there were all kinds of things attached to her skin, as if she were in a giant spider's web.

She was still weak, but the anger and fear that welled up inside her took over. She started to twist from side to side with the enormous force of all of her muscles, her eyes focused on the creature at her side.

The animal's own eyes widened, and she could see a strange white space around its pupils that was even more disturbing. It began crying out in some sort of incoherent high pitched babbling. She took no satisfaction at all from the fact that it seemed as frightened as she was. The only thing on her mind was breaking free.

"Doctor?" one of the anesthesiologists asked Pete in a very concerned tone. It was clear that he was anxious to get the order to sedate.

Pete didn't immediately answer. He was too mesmerized by what was happening.

The creature twisted and pulled with every bit of her strength and finally snapped the leather that had been holding her right arm and took a swipe at him.

"Okay," Pete said as calmly as possible, thinking that he had waited too long. He backed away from the table. "Okay. Let's see if we can slow her down some."

The dinosaur was just about to completely break out of the restraints. Pete could see that.

In a second, he and the two other doctors were going to be stuck in a room with this thing that was not only gigantic but pissed.

The three men watched as one of them carefully fed drugs into the IV.

The Arzat was still struggling to free her other hand when her body suddenly began feeling heavy. The sensation was very similar to the one she experienced when her mother and the other females had administered the drugs in the cave. She attempted in vain to get any part of her body to work but it was impossible, and she felt herself quickly drifting back to sleep.

Pete and the other doctors watched the heart and brain-activity monitors carefully to be sure that the anesthesia was not negatively impacting the creature before they could all breathe freely again.

"What do you think John?" he finally asked the doctor that had put the dinosaur under.

"I gave her just about the same dose as I would have given a full grown gorilla. Might keep her down for an hour or so, but I wouldn't know for sure Doc. I would guess shorter than longer," the anesthesiologist answered, still trying to recover from the scene he had just witnessed.

They all continued to look at the EKG and the other monitors.

Pete had been terrified to drug the creature—afraid there might be some negative reaction. Any kind of anesthesia was always dangerous, and they still hadn't done a full blood analysis. The doctors were shooting in the dark. Pete knew that he was going to need to act very quickly now. He didn't dare risk another dose.

"Hey, Ron," Pete asked the officer in charge of the area, "can you come in here please?"

Ron was another old friend of Pete's who had been working with him for many years. Ron had stationed himself just outside the operating room and had already given orders to clear everyone out of the entire section if necessary. He could see that this creature would rip the place apart if it ever got going, far worse than any angry full-grown gorilla. Unbeknownst to Pete, Ron had also stationed marksmen with high-powered rifles close by just in case.

"Yes, Doctor."

"Is this room strong enough to contain this thing when she comes to?"

"I am not sure Pete, but probably not."

"Well we can't keep doping her without killing her. I would like to let her regain consciousness without restraints, somewhere safe where we could still monitor her."

"We have a few rooms much better for that, my friend. Basically padded cells with one-way observation glass. They're in the primate compound."

"Let's get her moved."

CHAPTER 17

The Burial

M ot gave a light kick to "Senior" one more time just to be sure he was completely dead, then did the same to "Junior" as Alex looked on. She appeared to be in some sort of trance.

Mot took the time to study the long metal objects that the men had held like hunting sticks. He was particularly interested in the one that had made the great sound. His ears were still ringing. After what he had seen so far, he could only imagine how effective such a thing might be. Mot resolved to thoroughly question Alex about the weapons and their use, but he could sense that now was not the time.

The men were both dead all right. Mot was proud of himself. They had been very clean kills. But he was still a bit confused by Alex's reaction. Clearly, the human males had planned to kill her in a most unpleasant way, yet Alex seemed somewhat bothered that they had been eliminated.

Mot was still very hungry, and as far as he was concerned, although the males smelled terrible, if he could convince Alex to fire up that cooking contraption again, he might just gut both of these humans and have quite a nice supper. When Mot looked at Alex, he decided against asking her.

Mot was trying to be patient, but he sensed that this place was still very dangerous.

"Alex? What are we going to do?" he finally asked.

From the moment they had escaped the caves, Alex had been most concerned with protecting Mot. It was bad luck for the men that Alex really
hadn't been alone, and bad luck for Mot as far as keeping his existence
under wraps. The dead men just created a potential trail that might be
followed.

"We need to bury them, Mot, and get rid of them," Alex finally said, snapping out of her shock. "I think there is a shovel somewhere in the back of
the truck."

Alex turned to go see if she could find one—sure that Mot would have no
idea what she was talking about.

Now we've gone and killed someone, she thought as she rummaged around.
She found it interesting that she felt very little remorse about the dead men.
Alex was sure that had the tables been turned, it would have been she who was
now face down in the Utah desert. She shivered and returned to the bodies.

"Okay, Mot, we are going to have to dig a very large hole." She handed
Mot the shovel and then turned to survey the area. "Not here though. Let's
do it over there," Alex said as she pointed to another spot about fifty feet
away.

She didn't want to have to drag the bodies very far, but she also did not
want them to be buried right in the middle of things. They would be harder
to find in the place she had chosen.

"Just one last thing." Alex bent down over the men and reached in Senior's
pockets, producing a wallet and half a pack of Pall Mall cigarettes. "Pall
Malls? Who smokes those anymore?" she said absently.

She tapped one out of the pack and fired it up, and then flipped open the wallet. Anthony Albert Bradley, Blackhawk Boulevard, Mount Pleasant, Utah.

Alex had absolutely no idea where Mount Pleasant was. Probably some small, hell-and-gone place out in the middle of the state, she thought. It didn't matter, the picture on the license looked nothing like Senior, not by a couple of decades. Senior had obviously stolen it, and Alex shivered when she thought about what might have become of the real owner.

She went through Junior's pockets, as well, but there was nothing in them but a wad of cash. She shoved the bills in her front pocket, aware that she no longer had a wallet of her own. They might need the money along the way.

"Okay, Mot, let's bury these guys," she said, standing back up. "What do Arzats do? Do you bury the dead?" she asked, flicking the cigarette away.

"No, we burn them," said Mot, looking curiously at the tool Alex had just given him.

"That is a very common practice with humans, too," Alex said as she headed for the place she had indicated before. Mot followed.

"Let me see that thing," Alex said, pointing at the shovel. Mot handed it back to her, and she began digging in a spot that looked to be mostly sand.

"Ever used one of these, Mot?" Alex said, her breath already becoming strained after just a couple of throws.

Mot shook his head. "No, Alex, but I think I understand."

"Good," Alex said, handing the shovel back to Mot. "We need the hole to be at least three or four feet deep if you can get it there."

"Alex, what are 'feet'?"

"Oh, I keep forgetting."

How would Mot know what "feet" were?

Alex held her hand to her waist. "Three feet, okay? While you dig, I'm going to go get the truck ready to get out of here."

Mot was amazed by the tool. It was a heavy-duty, folding spade, an Army surplus job, virtually indestructible, but to Mot, the biggest news was that the blade was made of very hard metal.

In Mot's world, bronze had just been discovered and it was very soft by comparison.

He began to dig. Although there were many rocks in the soil, the material moved easily enough and—much to Mot's astonishment—the tool did not bend or break. Some of the bigger rocks he just grabbed and threw out of the hole.

Alex went back to the truck and finally retrieved her spare key from under the hood. She looked over and was surprised to see that Mot had already carved a hole that looked almost big enough to hold the two men. He was standing up to his thigh with a large mound of debris piling up. It would have taken her all day to do what Mot had accomplished in less than ten minutes.

She looked around again and made a mental note to someday go and get her motorcycle back from Tom and Batter.

Alex packed up anything else that was still on the desert floor and jammed it in to the truck bed. She wanted to be sure that once they pulled out, there would be nothing left of her camp. When she was certain she had thoroughly cleared the area, she went back to see about Junior and Senior.

The morning sun was already heating up the desert, and flies were beginning to swarm the bodies.

She shivered, knelt down beside Junior, and began to tug his body by the feet in the direction of Mot and the hole he was digging. Junior was not easy—he was probably 200 pounds of dead weight. Alex did have the advantage of sliding him over sand, but he was face down. She tried to roll him by pulling hard on his left arm and eventually she got him to topple over. Then she grabbed his boots and tugged again.

Alex knew in her heart that these were bad men and that it was very likely they had hurt people many times before without getting caught. It was probably a good thing that they would no longer be able to harm anyone. Still, she hoped that there wasn't a wife or kids at home somewhere that expected either of these two to show up.

"Cuz that ain't gonna happen, my friend," she said aloud to Junior, still disgusted, struggling to pull him through the dirt.

Alex had only been able to budge Junior about ten feet before she finally called Mot for help. He easily picked up both men, one in each hand, and walked them over to the hole and dumped them in, as if he were taking out the trash. As hungry as Mot was, the two had already passed smelling good to him and he was ready to be done with them.

Once they were in the hole, he looked at Alex.

"Okay?" he asked, indicating the shovel.

"One last thing," Alex said as she tossed the shotguns in with the bodies.

"What are those Alex?" Mot asked, very interested.

"What did you hunt with?"

"A long sharp stick, with a metal tip," Mot exaggerated.

"Well, those weapons are like that, but better. I will explain later. Now, let's cover them up."

In another few minutes, there was virtually no sign of Mot's hole or the dead men. Alex and Mot had carefully camouflaged their makeshift grave, and Mot had added his own final touch by rolling a boulder the size of a small car over the top.

The day was swiftly approaching noon. Alex looked to the sky and noted the time.

"Let's get out of here."

CHAPTER 18

Area Five-One

B atter's helicopter touched down on the west side of the Area 51 complex at 1130 hours local.

It was a trip he had made countless times over the years. He knew they were getting close when he saw Groom Lake appear on the right side of the aircraft followed by the massive crisscrosses of runways that made up a good part of the surface facility. They were so large they could easily be seen from space.

From the air, Batter thought, the runways and ramps looked like the giant X's of a target.

Area 51 was not only the emergency alternate headquarters for the U.S. government; it was also the predominant research site for government funded studies on everything from the atom to life in distant galaxies. Anything that was deemed "not safe for public consumption" occurred within the site. There was a primate lab, a lab that worked on viruses, advanced weapons, and lasers.

Batter could have named over one hundred other such specific areas of study, given the question. Most of the work was carried out underground, but the centerpiece of the facility was the ARC itself.

Batter, by order of the President and a secret congressional committee, and under the authority of the CIA, was somehow in charge of all of it, as well as the other three ARC unit sites.

What would the public think if they knew the actual truth about the extra-terrestrials that had been discovered in the fifties, he mused, making his way across the tarmac.

As he walked out of the wash of the blades, Pete Wilson approached and half saluted then shook his hand.

"Good morning, Mr. Batter," Pete screamed above the blast of the helicopter shutting down.

Batter noticed that Dr. Wilson, who was perhaps half his age, really looked barely old enough to be out of high school.

How in the hell does a guy like that get to be in charge of the whole scientific division, he wondered. Then he suddenly remembered that it was he, himself, who had appointed him.

Pete offered to help Batter with the one small bag he had brought, which Batter declined.

"Would you like some lunch, Sir, or would you like to get right to it?" Pete asked as they climbed into a Jeep and headed towards one of the buildings.

"Actually, I wouldn't mind a quick bite and perhaps you can fill me in, Doctor. I cannot remember the last time I ate."

"Likewise, Sir."

Pete would rather have gone right back to the observation room, but he really was starving, and he had instructed his people that he was to be paged immediately if the creature began to awaken. He hadn't wanted to leave in the first place, but figured it would be a big mistake not to see to Batter's arrival himself.

A few minutes later, both men entered a large dining hall five hundred feet below ground. There were probably two or three hundred uniformed and non-uniformed personnel having lunch.

How in the hell do we keep this place top secret, Batter wondered again as they made their way through the lunch lines. Some of the best food on the planet was served here, and almost no one in the world knew about it. Now, it might all be over in a few days. No more dining of this caliber, that was for sure, he thought.

They found a table and Pete proceeded to fill Batter in on all that had happened since they had returned from the Utah site, including the exact details of the accident. They ate quickly, then Pete got a page, the creature was coming around again.

"Mr. Batter, we have to go."

Pete took Batter deep into the heart of the primate unit and ushered him up some stairs into a viewing gallery that was raised from the main floor of the compound. There were just two entrances to the compound itself, along with a couple of pass-through drawers where food could be delivered or experiments could be carried out.

Even though Pete had already prepped him, Batter found himself amazed at what he saw on the floor of the room below.

At first glance, the creature looked to him like an alligator sleeping, but past the scaly skin and the obvious reptilian features, there was absolutely nothing else about this animal that resembled a gator, particularly the fact that the thing had no tail. In fact, its body looked far more human than most primates.

Another young doctor approached Batter and Pete in the gallery.

"Mr. Batter," Pete said, "this is Dr. Randall Philips. He actually discovered the heartbeat. What's the status Randall?"

"Well, Doctor, the creature stirred and then appeared to drop back to sleep. We are just waiting again now. The anesthesiologists say it should be any time," Phillips said, checking his watch. He glanced at Batter, clearly nervous about being in the man's presence.

"What are you going to do with her? It is female, I take it?" asked Batter.

Pete nodded. "Yes, we determined that when we first exhumed her."

"Anyway," continued Batter, "what are you going to do with her when she wakes up?"

Pete turned to Batter directly, "Sir, I have no fucking idea."

* * *

The Arzat could feel herself coming back around. This time she had convinced herself to be more careful. She was fully awake before she even thought about opening her eyes. Her mother had warned her that she might find things very different when she awoke, advice she had failed to fully take into consideration the first time around.

She decided to keep her eyes shut for the moment, pretending to still be asleep while she studied her surroundings. She had many other strong senses besides her eyes, and this time she planned to use them.

She had a good sniff around, but without flicking her tongue, it was difficult to isolate exactly what was where. Nothing was familiar at all.

Could she escape? Where were the other Arzats? Were there any others?

She was very disappointed that she could not sense any. If there were others, she should have been able to detect their presence, even if they were not nearby, and even without the use of her tongue.

She wasn't freezing now and she didn't think that she was still in the cave. Last time she woke up, she found herself on some kind of table, but now she felt like she was on a rock floor.

She did not sense the immediate presence of the strange creatures in the room with her, although she was certain she could hear many close by. There were definitely strong and distinct odors coming from them. She listened and felt.

How many were there?

One flick of her tongue was all she needed but it would be a dead giveaway that she was awake.

She finally risked opening her eyes, doing it ever so slowly, her retinas mere slits against the light coming from overhead. The brightest light the female had ever seen was direct sunlight and this seemed even brighter.

At first she could see nothing but glare, but gradually her surroundings came into focus.

She tried to move her body again, expecting restraints, but was surprised to find none. She actually raised her head slightly and there was nothing attached to her as there had been before.

Had she just been dreaming? Had she just imagined them?

As her eyes continued to adjust, she began to look around the chamber. Never had she witnessed any space so well formed. The room was square and smooth, the walls a perfect white—as brilliant as any clouds she had ever seen. At the top, high up on the wall, was a series of openings that went all the way around the chamber. They reflected light like still water.

Perhaps they were openings, she corrected herself. Be careful, and assume nothing, she reminded herself.

Batter and Pete watched as the dinosaur slowly gained consciousness. Pete was relieved to see that the creature had not become immediately violent and that his strategy of just leaving her alone so far seemed to be working. He did have two men prepared with tranquilizer guns stationed near the doors just in case.

"Extraordinary, Doctor!" Batter said as he watched the lizard awaken. "What do you know about her?"

"We carbon dated everything we could get our hands on in the cave. Some bone fragments and some items that we think were used as tools. There were also some carbon deposits we think might have originated from torches. Everything so far points to 65 million years give or take a million. You may not remember, but that was the period in the Cretaceous just before the infamous K-T event."

"Don't remind me." Batter replied under his breath.

At some point very soon, he knew he was going to have to break the news to Pete about the new asteroid, and he was not looking forward to it.

"Excuse me?"

"Never mind, Doctor, you were saying."

"Well, even more mind-numbing than the creature's apparent age, is the fact that her species appear to have been full-on *sentient*."

"Which in English means...?"

"Intelligent. I mean language, tools, fire, writing,'the whole enchilada,' as they say. There were engravings in front of all twelve burial plots which we assume might have been numbers or even their names. No paleontologists have ever even suspected... Well, you might imagine... I mean the whole thing is impossible." Pete shrugged, his eyes fixed on the female.

"One thing we now know for sure, is that cryogenics *is* possible, at least for her species. I sent a sample of the material she was packed in over to the lab and my guys are testing it now. I mean 65 million years! Can you imagine?" Pete went on, watching the creature, talking to himself as much as he was to Batter.

The Arzat rolled up into a squatting position and studied the room around her. Her joints were stiff and sore. She really needed to urinate, and she was extremely hungry and thirsty. She had the uncomfortable feeling again that she was being watched, though the room she was in appeared to be quite empty.

Finally, she couldn't hold it any longer and went to a corner.

The entire staff gasped. The creature's move was so swift it seemed supernatural. She had disappeared from the center of the room and reappeared on the side like a tiny lizard darting, all three hundred pounds of her.

The female sensed the reaction but continued to relieve herself, disgusted by the way her urine was running so uncomfortably close her feet.

The Arzats had a communal bath that had a stream of water running through it for this purpose, and since the females were seldom out of the caves for more than short scavenges, they were rarely forced to urinate outdoors.

She hissed and flicked her tongue, totally embarrassed, and looked up toward the glass.

Pete could have sworn the creature was looking right into his own eyes.

"Wow, I never even considered that," he said as he watched her urinate on the compound floor.

"I would probably have to go pretty bad myself after a few million years," Batter chuckled. "The next thing I would want is a glass of water or a Bloody Mary and a big-ass breakfast."

"No kidding," Pete said heading for the stairs. "Please, excuse me."

CHAPTER 19

Good Ole Truck

A lex and Mot put the finishing touches on the camp, doing their best to erase any obvious evidence that they had ever been there.

Mot was very familiar with what Alex was trying to accomplish. The Arzats attempted to always leave as little trace as possible after a hunt, and especially a kill. There were too many competing tribes and too many scavengers to advertise success.

He had expertly managed to remove any signs of blood from his kills by carefully scattering desert dust over the area. When he was finished, there was no indication that anything had happened. He showed Alex how he covered his own footprints, and put her to that task with the shovel.

For Alex, removing any sign of her camp was simply a matter of trying to keep Mot's existence secret as long as she could.

Her big advantage, if she had one, was that, for the moment, everyone probably thought she was dead. That would give her some time, but Tom or someone else was sure to eventually come looking for her dig site and start snooping around.

She made a mental note to call him as soon as they got to the ranch.

"Mot, are you ready?" Alex was standing by the driver's door of the truck.

"Yes."

"Mot, remember when I was trying to describe just how different this world is?"

"Yes, Alex."

"Well, if your mind wasn't already blown by what you've seen so far, meet this thing we call… well, we call it a lot of things actually, but let's just call it a truck. My good ole truck," Alex said, and gave the side a nice open handed pounding.

"Good ole truck," repeated Mot, confused again.

What he really wanted was something else to eat, and he had no idea what Alex was talking about.

"Mot, I imagine that you did a lot of walking where you are from, and we humans do too, but we also have invented several faster ways to get around from one place to another. This is one of them. Nothing to be scared of, okay?"

"I am not fearful, Alex." Mot said, standing by the driver door of the truck, watching her, wondering why they hadn't started walking.

"Okay, good. I am going to do what we call 'starting' the engine. There is some noise and stuff that happens but don't worry."

She got in the truck and turned the ignition. The old Ford's starter hesitated at first, then caught the beat and spun until the engine fired, much to Alex's relief. When she looked up, Mot was wide eyed. He cocked his head—a habit Alex noticed was indicative of him listening to something intently— and flicked his tongue.

"See how I am sitting? I need you to come around the other side and get in and sit like me."

Mot tentatively made his way around the truck as Alex reached over and opened the passenger side door.

Good thing this isn't a compact, she thought.

Even so, Mot was about all the old Ford could handle even with the seat pushed all the way back. The truck's suspension sank under his weight as Mot awkwardly climbed in. He was barely able to get his feet on the floor-boards and his knees in front of him.

Mot placed his huge hands on the glove compartment and waited. The smell of the truck's exhaust was interesting, if not overwhelming—like fire but with a sharp after-bite. Mot suddenly worried that the odor was going to make him sick.

"Ready?" Alex cautiously asked.

"Yes, ready Alex," Mot said, hoping she would hurry with whatever she was doing. He thought they were going to leave, not sit here roasting in this noisy metal box.

Alex pushed in the clutch and jammed the transmission into first gear. The truck protested as Alex let the gears take hold, and then it began moving forward. She was trying to be as smooth as possible so as not to alarm Mot, who was sitting stoically, suddenly wide eyed.

Alex thought that, if she could see deep enough below his green and blue skin, she might see a lot of white. He might be scared right now, but he is going to love this later when he gets the hang of it.

Mot felt his hands and feet digging for a better hold. The 'good ole truck' began moving at a pace that would equal his best for a long hunt, yet he was doing nothing.

"Is this magic, Alex?" he asked overwhelmed.

There seemed to be so many things in Alex's world that were completely inexplicable.

Alex laughed, "No, Mot, when we get to my father's ranch, I will try to show you how this works."

They were on a long section of the dirt road that had originally led Alex down to her camp. She was keeping an eye out for the dead men's vehicle.

They must have driven something to get here, she thought, now where was it?

Finally, just before the highway, she spotted a brand new Chevrolet pickup parked far off on the side, well out of view of the main road.

That must be it, she thought.

Alex considered stopping to take the registration and the license plates, but she was too worried about someone else coming by. She would just have to take her chances that no one would spot it for a while and get curious. Besides, someone was probably going to have to report the men missing before they came looking, and she doubted that anyone was going to miss those two very soon.

She shuddered again when she thought about how her encounter with them might have turned out had Mot not been there.

Now that they were about to get on the highway she was about to have another problem. If anyone saw Mot, they were not going to mistake him for just some ugly kid.

"How ya doin', Mot?" She looked over, he seemed better, but his eyes were locked on the road.

"I am fine, Alex. I wish to know what makes this move."

"I promise I will explain everything when we get to my house. In the meantime, I need to hide you," she said pulling on an old Indian blanket that was draped over the seat, "so can you kind of duck down a little and put this around your head." Alex helped Mot make the blanket look like a shawl.

"Boy, you make one ugly looking woman, Mot," she laughed when she was finished.

"I do not understand, Alex," Mot said, looking back at her with his reptilian eyes, his forehead shrouded by the blanket.

"Never mind. Let's just get you home."

When they reached the highway just south of Vernal, Alex made a right toward Price. It was about 110 miles to her dad's ranch, about two hours if she drove fast.

Alex was exhausted and she just hoped that she had enough adrenaline left to get them home before she passed out. There weren't a lot of cops out in the middle of the desert, which was good for fast driving, but she had to make sure that she didn't get stopped by a patrol car. That would be a disaster.

As the truck's speedometer climbed past sixty, she looked back over at Mot. He was still staring straight ahead.

"Home sweet home, here we come," Alex said with much more enthusiasm than she felt. Mostly she was nervous. There were a million more bad things that could happen along the way.

This is much faster than I could run, thought Mot, mesmerized by the pure speed.

He was relieved to find that the sickening smell had more or less disappeared as the wind flew through the open window of the truck. Mot stuck his arm out and was surprised when the wind slapped it back. He had never felt anything like it.

As he sat there, trying to imagine how the truck worked, a similar metal box buzzed past them going the other direction. Mot looked at Alex expectantly when this happened, imagining for a moment that they would collide.

Alex was busy looking forward and sometimes glancing into a shiny object above her head. She appeared to be worried, but not at all concerned about the thing that had almost hit them. Mot was very confused again, but as they drove on, the blanket was making him warm and the steady hum of the tires on the road was making him sleepy.

"Alex?"

"Yes, Mot."

"Will there be food there, at this place you call home?"

"Yes, Mot. I have a freezer full of venison that I think you are going to really enjoy."

Alex made a mental note to check when she got the ranch, but her caretaker tended to hunt deer at night with a spotlight, and he liked to keep his stash at her house in her dad's old chest freezer.

"Hum," Mot grunted, having no idea what venison was, but imagining it was meat of some kind. He was still very hungry. "Alex, how long until we get there?"

"I am not sure how to answer that Mot. How do Arzats mark time during the day?"

"We refer to all times as animals that are common to my world."

Like the Chinese, Alex thought.

"How many animals do you have for the day?"

Mot held up both of his giant hands and stretched out his fingers—this many for day and again at night.

Okay, thought Alex, so we have twenty-four and Arzats have sixteen, roughly eight to our 12 for daytime hours, and eight for night. Seeing Mot hold up his hands that way went a long way to explaining their base eight numerical system.

"Probably then, just about one of your 'animals' to get to my father's house," she finally answered.

"Will your father be there, Alex?"

"No, Mot, my father died some time ago."

"Do you have other family? Siblings, children, a mate?"

Alex shook her head, "No, Mot. I used to have a husband but no more."

"Husband?"

"Mate. I used to have a mate but no more." Alex said, thinking about Tom. She wondered what she would say when she called him.

"You must be very lonely. In this, we are the same," Mot said absently, looking out the side window.

Alex did not answer.

Mot felt his eyes becoming heavy when, just for a moment, he thought, that he could feel the very vague presence of another Arzat far, far away.

* * *

Alex didn't relax until they were only a few miles out from the ranch.

Mot had been asleep for a good part of the trip despite his interest in the truck and its workings. Fortunately, there had been very little traffic as Alex had pulled through Price, and then through even-smaller Wellington, where everyone knew her and definitely knew her truck.

She was low on gas but decided against trying to fill it at the only station in town, and having to risk explaining to Sally the station owner just what was *really* under the blanket. There was a two hundred gallon tank of fuel at the ranch if they could manage just a mile or two more. The gas needle sat precariously on E.

Just past the south side of town Alex turned off the road and stopped—the sudden change in pace and the gravel crunching under the tires waking Mot.

"Here we are," Alex said, relieved to be home. "Wait here, Mot. I am going to open the gate."

She opened the door and slid out of the truck seat and walked forward.

An old wooden sign hung in the western style above the road at the main gate with block letters IN SITU carved into it. You more or less had to be a scientist to get it, but the term meant "found and left in its original place," undisturbed, not moved, just where it belonged; like Alex's fossil before Tom and his guys destroyed it, like this home in the desert her father had created for Alex after her mother's death.

Alex could still remember watching as old Simon had patiently carved the words into wood with a hammer and chisel in his shop. She had been around the world and back again, but the ranch was still her favorite place on the planet. She had loved the place from the first moment she had seen it.

The ranch encompassed a full section of land—six hundred and forty acres—a mile by a mile of beautiful desert. The entire property was loaded with fossils and all kinds of great finds that, as a child, Alex had proudly hauled back to show to her father.

"What have you brought me this time, Alexandra?" she could hear him saying.

As Alex swung open the gate and was just about to jump back in the truck, she spotted a sheriff's patrol car coming around a bend in the road. Her worst fear, it pulled off directly behind her pickup and stopped.

As the officer exited his car, she was relieved to see that he was an old friend of hers, but she was worried about Mot. She gave him a silent warning not to move and hurried to the back of the truck to get between it and the patrol car.

"Hey, Gus!" Alex said, giving him the familiar hug of an old friend.

"Well, hey there, Alex, haven't seen you in a while."

Gus still thought Alex was the most beautiful woman he had ever seen. They were just about the same age, had gone to grade school together, and Gus had always had a mad crush on her. Alex's dad had often invited the kids in town to "big" science events at the ranch, which Gus had always attended, despite having no interest whatsoever in Simon's lectures. Gus spent the time secretly fantasizing about marrying Alex when they got older, but had eventually given up on that idea when Alex moved away.

He had ended up settled down with Sally, another local girl who had been part of his very small graduating class at the high school in Price. Now she helped her parents run the only gas station and convenience store in town, and Gus was the local cop.

"I've been up north on a dig for a week or so." Alex said, trying to distract Gus.

"Find anything good?" he asked.

Alex felt herself blush, well aware that she was a terrible liar, and nervous that Gus would look toward the cab of the pickup.

"No, not really," she said as convincingly as she could.

"Well, that's too bad." Gus seemed suddenly preoccupied, looking around in the bed of the pickup that was full of Alex's gear. "Hey, must be the first time I ever seen you go out without a dirt bike in the back. You haven't given up riding have you?"

Alex tensed, she felt any minute now Gus was going to look towards the cab.

"No, no. I'm still riding. You?" she added quickly, trying to steal his attention.

Gus kept looking around, uneasy.

"Well, I'm still trying to talk Sally into that Harley that Hank Mitchell has been trying to sell, but…"

There seemed to be a sudden gust of air, then everything was still again.

Alex and Gus both looked toward the source of the sound. The passenger door of the pickup had swung open.

Gus stood motionless, peering at the door, sure and not so sure that he had seen something move there. Whatever had happened, it had raised the hair on the back of his neck and his hand had instinctively felt for his gun.

"What the heck? That is just about the weirdest thing I ever…"

Alex knew that Mot was going to be discovered and felt helpless to do anything. She watched as Gus pulled his gun and flipped off the safety.

He cautiously walked up toward the open door of the pickup. Alex was about to intervene as Gus reached the cab, but something told her not to. She was surprised and relieved when Gus, looking in the cab, showed no reaction. She walked over and looked in herself. There was nothing in the cab but the old Indian blanket lying on the floorboard.

"You didn't have anyone with you, did ya Alex? I mean, I could a sworn I saw something, but it was just too fast. Did you see it?" he said, swinging the door of the truck back and forth as if he were testing it.

"No, Gus," Alex said honestly, in shock herself over Mot's miraculous disappearance.

He pulled off his hat and wiped the sweat off his brow. Alex noticed that he was prematurely balding.

"I still can't figure it. I had a mountain lion do something similar to me one time. Never saw her. Knew she was right there. In fact, I thought she was going to kill me. This felt just like that."

"Might have just been a gust of wind," Alex offered.

Gus stood staring out into the desert for a minute.

"Yeah, guess you could be right, Alex. But damned if I ever seen wind open up a car door. I seen it shut a few, though." Gus looked back at Alex and smiled.

"Well you look tired, and I best be getting back up to town. Anyway, it's great to see you," he said, giving her an awkward hug.

"You too, Gus," Alex said, still not believing her luck. "Say hello to Sally for me."

She gave him another quick hug then jumped back in the truck and started it.

"Hey, Alex," Gus said, suddenly back at her driver's side window.

Alex gulped and almost pissed her pants again.

"I near forgot," he said. "The real reason I stopped was to warn you about something."

Alex gulped again. Did he already know something about the men they had just killed? She looked at Gus and let him continue.

"There was a prison break down in Gunnison. Five convicts escaped, and so far they only rounded up three of them. Apparently, a father and son got away, and ended up killing a couple of people in Mount Pleasant, then stole their truck. Word is they started out north from there, an' that means they could come through here, 'specially if they're thinking to get cross't into Colorado. I just wanted to warn you to keep an eye out. They are very bad men, Alex."

"Thanks, Gus." she said, relieved. "I'll let you know if I see anything suspicious."

"Well... Good to see you again," Gus said, patting the edge of the window.

"I'll go ahead and get that gate closed back up. You take care all right? I don't want to have to worry about you being out here all alone."

"Thanks, Gus. I… I'll be fine."

Alex pulled the truck forward and waited as Gus swung the gate back in place. She gave him a little wave and rolled off, leaving Gus staring after her with his hands on his hips.

Now, she thought, where the hell is Mot?

CHAPTER 20

A Rose Is Still

"**D**oc, you can't just go in there!"

"Just do as I ask, please," said Pete.

It was a nicer way of issuing an order. He was standing near the entrance to the enclosure.

"But that's like going into a lion's den not knowing the lions!" said Paula, the team member that had patched up his eye after the accident. Besides her skills as an amateur nurse, she was actually an animal behavior specialist.

"Doc, you can't go in and just introduce yourself to an unknown predator with a piece of raw meat."

"That is *exactly* what I have in mind, Paula."

Pete had ordered some bottled water and a large bowl. He had also asked someone to run to the commissary and get some steaks and some fruit. Pete was sure that the creature was primarily a carnivore, but who knew?

"Raw steaks, Doctor?"

"Yes raw, of course raw," Pete had replied, fully aware that he had no idea what he was doing.

"So, you are essentially going to walk in there with a bunch of bloody steaks?" Paula tried to reason again, shaking her head.

"Look," said Pete, "if worse comes to worse just shoot her with tranquilizers and I will get right back out."

"That might not be so simple, Doc," said one of the marksmen who had witnessed the creature's earlier moves. "It could easily get you between itself and our line of fire."

"Pete," Paula tried one last time, "did you see how fast she was? If she comes after you we won't be able to stop her. Even with tranquilizers, she won't go down immediately."

"Well, you guys just do your best, and I promise you I will be right in and right out. I'll wear a headset so we can communicate. But do not under any circumstances fire at that creature unless I give the order. Is that clear?"

Pete got another very doubtful look from both Paula and the marksman, but they said nothing more.

When everything was finally in place, Pete took a deep breath, tested his radio one last time, and had his staff open the door. He walked through it slowly, a gallon bottle of water in one hand and, in the other, a large bowl full of raw steak and some apples and bananas. He felt as if he had a target painted on his shirt, but something in his gut told him things would be okay—that he was dealing with intelligent life.

The creature sat, watching him from the other side of the room. Her skin glowed under the lights, mostly golden but really the entire spectrum of colors. Her eyes were golden as well, with amazing flecks of blue and yellow accents around very linear pupils. Aside from their unique color, they could have belonged to python or an alligator or almost any other reptile, but they glowed with some sort of higher intelligence—Pete was sure of it. He imagined that the creature was actually squinting at him, sizing him up.

He slowly sat down with his back against the wall near the door where he had entered, never taking his eyes off of the creature, carefully placing the water and the food on the floor. His hands were shaking.

She was absolutely amazing. Beautiful. Deadly.

The Arzat sat as still as possible for the longest time, willing herself not to flick her tongue as she studied the little animal. She could smell the water and the meat and the creature itself, the latter two both seemingly good enough to eat, although neither had an odor that was completely familiar to her. She was very thirsty and very hungry, but sniffing with only her nose was like trying to see in the dark. Her tongue was where her primary receptors for heat and smell were. Despite herself, her tongue popped out, and she felt herself blushing.

Who was this little creature anyway, tempting her and scaring her, and forcing her to display bad manners? She was an Arzat, after all—a Zanta no less—from a proud lineage of excellent Hunters that spanned thousands of seasons. She wished her father were here. He would know what to do.

Pete was still trying to decide if he had really seen the creature flick her tongue.

"Paula, did you guys get that? Can you replay that and confirm?" he said, almost whispering into the radio.

"Yes, we are running it again right now and… Wow!"

"I take that as affirmative," he said quietly into his microphone.

"Yes, oh yes, sorry Doc. Definitely a tongue flick."

The female shut her eyes for a moment and focused all of her senses. She listened and felt, but sadly, she could still not discern the presence of any other Arzats, only the loud noises of these strange animals. The world had never been so loud. She could hear all kinds of inexplicable bumping and moaning, and the high-pitched chatter of the skinless creatures.

Hopefully, she thought, she would be able to eventually block some of it out, or it might drive her mad.

She turned her attention back to the one creature before her. She knew she would have to learn, and learn quickly, to survive. She could smell that the creature was a male and that he seemed to be trying to establish contact. Perhaps something could be done.

It was confusing though. The little male appeared to be communicating or trying to communicate, but she didn't get the feeling that the communication was directed toward her. This made no sense at all since the two of them were the only ones in the room.

She tested his mind a bit, probing.

Arzats could sometimes communicate with other creatures on a very limited basis. It just depended on the circumstances, and mostly on whether the other animal was willing and had some level of intelligence. Since a good deal of Arzat time was spent trying to hunt and kill most animals, the opportunity to have any meaningful interchange was limited.

But she was no threat to this little male—at least for the moment—and it was quite clear that it had some language skills.

Az mam Ra'a, imi agi metses moroc Zan. Kot en tew, tama azrew? "My name is Ra'a daughter of the great Hunter Zan. Who are you little creature?" She spoke with her voice and with her mind directly to the little animal. She tried to speak softly, so as not to frighten him.

Pete was so astonished he couldn't move: language? He recognized the clear pattern of speech immediately.

Of course, Pete couldn't understand any of it, but something else amazing was going on in his head. At first it was like he was being tickled, then a huge point of pain like a massive migraine came and passed.

Was she trying to say her name? It was as if he had actually understood her, but in a language that might as well have been Martian.

"My name is Ra'a daughter of the great Hunter Zan. Who are you?" Ra'a repeated the question, but this time with her mind only. All of the other little animals outside the room had burst into chatter when she had attempted to speak aloud. It was most annoying.

One thing about these creatures, she thought, they were very excitable and very noisy. She wondered if they ever slept, and if so, how?

Pete sat dumbfounded. He thought he had actually understood her. Did he? Was he just imagining it? He couldn't move. He didn't respond; he was too busy thinking. Impossible. Language?

Come on Peter, this whole thing is impossible. She, this creature, is impossible. Forget about impossible. The word no longer seemed to have any significant scientific value. Besides, you were the one so convinced of her intelligence. Why should you be so surprised about language?

Ra'a decided to get closer to the little male. Proximity did sometimes have a bearing on communication, although she wouldn't normally have a problem reaching another Arzat at even much greater distances. Anyway, the creature certainly didn't seem to want to hurt her, and she could see that it carried no obvious weapon.

In the time Pete might have blinked, the three hundred pound female had moved from thirty feet across the room to less than five feet away from him. She was already squatting, trying to bring her head down to the level of Pete's. Her speed was impossible, practically preternatural, and clearly too fast for anyone to have done anything.

She flared her neck and the skin on the back of her head spread much like that of a cobra's. The creature looked him directly in the eyes but her face remained non-aggressive and neutral.

Pete could only sit, watch, and attempt to stay calm. He had worked with many wild animals in his life, but he had never seen anything move like this one. It almost defied the laws of physics.

He could hear Paula on the radio calling for the marksmen to prepare for a shot.

"I am Ra'a daughter of the great Hunter Zan. Who are you?" Ra'a again repeated silently.

The language was foggy, as if it were covered with a blanket. The beast was speaking to him without saying a word.

"Don't shoot, do *not* shoot, Paula," Pete spoke into the radio as quietly and calmly as he could.

"What is 'shoot?' What does that mean?" Ra'a asked.

The creature kept looking directly into Pete's eyes, but he could tell that she was scanning the entire room as well.

"Do *not* shoot her, confirm please," Pete said again into his headset, as calmly as possible. It was as if the creature's words were suddenly coming into complete focus.

Ra'a was confused. Who was this creature talking to? She was aware of the entire room and could see nothing around that was a threat or that could "shoot her," whatever that meant.

Finally Paula responded. "Confirmed, Doc, but are you all right?"

"Can you understand me, little creature?" Ra'a continued, beginning to get annoyed. "Kak. I am Ra'a daughter of Zan," she tried again.

Ra'a thought that she might be getting through but she was not yet certain. What she was certain of was that the proximity of the food and water was making her salivate. She reasoned it would be much easier for her if she could establish direct communication with the creature, but if not, she would just have to come up with another plan.

Perhaps I will have to just take it from him, she thought to herself, knowing full well that such a move would be an unconscionable display of bad manners.

"Okay, Paula, the headset is not going to work," Pete finally said, mesmerized by the creature. "You guys will have to just keep a visual on me."

"But…" as she tried to respond, Paula could see Pete removing the radio slowly from his head. So much for that idea, she thought, as she watched her boss cutting off her only form of direct communication.

Pete looked the creature in the eyes, his heart pounding.

"My name is Pete," he said to the female directly. He watched and waited. The animal cocked its head to the side, studying him.

"Pete," Ra'a repeated aloud, but with so much accent, no one would have recognized it.

It didn't matter. Pete had heard it clearly in his head, and understood it perfectly.

"Yes, my name is Pete," he replied, his heart racing.

"Greetings, Pete. My name is Ra'a daughter of the great Hunter Zan."

"Ra'a?" Pete tested out loud.

"Yes, although your pronunciation is not quite correct."

"Well, I am going to have to work on that," Pete said, trying to suppress a smile, his heart slowing. He had been right: the creature was sentient and intelligent.

"This is not a big concern, Pete. Many of my own kind have difficulty with my name as well, but it is quite clear that we can speak non-verbally if you prefer. Simply make the effort directly to me to communicate as if you were going to say it with your voice."

"Okay, Ra'a. How can I help?" Pete tried to just think of the words.

"I am not familiar with the concept of 'OK' but will assume it indicates an affirmative. I must first know your father's name."

"He isn't alive."

Despite his excitement, the question stung Pete. He had buried his father less than a year ago.

"I am sorry to hear that your father has passed from this world," Ra'a replied, "but it is not necessary that he be alive to have had a name. We are all of our fathers, are we not?"

"Yes," Pete said, his head about to burst. "His name was Robert."

Ra'a seemed to contemplate this for a while. Pete couldn't have known that it was customary and a sign of good manners for an Arzat to fully consider a name for a moment when introduced, but Ra'a did.

In general, the manners of Arzat females were superior to those of the males, and Ra'a took great pride in the fact that she had been raised very correctly.

"Pete son of Robert then," she finally responded.

"Yes."

"Yes," Ra'a repeated.

Pete suddenly had no idea what to do. Ra'a had folded her mantle back into place, and both of them now sat looking at one another. Pete wanted to ask a million questions, but he found himself speechless.

"I am glad that I did not have to kill you earlier, Pete son of Robert" Ra'a said, remembering the first time she had awoken.

"Yes, me too."

Pete nervously cleared his throat despite that fact that he was not even speaking aloud. He had no doubt that the being in front of him could rip him apart before he could even blink if she wanted to; intelligent or not.

Ra'a stole a quick look at the water and the food. The smell of them was almost overwhelming. She was torn. It was extremely bad manners for an Arzat to ask a host for anything; it had to be offered. She waited, hoping that this "Pete" creature would get the hint and invite her to drink. Finally, when she could stand it no longer she asked, blushing with embarrassment as she did so.

"Tell me, Pete son of Robert, who might the water be for?"

"Oh, of course," Pete said, recovering from his stupor. "I brought this for you."

He gently removed the top from the plastic jug and pushed it towards the dinosaur along with the bowl full of meat and fruit.

"In what way does your species express gratitude?" Ra'a asked, relieved that she had apparently not offended.

She carefully removed the meat and the odd looking fruit from the bowl and placed the items on the floor, doing her best not to look too anxious, then carefully poured the water into the large container. She picked up the bowl with both hands and took a long sip.

"We say 'thank you'," said Pete, watching her intently, amazed that the plastic jug seemed to pose no problem at all for the creature to deal with. She had deftly picked it up with one of her large hands and poured half the water into the bowl.

Ra'a quickly drank the contents, then poured the rest of the water from the jug, and began to carefully sip again.

"Thank you, Pete," Ra'a said with her mind, testing the term even as she drank. "I was extremely thirsty."

"You are welcome," Pete said silently back, still in shock.

Ra'a looked at Pete carefully as she sipped. "Now tell me, Pete son of Robert, why do many of your friends seem to refer to you as 'Doc'?"

"Oh, it's just a nickname," Pete immediately replied, shocked, wondering where she had heard it. Then it occurred to him that she must have been able to detect Paula's voice through his headset!

Oh my god. How the heck do I explain what a 'nickname' is?

"It's short for Doctor. Easier to say," Pete added to try to clarify.

"Yes, it is much the same in my language," Ra'a said, setting the empty bowl back down on the floor. "We have many ways of referring to certain people. My given name, for example, was very difficult for my younger siblings to pronounce correctly, so when we were very little—instead of Ra'a—they simply called me 'Ara.' It means 'the wind' in my tongue, which they thought was very amusing until I proved to be faster than all of them. You may call me that if you wish."

"Ara," Pete tried to pronounce it aloud.

Ara slapped her thigh and laughed. "See, much easier, isn't it?" She looked down at the food on the floor and then back at Pete. "I hope you have a way to cook that meat, Pete, son of Richard."

Pete suddenly found himself speechless again.

* * *

In the gallery above, Paula had located Batter and sat with him as the events transpired below. Since Pete had removed his headphones, there wasn't much more she could do other than watch and hope he wasn't killed.

"I actually think he is communicating with her somehow," Paula said, looking down, shaking her head in disbelief.

"I agree." Batter said.

At any other time in his life, he might have had the luxury of being as fascinated at this discovery as everyone else, but unfortunately, he had an impatient President to deal with and a lot of work to do.

"As soon as he gets out of there, have him find me," he said to her, heading for the stairs.

CHAPTER 21

The Ranch

Alex watched Gus disappear from her rearview mirror as she slowly drove the truck around the first hill on the way down to the ranch house. The road was not paved, just a gravel path worn smooth with two distinctive ruts from years of carts and cars rolling down it. The main house itself was about a quarter of a mile from the gate.

Alex was worried, but she knew Mot must be somewhere close. She stopped the truck when she was sure she was far enough to be completely out of Gus's potential line of sight and stepped out. When she turned to look back down the road she was startled to see Mot right behind her. He had come out of nowhere.

"Jesus, Mot! You scared the crap out of me!"

"I am sorry, Alex. I was worried I might not catch up with you."

"Well, that's hardly likely," she said, calmer now that she had found him.

"I am a very fast runner, but not as fast as your good ole truck," Mot said so matter-of-factly that Alex laughed.

"Yes, Mot, that might be true. But you see, my house is right down the hill there." Alex pointed.

"What are those animals?" Mot had smelled them long before he'd seen them. He was still very hungry and whatever they were they smelled delicious.

Alex squinted down the road, trying to figure out what Mot was referring too.

"What? Oh, that is just Billy and Bobby. They're horses that I keep for the ranch. Mr. Garcia comes and feeds them every day when I am not here."

Alex made a mental note to call Mrs. Garcia and tell her that she had returned. The last thing in the world she needed was for Garcia to find Mot! Talk about a heart attack.

"And no, Mot, they are not to eat," she added. "Come on, jump in and I will take you down."

As Mot squeezed back into the truck, he was still gazing in the direction of Billy and Bobby. "You mean none of your kind eats those animals?"

"Well, they are okay for eating, but they are much better for riding."

"Riding?"

Alex just smiled, she was going to have to teach Mot *everything*, and she loved the idea.

The house was a classic western two story, which was one of the many things Alex liked about it. The front door was right in the middle of the bottom story, which included a covered porch and identical windows on either side. Just to the left of the house was a corral and a large barn, and just past them another building that was the high point of the ranch, her father's old library and lab.

As she pulled in, Alex realized she had underestimated the horse situation, not from Mot's point of view, but from the horses themselves. Billy and Bobby were stirred up, trotting back and forth and a making a lot of noise. They were so nervous they looked like they were about to try to bolt from their corral.

"Wow, they are all jacked up over you, Mot. Stay here for a second."

Alex slid out of the truck and walked to the corral, speaking in a calming voice to Billy and Bobby. Both of them were excellent ranch horses and they were used to a rattler or the scent of a mountain lion, but that didn't mean they had to like it, or that they wouldn't react if they sensed a predator. She pulled some sugar from a stash she had by the barn and eventually got them both to the fence and calmed. They happily licked the sugar cubes out of Alex's hand and relaxed.

Might as well try to get them used to Mot right now or there will be no rest for any of us, she thought to herself. She left the horses and went back to the truck.

"Okay, Mot, let's go see how we do together with these guys. We have to get them to calm down around you."

Mot got out of the truck and took a big sniff of the desert air, flicking to get the full flavor of it. He stopped for a moment to see what he could feel in the earth: the large animals, Alex, something much lighter scampering away somewhere beyond the wooden structures and some other very small animals foraging about. But there was something else. He could feel another presence close by, but he just couldn't identify it. Mot wasn't sure if it was dangerous or not, but Alex didn't seem to be worried, so he followed her, sniffing the air along the way.

As they walked towards the corral, Alex was speaking out loud in a very different voice than Mot was used to. Her tone reminded him of his mother for some reason. The horses settled and stayed calm. And even when Mot got very close, the horses, while bothered, remained relatively quiet.

Alex was a little confused because she had expected Billy and Bobby to get a little more worked up over Mot when he got near them, until the cougar made a break for it.

First, there had been an otherworldly growl, low and angry, and then the cat rolled out from behind a corner of the corral and ran swiftly for the desert. The horses had seen it, Alex had seen it, and Mot had instantly disappeared after it. Billy and Bobby went nuts, and Alex had her hands full trying to calm them again.

Good thing I don't have a dog, she thought, as she worked to sooth the two horses.

Mot eventually returned, walking swiftly back from the direction the cat had taken. Alex was relieved when she saw that he didn't have the cougar slung over his shoulder.

"The creature got away," Mot said as he approached, obviously disappointed.

"Well, they are very fast," Alex said, still wondering what the cat had been up to.

"Yes, I was only able to catch this part of it." Mot reached out and showed Alex a bloody wad that must have been the tip of the cougar's tail. "If I had my hunting stick it would not have escaped," Mot said. He appeared to be only mildly out of breath.

"I am sorry, Alex, if I knew the animals of your world better, I might have detected it sooner. It is obviously a predator."

Alex blanched as she reluctantly took the tail. Something else to bury, she thought.

"Well fortunately there aren't very many species we need to worry about around here. Come on inside and I will fix us both something to eat and then, I don't know about you Mot, but I have to sleep."

"I would like to sleep, but I am very hungry, Alex."

Alex disposed of the cougar tail and took Mot into the house, his huge bulk barely clearing the front door. There was a straight flight of stairs that lead to four bedrooms on the top floor with one bath. Downstairs, there was a parlor on one side, a large kitchen on the other, and another bath.

Alex had been around this house in one fashion or another for almost twenty years, so she was pretty certain that the chest freezer on the back porch would be full of Garcia's venison and was delighted to see that she was not wrong when she opened it. She grabbed what she thought must be four or five pounds of meat. Glancing over at Mot, who was watching her every move, she thought better of it, and pulled out another five pounds and threw it on the counter.

"Well Mot, let me just get some dinner started and then I can show you around." Alex unwrapped the meat from its white butcher paper and dumped it in a large pan and turned on the heat. This was not going to be a gourmet meal; she was more concerned with quantity than quality.

Mot was looking at everything at once and following Alex's *every* move.

She pointed at the oven and stove top. "Mot, this gets very hot, like a bigger version of the one I had in the truck. We cook almost everything on one of these."

"What is it called, Alex?"

"A stove."

"Stove."

Alex could hear Mot attempt to repeat the word aloud and she could hear him saying it in her head. She realized, or suddenly remembered, that she and Mot were communicating almost entirely non-verbally.

"Come on, I'll show you the house. This is our version of what I believe was your cave."

"Yes, Alex. It was far too dangerous to live outside of the caves. This would never keep out the predators of my world," Mot said, stooping over to peer out the windows and gently testing the wooden walls with his enormous hands.

"Well, we don't have anything like the kind of animals you had to face, and most of the ones we do have are usually frightened of humans, and they do their best to avoid us."

Mot just grunted a reply, completely distracted by the details of Alex' home as they walked through it.

Alex showed Mot the parlor and made a mental note to come back later and remove the dinosaur movie she had been most recently watching from the DVD player. That is the last thing I need him seeing, she thought, as if Mot could figure out how to work the thing by himself.

As she led him upstairs, Alex tried to do a quick mental inventory of the house, wondering what else it might be wise to hide from Mot. She quickly gave up, realizing that the entire place was packed with dinosaur paraphernalia.

When she showed Mot the upstairs bath, she was rigorously questioned about the toilet's function and operation.

"We had something very similar in the caves, Alex, water running through," he said, studying it intently. Mot turned to her. "I will use this toilet," he announced.

Alex laughed. "Okay, Mot, just don't forget to put the lid back down."

"I do not understand Alex."

"Oh never mind. Come back down when you are done and I will feed you," she said, walking toward the stairs to give him some privacy.

Alex went back to the kitchen. She was pleased to see that the venison was thawing in the pan and already beginning to brown. She turned up the heat, searing it lightly, and proceeded to cook the entire lot of it until it was quite well done. Alex figured there was enough for ten very hungry people.

When she had finished thoroughly cooking the meat and dicing it up, she placed the overflowing plate in front of Mot. His tongue flicked.

"Can I get you anything else with that?" she asked, smiling at the dinosaur.

"What about you, Alex?" Mot asked, focused on the meat.

"Oh, I couldn't eat a thing." Alex felt full just from cooking the massive dinner.

She grabbed a chair and watched as Mot nearly finished the entire plate. Alex hadn't thought to offer him a chair or any utensils and Mot hadn't asked, polishing off the venison with gusto as he stood at the counter.

As if he hadn't eaten in a million years, Alex thought, amusing herself as she watched him. She was so tired she was almost falling asleep.

"Thank you, Alex," she heard him say and she realized that she had dozed.

"Mot, I have to go to sleep," Alex said, fighting to rise from her seat. "I bet you are tired too. You can sleep wherever you wish, just please do not leave the house without telling me. We will be safe I am sure. Okay?" As she spoke, she rinsed what was left of dinner into the sink, and set the plate on the counter. Alex turned back towards him, "Mot, it is very important that you stay here in the house, okay?"

"Yes, Alex. I understand."

Alex felt like she should call Tom, but she was just too tired. She climbed up the stairs and fell into bed with her clothes on. Her alarm clock indicated 6:33 p.m. It had been a long 24 hours. She fell instantly into a deep sleep.

Mot wandered the house for a while, looking around at everything with great fascination. Finally, when he got drowsy, he walked quietly up the stairs and went to sleep in front of Alex's door.

CHAPTER 22

Batter Reports

A rthur H. Long had been President for only a short time, so Batter had some genuine empathy for the man was now dealing with the worst event in the history of the world.

Batter had been asked to report on two issues. The first, which might have been monumental news at any other time in history, was that, indeed, the specimen that they had found in Utah had somehow survived not only 65 million years of hibernation, but a massive traffic accident to boot. Even more incredibly, it appeared to be as intelligent as a human, not that that was necessarily saying much. And yes, it did seem as if the scientists had discovered a possible cryo-protectant based on the minor ingredients in the mixture the creature had hibernated in. They believed that it might actually work, but testing had just begun and they were running out of time.

The second and much bigger issue, was that the world was about end, and it looked like Batter was only going to be able to get three of the four ARCs functional in time for that unfortunate event.

Batter felt like he was failing on the Utah site, an emotion he was completely unfamiliar with. But the fact of the matter was that if the astronomers were right, they were only going to be able to save a small handful of people anyway, and who knew for how long? This situation made the plague or World War III or most any other disaster imaginable look like child's play.

"I am sorry, Mr. President, but the progress in Utah does not look good," Batter said. "We are 99 percent complete and have everyone available on it, but I just don't think we are going to pull it off. Are we still on the same schedule?"

"Yes, Batter, unfortunately nothing has changed. 2117 hours Eastern Tuesday is what they are saying. I am still waiting for the scientists to pin down a more precise impact point. So far, they are saying somewhere in the Pacific, maybe just off of Ecuador's coast. So that doesn't help us. The blast is expected to be several thousand times Nagasaki/Hiroshima, and it really couldn't be closer to North America without being *in* North America. Just the tsunamis alone will wipe out the entire West Coast. It truly looks like it is the end of the world, at least the world as we know it. I think you may want to just scratch Utah, and concentrate on the other three ARCs. I can't risk populating it, if you can't guarantee the site's integrity."

"I'll consider that. Do you mind if I ask, Sir, what the other nations have decided to do?"

"We are in agreement not to panic the public in advance of the event. This first asteroid is almost 1 kilometer in diameter, with the second one about three times that size. Between the two of them, they are probably going to kill everything on the surface no matter what we do. The more lead time we give the public the more unnecessary grief. Six hours is what was decided."

"What's that, Sir?"

"Six hours." The President repeated. "It's funny, there seems to be more concern about the potential behavior of the general population *before* the event than the event itself, and I am inclined to agree. In the meantime, internally, we are still calling it a drill, even with the some of the highest security personnel. Otherwise, as you know Batter, some will just panic, and it won't be good for anyone."

"I understand, Sir."

Batter had already imagined the rioting that would eventually ensue once the word got out. He made a mental note to keep close tabs on anyone on his staff who would be aware of the actual situation. People were people, always a frightening prospect.

"Also, Batter," the President continued, "I have arranged to send the Vice President in my place. I will be staying in Washington."

"I am sorry to hear that."

"It's not for me, Batter, this underground thing," the President said matter-of-factly.

"Let me know if there is anything else I can do," Batter said, in complete agreement. He was quite sure that it wasn't for him either, but it didn't occur to him that he had a choice.

"Just help everyone settle in. I assume that you will stay at 51?"

"Yes, Sir."

The President paused on the other end of the line. "Fascinating coincidence isn't it?"

"Sir?"

"That dinosaur you just woke up? Sounds like it was around the last time this happened. I wish I could be there just to see her. Perhaps you can send me some video?"

"Certainly, Sir. Regarding that issue, Sir, protocol has always dictated the elimination…" Batter caught himself, suddenly not knowing exactly how to say something. "Well, you know. 'Document then eliminate' I believe is how the policy is summarized. How would you like this matter addressed?"

"Oh, I suppose during any other time we might have had a wide-ranging conversation about whether or not we could risk the exposure. I mean, that is one of the main reasons we have always maintained 51, right, to 'shield the world from any evidence of other intelligence?'"

The President paused. It was as if Batter could see him shaking his head.

"I am going to let you decide this one, Alan, since I no longer think that it is an issue. I guess you'll have to figure out whether your dinosaur ends up being house guest of the Nevada ARC or not. But you will have some challenges with that as I am sure you are aware."

"Yes, Sir," Batter said, suddenly realizing this might be one of the last times he ever spoke to the man.

"Hey, what is it that they call that place again? I can never seem to remember the nickname."

"Dreamland, Sir. They call it Dreamland."

* * *

Pete had finally left Ara to the care of the other researchers so that he could go and give a full report to Batter. He also wanted time to pursue a theory he had developed regarding the cryogen projects, something he was very excited about. He had quite possibly identified the one problem that had been holding them back, and its solution.

He eventually tracked down Batter in one of the libraries reserved for ranking officers and was surprised to see him enjoying a cigar and what appeared to be a snifter of cognac.

"Sorry, Doctor, I went ahead and had dinner, and then…" Batter said, displaying his cigar and the giant balloon snifter. "What is that saying? 'You only go around once.' Isn't that it?"

Pete was a little surprised at Batter's mood. The bottle on the table was Remy Martin XO Premier Cru. Pete had been working closely with Batter for years and had never seen him relax at all, let alone smoke a cigar or indulge himself with something as expensive as the Remy.

Hell, smoking wasn't even allowed down here, now that Pete thought about it. He looked around but there didn't seem to be anyone else in the room.

"Oh, I sent everyone out so that we could talk confidentially, Pete," Batter said, noticing. "Can I get you a drink?"

Pete was anxious to get over to the cryo lab and back to Ara, and the last thing he wanted to do was get stuck with Batter for the rest of the evening. "No thanks," he said, still standing, hoping to keep the meeting short.

Batter offered him a cigar, which Pete also declined. He watched impatiently as Batter slowly poured more of the cognac for himself from what was rapidly becoming the bottom of the bottle.

As he stood, Pete considered Batter's comment about "around once," the cigars, the cognac, and the beyond amazing discovery of the Arzat which he had risked his life obtaining—and became suddenly hopeful.

Maybe he's finally going to give me a raise, he thought. Pete's oldest daughter would be going to college soon, and some extra money would sure help. He finally sat down to listen to what the man had to say.

"How's your dinosaur? Or should we be calling it something else?" Batter asked as Pete settled into the seat next to him.

"She's fine—remarkable. I have no idea how to classify her. She claims to have come from a clan of Arzats, a species she says was populous in the world of her time. We are actually able to communicate telepathically."

"Interesting. After all the science fiction and all the speculation, it's actually possible."

"She said that she thinks humans could telepath with each other as well, that we just need to be able to turn on that part of our brain."

"Sounds like you could study her for years."

"That's the plan. My staff is very excited. We just fed her dinner. An enormous amount of very good steak, and I should add, prepared well done per her request! And we've worked out lavatory arrangements."

"Lavatory arrangements?" Batter said, amazed.

"Yes, apparently she did not appreciate us forcing her to squat in the middle of the room to urinate. She said it would have been more embarrassing if she had needed to take a crap."

"Did she say that?" Batter laughed.

"Well, not in so many words. Remember we are communicating with telepathy, Sir. It's weird, general concepts are easy. We just have to explain unfamiliar terms to each other."

"But she has a spoken language as well, right?"

"Oh yes, and written apparently. It's amazing what I'm learning. For example, I believe her word for 'shit,' the expletive version, at least, is 'kak', or something close to that."

"Astonishing, really, that it took this long to find other intelligent life here on earth, isn't it?"

"Let's face it, no one wanted to. Can you imagine introducing Ara to the Pope?" Pete said, smiling.

"Yes. In fact, I know you are quite aware that, among other things, 51 was originally created to make sure such a thing *didn't* happen. As was the case with our visitors from space," Batter added.

"Yes, sir," Pete bristled. Had he underestimated the situation? Suddenly he was afraid of Batter's possible instructions.

The crash-landing of aliens so many years ago and many of the rumors that surrounded the event since that time were largely true, but only a handful of scientists actually knew that the aliens had been put down because of "protocol" and a profound fear that news of them might eventually become public. A "mistake" had been made, was all that had ever been acknowledged internally. The remains were still being studied, but to this day, they had not been able to figure out where the beings came from or what their mission was. There were still a handful of scientists working on the remnants of their vehicle as well, which had led to some interesting discoveries.

"Normally, Pete, I would probably be telling you to wrap up your investigation with this creature and to get her back on permanent ice. I mean, you are probably as familiar with the protocol as I am. But unfortunately for all of us, there has been turn of events that has probably taken that decision out of our hands."

"Sir?"

Batter took a deep breath. He had to tell him. Pete was critical to the operation of the ARC.

"Have you ever heard of a gravitational keyhole or the Torino impact scale?"

"Sounds like astro-speak to me, Sir. I am probably not as up on astronomy as I should be."

"I wasn't either until recently. Anyhow, as I am sure you are aware, some time ago the Pan-STARRS telescope identified a near earth asteroid—they call them NEOs—that was, er, *interesting*, shall we say."

"Interesting?" Pete began to brace himself. Batter rarely used the word "interesting" in a positive context.

"Yes, the astronomers were indicating that there was a small chance that it could impact the earth in 2036. 'Apophis,' they were calling it, which is the name of some Egyptian demon. In fact, it was around that time that I received orders to accelerate the preparedness of the other three ARCs. Apparently, there were some politicians who got pretty excited about it. In any case, we later discovered that the chances of impact with earth on this Torino scale were minimal, so everyone relaxed." Batter paused, took a drink and a long pull from his cigar. "However, the astronomers recently found something else."

"Sir?"

"A few days ago, they discovered two other asteroids, a pair on practically the exact same trajectories, and they are apparently headed our way." Batter looked directly at Pete. "They're calling the first one they found Diabolus, the Devil."

"How long do we have?" Pete said, assuming the worst, afraid that the answer might be in one or two years.

"For Diabolus?" Batter said as if he were distracted. "Twenty eight days."

Pete was speechless. "How big?"

"Big enough. Several hundred million times Hiroshima. Between the two of them, they each make Apophis look like a bad joke."

Pete got up and poured a drink. His hands were shaking.

"But, Pete," Batter reluctantly decided to continue, "Diabolus is not our big problem."

"Sir?"

"It's the smaller one, Depraedor they are calling it. It will arrive much sooner. They say that it is going to impact earth in," Batter looked at his watch, "two days, 11 hours and… 12 minutes."

Pete's drink fell to the floor and broke. He left it there, staring at it.

"I know you are aware that the first trains from Washington will start arriving tomorrow under the auspices of a National Emergency Drill, but this is no drill, Pete," Batter said, looking down at the broken glass as if nothing out of the ordinary had happened.

"I understand," Pete replied, but it was too much information. His head was reeling.

"Do you have family?" Batter asked, already well aware of the answer.

"Yes."

"I am very sorry, Pete." Batter took a long gulp from his cognac and tossed the stub of his cigar into a large ashtray. "One last question."

"Yes, Sir?"

"I'm just curious. Do you think there are any more of them?"

"Sir?" Pete was lost in the news of the asteroid, trying to focus.

"Arzats, dinosaurs, whatever you are calling them?"

"You mean, anywhere else besides what we found in the Utah site?"

"Yeah, I guess that's what I mean."

"Pretty unlikely sir."

"It's a weird coincidence isn't it?"

"What's that, Sir?"

"Your gal, your Arzat. Wasn't she around the last time this happened?"

"Well, yes, now that you mentioned it."

Batter leaned towards Pete. "I suggest you get some rest. We'll regroup first thing in the morning and figure out a plan. I am going to need your help with this, Doctor."

"You'll have it," Pete said, trying to regain his composure.

Batter got up. "I think it goes without saying that this needs to stay between us for the time being. There are only a few people in the world who have this information and probably even fewer who can handle it."

"Of course," Pete said as Batter left the room. He sat there, looking at the broken glass on the floor for a very long time. Then he thought about his family and cried.

CHAPTER 23

Pancakes

Alex thought she was dreaming that she heard the TV. She had been dreaming of water, lots of water, and now she thought she was dreaming TV. Then she realized she was awake.

She opened her eyes and took a minute to adjust. There was sunshine showing through her window. Alex was safe in bed and her clock said 6:15 a.m.

Had she really been sleeping 12 hours? Was she really in her bed back at the ranch? She had dreamt that she was drowning. Had she really left the TV on downstairs?

Then she remembered Mot, and the thought shocked her fully awake, like someone dumping cold water on her. She had a 65 million year old house guest, and he was obviously watching the dinosaur movie she had left in the player!

Alex popped out of bed and ran downstairs worried about what she might find. It was irresponsible to have left Mot alone last night to fend for himself and even more irresponsible to have left that damn movie out.

She was relieved to see that he was seated on the floor about three feet from the television with his legs crossed Indian-style watching like a little kid, but bigger by three hundred and fifty pounds, his eyes wide with interest. Mot did not move when Alex entered, nor did he take his eyes off the screen.

"Mot," Alex asked cautiously, "are you okay?" Alex continued berating herself for not removing the movie the night before when she had thought about it.

"Sorry, Alex, I got up and this box came alive." He silently said to her without looking away from the screen.

Alex noticed the remote upside down on the floor. She thought Mot must have accidentally knocked it over, and perhaps that is what turned on the TV.

Hell, maybe he just turned it on with his mind, she thought. She watched him for a moment.

Nothing different between him and a three-year-old on Saturday morning, she decided. I guess I worried for nothing.

Alex felt great after her 12 hour sleep. Now all she needed was a cup of strong coffee and a good hot shower. Then maybe she could figure out what to do next.

"Mot, I am going to make some coffee, take a shower, and then come back and make you a traditional country breakfast. How's that sound?"

"Mot?"

Mot telepathed something that resembled a "yes," but he was obviously distracted.

"I will be right back." When she got no reaction, she shrugged her shoulders and rolled her eyes, just as her father was so famous for doing.

Why am I not surprised, she asked herself? The movie had been a favorite of Simon's and hers for years. She often watched it when she wanted a mindless distraction. She went back upstairs, quickly made her bed, and turned on the shower.

"Heaven," she said after she had stepped in and let the hot water run through her hair and over her body. She took her time; washing and rinsing until she felt squeaky clean.

Occasionally, Alex thought she heard the phone ringing, but it was all the way downstairs and she was damned if she was going to ruin her shower running for it. I have to call Tom, she remembered.

There was no answering machine attached to the phone. That was technology her father had rejected for the ranch entirely. Of course, Simon had allowed Internet for research—but he frowned on email.

"Alex, the last distraction I need when I am trying to get something done is trying to answer twenty damn messages!"

Alex couldn't say he was wrong, so she had left his old landline alone. She thought about her cell phone that was lost somewhere hundreds of feet below the surface of the earth, and made a mental note to pick up a new one.

She dried off then threw on a robe and checked on Mot. Leaning over the banister she could see that he was still in place in front of the TV. She quickly toweled her hair, and changed into some clean khaki shorts and a work shirt with pockets, then hurried downstairs.

When she reached the lower floor, Mot looked up and his tongue flicked. Alex actually thought she could detect a hint of embarrassment cross Mot's face. Alex found it astonishing that she could even get his attention. The movie was right at the part where a gang of Velociraptors were in the kitchen chasing the kids.

"I cannot believe that you figured out how to turn that thing on," Alex said, standing with her arms folded in front of her, watching along with Mot.

"You smell... different," the Arzat stammered, looking up.

"You know that is not real, right?" Alex said, trying to ignore the remark and gesturing to the TV.

"Oh yes, Alex, I know. The animals look nothing like that," Mot said matter-of-factly, his attention already completely back on the television.

"Good," Alex said reaching for the remote, "then let's turn this TV off and see about some breakfast." The screen went blank and Alex headed for the kitchen and the hot coffee she knew was waiting. Mot sat for a moment staring at the blank screen, then reluctantly got up and followed her.

"You smell so different, yet the same. It is just so with Arzats after we bathe." Mot paused for a long time, glancing back at the box that was now black. "You remind me of Ara."

"Come on, Mot." Alex said, blushing. She led the way to the kitchen and poured herself a cup of steaming black coffee.

Alex seated Mot on a barstool next to a small island that doubled as a huge chopping block, checking the legs on the stool to be sure it would support Mot's weight.

"Okay, Mot," she said as if addressing a cooking class, "I know that you Arzats are pretty good at eating meat, and you liked that apple, but how about some other stuff? Other fruit? Maybe eggs? What else do you guys eat?"

"Yes, Alex. Many things. A number of the products of the trees-perhaps 'fruit' as you are calling it, and many of their roots. We dry some of them and store them for consumption at a later time."

"How about eggs?" Alex spun to the refrigerator and pulled a carton from the shelves and opened it. "These are eggs?"

"Yes, Alex, I am quite familiar with 'eggs.' I am 'of' an egg. All of our young, of course, are hatched," he said, looking at them with great interest.

Alex blushed. "Talk about foot in mouth," she said aloud. She closed the carton was about to put it back in the fridge when Mot grunted in a way that sounded like a laugh.

"It is 'okay,' as you say it, Alex. We also eat many eggs of other animals when we can find them."

"Do you grow anything?"

"You mean purposely?"

"Yes, we humans grow much of what we eat from the earth. We plant it, water it, and help it to grow. There is a garden out back of the house. I will show it to you later."

"No. We are hunters Alex," Mot said proudly, "the plants grow everywhere on their own. I live in a great forest. You would never walk through it but for the paths we cut or the trails the animals make for themselves."

"Hum… so, definitely hunter-gatherers. That sounds like pancakes to me," Alex said, amused with herself, her hands on her hips. She began to spin around the kitchen, grabbing a large mixing bowl from one cupboard and a large brown bag from another with the words 'pan mix' hand scrawled on the side."

"I'm sorry." Mot said, confused.

"Pancakes," she repeated, "Pan-cakes. And I bet you have never had pan-cakes better than mine, Mot. Actually, this is my father's recipe passed on to me. 'The best buttermilk pancakes in the entire southwest,' he used to say, and he was right."

Alex dumped a bunch of the mix into a bowl, added eggs and milk and used a wire whip to mix it. She managed to do all that and to turn on the cook-top to get the grill heating as well.

Mot watched, fascinated. So similar in so many respects to our females, he thought. Able to do so many things at once, while males seemed unable to focus on much more than one thing at a time.

"What was your father's name?" Mot asked. He flushed as he suddenly realized that the two of them had not actually been properly introduced

"Simon," she said, pausing to look out the window, "Dr. Simon Moss."

"Was he a Medicine Man?"

Alex paused, thinking fondly about old Simon. "No, more like a hunter—a bone hunter I guess you could say."

"Then in my world, your full name would be Alex daughter of the great bone hunter Simon."

Alex expertly dropped four large pools of pancake batter on the grill and then took a peek under it to make sure it was getting hot.

"I like that, Mot. I like that a lot." Her father, she thought, was definitely a hunter, as was she for that matter. Oh, how I wish ole Simon could be here now to see what I brought home to him this time!

She took another long slug off her coffee and expertly flipped all four pancakes, then turned and caught Mot flicking his tongue, apparently trying to make sense of what she was cooking.

"Don't worry," she added when she saw the look on his face, "I pulled a 5 pound ham out of the freezer last night as a 'provisional.'"

Mot took a long breath and flicked his tongue again, less self-conscious about it, vaguely wondering what the term "provisional" could possibly mean.

It was amazing how much the smell of the kitchen had changed as Alex prepared the food. First, there had been the clean fresh scent of Alex after her bath. Then the aroma of that dark and very hot liquid that smelled like the roasted nuts the Arzats females would sometimes prepare. Now, the goo that Alex had placed on the hot surface was changing into something solid, its smell wafting all through the room.

Alex expertly flipped the four giant pancakes off of the grill, placing one on one plate and stacking three on another. She put the stack of three in front of Mot, smiling.

"That, my friend," she said, her hands on her hips, "is called a 'short stack' and is ranked as one of the finest breakfast's in the world."

Alex suddenly remembered the three other critical ingredients. She quickly rummaged through the refrigerator and pulled out a stick of butter, a jar of peanut butter, and a bottle of maple syrup.

"Pancakes. Short stack. Breakfast," Mot repeated the terms, trying to commit them to memory.

"Okay, Mot, we gotta do this fast," Alex said excitedly. "First, we take a little butter and just slide it in there between the pancakes, like so. This has to be done while the pancakes are still hot so it melts the butter. Next," she continued, unscrewing the top of the peanut butter jar, "we take some peanut butter and sneak some of that in there too." Alex took a kitchen knife and spread a thick layer of the peanut butter between the pancakes as well. "Now, wait until that melts a little bit…" She tossed the knife nonchalantly in the sink.

"Finally, the pièce de resistance." Alex opened a bottle of syrup and ceremoniously poured a liberal amount over the pancakes, the excess running down the sides and onto the plate. "Voila! What do you think Mot?" she asked, smiling again.

Alex took her own plate and a fork, hopped up on the kitchen counter, and sampled a large bite of her own pancake. "Fantastic," she exclaimed, quite proud of her accomplishment. "Go ahead, Mot, try some. You can just pull it apart with your fingers if you want," she said, gesturing at his plate with her fork.

Her cheeks were puffed out trying to chew and talk at the same time, though she needn't have spoken out loud. For the first time in days, she was clean, rested, and now she was getting fuel. It felt good to talk with a mouthful of food.

The entire time Mot had studied Alex, watching the way she used the metal object to carve the food and place it in her mouth. Most interesting. Arzats sometimes used knives similarly but they were much larger and much more awkward.

"I would like to try your way," Mot responded, his eyes fixed on the movements of the eating tool Alex had in her hand.

"Absolutely!" Alex jumped down, fishing a fresh fork from the silverware drawer. She handed it to him handle first, wondering mischievously whether he would be right or left handed. Mot grasped it tightly in his right, the fork almost disappearing in his fingers. Alex leaned over and helped him hold it correctly. "Nice and easy. You don't need to squeeze it to death. Take your time."

Mot managed to cut a segment of the pancakes and then he carefully and very slowly took a bite. The combination of the syrup, peanut butter, and the pancakes almost immediately stuck the entire surface of his mouth together. It was quite shocking, but the sweet taste was delicious, one of the most amazing things he had ever tasted. Third most, he remembered.

"Good, isn't it?" said Alex, noting his reaction.

Mot could only nod, having already noticed that up-and-down was yes in Alex's world, and the Arzat affirmative of side-to-side was a negative to her. He hoped the nod was a polite answer. Mot was so busy smacking his lips and trying to get his tongue working that the words would not even form in his head-his brain stuck together by the peanut butter.

Alex proceeded to have one of the finest laughs of her life, and Mot couldn't help but join her. It was great to be alive.

She pulled the ham out, unwrapped it, and began cutting slices for Mot much to his further delight.

"Now, tell me, who's Ara?" she asked.

CHAPTER 24

The Call

Tom had gone back to his trailer to rest for a while with orders for his men to call him the minute they thought he could access the deeper sections of the caves. He was just drifting off to sleep when the phone rang.

He had pulled his crew back together as Batter asked, and gotten most everyone back on track, but Andy and a group of a dozen or so men peeled off to begin pumping the flooded caves.

Regardless of Batter's hurry to finish, Tom was determined to find Alex's body before he had to permanently seal off the last section of the ARC. Their search had turned up nothing so far, but his men still had not reached the section where Tom had left Alex.

The phone continued to ring and he tried to ignore it for as long as possible, his body desperate for sleep. "Hancock," he said when he finally picked up.

"Tom?"

There was a long moment of silence. "Alex, is it you?" Tom said, his voice shaking. He was suddenly fully awake.

"Yes."

"I knew it! I have been looking for you, or I should say, for your body for the last 24 hours and I… and I …" Tom was on the verge of tears he was so happy. "Alex, are you okay? Where are you? Are you calling on your cell? Do you want me to come and get you?"

"Yes, don't worry. I'm actually fine. Very lucky. But then you know me—I am a very lucky girl. Anyhow, I am down at Dad's ranch and…"

"Alex, how the hell did you get all the way down there?"

"Tom, it is a very long story and I will tell you all about it, but first I need to ask you some questions."

"Okay, okay, but I just don't get it," he was shaking his head. How had she gotten out? There was no way unless she had found a dry tunnel. The flood had been so sudden. Then he began to smile. Of course she got out. That's just Alex. It was totally impossible, so Alex would do it.

He was so relieved to hear her voice he was beside himself, as if his whole life had just begun again.

"Tom, I need you to focus for a minute."

"Alright, alright, but you can't really blame me for being happy."

"Remember when you told me about the science team that showed up and cleared everything out in the caves?"

"Yes."

"Where did they take everything?"

"Alex, I have no idea."

"Come on Tom." she said, not caring if it was classified information or not.

"Really, Alex, they didn't tell me."

"We have to find out. Batter would know, right?"

"Alex, I think Batter knows just about everything."

"Well, can you ask him?"

"I guess I can, Alex. Have to try to call him though. He's not here."

"Where did he go?"

"He left for Area…" Tom had to stop himself—this wasn't a secure line. "Alex, I really can't say. I think you know why."

Tom wasn't sure about his private cell phone, but he knew for a fact that all of the phone lines in the complex were monitored and recorded. Batter's whereabouts were classified.

Now that he thought about it, Alex was classified, as well, since she knew about the ARC. Batter and his gang would be looking to debrief her the minute they found out she was still alive.

"How did you get this number?"

"Tom, you gave it to me several months ago in case of emergency, remember?" she said, her voice now showing signs of irritation.

"Alex, who knows you're home?"

"Well, I happened to run into Gus Hooper. You remember him, he's deputy sheriff of Carbon County."

"Alex, I'm going to come down. In the meantime, don't let anyone else know you are there, okay?"

"I'm not so sure that's a good idea, Tom." She was looking at Mot as she was talking on the phone.

"I don't want you down there alone."

"Well, I'm not actually…"

"I'll be there in less than two hours. Don't go anywhere," he said, not hearing her last statement, and hung up.

Tom hurried and dressed. He instinctively knew he was in a race to get to Alex before Batter did.

Less than five minutes after Tom had hung up the phone with Alex, he was on his motorcycle and headed down to Price. He thought about trying to borrow an airplane, but then decided that by the time he got that accomplished he could be already be there.

Tom had been in the military for over six years—a ranger and special ops guy. He was notorious for his conquests of women, but even more notorious for the way he could fly anything from a Cessna to an F-15 to an Apache helicopter. When he felt like he needed to get somewhere fast, there was still nothing like an aircraft of some sort to accomplish it. He always felt like he could walk faster than he could drive. But a fast motorcycle, well, that was another matter.

He made the turn at Vernal and gunned his bike down the highway. It was midday and the road was radiating heat, blurring the lines far in front of him. When he reached 100 mph, he settled down and began thinking about Alex and watching for cops.

Something wasn't right. This whole thing with the caves, the way Batter had behaved. Tom wasn't really superstitious, but he was wondering if there was a full moon or an eclipse, or what was going on. One thing was for sure, this thing with Alex nearly dying had confirmed that he never wanted to be without her again.

He realized that he had made a huge mistake, and hoped that he could make it up to her. Tom knew that was not going to be easy. Alex was a tough case and he knew he had really blown it.

When Batter had originally offered him the job of constructing the ARC, he had been torn between the job of his dreams and Alex. He knew she would never accept the top secret nature of his classified position, so he had fabricated a story of infidelity in order to break the relationship: a huge mistake. A part of him, he supposed, had always hoped she would see through the charade.

As he rode, he turned his attention to Batter and thought back to the specimens and the way that whole K-T discovery had been handled. At first, he hadn't considered anything about the find to be that monumental simply because he had been so preoccupied. In fact, he had been more annoyed that it had temporarily stopped work. Initially, the project's construction was to have taken just a few days over three years to total completion, but delays had them at three years and just about three months at this point. Not bad, considering all of the contingencies, when you really thought about it.

What was the rush beyond that? What did Batter know? Surely, the world wasn't going to end in the next couple of weeks? Was it?

Tom looked down and noticed that he was going 120 miles per hour. A chill suddenly went down his neck that had nothing to do with his speed.

CHAPTER 25

Ara The Captive

"You seem bothered Pete," was the first thing Ara had said to him in the morning when they met. She had thought of several questions she wanted to ask him, not the least of which was where were the other Arzats? In particular, where was Mot?

* * *

After Pete had said goodnight to Batter, he had gone back to check on Ara. He had his staff provide her with a portable toilet and a mattress, and ordered them to feed her again. She was calm throughout the process and any of Pete's angst about her becoming dangerous had subsided.

Pete had gone to sleep knowing that the world was about to end and that his family was going with it. He thought about calling home before he went to bed, but he was afraid his wife would pick up on his mood. If Ara was a mind reader, then certainly his wife Hanna was the next closest thing. He would have to try to explain that nothing was really wrong and, in essence, he would have to lie.

Pete had slept fitfully, trying to decide what to do with the news. How could he save his family? Could he? No, was the answer that kept coming back to him.

* * *

There were no provisions for family at Area 51 other than a select few that might be coming with some of the political leaders. The entire purpose of 51 was to preserve the executive and legislative branches of the government and the judiciary.

The military was primarily to be housed in the Colorado ARC and Kansas ARC, with the as yet unfinished Utah ARC designated primarily for the science community. In fact, had Utah been finished, Pete Wilson and most of his team were to have been housed there. Batter had already informed him that would now not be the case and that he would remain at 51.

From the moment of their inception in the mid-90s, it had always been understood that the ARCs would be a last ditch effort to save mankind and, perhaps, some semblance of the U.S., were there to be a holocaust, pandemic, or other major disaster.

No one knew how long it would take the world to recover, or even if it would recover enough for life on the surface. But the ARCs would give them a shot, a few years to let things settle.

Despite the fact that family, in general, was not allowed, the support personnel for all four facilities had been carefully pre-selected, not only on qualifications, but for ratios of male to female, average ages, and other such factors. There was one thing no one doubted: the strong tendency of humans to procreate regardless of conditions. No room for lay persons, everyone had to serve a specific purpose.

* * *

"I have a lot on my mind." Pete didn't try to deny that he was bothered. Ara was, after all, a mind reader. "How did you sleep?"

"I am doing as well as any captive could be expected to do under the circumstances." She said it with no malice. "Thank you for the bedding."

"Ara, you are not a captive," Pete said, careful not to be defensive.

"Then, perhaps I just need instruction on how to operate the exits from this room. I found I was unable to open them of my own accord last night."

Her eyes bore into Pete.

Of course I am a captive, little creature, Pete son of Robert, she thought, carefully blocking, and if any of my clan had found you in our world we would have been just as quick to lock you up. That, or we'd have eaten you.

"Listen, Ara, you are not so much a prisoner as a guest. We are only keeping you here for your own protection. You would not last out in our world very long without some knowledge of it. I imagine the world as you knew it was a very hostile place. To you, right now, it is still a very hostile place. You'll just have to trust me on that. You were asleep for a very long time."

Ara considered what Pete had said. He was telling the truth, at least as far as he knew it.

"Do you know how long I was asleep?"

Pete had fortunately anticipated this question and had brought a bag of sugar with him.

"How do Arzats mark time, Ara?" he asked.

"There is an orb of fire in the sky. What do you call it?"

"We call it the sun."

"We call him Qa'aa. When Qa'aa rises, that we call a het. When Qa'aa rises again, that is another het. This het is divided further into smaller pieces according to the names of animals in the forest. Do you understand?"

"Yes."

"Now, Qa'aa likes to come up in different places," Ara continued, indicating a horizon with her hands, "but sooner or later he always comes up at the same place again, and this we call a season or a ra. I have lived for two eights of these seasons Peter."

My god, she is just a teenager, thought Pete. Of course, that is assuming the Arzat life cycle was anywhere near human. It was also starting to sound like their system of time keeping might have been a sophisticated as the Mayan's.

"So Ara, you asked me how long you were asleep." Pete said, showing her the five pound bag of sugar. He opened it carefully then dumped about half of the bag in a large mixing bowl. "Are you familiar with the idea of 'imagination' Ara, where you picture something in your head that you know may be different than reality?"

"Yes, Pete. I have done this often, mostly regarding food." Sometimes as of late, she wanted to add, regarding a few males of my clan, but she hid the thought from Pete.

"Our women, our females, are very similar in that way," Pete said. He held up one crystal of sugar on the tip of his finger and showed it to Ara. "Okay, Ara, imagine that this little tiny sugar crystal is a season."

"Yes, Pete. Not a het?" she said, carefully following. Ara had already come to the conclusion that her survival might depend on every bit of information she could glean from this human—Pete son of Robert.

"No. This is a ra." Then Pete held up the bag of sugar, "And imagine that these are ra, too." He dumped the rest of the sugar from the bag into the mixing bowl. "Now, Ara, imagine that I had many of these bags, all full of seasons—ra." Pete stopped to see if he had lost her.

"Yes," Ara said, understanding. "How many bags?"

"Many—many," Pete answered, sweeping he arms around the room.

Ara said nothing to Pete for the next few minutes. She turned slightly away and stared off into space.

"There were others who slept with me. Where are they?" she finally asked. "My mother and the other Elder females placed eight and five of us in the sleeping cocoons. What happened to the others? I can detect none of them around me."

Pete gulped. He had known the question would be coming and he had already dreaded answering it. He looked at Ara, genuine sadness in his eyes.

"Ara," he began, knowing he could not lie about what had happened, "there was an accident. We removed you and eleven… eight and three, others from the caves. On the way here, there was a terrible mishap and all of the Arzats with the exception of you were destroyed."

Pete watched as Ara's eyes narrowed. He could feel a strange tingling in his mind he hadn't noticed before.

Ara's heart began to race. Eight and three? Eight and three! Perhaps they have not found Mot, she thought, remembering his odd placement in the caves. She had to know. She just had to know!

Ara debated with herself for a moment, then looked Pete directly in the eyes and searched. She knew that he had no ability to block. Ara looked deep into his mind until she could see all that had transpired. There, in Pete's memory, she could see his vision of the eight and four spots that had been excavated in the cave, but there was nothing in his head regarding any discovery of Mot's location in the wall! She could see the truck burning in the night, and she could feel Pete's sadness. There were many other things in Pete's mind that were very disturbing as well, but Ara's heart quickened when she realized that Mot might still be alive.

"Did you have a mate?" Pete finally offered.

"Mate?" Ara said, surprised.

"You know, a male Arzat that you were attached to. Here we call that being married, or for you, having a husband."

Ara blushed. Perhaps Pete was probing her mind as well!

She could clearly remember the last time she had seen Mot, freezing in the caves together with her, sending her a signal just before they went to sleep. Oh Great Creator of All Things, let it be true that Mot has survived!

"No, but my potential mate was frozen with us," she said.

"What was his name?"

"Mot, his name is Mot son of the great Hunter Url."

Pete was beside himself with grief. "I'm sorry to hear that." I've killed her mate, he thought to himself.

"Perhaps not," Ara said, without thinking.

"I'm sorry?" Pete said, not understanding her response.

Ara had been probing Pete's mind again, despite herself. She instantly knew she had been caught. It was an atrocity in the Arzat culture to probe—and it was wrong—and she had been caught.

"I mean, that perhaps you do not need to be sorry Pete. It was an accident, no?" Ara said, trying to cover her indiscretion.

"Do you know if there were others, maybe in a different location?" Pete asked, hoping for a moment there might be a way to redeem himself. Then he remembered his conversation with Batter. What would be the point?

"No."

"You mean 'no, there were not' or 'no, you don't know'?" Pete said, suddenly curious about the Ara's tone.

Ara did not answer for a long time. She was angry with herself for probing Pete's mind, but furious that she had no way of knowing about Mot's fate. She resolved that she must think of a way to escape and to see if she could find him.

"I do not know Pete," she finally said, hoping that he would not see through her obvious lie. "I do know that there is no future for me without a mate."

* * *

Batter was in his quarters. It wasn't much, just the equivalent of a small one bedroom apartment, but it was going to be heaven next to the much smaller room he would be assigned in the ARC. He had been pouring over the details of the plans to populate the Colorado and Kansas units.

There was a knock, and he opened the door.

"Mr. Batter, sorry to disturb you, but a message just came in for you from your office marked urgent," a uniformed Corporal said.

Batter took the plain brown manila envelope stamped CLASSIFIED/

URGENT from him and shut the door. If he had seen one of these packages, he had seen a thousand. Most of them brought bad news, but what could be worse than what he already knew? He pulled out the papers, a note on top said: Boss: Thought you might want to see this—Mac.

Pat McCartin was one of Batter's favorite intelligence staffers, always looking for a needle in the haystack and often finding one, and for years Batter had always just referred to him as Mac. He got halfway through the reading and started to smile.

"I'll be damned." It was a transcript of the telephone conversation between Alex and Tom.

Batter finished reading and pondered the note for a long time. "Interesting," he said aloud when he was done, then picked up the phone. "Good work, Mac. Now, you know my next question. Who do we have... wait... where the heck is that place? Who do we have around Price, Utah?

"I have already dispatched a team, Boss."

"Excellent!" Batter said, still thinking about the conversation between Tom and Alex and the Arzat Pete had discovered.

"And Mac, tell the team be ready for anything." Batter proceeded to give Mac a long list of instructions before he finally hung up the phone.

CHAPTER 26

Can I Borrow Your Plane?

It was late afternoon when Tom finally rolled his motorcycle into the Servo Station in Wellington.

He decided to stop and quickly top off his gas. He had been running with the light on for several miles, and didn't want to risk running out. Besides, he was thirsty and needed a short break.

This will only take a minute, he thought to himself as he stopped in front of the pumps.

The second he turned off his motor he was sorry. Gus Bell pulled in right behind him in his patrol car, and Tom was sure he was in for a ticket. He had been running the motorcycle well over any reasonable speed limit the entire way down, and thought Gus must have seen him. Tom didn't know Gus very well, but he had met him a few times before when he had visited the ranch with Alex.

Maybe I can talk him out of it, he thought.

"Hey, Tom, I figured that might be you!" Gus said, climbing out of his car with a broad smile on his face. He put his hat on and held out his hand. "This is like old home week or something. I just ran into Alex yesterday.

Hey, nice ride man," Gus said, adding a low whistle, admiring Tom's bike. "Ducati? Never heard 'a that brand before. Looks real fast. Real pretty too."

"Thanks Gus," Tom said, relieved. Obviously Gus had not seen him speeding. Tom opened the gas cap and began filling.

"I'll be damned. I haven't seen you in... what? Must be a couple of years," Gus continued. "I know it's probably none of my business, but I thought you and Alex... well, I thought you were on the out-n-outs so to speak." Gus looked like he just could not wait to hear the reply.

Tom wasn't upset. This was the way of small towns—all gossip. If Gus weren't here he'd probably be up at the barber shop in Price trying to find out what was going on in the county: who might be pregnant, who's dog was about to have pups, who wasn't in church last Sunday.

"Well, Gus, we may be getting back together real soon here," Tom said, as he placed the hose back in its holder.

"That so?" Gus couldn't completely hide his disappointment. Just recently, he had rekindled his wild fantasy of divorcing his fat wife Sally and running off to Mexico or somewhere else with Alex. He knew it was just a crazy dream—they'd never even dated—but Tom had crushed it once again.

"I can't say as I blame you." Gus looked over his shoulder into the store and spoke more softly. "Don't tell Sally, but you know I have always thought that Alex was a real catch." He winked at Tom.

"Gus, you gonna talk that man's ear off or come inside and say hello to your wife." Sally's voice was low and full of authority.

Both men looked up and saw her rather large figure in the doorway. She had obviously been watching them for some time.

"Sally, this here is Tom Hancock. You remember, Alex's husband," Gus said, flinching, hoping Sally hadn't heard him talking about Alex.

"Oh, hey, Tom." Sally gave a short wave and a disapproving look at Tom's motorcycle. "Now, Gus, don't be gettin' any ideas. I got a list of things I need you to do for me up in town, and the day's getting late. Come on in here!"

Gus looked sheepishly at Tom. "Well, good to see you again Tom." He reached out and shook Tom's hand. "Boy, this has been a busy day. I had some government types come through earlier this afternoon looking for Alex too. In fact, they had me escort 'em right to the gate."

* * *

Tom hadn't heard anything else Gus might have said to him. He pulled his helmet on, jumped back on his bike and gunned it, fishtailing out of the store parking lot, riding as fast as he could to the ranch, which was just a couple of miles further down the road.

When he got there the gate was wide open—not a good sign. He rode on through it heading directly for the house.

As he approached, he anticipated seeing some sort of government vehicles, but there was only one unfamiliar truck parked by the corral. He could see Billy and Bobby with their heads over the fence. The ranch truck and Alex's SUV were in the barn. Tom stopped near the house and pulled off his helmet.

"Señor, Señor!" Tom could hear the familiar voice of Garcia coming from the barn. The old man was half running half limping toward him. "Oh, Señor Tom," Garcia said, now recognizing him, "there is no one here. I came to feed the horses, and they took her away!" he said as he approached out of breath. "Lo siento, Señor Tom. I try to stop them, but there were many men. They told me to stay away—with guns!"

256   David Samuel Frazier

"How long ago were they here?"

"Oh Señor, less than one hour. I was here, I heard nothing Señor. Then three black cars—grande cars—came fast fast down the road. They circle the house and then they shoot Señorita Alex!" Garcia pushed his hat back and wiped his face with his bandana.

Tom hadn't seen any cars. They must have left out the other direction.

"What do you mean, Garcia? They shot Alex? Is she dead?"

"I do not think dead, Senor Tom. I think maybe they shoot her with a drugs—like they do animals. Pero, Señor…," Garcia hesitated, as if he was sure that no one would believe him, "pero, Señor—they also shot a grande lizard, Señor! Muy, muy grande!

"A lizard?"

"Si, Señor. He was bigger than you, Señor Tom, and walked like you do and I do, Señor Tom!" Garcia went on, his eyes wide. "But faster, much faster."

"Wait, where was this lizard, Garcia?'

"En la casa, Señor, en la casa!" Garcia said, pointing at the farm house. "When Señorita Alex was shoot, he came from the front door with such speed that he catch her before she falls down. He was like a demon, a ghost. El Diablo, Senior, El Diablo!"

Tom could see the dust from another car coming down the road. Sure enough, it was Gus with his red lights on. He drove up next to Tom and Garcia.

"Wow, Tom, you pulled out so fast I got to worrying. Is everything okay?" Gus asked from his car window.

"Gus, take me to the airport," Tom said, coming around to the passenger side of the patrol car.

"Well, that'd be up in Price, Tom," Gus said, not understanding. "They have an airport up there, but it's really just an airstrip, if you know what I mean." He watched curiously as Tom jumped in the passenger side of his patrol car.

"I know where it is, Gus. That's where they took Alex."

"Whaddaya mean, Tom?"

"Gus, those government guys you sent down here earlier, they kidnapped Alex. They took her, Gus, and I know where they are taking her now. We need to get to that airport!"

Gus floored the patrol car in the direction of Price. As they sped past the market, they noticed Sally out in the driveway, with her hands on her hips, watching disapprovingly as they drove by.

"Oh boy," Gus said, "I'm in for it when I get home." He reached down and turned on his siren. "Makes it look more official."

                                    * * *

It took about twenty minutes to get to Price with Gus driving as fast as he could and Tom regretting that he hadn't taken the wheel.

As Gus finally made the turn for the airport, they passed three large black SUVs just leaving, standard issue CIA vehicles that completely ignored the patrol car's flashing lights and siren.

Tom had a sinking feeling that he was too late. The SUVs turned toward Provo, probably on their way back up to Salt Lake. No telling how they had gotten down here so fast.

The airport consisted of a small parking lot and two uncontrolled landing strips that intersected midway down their length. A yellow windsock dangled in the dead air of the desert. There were a half dozen aluminum hangars just off of the parking lot side, and two port-a-potties sat nearby.

Across the field, an unmarked Chinook was just rotating off of the runway.

Gus stopped the car still confused, but aware that they were too late for something. As if taunting Tom, the chopper lifted off and flew directly over the patrol car, then started climbing. He marked its' heading.

Tom noticed someone working on an old bi-plane in one of the hangars.

"Gus, drive me over there would you," he said, pointing at the plane.

"Sure, Tom," Gus said squinting in that direction. "I think that'd be old Matt Kosek."

"You know him?"

"Oh sure, Matt's born and raised here, just like me. His pop used to fly for the Air Force. He always kept that old Stearman around for air shows and such. Matt flies it around himself ever once in a while just to keep it fresh. Kids love it when he buzzes the school yard. Can't say as much for teachers."

"Gus, I am going to need to get my hands on that plane. We are going to have to commandeer it, and I need your help. I have to try to follow that helicopter and find Alex.

"Alright, Tom, but maybe we should just ask."

Gus drove across the airstrip and pulled the patrol car right up to the hangar. Just inside was a vintage Stearman biplane with the classic yellow and blue colors of the Army Air Corps. Tom noted that the plane appeared to be in mint condition.

"Hey, Matt," Gus said as they both got out of the car.

"Well hey, Gus, what are you doing out this way? I never seen this place as busy as it has been today." Matt said, gesturing towards the area where the helicopter had just taken off.

"Matt, this here is Tom Hancock. You remember Simon's girl Alex? Well this is her husband. Anyhow, Matt, we are having kind of an emergency, and Tom here needs to borrow your plane if that'd be okay with you." Gus looked him directly in the eye, his hand on his holster.

Matt stared back at Gus, sizing him up and letting his unusual request sink in. He had known Gus his whole life.

"Come on Matt," Gus said, dropping his hands to his sides. "It's not that much different from borrowing a car. You'd let Tom here borrow your car if I asked, wouldn't ya?"

"Well," Matt turned and looked directly at Tom as he finished wiping a socket with a red rag. "I guess you couldn't have picked a better time. I just fueled her and was getting ready to take her up. Then all that commotion over at the other end of the field started and I kind a got caught up watching."

"See anything interesting?" asked Tom.

"Yes, as a matter of fact. Looked to me like they loaded a couple of bodies on that chopper. It was a hard to see real clear from here, but that's what it looked like, couple of bodies. They really struggled with one, looked huge, like it probably weighed a ton. Those boys were having a real tough time with it," Matt said, shaking his head.

Tom looked over his shoulder and marked the current altitude and direction of the Chinook. It was definitely headed southwest, which gave him a big clue about its destination, but he needed to get going or he was not going to be able to tail it. Tom wanted to follow the chopper directly. He didn't want to take any chances losing it even though he was pretty certain of the course it would take.

"Thanks, Matt. I'll take good care of her."

"If you can push a grocery cart, then you pretty much ought-a be able to fly her. Somethin' tells me you've flown better, and maybe worse."

"Yes, Sir, I have."

"Well jump in and I'll fire this muthah up for you. Here, take this jacket. Gonna be cold up. Oughtta be some goggles in the cockpit somewheres. No radio though. Broke it a while ago and haven't got around to gettin' it fixed yet," Matt said.

Tom threw on the leather jacket Matt handed him, zipping it all the way, and hopped into the back seat of the plane. Draped over the throttle was a set of vintage goggles. He looked around the cockpit just to get his bearings, fastened the seat belts and tested the controls. Everything seemed to be working. He pulled on the goggles and flicked on the power switch.

"Contact!"

Matt bent down at the front of the plane and gave the propeller a hefty swing. The aircraft shuddered and popped, and then the motor came alive and began to rev.

Tom gave both Matt and Gus the thumbs up and rolled the plane out onto the airfield. He checked the windsock and made sure the runways and air space were clear, then gave the little airplane all of its throttle, ran it down the asphalt and rotated the nose into the air.

Tom checked to the southwest but could no longer see the Chinook. He would just have to fly as fast as he could and hope that he could catch up.

Gus and Matt watched as Tom headed for the horizon.

"Thanks, Matt," Gus said to his friend. "Tom was pretty certain that Alex was on that helicopter and that the guys took her were up to no-good."

Matt kept his eyes on the plane until it disappeared from sight. "Then, I have a feeling that's the last I'll be seeing of Dad's old plane," Matt said wistfully. "Hope the wife has kept up the insurance."

CHAPTER 27

Rendezvous

This was the second time in two days that she had been knocked out: the first time from a rock, and this time from a tranquilizer gun.

Alex had another splitting headache. She could hear the incessant vibration of helicopter rotors as she regained consciousness and she knew that the minute she opened her eyes she was going to feel violently hung over.

When she finally let her eyes open, she braced for pain, and found that she was facing a warrant officer seated directly across from her and that she was flying in the back of some massive military helicopter. The officer was reading something displayed on an electronic notebook.

Where the hell am I, Alex wondered. Worse, she worried, what happened to Mot?

She tried moving her hands but they were secured with plastic ties to the flight chair. The warrant officer looked up and smiled, nonplussed by Alex's struggling.

Mr. Cool Calm Collected. He wouldn't be if I could get loose, she thought, immediately irritated by the officer's passive demeanor. Oh my god my head hurts!

Alex tried to say something, but realized it was too loud in the helicopter to converse. The rotor thump was making her head throb.

The officer held up a single finger, and then grabbed a headphone set off a rack. He plugged them in and then gently placed them on Alex's head. He was actually kind of good looking, Alex noted, even though she was seething. He swung the microphone close to Alex's lips, continuing to smile as if he had been given the best job in the world.

"How's that?" she could read his lips but nothing was coming through. He reached over slowly and adjusted the volume on the headset slightly. "How's that volume, Doctor?" the officer asked again.

"Good," she said into the headset. But how does he know that I am a doctor? "Where is Mot?"

The officer looked puzzled.

"The creature? Where is he?" she asked.

"Oh, it's right behind you, Ma'am," the officer said, pointing over Alex's shoulder. "A little more sedated, but it is right behind. If you would like, I can remove your restraints so you can move around a bit?"

The Officer's tone revealed nothing about the orders he had been given to immediately use his Taser on Alex if she started acting up in any way.

The officer had called her 'Ma'am.' The kiss of death, thought Alex. I must look like shit. Ma'am! Jesus!

"Well yes, Lieutenant, that would be very nice," Alex said in the sweetest voice she could muster, resenting the new moniker, but realizing that she might need this asshole's cooperation.

"Stay calm, Alex, stay calm," old Simon warned.

The officer slid forward again and deftly clipped off the plastic ties on her wrists.

Alex immediately turned around the best she could in her seat. Behind her, further back in the aircraft, she could see Mot on a cot in the center and attendants on each side of him. He was not conscious, but he was very securely belted down.

She noticed that an IV hung on a rack at his side. It was clear that the doctors, or whoever they were... were ready to give Mot another shot of anesthesia if necessary to keep him down. His eyes were closed and he had the scary loose look on his face of someone who had been sedated.

Alex could only vaguely recall what had happened after breakfast with Mot. She could remember talking to Tom on the phone. There was something about him coming down to the ranch. Then she had seen Mr. Garcia and had apologized for not calling him sooner. She'd gone outside, intercepting him at the corral so he wouldn't see Mot.

Alex could remember walking back to the house, having the feeling that something was not right. Had Mot tried to warn her? Was there a pin prick in her neck? She had felt it, and then had pulled out the bullet-sized syringe just before passing out. As she sat there, trying to recover from the tranquilizer, the events of the morning became clear in her mind.

* * *

They flew on for some time.

Alex decided that it was pointless to ask any more questions of the officer. She would find out why they had been taken soon enough, and he certainly wasn't going to tell her.

Whatever was going on, she had a vague idea that Batter must be behind it. She was overcome by a huge sense of relief to find that Mot had not been killed.

From the position of the afternoon sun, Alex judged that the helicopter was heading west-southwest.

She looked out the window and could see a very large dry lakebed coming into view. At first she thought it might be Salt Lake, but then she spotted the mass of airstrips that appeared at its south end. She knew this place from the many aerial photographs that Simon kept in the shop for years. This was the infamous Area 51 her father had been obsessed with since she was a child.

Alex looked back at the officer. He was studying something on his note pad, but Alex was aware that if she made the slightest move he would notice. She looked back at Mot, and then back out the window.

She noticed a speck on the horizon that seemed to be flying approximately the same speed and direction. Probably a security tail of some sort, she thought. The object was too far back to identify.

* * *

Batter looked up into the late afternoon sky. A large patch of cumulus clouds were forming in the west, slightly obscuring the sun as it drifted slowly toward the horizon. He could hear the distinctive sound of the dual blades of the Chinook slicing through the thin desert air before he could actually see the aircraft. Pete was with him. They stood at the end of runway 14L/32R.

A row of giant hangars, each large enough to house a 747 or even a C-130, lined one side of the runway and ran for almost a mile like houses on a Monopoly board, but the proportions were epic. It looked like a neighborhood of giants.

Behind the hangars, were the many above ground barracks and service facilities for Edwards Air Force base, which had always ostensibly been the main purpose of the entire complex.

Below them, perhaps 500 feet, was the vast maze of secret facilities that had been under construction since the late 1950s. It was the single largest project ever undertaken, certainly by the United States, and probably by anyone anywhere in the world.

Except perhaps, by the Chinese. Never underestimate the Chinese, Batter thought as he watched for the helicopter.

He looked around and shivered.

Batter had been a part of the development of this base for the last 30 years, and had been totally in charge of it and the construction of the other three ARCs for the last 10. To him, the job seemed like a natural function of the CIA umbrella, and he had been honored and had felt an extreme sense of duty when he was chosen to oversee them.

His position, like a select few of his colleagues, was considered so top secret and so long range that it by-passed even the Director's authority. In fact, for all intents and purposes, *he* didn't even exist.

How fast the time had gone, Batter thought, looking around at the massive air base. In another 24 hours, he mused, this place will look exactly as it does now, but below these hangars, the entire government of the United States will be here; and suddenly, my problem.

Now Batter stood with the facility's top ranking scientist and several staffers waiting for two other very important guests.

Batter, despite all his pressing concerns, was very much looking forward to seeing Dr. Alex Moss again. He had been very attracted to her the first time they met, which in retrospect, he had to admit, had clouded his judgment—a rare occurrence to be sure.

But Batter was no misogynist. He loved women of all sorts and loved to be surrounded by them whether romantically or just in business. Never, he was proud to say, had he ever stepped over the line with any of them, despite the constant temptation.

Alex was not only extremely tempting; she was a very accomplished scientist and perfect for recruitment. He had been very disappointed when he heard she had died and had felt somewhat responsible. But now, it seemed, all was well. He might have her on his team after all, a prospect that made the idea of being locked below ground somewhat more palatable.

He could only imagine how thrilled she must be about the male Arzat. Too bad the excitement would be short-lived, and he meant that literally.

If there was one thing Batter was very good at, it was projecting. After everyone had settled into life underground, it would not be long until the issue came up of why they were expending valuable resources on lizards.

Batter could already hear the banter. An informal committee would be formed at first, then the Vice President would end up involved. The scientists would fight the decision, but sooner or later the dinosaurs would be put down. That was inevitable.

Hell, Batter thought, if things got bad enough there might have to be some other decisions about who else might have to go. People were inevitably always people, and it was hard to tell how even the best of them might act when it finally sunk in that they had essentially been buried alive.

Batter still wasn't even sure how he was going to take it despite the arrival of Dr. Moss.

No, he decided, better to leave the creatures out of the ARC in the first place. He would be doing them a favor in the end.

The Chinook was approaching. He patted Pete Wilson on the shoulder as the helicopter came in for a landing.

"Excited?" he screamed at Pete, trying to help him make the best of a bad situation. Pete had been lost in his own thoughts, looking out at the vast airfield. He only nodded.

Batter looked across the runway and noticed a couple of F-22s preparing for takeoff. It seemed unusual to have training flights this late in the day. A Sergeant ran up to him from across the tarmac.

"Sorry to interrupt, Sir, but we thought you should know. It appears that the forty-seven was tailed into our airspace."

"By what?"

The Sergeant hesitated, "Well, Sir, looks like an old biplane of some sort."

"A biplane?"

"Yes, Sir."

"You guys aren't too worried about that are you?" Batter asked.

"Sir, we are worried about everything, Sir," the Sergeant replied as if he were stating the obvious.

"Sorry, Sergeant. Yes, you are quite correct. Keep me informed."

The Sergeant saluted and walked away, and Batter was able to focus on the helicopter, which had just landed.

* * *

"Welcome, Doctor," Batter said as the roar of the Chinook's engines died down.

Alex had been first off the helicopter and personnel were already busily preparing to get the lizard off as well. Batter offered his hand to Alex which she ignored as she jumped down from the giant aircraft.

She stormed past him, out of the range of the rotor wash, then stopped when she realized she had nowhere to go. A large military ambulance was driven into place as Mot was wheeled back on a gurney to the loading gate of the chopper.

"Welcome, Doctor," Pete said, walking over to meet her.

He had not known what to expect of Dr. Alex Moss, and certainly was surprised by what he saw.

"My name is Peter Wilson. I am the SIC at this base," he said, also extending his hand which Alex refused.

"I am sure you must be very upset Doctor, but Mr. Batter assures me that everything regarding your specimen was done with the utmost care to safeguard both you and the creature."

"Well, I wouldn't call knocking us out with tranquilizer guns and kidnapping us to be the friendliest way of inviting us down," Alex replied sarcastically.

"Really, Doctor, would you have come any other way?" Batter said as he caught up with them, overhearing their interchange.

* * *

Tom was almost out of fuel.

He had used all of the engine's horsepower throughout the flight just to catch up and keep up with the Chinook. The fact that he had been forced to fly at full throttle hadn't helped with fuel consumption.

For an aircraft that was over seventy, the old girl had done a stellar job of keeping him in the game so far, he thought, but that wouldn't last long now.

He tapped his finger on the gauge and rocked the wings just to be sure he was getting an accurate reading. The needle moved slightly, but immediately drifted back toward zero. Maybe ten or fifteen more minutes, then that would be all she wrote and he would have to put the little plane down.

Tom relaxed a little when Groom Lake appeared far off on his starboard side. He was almost positive that was where they were taking Alex and whatever-in-the-hell it was that they had captured with her.

She had found something in the caves. He didn't doubt that, but Tom could make no sense of what it might be. He had left Alex in an area that was dated to 65 million BCE. Nothing alive could have come from that, could it? It was completely inexplicable.

But Area 51 was famous as the place for the inexplicable, and it was home to another of the four ARCs, which meant that Batter was probably in the mix.

It also meant that any time now, he suddenly remembered, his plane would be identified on radar and he would become a target. The facility was boxed by a 25 mile restricted airspace; a 'shoot to kill zone' where the rule applied to anyone who dared to enter without permission.

That was the one advantage of not having a working radio, he thought ironically. He couldn't ask for clearance or identify himself even if the wanted to. Tom scanned the sky. He was going to have company any minute.

Two dots appeared on the horizon and seconds later a pair of F-22s buzzed him head-on doing about 500 knots. The little Stearman took it in stride, but it did pick up some turbulence in its wings. Tom steadied the aircraft and looked back. He could see the fighters looping for another go round.

This time they approached from behind, doing their best to match the Stearman's slower speed. One jet trailed Tom's plane and one approached on his left wing. He imagined he could hear the missile lock indicator blaring in the fighter cockpit behind him.

The lead pilot gestured to Tom to follow him, then rolled his F-22 slowly to the left. Tom knew it was likely he would be shot down if he did not comply immediately and follow the fighter out of the restricted air space, but then he would never get back in and he would never get to Alex.

He pulled the throttle back on the Stearman, trying to lose a little altitude, and kept the plane on course for the runway where he had seen the Chinook land. He was almost there, another three minutes or so.

The engine sputtered once, trying to find the rest of the fuel in the tanks. Tom felt to make sure that his parachute was firmly attached, and hoped to hell that Matt knew how to properly pack one.

The F-22 returned, flying closer to Tom's wing, only forty or fifty feet between the pilot and himself. The pilot had pushed back his visor and was giving Tom a very unpleasant look. Tom could tell that this was his last and final warning.

He checked altitude.

They were only at about a thousand feet. If he jumped he would barely have time to get his chute opened before he hit the ground.

Perfect, he thought.

As the F-22 again eased left, Tom popped the throttle on the Stearman, pushed the nose up slightly, and proceeded to barrel roll until the little bi-plane was flying perfectly upside down.

"Sorry Matt," Tom said as he released his seat belt and immediately fell away.

The second he was clear he pulled the rip cord and heard the distinctive sound of a missile firing. He looked up just in time to see his airplane disintegrate into a fire ball. Tom covered his face and hoped that none of the debris would hit his chute and start it on fire.

Tom was very low when his parachute finally shook itself open, barely a hundred feet over some portion of the airstrip. The parachute was an old round para-commander version which tended to land hot, so Tom prepared. His legs hit the ground hard, but he was able to roll out and stop without any major injury.

Across the runway in the distance, he could see flashing lights of security vehicles racing across the asphalt bearing down on him. Back in the other direction, some of the wreckage of Matt's old bi-plane burned along the edge of the field.

"Boy, am *I* in trouble," was all Tom could think to say.

CHAPTER 28

Alex Interviewed

"So, Dr. Moss, we meet again," Batter said smiling, enjoying the pure pleasure of just looking at her, even with the rage burning in her deep green eyes.

I know she hates me now, but we are going to be down here for a long time. Who knows, he thought mischievously.

"Trust me when I say this, I am personally very happy to see you alive, Doctor. Until your telephone call, well," he held up both hands.

"Where's Mot?" she snapped back.

* * *

Alex had remained silent as Dr. Pete Wilson and Batter escorted her from the Chinook's landing area to a large hangar. Inside, trucks were rolling in and out delivering supplies to a bank of giant elevators that lined one entire wall. They boarded one of them, and began a descent that took several minutes to reach the bottom.

Pete then led them through a series of wide corridors, busy with hundreds of people and small electric vehicles loaded with equipment.

Eventually, they arrived in an area that transitioned from some very utilitarian back areas to a long section of wood veneered hallways with very formal office spaces. Pete had dismissed himself and disappeared.

Alex eventually found herself seated in some kind of conference room furnished with a beautiful and very long mahogany table surrounded by sixteen black leather chairs. Three of the walls were full of flat screens that were dark at the moment. On the fourth wall, a very nice map of the world was hung as the apparent centerpiece.

As Alex looked around, it reminded her of what she had always imagined one of those secret command posts would look like.

Her head still hurt and she was rubbing her wrists where they had been tied. She and Batter were the only ones in the room, and she wondered what he could possibly be up to. Her intention was to find out first, what they were doing with Mot, and second, why she was there.

* * *

"Alright, Batter, where is Mot?" she asked again.

"Pardon me?" Batter asked, momentarily preoccupied with a file he was examining.

"Where is… my specimen?"

"Oh yes, him," Batter finally looked up. "*He* is in a very safe and secure area, I can assure you, Doctor."

"Listen, Batter, I don't have time to play games here," Alex said, annoyed. "When that animal wakes up and finds himself in unfamiliar surroundings anything could happen. I need to be there."

"I understand, Doctor," Batter said, placing the file on the table, finally giving her his full attention. "I assure you I did not bring you here to play any sort of games. If you wish, think of it as an effort on my part to actually save you. We are going to be spending a lot of time together, and I wanted to give you the opportunity to fully understand the situation. I intend to put you with the creature the moment we are done here," he added, in an attempt to diffuse her anger.

Alex relaxed a bit. "Save me? What are you talking about?" she asked, now totally confused.

"In just a few hours, this room will be occupied by no less than the President of the United States and most of his cabinet," Batter continued patiently, falsifying the facts only slightly. "Additionally, I have a current count of forty two senators and about three hundred and ninety representatives who will be arriving here shortly along with most of the members of the Supreme Court. The rest of them, unfortunately, were too busy or irresponsible to heed a direct order from the Executive Office. And my office for that matter," he added as an afterthought.

Alex just looked at him, as confused as ever.

Batter hesitated, changing direction slightly, "I am sure, Doctor, that you are well aware that Area 51 has been, among other things, a research center for some time. What you may not be aware of is the fact that a large part of it has also been set up as an ARC, just like the site in Utah. This particular ARC is designated for the President, the Judiciary, and most of the rest of the government of the United States, as well as some intelligence personnel, such as some of my staff, and well, you get the picture."

Alex looked around the room.

"I know. It leaves one speechless." Batter bent forward and lowered his tone. "Now, Doctor, let me give you the most classified information of all. Can you imagine why the President would be coming here?"

Vice President—actually—Batter thought sadly, still choosing not to share that information.

Alex shook her head.

"Of course not, because the whole idea of it is just as impossible as those creatures down the hall."

Batter paused a moment, as if he were trying to get his own arms around what he was about to say.

"Because, Doctor—and you should be one of the few people on the planet really familiar with this due to your knowledge of the K-T event—because, Doctor," he repeated, "we believe that an asteroid of similar magnitude to the K-T is about to strike the earth. Two of them, in fact, to be more precise."

Alex figured that Batter could be a pretty good liar when he needed to be, but her gut told her he wasn't lying about this. What purpose would it serve?

She sat and looked at him for a long time, trying to evaluate him and his message. She wondered if she was beginning to be able to read human minds as well.

"When?" was all she could think of to say.

And had she missed something, or had Batter said *those* creatures—plural?

Batter nodded to the wall behind Alex and pushed a button on a remote control. A large digital clock came up on one of the screens. Alex turned in her chair.

27:31:43

The seconds were ticking away. She swung her chair back and faced him.

"You do realize that the K-T asteroid caused a blast something equivalent to 100 teratonnes of TNT? That is the equivalent of about one billion Nagasaki atom bombs going off at once."

"Yes, Doctor, I am well aware of the scale of the effects," Batter said, trying not to sound patronizing.

There was a sharp knock at the door and it opened. A young officer entered and spoke into Batter's ear.

Batter laughed, "Well, this just gets better and better."

"What do you mean?" Alex asked, unable to imagine humor in anything at the moment.

"Your *former* husband is here. Just 'dropped in' so to speak." Batter laughed again then sobered when he realized that the irony of Tom's sudden appearance was funny only to him. "Seems Mr. Hancock was concerned enough about your wellbeing that he deserted his post at Utah to come and find you here. I'm not particularly happy about it, but I would imagine that you should take it as a big compliment, Dr. Moss, since what he did is tantamount to treason."

Alex looked at Batter, but she found herself, once again speechless. Tom here? The world about to end? Treason? And God only knew where Mot was.

"Not to worry, Doctor," Batter continued, "I am not planning on charging him at the moment. In fact, I am having him brought down with practically a hero's welcome to see you now. In the meantime, would you like to hear about the other Arzat?"

* * *

It seemed a miracle but the security guards had not shot Tom when they finally caught up to him. He knew that if he were in charge of the base's security, he would have given the order himself.

Hell, he thought, I would have had that F-22 blow me out of the sky the minute I entered airspace.

Tom had untangled himself from the parachute as quickly as possible and stood on the runway with his hands held high as two trucks filled with security guards sped out to meet him. The guards poured out of the vehicles, forming a nearly perfect circle of assault rifles around him.

Tom was very careful and had followed their instructions to the letter. He invoked the name Batter enough times that he felt confident someone would alert the old man. He was now fairly certain they would at least hold their fire until Batter weighed in.

Nonetheless, he had been blindfolded and handcuffed, and pushed and shoved around a bit. Tom was transported across the airfield, and then he was aware of being put on an elevator. After a long downward ride, he had walked for quite a while/

Eventually, when his escorts finally decided to lift his blindfold, Tom found himself in a hallway that looked like it belonged in a posh lawyer's office. One of the men removed his handcuffs and opened a door, waving him in with a disapproving look. When he entered, he found Alex sitting there waiting for him.

She stood up when she saw him, shocked by his appearance. "Jesus, Tom, what the hell happened to you?"

His face was almost black from oil, with the exception of where his goggles had been, and there was a cut on his forehead that was bleeding slightly. He looked like a raccoon that just had the shit kicked out of him.

"Well, I don't suppose that's the very nicest way you could

greet me after all I have been through to get here," he said.

There was some humor left in him, Alex noted, which meant he was probably okay.

Tom didn't care about the comment, he was so happy to see Alex alive he hugged her and kissed her profusely.

To her surprise, Alex kissed him back just as passionately, then gently pushed him away, holding him by the arms. "We've got a lot to talk about."

She spent the next half an hour recounting the entire series of events since Tom left her in the caves, including Batter's recent revelation about the asteroids and the two Arzats.

The story was so unbelievable that Alex had to repeat parts of it patiently, some several times, until Tom fully understood her, particularly the news about the asteroids. He sat across from her amazed.

"Sounds like we need to go find Mot and Ara," he said when she was finally finished.

CHAPTER 29

Arzat Aware

P ete had gone back to Ara's compound after leaving Batter and the stunning Dr. Moss.

After meeting Alex, he no longer had any doubts why Batter had taken such an interest in her. The discovery that she was alive, and the even bigger discovery about the male Arzat she had found were simply incredible. Asked even a few days before, he might have even said, "impossible." No more.

Pete still wondered how his team could have missed Mot's sarcophagus. Under normal circumstances, there would have been some unpleasant meetings with them regarding the oversight, and someone would have been reprimanded, or worse.

Given the present situation, there was no point. Pete was well aware of the fact that most of his staff would not be invited into the ARC, which was very disturbing.

While the discovery of a second Arzat had been surprising, the fact that a team had been sent out to capture it was not. Batter had correctly guessed that Alex had been assisted out of the caves. How he had figured that out was a mystery to Pete, although the resurrection of Ara might have tipped Batter to the possibility. The man was that intelligent. And of course, even though there was only a short time left before the first impact, it was no surprise to him that Batter would have followed protocol and ordered both the Arzat and Dr. Moss brought in. The situation in the world was tenuous enough without taking the chance that a creature such as Mot would become public.

Perhaps, Pete thought, without much hope, the asteroid will miss altogether, and Batter's decision will prove to be monumentally correct. As it stood now, it didn't seem to matter much.

So, on what should have been yet another of the most amazing days in his scientific career, Pete found himself hopelessly depressed. The condition was made worse by the fact that he could never remember being in such a state in his entire life.

He knew that he needed to go in and see Ara, but he was worried that he would be unable to hide the truth from her about their fate. He did his best to shake off his concern as he prepared to face her.

Pete's staff had alerted him that Ara had been sleeping and then suddenly awoke. The timing had coincided exactly with the other Arzat's arrival in the complex. She had been pacing her compound since.

Ara had not chosen to attempt to communicate directly with anyone other than Pete, so they were left to guess about what was obviously bothering her until Pete returned.

"Be careful, Doctor," Paula cautioned him as she opened the door for him. "She seems to be very upset."

"Well, at least I have some semi-good news for her," he replied as he walked in.

Ara stopped pacing and faced Pete, her reptilian eyes narrowing.

"There is another," she said, with a note of accusation, the skin on the back of her neck flaring.

"That is what I have come here to tell you." Pete said, as calmly as possible. He was not worried. Even Ara knew that there was no way he could lie to her without being detected. "He just arrived here, Ara, and I only learned of his existence since we last spoke."

"He?" she asked, with a tinge of hope that Pete could not help but notice.

"Yes, according to the female that found him, it is Mot. Did you know?"

Ara did not answer immediately. She stood staring at Pete, thinking. It is true! Mot son of Url! Oh Great Creator!

"I can feel his presence. I can sense him. He is close by. I should be able to speak to him but for some reason I cannot. He must be asleep the same way I was put to sleep. This would prevent me from being able to reach his mind," she said. "Therefore, I could not be certain."

"Well, Mot is close by and you will see him soon," Pete said calmly, trying to reassure her. "I understand he was sedated for his own protection, Ara, but we will be reviving him shortly. When we do, I am sure he will be as happy to see you as you will be to see him."

Ara sat down on the floor. She suddenly had become quite calm, her stunning mantle folded neatly back into place. Pete had noticed that when Ara was agitated in any way, she would squat on her haunches like a Sumo wrestler; when calm, she would completely sit down on the floor and cross her legs. She beckoned Pete to sit with her.

Pete was hesitant, but he joined her and sat down close, crossing his own legs in the same fashion.

The Arzat looked deeply into Pete's eyes, her pupils dilating.

"It is good to tell the truth, isn't it Pete son of Robert?"

"Yes," Pete replied, curious about the question, worried about where the conversation would go.

"In my culture, telling an untruth is referred to as an atrocity. Our word for atrocity is mata. Do you have such a term, Pete?"

Pete thought for a moment. "I suppose we would call it a sin."

"I have committed such a thing, Pete, this sin, as you would call it."

Pete's heart began to beat harder. What was she getting at?

"You could not have known. Arzats communicate very carefully and are skilled at blocking out any thought they do not wish to reveal. Unfortunately, you do not yet possess these abilities and my curiosity overcame me the last time we met." Ara paused, ashamed, and took a deep breath. "I have looked deeply inside your mind, Pete. I have seen you as a child and as a young male. I have seen your family and even the small animal you care for. It is not right that I did this, but I now know almost everything that you do Pete. At least, most everything that is on the surface of your conscious-ness. I am sorry, but I felt the need to fully understand the situation."

Pete was awestruck. How was one to reply? Anything he might say now she was probably already aware of. It suddenly occurred to him that Ara must know about the asteroid.

"Yes, Pete, I also know about the great rock."

Pete looked into her eyes as if he were seeing the magnificence of them for the first time. They were golden, with flecks of blue and yellow like shining jewels. They actually sparkled. He knew that she was a very young female, but, as with some humans, she was very mature despite her age.

Ara blinked, and Pete was almost certain he could detect a tear.

"So you know about *everything*?" he asked.

"I know that our prospects for survival in here are small and outside they are non-existent. At least, that is what you believe. I even contemplated trying to escape before I sensed Mot's presence here in this place. But what purpose would it serve? I am afraid that all of our fates look sadly alike, Pete son of Robert. It is an unfortunate turn of events that I should be re-awakened to a second chance at life only to have it stolen away. Especially," she said wistfully, "now that Mot is known to be alive, as well."

"Ara, I will do everything I can for you... and for Mot," Pete said, knowing that Ara would fully appreciate the sincerity with which he was saying it.

"I am sure you will, Pete son of Robert, but in this matter—how is it you would say—the handwriting is on the wall, and I find myself, once again, helplessly in the hands of the Great Creator."

Pete lowered his head. Yes, Ara the Wise, he thought, you are quite correct. We are, all of us, helplessly in the hands of the Great Creator.

"I wish there was something I could do."

"You can. I wish to see Mot."

CHAPTER 30

No One Ever Uses It

B atter had left Alex and Tom to themselves in the conference room. He had not wished to experience their reunion. It had been completely obvious to him when they had all met in Utah, if not to Tom and Alex themselves, that the two of them were still very much in love.

Batter had so much personal relationship wreckage that he often wondered whether he was even capable of really loving anyone. His entire adult life had always been completely focused on his job—his true mistress.

Seeing Alex and Tom together was just another reminder of what a failure he was at genuine human relationships. Most of the time it didn't bother him—he just accepted it as a fact of his existence—but Alex had changed all of that in a way that even he couldn't quite figure out. No woman had ever affected him the way Dr. Alexandra Moss had.

* * *

Batter was standing at the train platform with a large number of the ARC personnel, waiting for the Vice President to arrive.

The platform might have been any subway station in New York, except that there was no graffiti on its pristine walls. The place looked brand new because it was, recently built to replace the antiquated rail system that was originally installed in the early 60s.

Batter checked his watch and looked up to a screen on the wall that tracked the train's progress from Washington to 51. It would arrive right on schedule.

There were several other trains en route for the Kansas and Colorado ARCs as well—different colored smaller dots moving slowly towards two other larger white squares. Many of the people who would be occupying those sites would be arriving by plane as well, depending on their rank or level of importance.

He was mildly irritated with himself when he noted that there were no lines headed for the fourth white square, Utah. It was his fault, but there was nothing he could do about it now.

Batter summoned one of his aides who stood close by.

"Is everything ready, Roberts?"

"Yes, sir."

"Good. Now just for your information, the President is not on this train, but the Vice President is. Please shift your priorities accordingly, and treat him as if he were the Commander and Chief. We will regard the President's absence as highly confidential. Got it?"

"Yes, Sir," Roberts replied without hesitation.

That's what I like to see, Batter thought, noting Robert's nonplussed reaction. The aide had not flinched at the new information.

* * *

The train arrived on schedule at 1811 hours, and Batter worked through the evening with all of the ARC staff to get the Vice President and all of the congressional and judicial members settled into quarters.

The attitude of most of the new arrivals was nonchalant and curious. Some laughed and joked as if they were on a paid holiday, inquiring about such things as where to get the best cocktail. Most had never imagined that such a place could exist, and spent a good deal of time pointing their fingers in multiple directions.

As they were led through the long corridors of the various areas within the ARC, they were not only amazed by its scope, but the scope of the mock drill.

Many of them quietly complained that they would have been content just to have had the information, saying it was hardly necessary to show off a facility that had such a very low probability of ever being needed. They were, after all, very important to the Washington community with a lot going on. This trip, while interesting, was killing three days that they could have used elsewhere.

Batter had followed along, watching each of them, coldly sizing up various individuals in the group as they toured.

Soon, he thought grimly, they will all wish they had provided better funding to NASA for NEO intervention.

* * *

After everyone had been fed and assigned quarters, Batter conferred with the President and the Vice President by secure videoconference link in the very room where Batter had earlier interviewed Alex.

There was to be a meeting of all of the delegates at 1200 hours Nevada time—noon the next day. That was when the other shoe would drop. The President would address the nation at that time from the Oval Office, and everyone in the world would suddenly know exactly what was going on.

It would give everyone on the "outside" only a few hours to say their good-byes. 24 hours was too much in a case like this, all of the sociologists had agreed. Once the general population had any time at all to get past the shock, the mobs would have time to form and riot. The crimes against humanity would be horrific if too much notice was given, and perhaps create a worse situation than the arrival of the asteroid itself.

The final advice of the human behavior experts was, "better to give them no notice at all."

After a heated debate, the world leaders had eventually compromised at six hours. They were all to begin their announcements at precisely 2000 hours Zulu-12 noon PST Nevada time.

For the new arrivals to the ARC, Batter knew he would likely be compelled to personally follow up on the President's comments with some of his own. Although every member of Congress had been advised of the ARC emergency plan in case of disaster, and they had all pledged to strictly adhere to it should it become necessary, the reality of what was about to happen would be too much for some of them.

Batter had a contingent of doctors and a huge security force standing by with sedatives and plenty of fire power to deal with the almost certain fallout.

The lawmakers would be forced to comply completely with the rules of the ARC or face severe consequences. Everyone's survival depended upon it. Any tendency to anarchy would be immediately suppressed with all means necessary.

Batter knew this was going to be very difficult for men and women who had largely lived their lives setting the rules for themselves and others. It was highly unlikely they would react well to their new situation.

* * *

"Well, Mr. Batter," the Vice President said to him as they ended the meeting with the President, "looks like we are going to have our work cut out for us tomorrow."

He was a 63-year-old politician with a full head of graying hair. He looked like he had aged ten years just since his arrival.

"Yes, Sir," Batter replied. "I have everything in place."

"I am sure you do, Batter. I am absolutely sure you do," the Vice President said. He swirled the ice that was the only thing left from a cocktail he had been drinking. "I have three brothers, a sister, four grown children, eight grandchildren and a slew of nieces and nephews. None of them is going to survive after tomorrow," he said with regret, looking into the glass. "Do you have family Batter?"

"I have no children, no siblings and no parents—just three lovely ex-wives who are no longer on speaking terms with me, and a German Sheppard by the name of Max that follows orders like a Marine. Max I will miss."

The Vice President chuckled slightly. "Well, let's hope everyone tomorrow takes a lesson from Max."

"Good night, Mr. Vice President."

"Good night, Batter." The Vice President rose and prepared to exit the conference room. "By the way, do you even have a first name?"

"I do sir," Batter responded politely, "but no one ever uses it." Almost no one, almost never, Batter thought, remembering his earlier conversation with the President.

The Vice President let the comment stand and walked out the door.

CHAPTER 31

The Rival

A lex managed to ask around enough to lead Tom through the underground labyrinth and get them to the Primate Research area.

They both clearly noticed, as they passed through some massive doors on the way, that their destination was not inside the protective confines of the ARC itself.

Batter had informed Alex to contact Pete Wilson when they arrived.

Pete was standing with a clipboard, just outside of Mot's enclosure when he spotted Tom and Alex making their way up the hall.

"How is he?" Alex asked immediately as they approached.

"I had the IV removed about an hour ago. The anesthesiologists think any time now he will awaken. I am very glad you are here, Doctor," Pete said, sincerely. Then he looked at Tom.

"I'm sorry, Doctor, this is my... this is Tom Hancock," Alex said turning back towards Tom.

"Yes, Alex, we've already met. Utah, remember," Tom said extending his hand. "Nice to see you again, Doctor."

"Oh, of course, I'd forgotten," she said, embarrassed.

"Welcome, Mr. Hancock. I heard about your grand entrance. That was really something. Can't say as I blame you," Pete said smiling, looking back at Alex.

"How do you want to approach this Alex? Are you able to communicate with Mot as I do with Ara?" Pete was aware that Batter had told Alex about the female Arzat and—for reasons he still didn't really understand—about the impending impact of the asteroids.

"He is going to be extremely disoriented and probably pretty upset. I think I had better try to calm him down by being with him when he wakes," Alex said.

"A note of caution, Doctor. Batter informed me that you and Tom have been fully briefed on the coming events. Ara was able to go completely past normal conversation and into the deeper parts of my consciousness. Suffice it to say, this means she knows everything about what is going on. Mot will probably be able to do the same if he chooses."

"How did you find out?" Alex asked, not completely surprised.

"She told me." Pete shrugged. "She seems as resigned to her fate as the rest of us, but, with Mot here, well, you never know."

"Mot would never hurt me," she said defensively.

"I know you believe that, as I do with Ara. But the survival instinct is a very powerful thing, as you know, Alex. Just be careful. I would hate to see you become a tool for an attempted escape. They are very intelligent," Pete added, knowing he was stating the obvious.

"What will become of them, Pete? We noticed as we walked over that this section is definitely not part of the ARC."

"I think, Doctor, that it is better if I do not answer that question just yet," Pete said in a way that begged her not to insist on an answer.

Pete and Tom went to the gallery above the room Mot was in. The facility was almost identical to Ara's compound and had been set up with a bed and a lavatory.

Mot was lying face up on a large mattress that had been placed on the floor, his feet hanging conspicuously off the end. The two men watched as Alex entered the room and made her way carefully over to him. She sat beside the bed Arzat-style and placed her hand on the side of his head.

"Mot son of Url, this is Alex daughter of Simon. I am here," she said, tears suddenly streaming from her eyes. The sight of her giant Arzat lying there, helpless, was almost too much for her to bear. She repeated the message several times until she saw his eyelids flutter.

Come on Alex, she admonished herself, pull it together.

Mot first heard Alex as a dull echo in his head. He tried to awaken immediately, but the drugs slowed him.

Gradually, he regained consciousness, and completely recognized her voice. His heart beat harder at hearing her, because he had thought she was dead. He vaguely remembered the sound of the human fire sticks and Alex falling, but little else from the incident at the ranch.

"Alex?" he asked hopefully, still only halfway to consciousness.

"Yes, Mot. I am here," she said gently as she watched him open his eyes.

Mot slowly rolled upright on the bed, his head pounding, and faced Alex.

"I am sorry, Alex. I failed to protect you," he said, trying to shake the anesthesia, his eyes blinking to clear the fog.

"We are safe now, Mot. Everything is okay."

Mot looked around the room, trying to get his bearings. He did not like what he saw or felt. He could sense the presence of many other humans. The room was shocking, white and barren.

Then, he suddenly recognized the strong presence of another Arzat. He flicked his tongue and smelled the air deeply. It was unmistakably the scent of Ara.

"She is here?" he asked, wide eyed, becoming fully awake and sitting upright.

"Yes, Mot, she is alive and well, and she is here," Alex said, wishing to calm him. "You will see her shortly."

Mot sat quietly trying to piece together all of the information, his head still swirling from the drugs.

Before the news of Ara, he had felt there was little hope for him in this new world, but now, well, anything was possible. He could feel his heart beating faster as he thought of her.

But there was something very different about Alex, something dark and hopeless, something very disturbing. Mot wanted to probe, knowing he could, but held himself back. Still…

Then a wave of jealousy that he could not explain overtook him. He looked into Alex's eyes, and he could "see" another male there.

"Someone is with you now. Is it your mate?" he asked, his eyes narrowing.

Alex tried to stay calm. There was no possibility of hiding anything from him.

"Yes," she answered slowly, "you remember the man I spoke of earlier? He is here."

It was not fair, Alex belonged to him, he thought, realizing the moment it crossed his mind that it was wrong-headed. She is a human, and of course she should have a mate. Despite his own reasoning, Mot still did not like the idea.

"Oh," or something close to that, was all he could say.

"Would you like to see her?" she asked. Alex was dying to meet the female herself.

"I'm sorry? Oh, yes. Yes, I would like to see Ara," he paused, "but first I would like to meet your mate. What is his name?"

"His name is Tom," she responded awkwardly.

Mot sat patiently. Oh yes, thought Alex, what is Tom's father's name for god's sake? He is waiting for his full name. "Tom son of Richard," she finally managed.

Mot contemplated the name for some time.

"Tom son of Richard," he repeated. "Alex, may I please meet Tom son of Richard?"

Tom and Pete had been watching Alex and Mot intently from the gallery. Tom was so astonished that he had not uttered a word to Pete. This was the first time he had actually seen Mot, although Alex had perfectly described him when she had told him about the giant Arzat earlier. Even so, the creature was astonishing in the flesh. He was huge and could have broken Alex in two with a flick of his wrist, but for some reason Tom was not worried.

Pete, on the other hand, watched quietly as well, but he was worried the entire time about what might happen.

He had a radio with him, and had quietly ordered marksmen with tranquilizers to station themselves outside the room just in case.

We really know nothing about them, he thought, wishing more than anything that he might have had time to learn more.

Alex looked up at the one-way glass and gestured.

"Tom, can you please come down? Mot wants to meet you," they heard her say through a speaker in the wall.

Tom looked at Pete, questioning.

Pete shrugged. "You will have a headache like the worst migraine you have ever imagined, which will pass in about a minute. He will ask who your father is," was all he could think to say.

Tom made his way down a flight of stairs and reached the door of the enclosure. One of the assistants signaled him.

"Are you ready?"

Tom nodded doubtfully, took a deep breath, and reached for the door. The assistant pushed a button and the door swung open. He walked in slowly and approached Alex and the giant beast beside her. His was heart racing as he began to fully appreciate Mot's size and obvious strength. The beast looked like the biggest linebacker he had ever seen, but clothed in alligator skin.

Mot watched as the male creature entered the room. He was much smaller than Mot expected. Really, though, he was about the size of most of the other human males Mot had encountered.

He beckoned Tom closer to where he and Alex were sitting. Although there was nothing directly threatening about this male named Tom, he could still feel the scales rising slightly on the back of his neck.

"Please tell him that he is welcome to sit, Alex," Mot said to her, trying to sound as friendly as possible.

Alex simply patted the floor next to her. Tom took the hint and sat in the same style as Alex and Mot, which took some doing. He realized he was very sore from his little escapade with the airplane.

Mot looked into Tom's eyes directly for an uncomfortably long time, tilting his head slightly.

"Alex, would you please ask Tom son of Richard, if he would like to communicate with me directly. It would not be polite to attempt to do so otherwise."

Alex had never felt so completely out of control with Mot before. She realized he had somehow taken total charge of their meeting. Is that a bad thing, she wondered?

"Tom," she asked, "Mot would like to try to speak to you directly. Are you up for that? Might hurt a bit at first," she cautioned, willing him to say "yes."

Tom nodded towards Mot and looked him in the eyes. The creature's pupils seemed to widen, and their color seemed to intensify.

Tom felt his head begin to throb, worse than any headache he had ever experienced, then the pain lessened and gradually disappeared. Mot's voice was like an echo at first, but soon became clearer and clearer.

"I am Mot son of the great Hunter Url," Mot had been repeating.

Gradually, the fog around Mot's unspoken words lifted, and Tom could completely understand him.

"I am Tom son of Richard," he finally said. "My father was a pilot," Tom added, recalling Alex's story about her own father.

Mot slapped his own knees in delight, as if he had surprised himself with his success.

"Very good, Tom son of the pilot Richard. It is a pleasure to formally meet you."

Mot wondered what a "pilot" could possibly be, but he held the question for later. Despite himself, he could already feel himself starting to like this little human.

Alex sat, only aware of Tom's comments, which he had spoken aloud. She was completely cut out of Mot's end of the conversation for some reason, but she assumed from his reaction and what Tom had said that they had succeeded.

Why is Mot blocking me out, she wondered?

Mot leaned forward towards Tom.

"Tom son of Richard, Alex cannot hear us so long as you do not speak aloud in your tongue. Do you understand?"

"Yes," Tom answered without speaking, still in awe of Mot's presence.

"We do not have much time. I do not know why I know this, but I do. This fact has become clear to me after speaking with Alex, and now even clearer after meeting you. I am aware that the humans outside this room have a plan that does not include the Arzats, Mot and Ara."

Tom did not know what to say. Mot knew. He wondered what Alex had told him but he doubted that she would have mentioned anything directly.

Alex had already cautioned Tom about trying to lie about anything—it was impossible and would be detected by Mot immediately if he tried.

Perhaps he has already probed my mind, he thought, recalling Pete's warning.

"Tom son of Richard, I do not hold you or Alex responsible," Mot continued reassuringly. "Something of importance is about to happen that is beyond our control and in the hands of the Creator. I must admit, I thought about trying to escape, but I have seen the fire sticks you humans possess and I realize that any attempt would be futile. We are not of your clan. It would probably be the same for you, if not worse, were you in the hands of my people."

Tom looked to Alex and realized she was completely unable to help him. For an adolescent, he was obviously wise beyond his years.

"I do not know how to answer you," he said to Mot, trying not to have any thought of what might really happen to the Arzats when they got to the end and locked down the ARC. He looked back at Alex.

"There is no need. It was only a statement of fact. I wish only your commitment, Tom son of the pilot Richard," Mot said.

"I will do anything for you I can, Mot," Tom replied, meaning it.

"You will protect Alex daughter of Simon, with your life, no matter what happens. You will be good to her and make sure no harm comes to her that you can prevent. This is your duty as her mate, and can no longer be my responsibility."

Mot paused, and looked over at Alex, then back at Tom. "She has protected my life. She has fed me and taught me many valuable things. She has led

me to Ara. She made me the pan-cakes, the best meal I ever had. She..."
Mot's voice trailed off and disappeared.

Tom wanted to laugh and probably would have were the situation not so dire. He glanced at Alex. She had a confused look on her otherwise beautiful face.

Tom realized again in that moment, more than ever, how much he loved her. He also realized that there was no way in hell she would ever allow Mot to be locked out of the ARC. Whatever happened, she would be going with Mot, and Tom knew that he would be going, as well. This revelation sent shivers up his spine, but he no longer felt any fear about the future.

He looked back at Mot. "We humans have a saying Mot, that 'it's not over till the fat lady sings.' Anything might happen. But I will keep the commitment you have asked of me freely."

"Good," Mot replied, "then I have done all I can do and said all that I can say, Tom son of Richard." Mot extended his hand in the way he had seen the humans. "Let us 'shake' on the matter, as humans do."

Tom slowly placed his hand in Mot's, watching it disappear behind the huge fingers. The creature shook Tom's hand firmly, and Tom was quite relieved that he did not crush it.

"Now," Tom heard Mot say to Alex, "I wish to see Ara."

CHAPTER 32

We Meet Again

M ot's heart was beating harder than it had when the Evil Ones had chased him and tried to have him for dinner.

He was standing by the door that linked his enclosure with Ara's. Alex had informed him that all he had to do was raise his hand and the humans would open the door.

* * *

Although they had grown up in the same clan and the same caves, Mot and Ara had had almost no interaction whatsoever in their entire lives. The young Arzat males and females were basically raised in separate areas, almost completely isolated from one another. Females were to learn the duties of females. Males were to learn the responsibilities of being the providers for the clan. Some, in the case of the females, would be taught different specialties, such as tanning or cooking or foraging for fruit and other forest edibles. Some, in the case of the males, would be taught the ways of medicine, to forge metal, carve stone—or, if they were talented and showed promise— they might have the opportunity to become Hunters. This, of course, was by far the most prestigious position a young Arzat male could aspire to.

So, before his great 'atrocity' and the disgrace that had accompanied it, Mot would have been 'a catch' for any young Arzat female. Her privileges as the mate of a Hunter would be much greater in every respect.

Now, Mot suddenly realized, he had nothing to offer her. What if she rejected him completely, he worried.

* * *

"What is he waiting for?" Tom asked Alex, as they watched from the gallery.

Alex gave Tom a knowing look. "Just be patient."

She turned back, mesmerized by the female Arzat's obvious strength and beauty. No wonder Mot's nervous, she thought.

Mot finally raised his hand halfway, and the door lifted. Ara was standing across the room.

Pete had told her about Mot's request to see her. Of course, she had readily agreed. She was just as nervous as Mot, but, unbeknownst to him, she didn't care at all about his status. Ara had been attracted to Mot for what seemed forever and she had never cared about where he would land in the Zanta hierarchy. Not that any of that mattered now, anyway. It had always been her parent's plan to offer her to Mot as a mate. But an offer did not necessarily mean acceptance in the Arzat culture. He could turn her down.

The fact that she was probably the only female Arzat in existence somehow did nothing to dispel her anxiety.

Mot crossed the threshold and stood by the door. They faced each other for several minutes.

Finally, although it was not proper Arzat protocol in the slightest, it was left to Ara to break the silence.

"I am Ara daughter of the great Hunter Zan," she said proudly. "Who are you?"

Mot felt his throat go dry. She was more beautiful than he remembered, the bright lights of the room glistening off of her golden skin, her eyes matching the highlights of her body.

"I am Mot son of the great Hunter Url," he croaked, formally replying, as he should.

"Come," Ara beckoned, "sit with me Mot."

Ara moved to the center of the room and seated herself. Mot followed.

"I understand that it has been many seasons since we last spoke though it seems like it was only a short time ago, Mot son of Url. Do you remember?" she asked, her eyes melting Mot's.

"I… Yes, I… I remember," Mot answered, feeling embarrassed for reasons he could not explain.

"It is good to see you are alive," Ara said. "I have heard that it is not so with the others."

"This seems true. There appear to be no others."

"Then let us rejoice in the fact that you and I have been chosen by the Great Creator to survive, as our mother's had asked, and the Astrologers had foretold." Ara leaned forward, her wonderful scent almost overwhelming Mot. "Listen, Mot son of Url," she said to him earnestly, "I have spoken to these humans and it seems that we have awakened at a bad time. Are you aware of this?"

"I know something of it, but not all," Mot said.

"Well, I have committed a mata with one of the humans, Mot," Ara hesitated, still ashamed of her indiscretion with Pete.

Mot's eyes narrowed. "A mata, Ara?"

"Yes," she said, worried she would lose face with Mot from her admission. "Their thoughts are very easy to read and I could not stop myself. I have probed the mind of one of the humans," she said, fully confessing.

Mot relaxed. "Continue, Ara."

"The humans believe another death star is approaching. Apparently their plan is to hide in these caves they have constructed just as our fathers and mothers would have done. I have examined every possible avenue of escape for us, and I cannot find one. It seems that the world outside is about to die again. It seems that our future is to be short. This Pete, the human I..." Ara stopped herself, not wishing to repeat her admission of the "mata." "This human, appears to have no ill intentions for us, but it is clear in his mind that he will also be able to do nothing to protect us. The will of his clan supersedes his own, as it should."

"I cannot believe that the Creator would have brought us all this way for an ending like this, Ara. Perhaps there is a way. The two humans I have been with seem to think there might be," Mot said, trying to be hopeful.

"Perhaps," Ara said doubtfully. She took a deep breath. "But, if our time is really to be so short, Mot son of the great Hunter Url, I propose that you take me for your mate immediately."

Mot was lightheaded. Had she really said that? The offer was always from the side of the female, but Mot was still surprised at the suddenness of her words. He looked into her beautiful golden eyes, unable to reply immediately.

"Then, you will be my mate," Mot finally said, his heart beating hard in his chest.

Ara reached out and touched his face. "In this, the Creator has fulfilled my greatest wish. Perhaps you are right, Mot son of the great Hunter Url. Perhaps there is a future for us that we cannot see," she said.

Mot was brimming with pride. Ara, daughter of the great Hunter Zan—as my mate! Yes, the Great Creator must be watching over me, he thought.

"Now," Ara said, "tell me everything that has happened and all that you know and I will do the same. Then, perhaps we can get these humans to provide us with a meal, and," she said suggestively, "perhaps we can get them to give us some privacy."

CHAPTER 33

Will There Be Anything Else?

B atter hung up the phone for what seemed to him at least the millionth time.

He had been busy checking on the status of the Kansas and Colorado ARCs and trying in vain to convince the President to take refuge. The President of the United States was probably one of the few men on the planet that Batter could not force to do anything.

For some reason, unknown even to him, Batter had also called all of his ex-wives. One he had been unable to reach, and had simply left a message of apology. It had been vague and general, but he had apologized nonetheless for basically being an asshole. The other two, he *had* reached, and had stammered his way through the awkward conversations, essentially doing his best to say the same thing without revealing the real purpose for his call. When he was done, he felt better. Batter couldn't remember ever really apologizing for anything. It wasn't nearly as painful as he had expected.

Batter glanced at his watch. They had passed the 24-hour point.

One day to go, he thought. Tomorrow at this time, there was going to be one hell of a sunset.

He went to the bathroom and checked himself in the mirror. It was the first time he could remember ever noticing his age. He prodded his face a bit, examining it closely, then shrugged as he grabbed his sport coat and headed for the door.

Batter had arranged a dinner date with Tom, Alex, and Pete. He was interested to hear about the Arzats, and he knew it was going to be very difficult to get Alex—and possibly even Pete—to let go of them tomorrow when the ARC locked down.

Might as well get a head start, he had reasoned, heading out the door.

* * *

Batter's dinner guests had already been seated by the time he arrived. He noticed that they were in a lively conversation that abruptly ended as he approached the table.

If he hadn't known otherwise, Batter might have thought they were in any busy fine-dining restaurant. There were five different commissaries within the ARC and this one was styled after a famous restaurant in DC. He considered it a ridiculous waste of funds, but it was there, so he figured he might as well take advantage of it.

Batter pulled up a chair and sat.

"What's everyone drinking?" he asked as affably as possible, feeling as if he were the odd man out. Once everyone had cocktails, the discussion opened up again.

"They are simply amazing," the beautiful Alex Moss was saying, her green eyes sparkling in the light of the restaurant. "Tom had no problem communicating with Mot at all. Did you Tom?"

Tom only nodded.

He had been very quiet since they had left Ara and Mot, and Alex had begun to worry about him. Usually, she could read his mind almost as well as she could Mot's. Something was going on, some wheels were spinning about something, but she did not know what.

She resolved to make a point of asking him after dinner, but at the moment, she was preoccupied with convincing Batter to allow them to move the Arzats into the ARC.

"How about you, Pete? What are your thoughts?" Batter asked.

"Well, I finally received the results back from the lab tests of the mysterious goo they were packed in. Mostly it consisted of some kind of prehistoric animal fat. But there was also a high content of a glycerin molecule in the material that appears to have come from a plant species that is probably extinct.

It might just be the 'missing link' for the cryogen project we thought it was. Some of the scientists have already tested it on individual cells and there is no apparent breakdown whatsoever under freezing conditions. It seems to be the ultimate cryo-protectant we were looking for. Of course, we still need to do a lot more testing, but it shows real promise."

"Very interesting," Batter said as their entrees arrived.

"Oh, one more thing," Pete added, "we have also determined that we were over-freezing. There is no need to go nearly as low in temperature. It now looks like the ideal point is right around zero degrees Celsius, with a very slow cooling of the body. It appears that the caves must have somehow managed to hold around that approximate temperature all of those years."

"Any idea how that might have happened, Tom?" Batter asked, trying to draw him into the conversation.

"No," he said, shaking his head, "it is just about as close to a geological impossibility as the resurrection of Christ—or for that matter—the resurrection of the Arzats. There are a lot of mysteries about that site, like where in the hell that hot spring came from."

Tom was obviously still very bothered by the unexpected turn of events that had almost killed Alex.

"Well, you needn't worry about it anymore," Batter announced. "I ordered them to shut down the entire Utah operation right after you showed up," he said, finishing a bite of New York steak.

Tom gave him a guilty look.

"Hah, don't worry about it Tom," Batter said, noting his reaction. "It was a lost cause before we knew about this new asteroid. At 28 days, we were still way out from having it complete in time for it to be useful. At two days? No sense in prolonging the pain, right? I figured I might as well let everyone who could get home to their families. Of course, they have no idea why, but that's the way it has to be," he said regretfully.

"On the bright side, Tom, you seem to have inadvertently won an invitation to *this* ARC. Pete and I are sure we will be able to use your expertise as well as Dr. Moss's in the future. Right Pete?"

Tom just took another bite of his dinner. Why am I not grateful for that, he wondered.

Now or never, Alex thought.

"Batter, we have to figure out a way to save the Arzats."

She had been waiting the entire dinner to say it. She looked hopefully to Pete for backup, but he had a sad look on his face that was less than inspiring.

Batter took a long sip of wine and slowly set down his glass. He looked directly at Alex.

"I am sorry, Doctor, but that is not going to happen. If it were up to me…"

"But it is up to you," Alex interrupted, pleading.

"No, Alex," he continued. "It is up to these people," he said, gesturing around the crowded room. "Look around, Doctor, and tell me if you think your two friends will really have any chance in the days and weeks and months to follow with these people. I am a student of human behavior, Doctor. Your Arzats will have no chance with them. I think even you know that," he finished, taking another bite of steak.

Alex could say nothing. She knew that Batter was right and she knew how things would go. First, there would be seemingly innocent questions about who or *what* they were keeping. Then inquiries would arise about the resources being *wasted* on the "lizards."

It all became clear to her. Batter was right, but still.

Batter finished chewing and calmly took another sip of wine.

"Frankly, Doctor, I am worried enough about your friends in this room. And I'm not, of course, referring to Tom or Pete. When these people find out the severity of the situation tomorrow and the place actually locks down, there may be more than a few of them who will be unable to adjust."

All of them at the table knew exactly what Batter meant. After the President's speech there was no telling what would happen.

Alex suddenly found that she had tears in her eyes. She was tough and not one for crying in public. She tried blinking them away but neither Batter nor anyone else at the table failed to notice.

Batter took another large sip of wine.

"I'll tell you what," he said, trying to appease her, "tomorrow is a long way off. Let's sleep on it and regroup after the general meeting. It has been a long tough ride for everyone. There is time enough. For now, I think we could all use some rest."

Alex looked up hopefully.

"But, Doctor, I hope you will strongly consider what I've said, if not for your sake, for the sake of your Arzat friends. Let's wait until after the President's speech to make the final decision. Right now," he said, rising from the table, "I think it is time to say goodnight. Pete, would you be so kind as to help Alex and Tom locate their quarters and perhaps," he said, eyeballing them, "a change of clothing? I hope it is not too much of an inconvenience to share a room. For the moment, we seem to be short on space." Batter winked at Tom and Alex and walked out.

Pete led Alex and Tom back through the maze of corridors and helped them find their room.

"He's right, you know," Pete said to Alex sadly as he left them.

She knew that the idea of locking out the Arzats was bothering Pete as much as it was her, so she did not respond. She watched him as he disappeared down the long hallway.

Alex took a shower that was automatically timed at one minute and Tom did the same. It was barely long enough to scour off and rinse. Tom tried to explain some of the fantastic recycling features of the ARC, but it did little to impress her. An aide arrived sometime in the process and delivered some fresh clothes. Aside from the obnoxious shower, the place operated like a five star hotel.

I wonder how long that's going to last, Alex mused as she pulled on a large military T-shirt.

"What are you thinking about?" she asked as Tom as they got into bed.

"Not what I should be," Tom said, looking her over.

"Come on Tom," Alex said, dismissing his weak attempt to be amorous rather than answer her real question. "I know that mind of yours. You are up to something," she said, laying her head close to his.

Tom looked at her. She did have the most beautiful eyes. "I'm trying to figure a way out of this mess and into your pants."

"Of course you are. You wouldn't be the man I know if you weren't doing both. I'll tell you what: you get the first part of that worked out, and we'll talk about the second," she said, turning off the light and pressing close to him. "What's that you're always saying? 'It's not over till the fat lady sings,'" she said, instantly asleep.

Tom lay awake for some time, running his plan over and over in his mind.

* * *

Pete had gone back to the compound and checked to make sure that Ara and Mot had been fed and that they were given control of the lights in their enclosure.

He walked up to the gallery and the enclosure was dark. The only way he knew for sure the Arzats were there was the infrared imaging that was displayed on one of the monitors. It appeared that the two were sleeping very close to one another.

Pete smiled as he left them, thinking of his own wife Hanna and his children, picturing them asleep.

He had struggled through a phone conversation with Hanna earlier in the day, attempting to sound normal, fighting his desperate desire to warn his family.

It was better this way, he continued to try to convince himself. There was no hope for them, so why worry them needlessly?

He had, on several occasions, struck out for the entrance determined to head for home, but he had ultimately turned back each time.

This was always a possibility, Pete reminded himself, and he had sworn to do his duty in exactly this kind of situation.

When he eventually reached his room, he calmly prepared for bed, then got down on his knees and prayed for the asteroids to miss. Pete was an avowed atheist.

* * *

Batter was in his quarters, working his way through the last in a series of novels about vampires. He was already a chronic insomniac, but in the last few days he found that he could barely sleep at all. He found that such fantasy books required little thought and allowed him to relax.

Batter eventually put the book down and was about to doze when the phone beside his bed rang. He was used to hearing bad news and instinctively prepared himself for more.

"Sorry to disturb you, Sir, but I have a secure call for you from a Dr. Jennifer Daniels from the Haleakala Observatory. She says the matter is urgent," the operator said.

"Send it through," he said, then hung up and waited. The phone began to ring again, and Batter reluctantly picked it up. "Batter here."

"Mr. Batter, this is Dr. Jen Daniels, I am the chief astronomer for Pan-STARRS," she said, her voice shaking. "I just got off the phone with the President, and he said that I should call you directly, Sir. He said," she continued, "'Batter will know what to do.' He asked me to repeat that to you when we spoke."

"Go ahead, Doctor. I'm listening," Batter said as gently as possible.

Whatever this young lady's message was, she was delivering it with a death warrant on her own head that she would be well aware of, yet here she was still at her post reporting.

"I am sorry, Mr. Batter, but the computers have just recalculated the projected impact of the asteroid." The statement was followed by a long silence.

"And?" Batter finally mustered the courage to ask.

"Well, Sir, it appears now that it will touch down somewhere very near the coordinates of thirty nine degrees north by one hundred and fourteen degrees west," she said, her voice cracking. Batter could easily imagine the phone shaking in her hand.

"Pardon me, Doctor, but could you fully translate that?" but he already knew the answer. Batter was very aware of the longitudinal and latitudinal coordinates of the Nevada ARC.

"Very close to your current location, Sir, with a plus or minus variance of only two or three degrees." Jen paused.

Batter did not answer. He was immediately busy trying to come up with a solution, any solution, but at the moment he couldn't think of one. The Colorado and Kansas ARCs were already full and too far. Utah wasn't finished. There was basically nowhere to go.

"I am sorry to say, Sir, that with an impact so close the chances of survival are… uh, minimal."

Batter tried to answer, but he suddenly found himself without words.

"Sir?"

"Oh, ah, yes, Doctor?"

"Sir, will there be anything else? I mean, we are all preparing and…" the Doctor had just delivered a death sentence, and hers was on its way. She was finding it difficult to speak.

"No, Doctor. Jen is it? Thank you, Jen. Good luck."

"You too, Sir."

He held the phone to his ear and listened as the line clicked and the phone went dead.

CHAPTER 34

Where Is The President?

T hey were almost late for the meeting.

Alex and Tom had slept in and grabbed a quick breakfast at one of the commissaries, then stopped by the Primate Compound to check on Mot and Ara. They avoided direct contact, not wanting to speak to the Arzats until after they heard the official word from the President, and had met with Batter.

The meeting was set for 1200 hours, Area 51 time, and when they finally arrived it was already 1154.

The chamber was packed, with the House and the Senate on the lower floors and the rest of the attendees in the wings and on the balconies.

The room very closely resembled the Congressional Chamber in Washington, with the exception that it was much more modern and had two very large screens right and left of the stage.

As they were seated, Alex looked around the room. She guess-timated that it could probably accommodate a thousand, and the place was packed.

She could see Batter, standing off to the side of the Vice President's podium, watching everyone closely.

By the doors, she noticed two or three-dozen security personnel standing with their hands behind their backs wearing side arms.

Batter's riot police, she thought.

The mood in the chamber was anything but somber. Old acquaintances met, and the room was a cacophony of happy chatter. Most were under the impression that immediately after the meeting, they would be heading back to Washington and home.

When Alex glanced back towards Batter their eyes met for just a moment, then he looked away.

A large digital clock was displayed on one of the screens. When it rolled to 1200, the VP rose and rapped his gavel on the podium.

"Good morning, ladies and gentlemen of the Congress, the Court, and all. Let me be brief. We are about to hear from the President of the United States. After that, I will have a few comments and will be available for questions."

Just as the Vice President, stepped away from the podium, the giant screens flashed to the Oval Office. An aide was still fitting a microphone to the President's lapel.

"Good morning fellow Americans," he said in a somber tone looking directly into the camera. "A few weeks ago, one of our most advanced telescopes, known as Pan-STARRS, identified what the astronomers refer to as an N-E-O, a near-earth-object. In less technical terms, it means an asteroid or meteor that will pass close to our planet. At first, there was little concern, but, as time passed, our computer system plotted a complete map of the arc of the object's orbit that suggested a high probability of impact here on earth sometime 28 days from now."

There were startled looks in the Chamber, but no one moved, their eyes locked on the screen.

"If that were not bad enough," the President continued, "our astronomers have now determined that a 'shadow asteroid,' that could not at first be seen, is traveling right in front of the one first discovered. It will arrive much sooner."

There was a gasp in the room. Some people started moving in their seats, some tried to head for the doors. The security teams stopped them with weapons raised and waived them back to their seats.

"The exact scope of the damage these asteroids will inflict is not precisely known, but it will be substantial, and will affect the entire planet and the environment we live in. Our scientists have been working around the clock, trying to find a solution, but so far they have found none. We simply do not have the resources to deal with this kind of situation," the President paused and took a deep breath. "It is with great regret that I must announce that at approximately 9:17 pm Eastern Standard Time we anticipate an asteroid to strike the Pacific Ocean just off of the coast of South America. Other authorities, from around the world, are making similar announcements as I speak."

The President stopped looking at his notes, and took off his glasses. He had just lied. He knew the scope and the damage, and exactly where the asteroid was going to hit-and it wasn't in the Pacific Ocean.

"I wish there were something more to say, some thread of hope I could pass along, but the situation is dire. The future of mankind is in jeopardy, along with the lives of all living things on the planet. I hope you will all help each other. The government of the United States will do all that it can while it can. Since our communications system is likely to be a casualty, I wish to express my deepest regrets and concerns to all of you at this time. While they are able, every major radio and television station will be broadcasting the latest status. May God bless you, may God bless the United States of America, and may God bless this world."

The screen went blank, and the room erupted in utter panic. It was left to Batter to restore order.

He calmly stepped up to the podium and fired several rounds from an assault rifle into the air. They were blank rounds—only Batter knew that—but they did the trick. He had a full clip of live ammunition in his pocket, just in case.

The room went quiet immediately.

Alex noticed that Batter's security guards had all magically been able to produce assault rifles of their own, and were now very conspicuously blocking the exits.

Batter approached the front of the stage and awkwardly lowered his head over the podium.

"Aaahumm," he cleared his throat directly into the microphone. "Ladies and gentlemen, my name is Batter and I am in charge of this facility. I work under the direct orders of the Commander and Chief. I know you must all be in quite a state of shock. I myself was when I heard the news that the President has just relayed, so I am quite empathetic to your situation. However," he said, now looking around the room, "make no mistake, we must all maintain complete order for our own survival. On this, I must absolutely insist," he finished. "Now please, ladies and gentlemen, the Vice President."

Batter stepped aside as if he had not spoken a word.

Alex looked down from the balcony. There was something about Batter that commanded abeyance. Maybe it was just the way he wielded the semi-automatic.

The room was silent.

The Vice President looked to Batter as if for permission, then walked back to the podium.

"I would like to remind everyone of the oath you signed regarding this unfortunate possibility," the Vice President began again. "Never was it imagined that such an event could come to pass in our lifetimes, or the lifetimes of many generations. We are fortunate to have the protection of the ARC. For those of you who wish, we have arranged open phone banks so that you may speak with your loved ones. However, I would like to remind everyone that this location is still classified, so you are not at liberty to disclose that bit of information. For those of you who are not willing to comply with the rules of the ARC... well, as Mr. Batter has indicated, we must insist that you do. From this point on ladies and gentlemen, like it or not—and believe me I do not like it myself—this will be our new home," he paused. "Now I will entertain some questions."

Silence, as if no one was even breathing. Many of the attendees were keeping a wary eye on the security forces at the doors.

Then one of the Senators rose from his chair to be recognized.

"Yes, Senator Bean," said the Vice President.

Senator Bean had been a member of Congress for thirty years. He was sixty-five years old and past taking shit from anyone, but as an ex-military man he had learned decades ago to be careful around young men in uniform with guns. This was serious business.

"Mr. Vice President, we were tricked. I'd never have come here if I had known this was happening. I wish to return home immediately."

"That makes two of us, Joseph," the Vice President responded, dispensing with protocol and using the Senator's first name. They had known each other for years, fished together, and dined together with their families. "And that is despite the oath I've taken to defend the Constitution and to do my duty to the best of my ability to preserve the Union," he added. "There is no one in this room who hasn't taken a similar oath as far as I know. Perhaps I should remind everyone that the main purpose of this facility is to preserve the Government of the United States in an emergency. I think the events that are about to transpire more than qualify."

"So we're trapped here?" someone called out from the floor.

The Vice President looked out into the audience trying to find the culprit and then to Batter, but the crowd maintained order, so he decided to reply.

"The asteroid is expected to create an explosion that is on the order of several hundred-thousand nuclear bombs all detonating at once. I believe this has all been covered during earlier briefings with most of you," he said wearily. "In a few hours, there will not be much to go home to. In fact, it might be impossible just to take a breath of air."

The Vice President had chosen to ignore the other possible interpretation of the question, the one that was likely intended. "Do you have enough men and guns to keep us here at all?"

There was another rumble in the room, but it quieted.

The Vice President recognized a raised hand. It was a freshman Congresswoman that he did not know.

"Sandy Miller from Mississippi, Mr. Vice President," she said with a heavy southern accent. "I have two questions, Mr. Vice President. How long will we have to stay down here, and how long for goodness sake can you keep us? I mean, there are an awful lot of folks here," she said, looking around the room.

"I wish I could answer the first question, but, we do not know. There are monitors on the surface and we have the ability to send out teams in special gear to report on conditions. Regarding the second question, we are provisioned for twenty-five years, but we also have the ability to produce our own food supply and we have power for, well, let's just say well beyond anyone's lifetime. So the answer really is 'indefinitely.'"

The room erupted in conversation and chatter, and the Vice President was forced to rap the gavel again to restore order. "We will have another meeting at 1730 hours to inform you further of the situation. Until then, we are adjourned."

The doors to the chamber were opened and people scrambled to get out. Alex and Tom watched from the balcony, afraid to move lest they be trampled. The fear was so thick it would have taken a diamond blade to cut through it.

She looked down towards Batter and their eyes met again. He gestured, indicating that he was ready to meet. She could see Pete was already standing near Batter.

"Thanks, Batter," the Vice President said as he was leaving the room, "that was close."

"You're welcome. I'm surprised no one asked the most obvious question," Batter said.

"Oh yeah, what's that?"

"Why the hell the President isn't here?"

CHAPTER 35

Tom's Big Idea

Alex and Tom located Batter and Pete, and the four of them pulled off into a small conference room that was near the main chamber.

"Well, Dr. Moss," Batter said as they sat down, "what did you think about the meeting we just had with those people?"

Alex knew that she had pretty much lost the argument of trying to save the Arzats based on the behavior she had just witnessed. Batter was correct, the Arzats didn't stand a chance in this environment, probably not in the short term, certainly not in the long term.

"Scary," was all she could think to say.

"Exactly," said Batter, looking at all of them, "and they haven't even gotten started. I predict that before the end of the day we will already have some of them incarcerated. Hell, we might even have to shoot someone, who knows?" he continued, quite clearly not entirely kidding. "Honestly, Alex, Pete, I wish there were something I could do but the situation…," he stopped himself, raising his hands off the table in a gesture of hopelessness.

Batter had thought about just conceding after the news last night. What did it really matter? In a few hours it would probably be all over for all of them. But, there was still a chance the asteroid might miss. Then what? He knew he was grasping at straws, but it was still *his* responsibility.

"Well, regardless," Alex fought back, "I am not leaving them." She turned to Tom, "Tom, I'm not leaving them. I'm sorry. I love you, but I'm not leaving them, whatever happens."

"I know," Tom said, looking lovingly into to her fiery green eyes. He turned back toward Batter. "You *can* help us."

Batter craned his neck and looked back at Tom, sizing him up.

"I don't see how Tom," he replied, obviously annoyed.

Before this morning's call, Batter had no intention of letting Alex or Tom stay out of the ARC. He would have drugged them, or shot them, or beat the crap out of them, but he had not been about to leave them outside.

"You can let us go," Tom said, looking Batter directly in the eye.

"Hah," Batter responded, surprised. "Look it, Tom, there is no place to go! *Haven't you heard?*" he said, not able to completely hide his total frustration.

Be careful, he thought, you are losing it old boy. Batter found it to be an interesting self-admission. He could not remember ever experiencing such a loss of control before.

"Might I also remind you, there is not just one asteroid on the way. There are *two!*"

"Utah," Tom said.

"Utah," Batter repeated, still irritated, and waved his hand. "I shut the whole thing down Tom. It's not finished. It's a lost cause. There is nothing there. You, of all people, should know that."

Batter was still smarting from his utter failure at the Utah site, and a part of him considered Tom as the reason.

Tom looked over at Alex and Pete, and then back to Batter.

"Batter, I know the place like a book. It is already provisioned and it's almost ready to go. Hell, we could live for years. The place is stocked with supplies for hundreds of people."

"Of course!" Alex chimed in. "Utah!" She squeezed Tom's arm. Why the heck hadn't he just told me?

Batter sat and carefully considered what Tom had said. Actually, it wasn't a bad idea. Maybe Tom wasn't such a dumb shit after all—except.

"Interesting idea Tom, but there is a problem," he said.

"What's that?" Tom said, suddenly worried that Batter was not going to give them permission to go. He immediately started to consider how they could fight their way out.

"The breach? Your little paleontological hole in the wall? I don't think they contained it. The place is not airtight Tom," Batter said testing him, having already thought of a solution.

"I'll fix it if it's not," was all Tom could come up with.

Bingo, thought Batter. Maybe you weren't my worst mistake after all Tom.

He glanced at Alex who had been watching Tom as he spoke, the look of absolute love in her eyes unmistakable. Tom had definitely gotten one thing right, Batter thought, with no small amount of envy.

"Look, Batter, I know Alex, and when she says she is not leaving the Arzats, she means it. And I am not leaving her. So we are both dead anyway if we stay here. At least give us a chance."

No, we are *all* dead if we stay here, Batter thought. He began to think of who he could send with them. Was there any point? Send them with a few pissed off politicians? Himself? No.

He checked his watch. It was past 1300 hours. Just over four hours to go. The ARC was going to begin the three-hour process of lock down at 1400. Regardless, they barely had enough time to make it themselves.

Decide Batter, decide, he told himself.

He looked at Alex and Tom and then turned to Pete Wilson.

"Pete?" he inquired, obviously asking if he wanted to go with them.

Pete had already considered that option as he sat and listened, but his family would be gone soon and his only point in living past that was his duty to Batter and his own staff at the ARC.

"No, I'm staying. Too much to do here," he said with a fake smile. He knew Batter would have already considered going as well, but would be staying for the same reasons.

Batter checked his watch again.

"Well then," he finally said, rising up, "I guess if you are going to go, then you'd better get on it."

Batter found himself suddenly liking Tom very much, although he still was not exactly sure why.

"I'll go see about getting that Chinook warmed up for you, the one you chased down earlier. I'd give you something faster but I evacuated all of the other aircraft to the East Coast. You'd better hurry—you only have 49 minutes," he said, checking his watch.

* * *

They were racing down the hall. Pete was with them guiding them back to the enclosure.

"Pete, did you say you thought that you had the cryo problem worked out?" Alex asked, out of breath from running.

"Yes, as a matter fact, I just met with the lab techs working on it. That glycerin we identified is fantastic. It seems to perfectly preserve cell tissue with absolutely no crystallization. We think it must be from a now extinct plant species, but the good news is that it was fairly easy to synthesize. We just prepared a large batch of it to experiment with on some primates, but I'm almost certain it's going to work. Too bad, though."

"Why's that?" asked Alex.

"The main bank of cryo units is in…" he stopped himself and looked at Alex. "Utah," Pete said, surprised at his own answer.

"I love you, Alex, but I'm not going to go in *any* cryo unit with you," Tom said, overhearing the conversation as they rushed down the corridors.

"It's always good to have a Plan B, Tom," she said to him over her shoulder. "Pete, think you can get me enough for four units before we get out of here?"

"I'll do my best."

* * *

Mot and Ara were sitting together in silent conversation when the three of them arrived.

Alex looked at both of them and knew instantly what had gone on the night before. The Arzats were beaming, but there was no time to talk.

"We're leaving," she blurted out, still gasping from the trip over.

Mot and Ara instantly got up.

"Where are we going, Alex?" Mot asked.

"Somewhere we can all be safe. Very near the caves where I found you."

Ara was unaccustomed to any female exerting so much authority and her defenses were immediately raised. Mot had explained everything about Alex to her, and it was clear that this little female, human or not, was potential competition for his affections, species differences notwithstanding. She relaxed when she searched Alex for any ulterior motives, and could find none.

"Why will Pete not join us?" she said, realizing she had given away the fact that she had probed Alex's mind. Alex had said nothing about Pete not going.

Alex simply looked at her. She knew she could not afford a confrontation with a jealous teenager at this point, especially one three times her size.

"I cannot go with you, Ara," Pete said, trying to save the situation. "My duty is to this place. But Tom and Alex will take good care of you."

Ara looked at Alex, then Tom, and finally back to Pete. "This makes me sad, Pete son of Robert. But we certainly understand duty."

"When are we leaving Alex?" Mot asked.

"Right now, we only have a few minutes," she answered, looking at Ara, directly in her golden eyes. I must have Mot teach me how to block, she thought.

"I will teach you, Alex daughter of Simon," Ara said, a smile in her voice. "This, I think, will be very necessary for us to survive each other."

"How will we get there?" Mot asked.

"I'm going to fly you," Tom answered.

"But that is not possible," Mot said, obviously having no recollection of his earlier experience in the Chinook.

Tom looked at his 65-million-year-old new-found friend and almost burst into laughter. "You're right," was all he could come up with.

* * *

The ARC was in the process of staged final lockdown. Personnel were rushing down corridors, checking last minute details, as they had in hundreds of drills, the look on their faces somber and determined. This, they now knew, was no drill.

Pete stepped out of the enclosure first, with Alex and Tom behind him, followed by Mot and Ara and two of Pete's own security personnel bearing assault rifles. Batter said he would do his best to clear the corridors, but there was simply too much activity for this to have really happened. They had considered trying to disguise the two Arzats, but their enormous size made it impossible, and, there was no time.

As the seven of them made their way down the through the long corridors people were stopping in their tracks and hugging the walls, some in curiosity and some in total fear.

Who could blame them, Alex thought, smiling inside as she pictured what they must look like to the uninitiated, as they hurried for the elevators.

When they neared the labs, Pete peeled off from the group and disappeared.

"T minus 30 minutes to perimeter lockdown," a synthetic voice announced over the loud speakers as they boarded the elevator. It was an automated ARC shut down warning.

* * *

As Batter had promised, the Chinook's blades were already rotating when they finally made the surface.

Mot and Ara were petrified when they first saw the giant helicopter, but Alex talked them through their fear enough to get them on board and buckled in.

Tom was in the cockpit, strapping on a helmet and getting some last minute instructions from another pilot.

Pete approached the helicopter door and held up a bag. "Here it is Alex. Guard it with your life. There is a disc in there with instructions and a full program for the cryo computer."

"Thanks, Pete," she said gratefully. "How confident are you this stuff will work?"

"See those two?" he said, indicating Mot and Ara. "It's *their* recipe." Pete smiled at Alex and winked.

Ara sat watching. She was sorry she had not had time to say a more formal goodbye.

Pete looked up at her and smiled. "I hear you, Ara daughter of the great Hunter Zan. I will miss you."

"And I, you, Peter son of Robert," she replied with great respect.

Ara was suddenly aware of the fact that this was the last time she would ever see him. He was a good hu-man, this Pete.

Alex really didn't know why, but she was surprised when she saw Batter appear on the tarmac. He was standing at a distance, watching.

"I'll be right back," she said to Mot and Ara. She jumped off the helicopter and rushed over to him, embracing him. "You know what, for a complete and total asshole, you turned out to be a pretty nice guy," she said directly into his ear.

Batter stood there, stunned, his hands to his sides. Then finally, he lifted his arms and hugged her back. It was for him, one of the most pleasurable moments of his life.

"Good luck Alex," was all he could manage.

"You too, 'Mister' Batter. Don't worry about me. I am a very lucky girl," she said, winking at him and holding up the crossed fingers of her right hand. Alex started back toward the helicopter and then turned. "Hey, I don't think you ever told me your first name," she screamed over the roar of the chopper blades.

"Don't worry about it, Doctor," Batter said, screaming back, smiling at her, "no one ever uses it anyway."

Alex climbed back aboard and shut the door. Tom gave Batter a thumbs up from the cockpit and expertly lifted the Chinook off the ground, spinning it to the northeast.

Batter stood and watched as the helicopter gained altitude and eventually disappeared over the horizon. He felt a tug on his shoulder.

"Come on," said Pete, "we've got to go before we're locked out."

CHAPTER 36

The Back Door

I t had taken over three hours to make the flight.

Tom nervously watched the digital clock in the cockpit clicking off the minutes as they made their way back into Utah, willing the Chinook to go faster, fighting unexpected headwinds.

Beneath him, the terrain was mostly desert and lots of open land criss-crossed by an occasional highway with very few cars on the road. He tried not to think about the panic that was undoubtedly ensuing below. From his current vantage point, the world seemed no different.

When they passed through to MST, Tom adjusted the clock and his wrist-watch to the new time zone. He could not afford to make a mistake. There would not be a minute to spare.

Alex stayed in the back, trying to comfort Mot and Ara as much as pos-sible. The Arzats had both been stoic, clutching each other's hands the entire time, never relaxing. Alex tried to assure both of them about the overall safety record of flight, but neither one of them seemed to be buying her story, even though they knew she was telling the absolute truth. They looked better when she finally announced that they were almost there.

Alex left them and climbed up into the cockpit with Tom, throwing on some headphones in the process so she could talk to him without screaming.

"What do you think?" she said, noticing that they were almost directly over the site.

"Looks like Batter was right. The main door is sealed and the place looks deserted. I guess we'll just have to get down there and see. He gave me all of the emergency access codes but I'm starting to wonder if we are going to make it Alex," he said, not looking at her, knowing how much she frowned on any negativity.

Tom knew it would take at least half an hour to get the huge main door open, but he was most worried about getting it closed again. He was trying to remember how long it had taken when they had tested it. The cockpit clock read 1743. They had thirty four minutes. There was no way.

"We'll make it," she said, patting him on the shoulder.

As Tom brought the chopper in for landing he noticed a familiar pickup parked outside the main control room.

What is Andy doing here, he wondered, worried.

He landed and quickly unstrapped himself and tossed off his helmet, purposely leaving the helicopter's engines running—his years of military training taking over. It was protocol never to shut down your aircraft before you knew an area was safe and secure.

"Alex, stay here for a minute, would you? I'll be right back."

Alex looked at him curiously, but figured this was no time to bug him with a bunch of questions.

Tom climbed out of the Chinook and ran over towards the control room. Andy met him at the door.

"Tom, what in the hell are you doing here?" Andy said, looking curiously out at the chopper, its blades still spinning.

"Same to you, my friend," Tom responded, glad to see his familiar face.

Andy shrugged, "Batter put me in charge of closing the place down, and, well, I've got really nowhere else to go. Seems like this is as good a place as any to watch the world end," he said, obviously aware of the news.

"Well, did you think about maybe going inside?" Tom asked more sarcastically than he meant to, gesturing towards the ARC.

Andy looked at him thoughtfully for a moment. "It's not for me, Tom. I get claustrophobic enough when the doors are open."

"Andy," he said, grabbing both of the man's shoulders, "Alex is alive. She's in the chopper. We need to get in."

Andy smiled and then his face darkened. "That's great Tom, but…" he said, checking his watch, "I'd never be able to get the main door open for you and then shut back down in time. That thing takes forever. And don't forget, there is another huge lock out at the bottom of the ramp."

"What about the emergency exits?" Tom said, having completely forgotten about the second interior door.

A frown crossed Andy's face. "Tom, don't you remember the big argument we had with the designers? The exits only work from the inside. There is no way to access them from the exterior. We'd have to cut through a couple inches of solid steel."

"Andy, did you guys seal the entrance to the caves?" Tom asked, looking for another way, knowing he was making a life or death decision.

"Well, we were working on it when Batter called us off. I gotta tell you, Tom," he said, scratching his head under his cap. "I'm not sure. We got the last reactor in, but the boys ran out of here so fast, I never did get a briefing on their progress with the breach."

"Did you get the caves pumped out?"

"Yeah, dry as a bone as far as I know. Never did find Alex. Now I know why," Andy said, smiling again.

"Is there any heavy equipment still inside?"

"Well, as I said, the boys ran out as quick as they could. So, maybe," Andy said, looking around the large construction area.

"How about gear? Where did you put the gear those scientists were using?"

"Oh, that stuff is still in the back of my truck. Never did take it out."

There is a god, thought Tom, but he's a mean bastard.

He ran to the back of Andy's truck and grabbed a couple of flashlights and a long climbing rope. Tom remembered Alex's story about the crevasse. This is going to have to be enough, he thought.

"Andy, sure you won't come along?"

He shook his head. "Never fancied living underground like a rat. No offense, Tom," Andy said.

"None taken," Tom said, forcing a smile.

Tom wanted to say more, but there just was not time. He said goodbye to Andy and ran for the chopper, dumping the gear in as he passed through toward the cockpit. He avoided Mot and Ara, knowing they were going to be very upset when he took off again.

"Alex, do you remember where you came out of the caves?" he said as he strapped himself into the pilot seat.

"I think I could find it. Why?"

"Looks like we are going to have go in through the back door," he said, running up the throttles on the Chinook's huge turbines.

Come on baby, Tom thought, willing the giant helicopter off the ground.

The clock turned to 1800. They had seventeen minutes.

"Alex, go back and calm down Mot and Ara. We're just going to the area where you and Mot came out. Tell them to be ready to run when we land and then get back up here."

"Got it," Alex said, throwing off her headset.

"Wait," Tom grabbed her arm, "which way?"

Alex scanned the countryside, knowing that she could not make a mistake.

"There," she said squinting to see, recognizing her canyon. The sun was about to set, just lingering on the horizon above the site.

She headed to the back and passed Tom's message to Mot and Ara, which was met by frightened silence. By the time she returned to the cockpit, Tom was practically over her original dig site.

"That's it," she said pointing down.

"Are you sure?" Tom said, eyeing the narrow canyon.

"Yes, I'm sure," she said, recognizing the boulder Mot had placed on the spot where they buried the escaped prisoners, her pulse quickening from the thought of her altercation with them.

Tom swooped down into the abyss, maneuvering between the solid walls of rock the best he could, but the rear rotor caught part of the mountain. It screeched sickeningly as steel struck stone and pitched the chopper sideways.

"Hold on Alex," Tom said with a fantastic note of calm as he fought the controls. He managed to get the helicopter almost completely upright before it hit the ground hard, snapping the legs off the landing skids. The main rotors bit into the desert throwing sand and rock until they finally lost momentum and stopped.

"Not your best landing, Thomas," Alex said, when the chopper had stopped moving, amazed again that she was still alive. She looked back and could see that Mot and Ara appeared to be unharmed as well. They were wide-eyed, but okay.

"You should have seen my last one," Tom replied matter-of-factly, tossing off his helmet, preparing to exit. He glanced for a last time at the clock.

It had just turned to 1811. Seven minutes.

"Sorry about that landing guys," Tom said as he helped Alex get Mot and Ara unbuckled. They looked white as sheets beneath their reptilian skin but said nothing.

"Alex, grab as much gear as you can and let's go. We've got to hurry."

"Roger that," she said, appreciating Tom's statement of the obvious. She was madly in love with him all over again and scared to death they were not going to make it.

As they emerged from the helicopter, the canyon walls had already grown dark grey in the dusk. Mot and Ara instinctively sniffed the air for danger, still trying to shake the effects of the horrible fumes from the helicopter fuel, their bodies adjusting to solid ground.

"Mot, we need to get to the entrance," Alex said to him.

"This way," Mot said.

"Ne," Ara said aloud. She grabbed Mot's hand and stopped him as he started forward. "I smell death here, Mot," she said, concerned.

Mot had sniffed out the odor as well, remembering the two humans.

"Never mind, it poses no danger. I have been here before," he said, carefully blocking the recollection of the event from Ara.

He could see the cave entrance as they started up the hill and naturally broke into a swift trot, bounding effortlessly over the terrain.

When he was halfway, Mot turned and realized that Tom and Alex had fallen back. Mot had no real sense of how much time they had, but his instincts told him that there was not much.

"Ara, we must help the humans. They are too slow."

"How?" she said, looking back down the path.

"I suppose we will have to carry them," he shrugged.

Ara looked at him doubtfully, but she knew he was correct. She turned to follow Mot back down the hill.

Tom and Alex were shocked to see the two Arzats running back towards them at full speed. It seemed impossible that they could have stopped when they reached them.

Mot turned his back to Tom. "Climb on, Tom son of Richard, or I fear we shall not make it."

Tom threw the climbing rope over his shoulder and handed two flashlights to Mot.

"This is embarrassing," he said as he hoisted himself up. Mot's back was rock solid. It was like climbing on a Brahma bull.

No sooner was he on than the Arzat took off faster than any horse he had ever ridden, and Tom struggled to hold his grip.

Ara watched, shaking her head. She swept Alex up into her arms like one would a small child, and set off after Mot, determined to beat him to the caves. Though the terrain was strange and barren, she sensed she was almost home.

Ara managed to set Alex down just as Mot arrived with Tom. She had somehow passed Mot, although Alex had no recollection of it. Neither of the Arzats seemed winded, while she and Tom had to bend over to catch their own breath just from the ride up.

Tom managed a look at his wristwatch, still bent over. They had two minutes left. They had made it.

"Oh my god," cried Alex. "I forgot Pete's cryo bag! The canisters!"

Tom was not concerned, even a bit relieved. "Alex, we don't need them. I told you," he said, beginning to recover.

"Yes, we do, Tom," she said, obstinate.

"I will go," Mot said, not wishing to waste any more time, remembering the bag Pete had given to Alex. Even on the surface of her mind, it was clear to Mot that the bag was important to Alex. As he turned to go, he saw Ara was already halfway down the path.

"Stay where you are, Mot son of Url," he could hear her saying as she ran, her beautiful long legs carrying her easily down the mountain. "There is no future for me without you."

Ara remembered the bag as well. If Doctor Pete thought it was important, that was good enough for her.

She reached the helicopter and found the bag, mildly irritated at Alex for forgetting it in the first place, and headed back toward the cave, managing to run faster uphill than she had down. When she was almost to the top, she stopped, dead in her tracks.

Ara had smelled it and heard it before her sharp eyes had seen it. A rattle snake had slithered onto the path and was blocking her way. Ara was very familiar with snakes, they could be delicious or deadly depending on the circumstances, but she knew she had no time for this one either way.

The snake was poised to strike, just beyond the range of Ara's powerful legs, its black reptilian eyes boring into hers. Ara spread the mantle on the back of her head and flicked her tongue as a challenge. The snake continued to look at her, sizing her up, then quickly lowered its head and moved on.

As they watched from above, Ara's movements had been so swift that Tom and Alex had a hard time following her with their eyes.

Why had she stopped?

Mot was just about to go after her when, miraculously, she had continued toward them. One minute to go, Tom thought, looking at his watch as Ara reached the entrance for the second time. Impossible.

Ara held out the bag to Alex, hardly breathing, a look of triumph behind her reptilian eyes.

"Thank you, Ara," was all Alex could say.

A strange stillness filled the air. The desert had become mysteriously silent. It was as if movement of any kind had become impossible. The sky had grown orange as twilight began to take over the early evening. Mot and Ara instinctively sniffed and flicked their tongues.

"It is happening," Ara said.

A streak of light passed over them, heading southwest, a shooting star before day had completely turned to night. It lasted less than a second before its path merged with the horizon.

Mot and Ara were the first to feel the ground shudder. A great light gradually emerged that was as bright as any sunrise they had ever witnessed, throwing a million trails of fire high into the evening sky.

All of them knew they needed to go, yet none of them were able to take their eyes off of the spectacular light.

"Come on," Tom finally said, tugging on Alex.

As they turned, Mot remembered the cave door. "Ara, help me."

* * *

Mot and Ara easily rolled the ancient stone back into place as Tom and Alex watched the last natural light they might ever see disappear around its edges. The door snapped into its 65 million year old cradle with an ominous groan of finality.

Tom switched on the two flashlights he had brought and handed one of them to Mot.

"Do you remember the way?" he asked.

"Of course," Mot said, happy to finally be back on his own turf regardless of the circumstances. "Follow me."

Mot led them down the stone corridor that eventually put them in the Great Chamber. He looked up at the small opening that the Arzats had formerly used to let out the smoke from the fires expecting to see light, but the sky was completely black and he could smell fresh ash in the air.

Ara stopped next to him, able to see everything in the room just from the ambient light that was cast from the human's magic torches.

It saddened her to see the Great Chamber, once so alive with Arzats, now so cold and empty. She remembered the sweet white sand that Pete had shown her when he was trying to explain the passage of time. The full weight of his lesson began sinking in as she looked around the deserted room. It was no longer home.

"Which way?" she asked Mot, anxious to move on, sniffing the ash.

As Tom panned his own light, he could see the gaping holes of several tunnels that branched off and he was glad that Mot was there to lead them. They looked like giant mouths ready to devour the four of them.

"There," Mot said, pointing his light in the direction of one of the openings.

As they left the Great Chamber, Ara looked back one more time. For a moment, she almost thought she could hear the echo of a group of Arzat Hunters.

* * *

They began to descend the long series of switchbacks and stone stairways that Alex and Mot had climbed to escape the caves just days before, the Arzats moving slowly so the humans could keep up.

Mot and Ara could see perfectly, but Alex and Tom were limited to just what they could detect of the steep terrain in the direct beam of the flashlights. Alex slipped and almost fell on several occasions but Tom had been there to catch her. He had offered his arm which she had refused, preferring to walk on her own.

When they reached the crevasse, Mot easily crawled down into it, performing a monumental leap from one side to the other when he was only half way down. He scrambled up the other side effortlessly.

"Show off," Tom said quietly with no malice. He shook his head, amazed at the Arzat now standing thirty feet across from him as if by magic.

"I do not understand 'show off,' Tom son of Robert,'" Mot said innocently. "Now, Tom, please tie the cord around Alex. Ara will lower her to the same place, the flat spot there," he said, pointing down.

"Then what?" Alex said, already worried.

"Then Alex," Mot continued patiently, "Ara will throw me the cord and I will pull you up."

Alex knew the maneuver would force her to have to swing across the crevasse, but it was all the rope they had. Tom carefully tied it just under Alex's arms and gave the other end of the rope to Ara. Alex stepped over the edge, almost immediately losing her footing, and slipped awkwardly down to the outcropping, slowed by the tension of Ara's grip on the rope.

"Do not worry, Alex, daughter of Simon, I will not drop you," she heard Ara say inside her head.

When she was safely on the ledge, Ara tossed the rope to Mot, who snatched it easily. He wrapped it around his wrist, and beckoned Alex to swing across. Tom was doing his best with the flashlight, but she would be forced to jump into almost total darkness. She grabbed the rope with both hands and prepared to launch.

"No, Alex," Mot cautioned, "hold your hands and legs out, they will protect you from the rock."

"Oh shit," Alex thought as she released her hold on the rope, sure she would slip through.

"Now or never Alex," she could hear old Simon whispering in her ear. "Damn you, Simon," she answered.

Alex threw her arms apart and stepped off, closing her eyes despite the low light. She hit the wall on the other side much more softly than she had anticipated, and by the time she got her bearings, Mot had already pulled her to the top.

"Very good, Alex daughter of Simon," Mot said approvingly as he untied her.

He tossed the rope back to Ara and they repeated the whole process—Tom with the climbing rope and Ara easily making the same spectacular leap that Mot had done earlier—until all four of them stood on the other side of the crevasse.

Tom had not gone into detail about the pumping of the caves, so Mot and

Alex were both very relieved when they found them dry, realizing that they would not have to swim through them again.

They eventually reached the chamber where Mot and Ara had been asleep all of those years, Alex explaining exactly how she had found Mot and pointing to the area where Ara had been as they passed through.

As they began to climb back up the original tunnel that Tom and Alex had taken down, the earth shook violently. They all fell to their knees and instinctively covered, but the shaking stopped, and the caves miraculously held together.

"Aftershock?" Alex asked Tom when the caves had quieted.

"Let's hope," he replied, getting back up and dusting himself off. He offered Alex his hand.

"What do you mean?"

"I hope it's not a 'before' shock," Tom said, panning his flashlight overhead, looking for cracks in the stone. "Come on, we need to get to the ARC."

CHAPTER 37

Welcome To My Cave

The four of them stood in the small chamber, looking at the several hundred tons of rock and stone that had been shoved into the entrance.

Tom's worst fears were coming true. It appeared as though his crew had managed to seal the breach in the ARC from the other side after all. If that were the case, then they were not only facing having to dig through the mountain of debris in front of them, but there might be several thousand cubic feet of cement and aluminum rebar already drying on the other side.

His heart stopped just thinking about it. Their little foray to the safety of the Utah ARC might just be over. He began to think he had made a huge mistake.

"What's wrong, Tom?" Alex said, watching his reaction.

"I don't know, Alex. It doesn't look good," was all he could say, panning his flashlight over the pile of boulders.

Mot stepped up onto one of the larger rocks and looked around. "What is the problem, Tom?" he asked, sniffing the air and flicking his tongue.

Tom just kept looking.

Ara, concerned, had once again probed deeper into Tom's mind than she should have.

"He's saying we are trapped," she said, her eyes narrowing. After coming all this way, they were trapped, she thought. Her future with Mot, which she had been contemplating with great joy, was suddenly doomed. No way forward and now, because of this human-Tom's bad judgment, no way back.

Alex looked over at her, upset that Ara had obviously probed Tom's mind. The two exchanged glances.

"Well, it's not Tom's fault," Alex said, irritated.

Ara stared at Alex, her eyes almost glowing in the dark, resenting her and all of the rest of the humans who had put her in this predicament.

"You should just have left us alone," she finally said, her anger turning into sorrow.

"Ara," Mot said, jumping down from the stone he had been standing on, "remember, we are Zanta. Where are your manners?"

Ara immediately realized that Mot was correct.

In the Arzat culture, particularly in the Zanta clan, it was considered an atrocity to disrespect an elder in any way. Ara wasn't sure how that applied to humans, but it certainly applied to the opinion of her male mate who had just pointed out her fault.

"I am sorry, Mot," she said, her head hanging. She turned to Tom and Alex. "Please, forgive me. I know you have done all you can."

Mot reached out and gently lifted Ara's chin. "Can you not smell it?" he asked her, a hopeful look in his eyes.

Ara sniffed the air deeply, flicking her tongue in the process, examining all of the elements. She looked at Mot and her eyes opened wide. "Yes, Mot son of Url, I smell it."

"Smell what?" Tom asked.

"Your cave Tom, your cave!" Mot said, turning back to him. "And I smell meat, lots and lots of meat!"

Mot scrambled up easily over the large pile of rocks, his nose working in tandem with his tongue, searching for the source of the delicious smell. He was very hungry. It had been hours since they had eaten.

"I have found it," he eventually said. A large rock, wedged between the top of the pile and the stone ceiling, was the only thing blocking his way. Mot jammed his feet securely against it, using the rocks behind him for leverage, and kicked the boulder back into the darkness on the other side. His nostrils filled with the scent of food.

Mot led his three companions over the rubble, through the small opening he had created, and down into the ARC.

Tom was able to locate the main control room, and they all watched as he threw switches and gradually powered the place up, until the entire facility was lit like a small city.

"That should do for now," he said, looking around proudly at his creation.

The Utah ARC had been designed much differently than the Nevada site. The Area 51 ARC was much older, and consisted only of a series of many rooms linked by miles of corridors. Tom's ARC was wide open, with bright white buildings and actual streets. It had been built to house fifteen hundred souls. Eventually, the other three ARCs, including Nevada, were to have been replaced by this new design.

It looks like a snow globe that I had as a child, thought Alex.

Ara and Mot gazed at the white city, speechless.

"Welcome to *my* cave," Tom said proudly to all of them, immensely relieved. "Now, let's go see about some dinner."

Tom led them to one of the commissaries that, like some in Nevada, had been built to resemble a restaurant. Among his many talents, he was a very skilled chef, having pulled more than his fair share of shifts in the military mess halls for his occasional minor acts of insubordination.

He pulled out 20 pounds of rib eye steaks from one of the massive freezers in the restaurant kitchen and proceeded to thaw them while he prepared instant mash potatoes and several cans of vegetables. He resolved to attempt to get the ARC's hydroponic farm going as he opened the last container and dumped it into a pot.

Tom wasn't quite sure about the Arzat's dietary preferences aside from meat, but he thought, what the heck, might as well find out.

While Tom prepared dinner, he sent the Arzats and Alex out on a reconnaissance mission to see if they could spot any heavy equipment and to select quarters. By the time they returned he had set one of the restaurant tables and laid out his massive feast, complete with artificial candlelight that was flickering in white glass. He turned on some background music and ceremoniously invited them to sit down.

"We could have helped you," Alex said, taking a seat, secretly glad that Tom hadn't asked. It felt so good to sit that she immediately wondered if she would ever be able to rise.

Ara was initially quite confused by the chairs and watched Alex closely before she tried hers, sure that it would collapse beneath her.

"What do you think?" Alex asked once they were seated.

"Quite comfortable," Mot said, his eyes fixed on the large platter of steaks.

"We can move to the floor if you wish," Alex suggested, embarrassed that she might have put Ara in a very awkward position.

"No," said Ara quickly, "thank you." She was determined to try the human way, including the strange metal tools they used to feed themselves.

* * *

"Well, Alex, did you have any luck?" Tom said as they were finishing dinner, referring to the heavy equipment he had sent her to find.

Alex fished in her pocket and threw a pack of cigarettes on the table in front of her.

"What's that tell you?" she said, beaming. "Matches too," she smiled, holding up a book of them between her fingers.

"Alex, I thought you quit," Tom said.

"Oh, come on Tom, after all we've been through. Heck, there's only half a pack here and when they're gone they're gone. I didn't see any mini marts around this place, I can tell you that, but there is one big-ass loader parked over by the main ramp," she added, smiling.

Tom wasn't about to argue with her. Alex did what she wanted. That was how it had always been, and he liked it that way. He just looked at her, happily defeated.

He still couldn't believe their luck. The loader would make the job of sealing the ARC about a million times easier.

"Mot, we have one more thing to do tonight that I don't think can wait," Tom said to the huge Arzat who had just polished off several pounds of meat.

Mot had very much enjoyed the dinner Tom had prepared. He had never seen a male cook anything in his life. These humans are so odd, he thought. Now that his stomach was full he was eager to return the favor.

"How can I help, Tom son of Richard?"

"We need to go and plug that hole in the wall you knocked out. How are you at operating heavy equipment?" Tom said, reaching up to pat the shoulder of the huge Arzat.

The two males left the room and Alex and Ara found themselves suddenly alone with each other for the very first time. The silence was deafening with the exception of some classical music playing lightly in the background.

Alex didn't know if the music was Beethoven or Bach. The only classical composer she could readily identify was Mozart, who had been her father's favorite and was hers.

"What do you call this sound?" Ara asked.

Oh my god, she's reading my mind again, thought Alex. She glanced at Ara.

"I am sorry, Alex, it is too easy," Ara said, embarrassed, as if it simply were not her fault.

"Don't worry about it." Alex poured a half inch of water into a short glass to use as an ashtray and fired up a cigarette, blowing the smoke luxuriously into the room. "We call it 'music.'"

The aroma of Alex's cigarette was actually quite pleasant, thought Ara. It vaguely reminded her of the Great Chamber. "We too have such a thing, like this 'music' as you call it, although we must have Arzats to create it. The sound is different... yet much the same."

Alex let the comment pass, as much as she was interested. She wished Tom and Mot would hurry and get back so she could go to bed. She could feel her eyes getting heavy.

"I am sorry, Alex," Ara said again.

"Why are you so sorry, Ara?" Alex scolded her. "You have been through, well, I cannot even imagine."

"I am sorry for my behavior in the cave. Mot was correct. In my culture, you would have every right to kill me or banish me. It is an atrocity to show such disrespect to an elder. I'm afraid I was overcome with, something I think you humans call 'emotion.'"

Alex couldn't help but laugh. "Well, I certainly have no intention of killing or banishing you. We females have to stick together now, don't we?" she said, liking Ara again very much. "And," she added, "I am *not* your elder."

"Oh, yes," Ara said. "Mot has told me of your many seasons. You are almost as old as my mother."

"Ouch." Alex looked at Ara closely, squinting over her cigarette, sizing her up. "Okay, what is still bothering you?"

"I have conceived Alex. Mot and I have conceived," Ara finally said, as if she were afraid to admit it.

Alex almost choked on her cigarette. She looked at it scornfully, and threw it in the glass of water. "You are going to have a child? Already?"

"Yes, Alex," Ara said, her eyes now glowing.

"How long, I mean, how…, er?" Alex stammered.

"Several," Ara hesitated, "several of your 'weeks' for the egg, then several more for the child. A half of one season."

Alex rose from the table and approached Ara. She dropped to her knees and put her arms around Ara's massive midsection. She stayed that way for a long time then looked up at the female Arzat.

"Now, so we can survive each other, will you teach me how to block?"

* * *

When Tom and Mot had finally returned, the couples headed for the quarters they had chosen, which were close but not too close to each other.

Tom was able to turn off the obnoxious automatic timer on the shower for Alex, and she had stayed in it for a very long time. When she came out, she approached Tom aggressively and made love to him until they were both exhausted and fell asleep in each other's arms.

CHAPTER 38

Cross Your Fingers

For the next few weeks, their lives were like a holiday. Tom taught Mot the game of tennis and Mot began to beat him severely within a few days of his first lesson. Alex and Ara commiserated about the baby Arzat and began making plans for a nursery.

Ara had been very curious about Alex's clothing, and they had spent a good deal of time fashioning some things for Ara to wear. Eventually, the two of them had convinced Mot to join in, although he still preferred his loincloth. Shoes, of course, were out of the question.

Alex had recently developed a glow of her own, and although she hadn't said anything yet, Tom began to wonder if she too, was pregnant. If so, he thought, he would find out soon enough. He was smart enough not to ask.

The four of them would have long dinners where Tom and Alex would tell the Arzats about everything human, and Mot and Ara would describe everything Arzat.

The Arzats marveled at human technology, and the humans marveled at the complexities of the strict Arzat culture, as well as the extremely dangerous world they had come from.

When Mot had told them the story about the night he had slain the dreaded beast, Alex couldn't help but wonder if the creature he had killed was not the very same dinosaur she had found in front of the caves.

Mot, of course, was ecstatic about his soon-to-be child. He told Tom that, if it were male, he would teach the child to hunt and all the ways of the Arzats. If it were female, then, well, he would leave the matter to Ara and Alex.

Tom would just nod and shake his head, not wishing to remind Mot that their hunting days were over, praying for a female.

Mot had described his hunting stick to Tom in detail and had questioned Tom intensely about the 'fire sticks' of the humans. Tom considered actually showing Mot the arsenal, but refrained when Alex had asked him not to.

"The last thing I want to see in here is a gun, Thomas," she told him sternly. "I have had enough of them and I would think you had too."

For the most part, he and Alex tried not to imagine what might be happening on the surface. None of the video monitors worked, but the atmospheric sensors continued to function, and Tom found himself checking them often. The carbon monoxide and carbon dioxide levels were astronomically high on the surface, and he doubted if anything above them that required a breath of air was still alive.

Even more disturbing was the fact that he had tried to connect with all three of the other ARC units, but was unable to. Perhaps something had happened to sever the lines during the earthquakes. Perhaps it was something electrical, he could only wonder.

* * *

Then one day, a warning siren went off. Tom ran to check on it and found that the levels of CO and CO2 were off the charts inside of the ARC. He examined all of the air scrubbers and found them to be functioning perfectly. Then he ran a system check on the entire ARC but all of the reports came back negative. There had to be a breach somewhere in the ARC itself.

His first thought was that it might be coming from the cave entrance that he and Mot had plugged, but they could find no evidence of a leak when they tested the air directly around it.

They spent over a week, crawling through the complex, checking everywhere, but still they could not locate the source of the poison air. Soon it would begin to affect their breathing. Then, Tom thought, it would eventually kill them.

"We might have to go into the suits if this keeps up Alex," he said to her one night just after dinner. "I am so sorry, Alex, but I just cannot find the leak, and I don't know if I have the resources to fix it even if I do find it."

"I don't think that I wish to live out my life in a plastic suit, Thomas. Anyhow, Ara's pregnant and about to drop an egg any day and," she paused, touching his arm, "I think I'm pregnant, as well."

Tom smiled at her, speechless.

"Besides, living down here is all well and good assuming you could fix the problem with the air quality, but I can't really see raising a child down here, can you? I don't think Mot and Ara really like the idea all that much either. And," she added, "we still have another problem."

"What's that?"

"There is a second asteroid coming, remember? I haven't brought it up, but if I have my dates right, it will impact sometime day after tomorrow. It might give us another earthquake and make the situation worse."

"What do you want to do Alex?" Tom said, afraid of her answer.

"There is another option."

* * *

It took some convincing, but Mot and Ara totally trusted Alex now. If she said it must be done, then it must be done. The world above them had ended once again, and their shelter was now in jeopardy. As before, there seemed to be no choice. As far as Mot and Ara were concerned, the whole process they had been through the first time only involved taking a short nap.

"What about my child Alex?" was Ara's main concern.

"I don't see why this won't work just the same for your child, Ara. Doctor Pete told me the cryo-protectant was the most amazing preservative he had ever imagined. He based his version on the formula created by Fet the Wise Mother. Pete told me that it should perform every bit as well as the stuff she concocted, and this time, you won't have to even get wet."

Alex had gone to work closely studying everything she could about the cryo units. One of the features she found far more appealing than the prospect of being packed in the goo that had served Mot and Ara so well, was that Pete's cryo-protectant was applied as an aerosol—no "packing in goo" required.

Tom had gone to work learning everything he could about the reactors and figuring out how to tune them to last as long as possible. He came to the conclusion, that under very low draw, one of them might be able to power their needs for twelve to fifteen hundred years or so. That was if nothing went wrong. He figured out how to set the defaults to the other reactors, if and when the first one failed, but that was an even bigger risk—the backup reactors might be anywhere from a few decades to a thousand years old by the time they were needed.

Their cryo experiment also demanded that the computers that controlled the units continue to function for centuries, as well. The computers were all hermetically sealed and had several backup systems, but they were risking everything on the computers' performance. In short, there was a lot that could go wrong.

* * *

"I'm not real comfortable with this Alex," he said, when he had finished all the calculations and setting up all the systems. He explained the tenuous power situation to Alex.

Alex was less worried. The cryo units had a battery back up and she had discovered that they were designed to shut down and open were there ever a permanent loss of juice.

"We'll be okay Tom," she just kept saying to him, as he watched her carefully loading the canisters of cryo-protectant Pete had given her into each of the four beds they would be using.

She put Mot and Ara in charge of food supplies. Tom had located a bank of hermetic safes and Alex had sent the two Arzats out to find anything and everything they could that was dry to stock them. Dry nuts, dried fruit, pasta, flour, anything and everything dry was the assignment. Alex figured with their noses, the Arzats wouldn't miss much.

She was only mildly annoyed when they showed back up from their first trip with a huge load of beef jerky and not much else.

She sent them out a few more times, and eventually, there was a nice stockpile of dry edibles packed into several of the safes.

Alex smiled when she noticed that Mot seemed to have inadvertently brought back several boxes of pancake batter mix, until she realized that there was a picture of pancakes on the box.

Tom was doubtful if there would be anything left of anything when or if they finally awoke, but he hadn't bothered to say it. Alex noticed that he had placed his own stockpile of duffle bags stuffed with something in the safes, but she hadn't questioned him about them.

When they were finally finished with all of the preparations, Tom cooked the four of them another lavish dinner, mostly meat, but complete with ice cream sundaes for dessert, which Mot and Ara claimed were delicious. They chatted and laughed throughout the evening until their last bites, then the dinner table became suddenly quiet.

"It's time," Alex finally said, when she was sure everyone had finished.

The four of them slowly cleaned up the table without speaking another word to each other. Alex wandered off somewhere with Ara after giving Tom and Mot instructions to meet them shortly.

All of them eventually made their way back to the area where the cryo units were open and waiting. Alex helped get everyone settled, double checking each of the individual cryo beds as she did so.

"What happened to your hair?" Tom asked, settling into his unit.

"Thought I would go for a new look, like it?" Alex said, modeling her shorter cut. "Ara did a good job, don't ya think?"

"Al, I don't care about your hair, long or short. The one thing I want you to know is that I want to be with you forever," Tom said seriously as Alex leaned over him.

"Well, looks like we are off to a pretty good start," she said, winking.

Was it just her imagination, she wondered, or was he actually getting better looking with age. Carbon fiber beams, she mused as she gazed at him, his damn mistress had been carbon fiber beams.

"Will you ever forgive me for being such an asshole?" he said, looking up at her.

"Not in a thousand years." Alex kissed him deeply. "See you in a minute."

"Thank you, Alex," Ara said, as Alex checked on her.

"For what?"

"For Mot, for bringing him to me. Without you, Mot would not have survived and I would have no mate and no chance for a child."

"You give me too much credit. I'll see you soon." Now, scoot up in the bed just a bit, Alex thought, deliberately blocking her thought the way Ara had taught her.

The Arzat did not move. "You look very nice for a human Alex," was all Ara said.

Alex just smiled, liking her new female friend very much. Gotcha, she thought, still blocking.

"Have I done something wrong again Alex?" Mot said as she approached him.

"Why would you say that Mot?"

"Oh, I was just wondering."

Alex bent down and looked directly into Mot's reptilian eyes amazed again that such an incredible being could exist.

"No, Mot, maybe just a bit unlucky. You've somehow managed to show up right before the end of the world, *twice*," she said, smiling at him.

"Maybe next time will be better?"

"Well, we humans have a saying: 'the third time is a charm.'"

"What does that mean, Alex?"

"Oh, never mind, Mot, it's not important." Alex said, her eyes were full of tears.

"Alex?"

"Yes, Mot."

"Do you believe in the Great Creator?"

Alex put her hand gently on his forehead.

"Well, I have to tell you, Mot, I didn't before, but you definitely have me leaning in that direction. I'll see you real soon, okay?"

"Yes, Alex, perhaps you will make me the pan-cakes?"

"Yes, Mot son of Url, nothing would make me happier," she said, gazing at the amazing Arzat that had so changed her life.

Alex did a check, and then another, as any good scientist would have done. She ran through the cryo programs according to Pete's instructions, and she adjusted the temperature settings to -1 degree centigrade, just as Pete had suggested. The only thing left was duration of sleep cycle. The computer icon was blinking in the box, daring her.

You should be a lot more scientific about this Alex, she thought. She typed in: 10000 years / 0 months / 3 days / 0 hours / 0 minutes—*ten* times longer than she had originally intended.

That will give me an extra few days to forgive Tom, she thought, smiling in his direction as she key stroked the command that would begin the sequencing, hoping he was right about the reactors and the way they were linked.

Might as well come back to something, she thought. She knew that one thousand years wasn't nearly long enough based on the damage the two asteroids might inflict.

Alex walked to her own cryo bed and lay down, trying to slow down her heart, which was beating wildly with anticipation.

"Alex?" she heard Mot say quietly into her head.

"Yes, Mot?"

"Thank you, Alex daughter of Simon. Thank you."

Alex took in a deep breath. She was going to ask Mot why he was thanking her again. But then she thought better of it.

"You're welcome, Mot."

The glass shields automatically lowered and Alex could immediately feel herself getting sleepy and the cryo unit cooling.

Alex wasn't worried, she was excited, like the first day of school or the night before Christmas. She was in love with Tom and someday, god knew when, she was going to have his child.

And the Arzats, those fabulous Arzats—Mot and Ara and their child—would be with them when the world began again. She was absolutely sure of it.

"You're a very lucky girl Alexandra Moss," she could hear her father saying as she was drifting off. Yes, I am, Simon. Yes, I am.

She crossed her fingers and slipped off to sleep.

Epilogue

Last Time For Everything

At 1735 hours on the day of the blast Batter had quietly escaped the ARC through one of the emergency exits and had climbed the nearly fifty flights of stairs to return to the surface.

There was no going back. He had locked himself out, purposely.

Batter pushed up a cover and emerged somewhere, he figured, on runway 03R/21L.

He sat with his feet hanging in the manhole and looked up at the sky, trying to catch his breath. The sun was just setting and the sky in the east was already growing dark.

He looked at his watch—1809 hours—still 8 minutes to go.

Batter fished a cigar, a short glass and a bottle of bourbon out of a small paper bag he had brought with him. He fired up the cigar, poured the bourbon straight up, and watched the horizon as the final rays of the sun disappeared.

As the last of the sunlight dropped below the mountains, he looked for the mysterious green flash of sunset that everyone had reported seeing at some time in their life, and was surprised when he actually thought he might have finally spotted it for himself.

It is a profound and amazing thing, he mused, to be fully aware of the last time you will ever do something. He could remember firsts, lots of them—his first kiss, his first love, his first day at the academy, and now, even his first damn green flash-but not a lot of lasts. Batter regretted that he hadn't paid more attention to those, because they suddenly seemed much more important.

One 'last' he would never forget was the last time he saw Dr. Alexandra Moss and her very unlikely trio of companions as they climbed aboard the Chinook.

Batter took a couple of long puffs from his cigar and blew the smoke out into the desert air. He watched as the grey wisps rapidly faded and disappeared altogether, then raised his glass skyward.

"Here's to you guys. Hope you make it," he said, realizing as he uttered the words that he meant them more sincerely than any statement he had ever made before in his life.

Batter took a long sip of the bourbon—it was the most delicious thing he had ever tasted. He laughed.

"Fuck protocol and the horse it rode in on," he said to the oncoming night.

Out of the corner of his eye, he thought he might have seen a star falling.

"Interesting."

* * *